Bevan McGuiness lives near Perth with his wife and daughter. Although he has worked as a factory hand, geophysicist and laboratory assistant, he is now a teacher of chemistry at a boys' school in Perth. He has been writing for fifteen years and has published short stories, book reviews, a novel and pieces for texts on science education. You can contact Bevan at bevan.mcguiness@optusnet.com.au

The Awakening

THE TRIUMVIRATE: BOOK ONE

Bevan McGuiness

HARPER
Voyager

Harper*Voyager*
An imprint of HarperCollins*Publishers*

First published in Australia in 2007
by HarperCollins*Publishers* Australia Pty Limited
ABN 36 009 913 517
www.harpercollins.com.au

HarperCollins*Publishers*
25 Ryde Road, Pymble, Sydney, NSW 2073, Australia
31 View Road, Glenfield, Auckland 10, New Zealand
77–85 Fulham Palace Road, London, W6 8JB, United Kingdom
2 Bloor Street East, 20th floor, Toronto, Ontario M4W 1A8, Canada
10 East 53rd Street, New York NY 10022, USA

National Library of Australia Cataloguing-in-Publication data:

McGuiness, Bevan.
  The awakening.
  ISBN 978 0 7322 8549 4 (pbk).
  I. Title. (Series: McGuiness, Bevan. Triumvirate; bk 1).
A823.4

Illustrations by Greg Bridges
Cover design by Gayna Murphy, Greendot Design
Typeset in 10/13pt Sabon by Kirby Jones
Printed and bound in Australia by Griffin Press.
50gsm Bulky News used by HarperCollins*Publishers* is a natural,
recyclable product made from wood grown in sustainable plantation
forests. The manufacturing processes conform to the environmental
regulations in the country of origin, New Zealand.

5 4 3 2   08 09 10 11

For Lindsay

The World of Ceandia

Guvor.

Njord

Sigvaard

Gudrun
Sea

Bothildir

Einar

Eysteinn

Southern Raiders'
Island

Kepompong

Hope

Evening

The Stragglers

Mei Mei

Wrested Archipelago

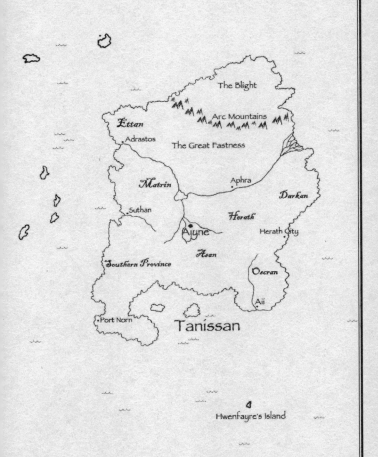

1

The first time she saw him, he was standing dawn watch on the wall.

He was a big man with coarse, almost brutish features. His untidy black hair was whipped back by the bitter wind that blew in from the sea. From his shoulders hung the dark blue cloak that identified him as a member of the City Guard. He walked slowly along the rampart, watching the endlessly heaving sea.

The young woman shivered and pulled her cloak tighter around her. She had lived in this fortified town all her life and the sea was ever part of her soul. Its constantly changing moods, its colours and its energy both frightened and compelled her. Often, she would come out onto this part of the ramparts just to stand and watch the sea as it moved in its never-ending quest, always moving, never still. This day, like so many others, she came to stand and watch.

Seeing the strange man, she stopped and pulled back, hiding in the darkness. He walked towards her with the smooth, easy tread of the warrior, ever alert, ever ready for violent action. His hand rested familiarly on the hilt of his sword, his grip steady. As he walked by her, he nodded, grunting a companionable greeting, turning his face towards her slightly. Startled, she smiled briefly. The smile, albeit fleeting, transformed her face, taking it to one of startling beauty. He walked on, neither pausing nor hesitating in his steady pacing of the wall. She watched him go on his way.

With the sole exception of the Coerl — the ranking Soldier in charge of the City Guard — never before had one of the guards as much as acknowledged her. It was one of the results of living in a closed community, that a reputation once gained, be it fair or otherwise, was nigh on impossible to escape. So it was with this woman. As a child she had been regarded as a 'strange one' with her lavender eyes and unpredictable moods. It was often said of her that she resembled her father, the Southern Raider who, it was believed, had taken her mother by force.

It had happened during one of many lightning-fast raids that had been so common at that time. The Southern Raiders had grown bold, even attacking the coast of the Empire of the World. They came at night with their swift black warboats and brutal war axes. The strangled cry of a sentry, killed by a single vicious blow, had been the town's first warning. His was neither the first nor the last life snuffed out that blood-soaked night, but that particular raid also brought to the town a new life. Some time later a poor woman of the town gave birth to a fair-haired, lavender-eyed daughter. To her daughter, she gave the name Hwenfayre, which in the language of the islands from where she herself came, meant *child of the sea*, for as she said, 'This child is none of my doing, she is got from the sea.' Thus it was that Hwenfayre came into life, never truly wanted, nor truly understood, for many things are told of the evil of the southerners who raid the coastal cities.

As a girl, she grew up knowing only veiled hints and innuendo. Her hair grew long and wild in its neglect. All the girls around her had the dark brown hair and olive complexion common to the people of the land, but Hwenfayre, with her pale skin and fine, white-blonde locks, shone as a lantern in the dark among them. It mattered not where she was or who she was with, Hwenfayre never blended, never fitted, never faded into the background. Yet she never seemed to make a great effort to do so. Her strangeness was not just a result of her appearance. There was something distant, something 'other' in her that drove others away. The other girls, as befitted the women of a poor town, displayed the properly demure, submissive attitude required of them by their men. Hwenfayre behaved exactly as she pleased, or, more precisely, exactly as she saw fit in any given situation. Even her mother, in one of her rare talkative moods, had commented, 'Hwenfayre, could you at least *try* to act like a normal child? You might even make a friend if you wanted one.' But this meant little to Hwenfayre.

Another man had seen this brief, apparently inconsequential meeting between girl and guard. The Coerl sighed as he stood motionless, hidden in the shadows. He had watched this scene played out many times before. Hwenfayre often came onto the wall at this time, just before the sun's rays took the sea's inky-black swells and turned them blue. She came to watch the change from darkness to light and the sea's transformation from a thing of shifting black mystery to a manifestation of blue-green beauty. He stirred as he waited for the next stage of the morning's drama to be played out.

Sure enough, when the new guardsman had passed out of sight, Hwenfayre walked quickly out of her partially hidden niche and stood at the ramparts, staring out at the sea. After a few minutes, she took out a small harp from under her cloak. With a smooth, practised movement she caressed the strings, producing a rippling, almost ethereal sound. She began to play a haunting melody. Although the Coerl had been listening to that same song for several years, he had never heard it played by anyone else, nor had anyone ever been able to identify it for him. It was a strangely compelling, melancholy song that drew out his emotions in a way that nothing else could. He had often wanted to ask her about it, but whenever he spoke to her she would stop playing and flee.

For some reason, this morning seemed to be somehow different, somehow full of meaning. As if, in some way, anything left undone now would never be done. The Coerl hesitated, then stepped forward. Immediately Hwenfayre stiffened and stopped playing. But unlike previous times, she did not turn and run. Instead she slowly turned to face him, her harp held protectively before her breast, as a mother would shield a child.

'Don't go,' he said. 'I just want to talk to you.'

Her eyes tightened suspiciously and she shifted her feet as if to take flight. In her every movement, she reminded the Coerl of a frightened deer, trembling and prepared, tense with energy to be released in a single bound.

'That is a beautiful song. What is it called?' he asked slowly, softly.

'What would one like you know of beauty?' she answered. Her voice was gentle, almost lyrical. It carried a hint of exotic places, of sights never seen, of a world unexplored. It was a voice that could entice and bewitch.

'Perhaps you could teach me.' The moment the words left his lips he realised his error and instantly regretted it. Her face closed and her eyes went hard. She turned and walked swiftly away, not looking back. He wished he had the courage to call her, to somehow make her turn around, to take back, to erase his hasty words. But knowing how she would continue walking without even acknowledging his words made his courage wither and fade. Watching her disappear away into the shadows of the pre-dawn, he felt a brief pang of indescribable loss.

As she hurried down the steps that led away from the wall, Hwenfayre put her harp back under her cloak. She paused and looked back sadly at the sky above the wall, lightening with the coming dawn. Another day had gone by without being greeted properly. Another day that must go on incomplete, ungreeted, unheralded. Somehow she knew how important it was for a day to be greeted and honoured. Now that another day had gone unrecognised, she knew that the hollow aching in her heart would be with her until she had the opportunity to welcome in the next dawn.

Behind her, and unnoticed by anyone, a tall, heavy-set guard with thick, unruly hair paused in his steady walk to turn and watch her go. A long, even stare and an unseen frown followed the fair-haired woman down into the dark streets. When she had vanished from view, he resumed his measured pacing. There was no one there to observe or comment upon the change that seemed to affect his whole bearing.

Scurrying through the suffocatingly narrow town streets with their overhanging buildings and dirty walls, Hwenfayre thought back to the two men she had met, albeit briefly, on the wall. She had surprised herself with her strong reaction to the Coerl's almost certainly innocent remark. She realised as she hurried home that she had been confused by the new guard. There was something different, something compelling about him. Despite herself, she felt a desire to learn more about him grow within her.

With her mind otherwise occupied, Hwenfayre stumbled on a broken flagstone and almost fell. Instinctively she grasped her harp close to her breast. The harp was her most treasured possession. Cradling it protectively, she regained her balance and hurried home, all thoughts of guards and Coerls banished.

She walked swiftly through the streets, between the buildings that rose two or three storeys above the cracked and dirty flagstones and seemed to be closing in over the top of her. All the buildings in the Poor Quarter, where she lived, were joined at common walls, and it often felt to her as she walked along that she was intruding in the vast home of a large family of which she was not a part. Every time she made her way along the streets she could feel the stares and hear the women who never bothered to lower their voices except when she was close enough to reply. Then they would fall silent and watch through hard eyes, with faces devoid of welcome, devoid of interest, devoid of any feeling whatsoever. But as soon as she walked past, it all started again.

'Isn't that ...' 'There goes that ...' 'Yes, I hear she does ...' 'Where's she going at this time of the day?' The voices, the words, the rumours never stopped. Not having a husband meant Hwenfayre did not have the common tasks of the other women, the endless washing, the constant caring for a man and children, the need to be forever engaged in work. She had nothing to share with these women, old before their time and bitter with unrealised dreams. They in turn despised her apparent freedom and carefree existence that allowed her to be on the wall watching the dawn, rather than up working before the dawn's early light brightened the skies.

On this day, a day when she had not been able to herald the coming day and welcome it as she ought, as it deserved, she felt the sting of unshed tears. Unable to contain the sorrow, she sobbed and broke into a run.

She arrived, breathless, at the old building that she called home, where she had lived all her life. It had three storeys. Hwenfayre lived alone on the ground floor. When she was younger, two other families lived in the floors above, but they moved out and no one else had ever moved in. Closing the door behind her, locking out the stares and the whispers, she busied herself with the business of the day. To occupy her days and keep body and soul together, she made and sold small pieces of jewellery in the bustling main marketplace. She collected small scraps of metal and brightly coloured stones, together with feathers and fabric, and fashioned them into complex patterns of interwoven spirals and curves. The brooches and earrings often reflected the moods of the sea. More than one potential buyer had commented on how they reminded her of the weather on the previous day, and more than one potential buyer had looked at who had made the jewellery and then hastily replaced it, scurrying away.

As she sat working, she allowed her mind to drift and roam freely through the distant paths of memory, along the softer trails of the remembered and the hoped-for. She wandered free and alone, past the sadnesses of her life to her childhood. For some reason, today she was drawn to the day, years earlier, when she found her harp.

It had been a hot, steamy day. Barely a breath of wind disturbed the air and there was a shimmer over the roofs. Hwenfayre had escaped the stifling heat of the town streets by stealing away to stand on the wall, watching the long languid swells roll in from the hazy horizon. Breathing deeply, she could almost smell the wonders that must exist beyond that mysterious line separating sea and sky. On such a day as this, when the horizon seemed to blur, Hwenfayre often imagined an intermingling of those two great forces, and for a time she could feel the sea on her skin by allowing the air to embrace her as she stood. It was a wonderful feeling, imagining the sea stroking her skin, lifting her hair and caressing her face.

She stood still, arms spread wide, feeling the soft gentle breeze ruffle her hair and cause her skirt to billow and swirl slowly around her legs. The feeling of the loose-weave cotton moving against her skin always made Hwenfayre imagine she was flying. Far below her the waves, carrying the secrets of far places, called to her with enticing sounds as they lapped ceaselessly at the rocks. Hwenfayre looked down at them fondly for they had borne her soul on many wonderful journeys. As she looked, as if in answer a larger wave crashed into the rocks, sending a plume of spray high up towards her. A seabird cried mournfully as it drifted, wings motionless, ever higher on an updraught rising from the cliffs. It passed closer to the wall and Hwenfayre sent a silent prayer out to its spirit for a long and safe flight. The bird cried once more and wheeled back out to sea.

'Hwenfayre!' Her mother's strident call shattered the afternoon stillness. 'Hwenfayre! Now you come down from that wall this instant!'

Sighing, the fair-skinned girl with the long white hair turned from the sea, back towards the town and her tall, raven-haired mother. She was standing with her hands on her hips, in that particular stance that said 'annoyed' but not quite 'angry'. Still, it was a stance to be obeyed, so the girl took one last look at the sea and skipped down the steps.

When she reached her mother's side she sensed something unusual, something that hovered at the edges of being understood.

'What is it, Mother?' she asked.

'What's what?' came the taut reply.

'You seem ...' she paused, 'upset.' *Yes, that's it, upset.*

'I'm not. Now come with me.' Her mother reached down and took Hwenfayre's hand. Immediately she knew something was wrong, for her mother generally eschewed physical contact with her. It felt strange, and Hwenfayre could sense the tension from the fingers that gripped tightly and from the perspiration in the palm pressed so close to hers.

'Where are we going?'

'Home, there's something I have to show you. Now be quiet and no more questions,' her mother snapped back. As if in response to the question, she increased her pace and Hwenfayre was forced to skip along to keep up with her. They went the rest of the way in silence, ignoring, as always, the stares and mutters that followed them wherever they went.

When they reached their small home, Hwenfayre's mother released her hand abruptly and sat down in her chair by the empty fireplace. She gestured for her daughter to sit at her feet.

'Child, it's time that you knew a thing or two,' she started. 'I guess you have heard rumours about your ...' she paused, 'your father. Well, I think it's past time you knew the truth. Your father was a rootless vagabond, a man of no means or station. He came to me by night and told me pretty lies. When he had bewitched me with his inventions, he took from me what he had no right to. Then he left and I hope he has died.'

Hwenfayre had indeed heard rumours about her father, but they had all been much more interesting than this bald, prosaic tale. She wondered why it was today that her mother had chosen to tell her about her father, but, knowing her mother there was probably no reason.

'You were born as a result of a lie and a betrayal,' her mother continued, 'and you seem much too much like your father for my liking. He loved the Sea and the dawn too. Many times he rose as you did and greeted the dawn as you do. The only thing he left behind when he left was that, over there.' With a dismissive gesture Hwenfayre's mother waved at the box that had stood in the corner of the room for as long as Hwenfayre could remember. It was of a dark wood, plain and unadorned except for a single spiral carved into the wood near the lock. A lock that, as far as she knew, had never been opened.

'It belonged to your father, child. It may as well be yours. I haven't opened it, never wanted to. Take it to your room. I never want to see it again.'

'Why not?' Hwenfayre asked.

Her mother looked at her, looking as close to tears as Hwenfayre had ever seen her. 'One day, child, you will understand about betrayal and desertion. I hope it will never happen, but it will. Then, Hwenfayre, you will understand why I have never opened this box.'

She stood abruptly and walked over to the box. With a grunt, she pulled it away from the wall and gestured curtly for Hwenfayre to help. Together they pushed it into Hwenfayre's room, then her mother left, closing the door behind her. From beyond the door Hwenfayre heard her mother cough. It was a harsh, racking cough that had only developed recently. Her mother had dismissed Hwenfayre's questions about it, so she had stopped asking.

From that day, until the day she died two years later, Hwenfayre's mother mentioned neither the box, nor the man who had left it behind. There were times when Hwenfayre's curiosity got the better of her and she ventured a question about her father. Her mother's hard glares and occasional rages prevented further enquiries. Hwenfayre sometimes wondered why she was so uninterested in her father; for some reason he rarely seemed important.

Once it was in her room, Hwenfayre was able for the first time to examine the mysterious box. Despite its having been in the room where she cooked, ate and spent most of her time, Hwenfayre had never felt free to look closely at it before. It was almost as though there had been a curse or a spell of some kind on it, keeping her away from its secrets. Now, though, it felt welcoming. She felt that the time had come for her to explore the mysteries and plumb the depths of her past.

Fingers trembling, she traced the outline of the lock and the the carving; everything, even the hinges, gave her a feeling of something forbidden, something arcane. The box was smaller than it had appeared. It stood just lower than her knee and was as deep as it was high. In length, she could stretch her arms out and touch each end.

After feeling the outside, running her fingers over the smooth, hard wood, she turned her attention to the lock. At first it was puzzling as it had no apparent keyhole, but she quickly discovered that it was a clasp, not a lock, and it was a puzzle-clasp. She tinkered with it for a few minutes and it fell apart in her hands. The pieces tumbled to the floor where they lay in intricate disarray. For a moment she looked at the pieces, distracted by the strange pattern they made. A peculiar dreaminess stole into her mind as she stared. She felt herself becoming light-headed, almost weightless; the room seemed to fade, drift away, swirling around the scattered, glinting pieces of metal on the floor. They shifted, moved, forming into a new pattern, a striking, strong pattern, an image of power and magic. A deep shudder shook the girl's slight frame as she watched, entranced by the shifting of the glinting fragments. Her eyes became unfocused and she grew giddy with the power of ancient mysteries that swept through her.

Hwenfayre shook her head. The room was real again, and the mystical pattern became the scattered pieces of a child's toy once more. Shaking her head a second time, she cleared away the last remnants of the disturbing feelings and lifted the lid. It moved easily, hinged at the back, to reveal the contents that had lain undisturbed for twelve years. Despite herself, Hwenfayre was breathing quickly and her heart was pounding as she gazed into the dark interior of her father's box.

Inside, there were three items: a small bag, a roll of parchment and a harp.

A heavy knocking on her door brought Hwenfayre out of her reminiscences. Startled, she turned away from the cold fireplace to the door. She put down her drink and rose to her feet.

13

'Who is it?' she asked.

A gruff voice muttered something indistinct. Puzzled, Hwenfayre moved quickly to the door and, pressing her ear to the heavy wood, asked again.

'My name is Wyn. I am a guard. We met this morning on the wall.'

His voice was deep, muffled by the door. Despite that, she could detect an unusual accent, a hint of mystery, something exotic.

'What do you want?' she asked, unable to entirely hide the interest in her voice.

'I thought that perhaps I might talk to you.'

'What would you have to talk to me about?'

'That song you played this morning. I recognised it. I thought that perhaps we might be kin.'

Hwenfayre cautiously opened the door and looked out at the big, heavy-set man who had greeted her that morning. In the evening light his coarse features were softened somewhat and he had tied back his mane of thick black hair with a leather thong. It was unusual to see a soldier with such long hair; normally they kept it close-cropped. He stood solidly, confidently, with his hands clasped behind his back. His stance and features made him look menacing, dark and somehow threatening. Her first instinct was to close and bolt the door. But there was something about his intense grey-green eyes that made Hwenfayre pause. She decided against closing the door in his face, and opened it wide and stepped aside. He hesitated, then walked in. As he passed her, Hwenfayre could smell the brine on his cloak.

He sat awkwardly on the single chair and waited as Hwenfayre dragged an old box out of the next

14

room to sit on. They sat for a few minutes in a strained silence, looking at each other. Then Wyn coughed, clearing his throat, in an attempt to make some sound, preparatory to speaking.

'Where did you learn that song you played this morning?' he asked diffidently.

'I didn't learn it, I made it up myself. Years ago, just before my mother died. It seemed to fit my mood at the time.'

'That is strange. It is an ancient song of my people, played at our most important ceremonies. To the best of my knowledge, it has never been played or heard by any not of our race. Hearing it played this morning, so beautifully, and by one who looks as though she belongs in the robes of a Priestess, was,' he paused, searching for the word to express his thoughts, 'unnerving. To say the least. I felt I had to seek you out and at least find out how you came to be here.'

'I live here. Have done all my life.'

'But surely many outlanders have visited this place? People who have brought their music with them?'

'No. Not many at all. Visitors travel here for market days, but none ever stay. On occasion travelling minstrels may visit, but their stays are brief, and their visits rare. We are not a rich town. But what of you? You are not from this town. Where do you hail from?'

'Everywhere, and nowhere. I travel much.'

'By sea?'

'Yes, mainly.'

'Tell me of the sea,' Hwenfayre almost begged.

'Ah, the Sea. What can be said of her? She is the loveliest maiden, the harshest witch and the gentlest mother. She gives, she takes, but ever she remains the same. Let me tell you of the time . . .'

For several hours, Hwenfayre sat entranced as the guard spun tales of rolling swells, fearsome beasts, mysterious islands and terrible storms. He spoke with a wonder and a love in his voice that touched her soul and lifted her heart. At some stage during those magical hours she picked up her harp and found herself playing some of her own songs, almost in accompaniment to the stories being told her.

Finally Wyn stood up, preparing to leave.

'Well, Hwenfayre, for all the talk of you in the town, you're a good listener, and that's the truth. And as fine a harpist as I've heard in many a year. But now I must take my leave. I have the dawn watch again, and that Coerl, he's not a forgiving man. So sleep well, and dream. Goodnight.'

And he was gone.

2

The slave was taking forever to die.

Shanek, Son of First Counsellor Sandor, hereditary advisor to Thane Kasimar IV of the Asan peoples, shifted uncomfortably in his chair. He had seen this display before. There were, he decided, only so many ways that a slave could die on the Axle. And once you'd seen them all, they became repetitive.

Admittedly, this slave was showing more resilience than most, but death would come to her soon enough and the show would be over. And then it would be back to the studies; the interminable, execrable studies. Once more he would have to listen to Domovoi the Appointed One, his teacher in the Arts of Leadership, droning on about duty and noble tasks.

'Attend me, Son of the Counsellor,' the 'Annoying One' would pronounce. 'Yours is a sacred destiny, to continue the honourable line of First Counsellors, the line that has extended back as far into our history as records are kept.'

And how dull that history had become. Year after year of massive victory following massive victory until the entire continent lay under the benign rule of the Thanes of Asan, where it had continued, quiescent, for all these long, insufferably boring centuries.

How he longed for something, someone, anything that would break the monotony!

But no, the conquered remained conquered and the enslaved rested easily under the light yoke of Asan slavery. Of course they rested easily; the alternative waited here in the Arena, together with the Axle, the Maiden and the various other devices of slow death.

Today was a special show. The leaders of the most recent abortive attempt at uprising, together with their wives, children, family and most of their friends, were being executed for the private viewing pleasure of the nobility. Most of the would-be revolutionaries had been disappointing. Several, knowing what lay ahead, had passed out at the sight of the Maiden as she rumbled out into the Arena. The Maiden earned her name from the large X-shape onto which her victims were strapped. Around the four arms were blades and other devices that slowly closed upon the bodies of her lovers, completing her harsh embrace. One or two had apparently died of fear, for they remained still and silent when their bodies were slowly broken and torn apart in the Maiden's embrace.

The memory of disappointment was as pungent as a taste in Shanek's mouth. To their credit, the Torturers recognised the poor showing of the slaves and dragged out a few more to finish up with. Some of them had never seen the Axle before so they were at least conscious before it started. For some years this display had been his only real pleasure. It was something he would never admit, but lately he was finding even the Arena dull and lacking its usual appeal. Looking around at the gathered nobility, he wished he could recapture his old fervour for the kill, as those here still had, but he feared it was gone.

A respectful sound at his elbow roused him. He turned to see a liveried servant hovering nearby. Shanek's raised eyebrow prompted the servant to speak.

'A drink, noble Sir?' He offered Shanek a tray on which were several gold goblets containing a range of exotic beverages. The Son of the First Counsellor selected one and waved the man away.

It was one of his favourites, rioko, a rare mix of a powerful liquor brewed only in the western provinces and a seductively sweet blend of herbs. Served warm with shredded mint leaves floating on the surface, it was a potent drink that cost about a week's wages for an artisan. Shanek enjoyed both the taste and the cost; that, and the fact that it was one of the few drinks of which he could stomach enough to get drunk. One of the many annoyances of being in his family was this hereditary intolerance of alcohol. It was not that he could not hold his liquor; quite the contrary, he was mildly allergic to it. Any more than two or three drinks and he was ill for days.

He sipped the drink, savouring the sweet burn, relishing the sensation of intoxication that followed almost immediately. It almost took his mind off the tedium of the dying slave. If only she'd hurry up and die. Couldn't she understand how hopeless it was to struggle on? Death would be a relief; at least to him; he was becoming bored.

Finally, she died, her last scream filling the Arena. The gathered Noble Families clapped appreciatively as Akem the Master Torturer bowed. The Thane waved his acknowledgment of the Torturer's performance.

With a perfunctory nod to his father and the Thane, Shanek rose from his seat and left the viewing area, accompanied by the latest of his entourage of flunkies and lickspittles. This collection had little to recommend it. There were the requisite climbers and social graspers, together with a couple of military types who sought power the same way many sought sex. Shanek considered one or two of the climbers interesting, mainly due to the sisters they brought with them.

He knew his father had hopes for a suitable marriage, but given the utter invulnerability of his family's position Shanek wondered why. With a certain justification, he felt he could marry the cheapest whore from the most rat-infested tavern on the continent and still maintain his position and power, so the petty manoeuvrings did little but bore him.

There was one man, however, who had managed to attract his interest slightly. He was new to the Capital, the youngest son of some outlying neo-nobility who had their roots in a robber-baron past. They had established something of a foothold in the wilderness and displayed intelligence when the benevolent armies of the Asan had advanced upon them. They promptly surrendered and handed over all control to the Commander of the Army. In recognition of their intelligence, the Commander had generously left one or two of the ruling family alive.

Now, several tamed generations later, a scion of this might-be noble line was here seeking his fortune. Shanek turned to regard Zahir closely. Perhaps he was not here for that purpose. There was something cunning about him. He lacked the simple, wide-eyed sycophancy of the other climbers. As he walked from the Royal enclosure, Shanek gestured for Zahir to walk beside him.

'What did you think?' Shanek asked him.

Zahir frowned. 'I am new to the Capital, First Son. I lack the appreciation of the Torturers' art.'

Shanek nodded. 'It was a poor show,' he agreed. 'Tell me,' he asked, 'what entertainments do you enjoy in the hinterland?'

'Riding, hunting the great wyvern and singing.'

'Singing?' asked another of the entourage. Shanek flicked the outspoken man an annoyed glance. Remembering his face, he marked him for an early grave. How dare he interrupt!

Zahir missed the glare and displayed no displeasure at the man's rudeness. 'Yes, singing, noble Sir. Our choirs and soloists are highly regarded. Several are even performing in the Capital at present.'

'Hmmm.' Shanek was already losing interest. *Maybe this one is not so different after all. Singing, indeed!* He waved him away, his mind drifting to other, more engaging thoughts. When his gaze left Zahir, he failed to see the satisfied smile that flickered across the young noble's face.

'A good day in the Arena.'

The voice startled him out of his thoughts. He looked around to see the daughter of one of his father's toadies smiling at him. She was about his

21

age, and one of the renowned beauties of the court. With her jet-black hair curled in the latest fashion, her flashing white smile and her sparkling blue eyes, she was eye-catching enough. Her body, full and willing, was memorable, but her mind was as empty as the pleasure he had taken from her. *What is her name?*

'Marcene!' Her father called. She spun around, her hair flying.

Marcene, of course! She has a sister. Shanek frowned. He could not remember her sister's name, either. And he should; he'd had her too. Marcene was having a low, intense conversation with her pompous father. Shanek shrugged and turned to walk away.

'First Son,' Marcene said. 'Did you enjoy the Arena today?'

'Not particularly,' he said, turning back to her. 'I thought they were a bit dull. Only three made it to the third stage of the Maiden.'

Marcene frowned, putting a small crease in her perfect forehead. 'True,' she agreed. 'But that last female was strong.'

Shanek shrugged, hoping she would go away. 'Seen worse.'

'You're thinking of that barbarian chieftain, aren't you?'

Despite himself, Shanek grinned at the memory. 'He was good, I have to admit.'

Burgen, the barbarian chieftain, was a warrior of repute who had led a rebellion against the benign rule of the Asan. For just under a year, he and his band of rebels had made audacious raids against

22

outlying towns. They overran a number of military outposts and caused a minor headache for the Commander of the Army of the World.

When the army finally caught up with and destroyed the rebels, they brought Burgen back to the capital in chains. He was a magnificent specimen of a man, huge, with the long white hair characteristic of the Tribes and eyes burning with rage.

The few remaining rebels were dealt with quickly by simple methods for the pleasure of the crowd. They roared in appreciation as the last fell lifeless to the blood-soaked sands of the Arena, then stilled as the huge barbarian leader was led naked into the sun. He was chained to four soldiers, two at each wrist, and they struggled to hold him as he surged across the Arena, shouting his defiance. He glared disdainfully at the Master Torturer as Akem examined him.

The crowd screamed in exultation as Akem turned to the Royal Quarter, where Thane Kasimar IV of the Asan peoples sat comfortably.

'Thane,' Akem bellowed in his powerful voice, 'I feel this man deserves nothing less than the Axle.'

The Thane nodded. 'So be it,' he called back.

The barbarian stood calmly as the Torturers scurried about, preparing for the entrance of the most hideous of their devices. It was a large, cumbersome machine, but what it could do to a human body had to be seen to be believed.

At one stage the machine stopped, overbalancing slightly as it ran over a slave. Burgen actually laughed as the Apprentice Torturers struggled to right it before it fell over. Akem, Master Torturer to two Thanes and three First Counsellors, regarded the laughing man with a thoughtful gaze.

'Perhaps,' he called to the Thane, 'our guest does not fully appreciate the Axle's capabilities.'

The Thane, knowing what was coming, waved his agreement. The Master Torturer nodded and turned to his Apprentices. Slowly, he walked along their ranks until he stood before a big man. He was a final-year Apprentice, a very promising torturer about the same size as Burgen. Akem spoke softly to the young man and then gestured to the guards.

Before the crowd knew what was happening, the Apprentice was hustled across the Arena and strapped into the Axle.

He lasted all the way to the Sixth Level, something rarely achieved. The Master Torturer was well pleased with his training, as the Apprentice only screamed once, just as he died, but the effect on Burgen was devastating. The big chieftain had gone noticeably pale, and, just before the Apprentice reached the Third Level, lost control of his bowels.

Shanek almost laughed out loud at the memory of Burgen's dying screams. 'Yes,' he agreed. 'I was thinking about the barbarian. He was good.'

'Much better than the Commander of the Army,' said Marcene.

Shanek grunted. 'He was feeble. No wonder it took him so long to capture Burgen. I think he should have been allowed to watch, though. Rather than starting the proceedings.'

Marcene smiled, but her smile faded as Shanek, with calculated rudeness, turned his back on her and walked away, his keen entourage following.

Putting her from his mind, Shanek made his way past the rest of the obsequious crowd of lesser nobility to where his own Fyrd waited. They were superbly trained soldiers, hand-picked by the new Commander of the Army for their skills and discretion. As he approached, the Coerl of the Fyrd snapped to attention. Behind her, the twenty members of the First Son's Fyrd fell into perfect line, their breastplates gleaming, their weapons close to hand.

Leone, Coerl of the First Son's Fyrd, was a striking woman who had earned her rank by skill and intelligence. Confident dark eyes gazed evenly at the world around her, aware of her superiority. She carried herself as a wolf among dogs, knowing that the first man or woman to challenge her would be the first to feel the edge of her blade. Her long black hair, tied back by a leather thong, fell to her waist in defiance of the accepted warriors' tradition of wearing the hair short.

There was nothing humble or apologetic in her even stare as she regarded Shanek's approach.

'First Son,' she said, saluting sharply. Her voice was soft, but carried easily across the noise of the crowd.

Shanek nodded in deference to her. 'Coerl Leone,' he replied. 'Here to rescue me from another dull day of ritual torture?'

Without a hint of a smile, the Coerl nodded. 'If such is your wish, First Son.'

'Sadly, Coerl, whilst it is my wish, it is not my lot. More ritual torture awaits me. The Annoying One, Domovoi, hankers for my presence.' Turning to those who still followed him, Shanek made to speak, thought better of it and turned on his heel,

25

dismissing them from his presence and his mind. He strode out into the street.

It was an indication of the level of their training that the Fyrd required no more than a look from their Coerl to form a defensive ring about the First Son before he had put his foot on the paved surface of the road. As was appropriate to her station, Leone walked at Shanek's left shoulder, one pace back.

'Tell me, Leone,' Shanek said without turning his head, 'exactly how far does your devotion to me extend?'

'First Son?' Leone asked.

'Well, let's say that, for example, I said take me away from all this.' He gestured at the teeming streets around them, taking in the grand architecture of the Capital, the thriving commerce, the swarming masses. 'Would you take me?'

'Where would the First Son wish to be taken?'

'How about the home of that new fellow, Zahir?'

'The Ettan city of Smisha? We could be ready to travel with you in one hour, First Son.'

Shanek stopped and turned to face her. The Fyrd halted around him, without seeming to hesitate. 'Just like that? In one hour?'

Leone nodded, her eyes steady. 'One hour,' she repeated.

'But don't you have families, friends?' He regarded Leone inquiringly, 'Or lovers?'

'If we do, First Son, they are secondary to our duty.'

'So you'd just up and leave home if I told you?'

'Naturally, First Son. Of course I would have to inform the Caldorman of my Hearthreu of my movements, which would explain the delay.'

'And that would only take one hour? You would not have to make an appointment? He is in command of twenty Fyrds himself.'

Leone allowed herself the smallest of fleeting smiles. 'Yes, First Son, but whilst he commands nineteen other Fyrds apart from this one, I allow myself the vanity of believing this one to be somewhat more important than the others.'

'What about supplies? Travelling gear? That sort of thing?'

Leone blinked in surprise, almost as much emotion Shanek had ever seen her display. 'No, First Son. Anything the Army of the Thane require is freely supplied by any who are asked.'

'So you just take whatever you want?'

'Not at all, First Son. The people are charged with the support of the Empire, and all they own is the Thane's by right. They are honoured to aid us in their defence.'

'But how is taking me to Smisha a part of their defence?'

'You are First Son. There can be no doubt that any action of yours would be motivated by anything else but the welfare of the Thane and the Empire.'

Shanek's heart sank at Leone's words. She was another who believed in his 'duty', the duty of First Son to Thane. There was no escape, no hope of his living any life but this one.

There were occasions when he felt humbled by the thought that a superb human being like the one who stood before him would happily devote her life, even sacrifice it if necessary, for his wellbeing. The thought that Leone held her own life as secondary to his every whim was sometimes almost overwhelming, but not now. He was suddenly filled with anger at the complete pointlessness of it all. The waste of a life like Leone's was too much to contemplate. He turned away from her and stalked off.

The Fyrd resumed its protective mission, surrounding him with a ring of razor-sharp steel linked to minds and bodies ready to kill. Leone matched his stride, one pace back at his left.

3

Hwenfayre did not dream that night. Neither did she awake before the dawn and make her way onto the wall to greet the new day. Instead, she opened her father's old box and read again the letter that he had left for her. The parchment crackled as she unrolled it and laid it flat on the table. Its smell and texture were familiar, sending a tantalising thrill of the mysterious through her, as it had done every time.

To my daughter Hwenfayre,

No doubt when you read this I shall either be dead or long gone from your life. You are not yet born and as I write this you rest beneath your mother's breast. Every day I can see you growing, and every day your spirit becomes stronger. You are going to be a fine girl, and we shall call you 'daughter to the Sea', for you are the very spirit of all that is magical about the Sea. I shall leave you my harp when I go and she will teach you of the mysteries. Be assured that when I leave I shall still love your mother. The love we share will

*outlast the Sea itself, but I can stay in this
place no longer; I must leave. My Mistress is a
kind one, but a demanding one. I speak not of
a mistress in the carnal sense but of the One
to whom I and all my people have willingly
given our hearts. She calls me back, as She
will call to you one day. You will not be one
with the people about you, and one day you
must leave, as I must now. Perhaps, if She
wills it, we may meet again. But if we do not,
know always that my love and that of my
Mistress will be with you.
      Your father, Feargus.*

It was a different story from the one that Hwenfayre
had been told all her life, even by her mother. It
raised many questions, not the least of which being
the prescience of her father. Certainly, she was not
the product of a Southern Raider's rape, but who
was she? Her feelings of not belonging, of difference,
of otherness, remained obdurate and indecipherable.

She spent the whole of that day, and the next,
making brooches and matching earrings. For
inspiration, she used the ancient and peculiar designs
of the jewellery her father had left in the small bag in
his box so many years before. Those pieces had
profoundly affected her in a way that she could not
fully articulate. In a way, they encapsulated her
feelings for the wildness and freedom of the waves.
She longed for the freedom which she had never
experienced.

Her thoughts turned often to Wyn, a strangely
compelling man who spoke to the emptiness in her

soul. His tales of his life on the sea, his adventures and his journeys, had touched her in a profoundly disturbing way. Hwenfayre felt herself torn between a need to hear more and a fear of learning too much.

She lay in her narrow cot staring at the ceiling above her head, a ceiling that she knew so well, a ceiling that had been her companion through many a long, dark night. She knew every crack, every line, every spider web like an old friend. Each time a new mark appeared on that ceiling, Hwenfayre felt as though her family had grown. But this night as she considered it, the ceiling was as new to her as though she had never seen it before. Each mark took on a new meaning, each crack was a wave, each line a trailing, windblown stream of spray. Hwenfayre was drifting, losing herself in the endless tides of her memory. She allowed herself once more to wander through the distant paths of her secret reminiscences.

It had been a good day and she left home on an errand for her mother after spending time with her while she worked with the other women. Despite her mother's bitterness about her status, she did have friends among the women of the town.

She skipped happily along the narrow alley thinking of the good times ahead when a hard shove caught her unawares, sending her to the ground. She fell heavily and cried out in pain. Despite the often happy times she spent with her mother and some of the women of the town, her differences were marked enough to make her a target for taunts from some of the boys of the small town.

31

The scrape on her knee bled freely; the bright red trail trickling down her shin, making its way past old scars and half-healed wounds. She looked up past her tangled white-blonde hair at her tormentor. He was a big solid boy, a year her junior and half as big again as she. His thick black hair and dark skin marked him as a local boy, born and bred to the life here in a frontier town. He, together with two or three fellows, had come upon her in ambush.

The taunts were nothing new, just the usual — 'whore child', 'white freak', 'witch' — nothing to worry her; she'd heard worse. What made this day different was the new boy. Something in his eyes made Hwenfayre flinch. Never had she seen such naked hatred. He had the look of the vicious bully, the cornered cur, about him. He bunched his fist and drew it back. The other boys urged him on, clapping and yelling.

'What's this?' A heavy hand grabbed the fist as it started down towards Hwenfayre's face and a deep voice cut across the boyish cries. Startled, the bully turned to see a pair of implacable eyes boring into him.

'I think we can leave the girl alone, can't we, boys?' he said, not once taking his eyes from those of the bully. As if by magic, the others melted away, leaving only one of Hwenfayre's tormentors, his hand still firmly clasped in the newcomer's strong fist. He gave the boy a shake and released him. 'Now, be off with you.'

With a single backwards look, the boy scampered away down the dirty street, disappearing into the deep shadows that filled the Poor Quarter.

After watching him flee, Hwenfayre turned to consider the man who had intervened for her. He was a tall man with strong features. He wore a traveller's cloak, which was stained with the dust from the road. His boots were black and dusty and his clothes were sturdy and worn, but his face was kind and Hwenfayre felt strangely warmed when he smiled at her. His clear blue eyes sparkled as he held out his hand to help her to her feet. Reaching out, Hwenfayre took his proffered hand. It was warm and strong, with calluses on palm and fingers. He easily lifted the slight girl to her feet.

'It's Hwenfayre, isn't it?' he asked.

'Yes. How did you know?'

'It's a long story. Come, let's see to that knee. And I think you could do with a meal.'

She looked up at him with surprise, but there was no guile in his eyes so she smiled and nodded. He did not release her hand as he started to walk away. Hwenfayre went with him, skipping along in an effort to keep up with his long strides. She was touched by his thoughtfulness when he shortened his stride and slowed slightly to allow her to keep up.

He led her to a corner of the market where a large tree stood. Its shade often sheltered young couples who sought its cool dimness to sit close together. Hwenfayre quickly forgot the pain of her scraped knee and the tormenting boys when the man eased the pack off his shoulder and opened it. Inside she saw a harp and some food. With a quick grin at her, he started to unpack the wrapped food to reveal bread, some cheese, a bottle of water and a wineskin.

A young couple, also seated under the tree, watched as the man started to prepare a simple meal. When it became apparent that Hwenfayre would be staying, they stood and walked away. With a puzzled look on his face, the man watched them leave.

'And how, pray, can such a young and small child be such a deterrent? What are you, ten, eleven summers?' he looked gently at Hwenfayre.

'I prefer to measure in winters, kind sir, and I have endured thirteen.'

'Hwenfayre, I suppose you would like to know how I know your name and why I sought you out?'

She nodded slowly, not taking her eyes from his face.

'First, my name. I am called Adam. Some have called me Adam the Nimble-Fingered, but around market towns like this I tend to leave that addition out. I travel, tell tales and play the harp. Enough of me; do you know that you are famous?' He paused and raised his eyebrows at her, quizzically. 'No, I didn't think you would. It's true; a friend of mine was in this town a month or so ago and told me to look for you. Apparently, you play the harp. My friend was most impressed with your skills.'

'Your friend was mistaken and you have wasted your time, for I am no minstrel,' replied Hwenfayre.

In response, he merely twitched his eyebrows and knelt to dress her still-bleeding knee. Taking a cloth from his pack, he wet it and gently washed her wound. He wiped the blood away and cleaned the dirt and small stones that had been left embedded in her flesh. His hands were strong and his fingers deft. As she watched his head, bent over as he tended to

34

her knee, she noticed that he was starting to lose his hair, forming a small bald spot. In a peculiar way that, more even than the gentle hands or the kind words, endeared him to her. She found something real, something inherently *human* in a man who was losing his hair.

'Adam,' she asked suddenly, 'are you a good minstrel?'

'Aye, I am. Very good. In fact, without foolish modesty, I am regarded as one of the best. Why do you ask?'

'You don't dress like a successful minstrel. And you are not arrogant and rude, like most minstrels.'

'And you have met so very many of them, haven't you?' replied Adam, teasing her gently. 'There,' he said straightening up, 'I think that should do very nicely. What do you think?' He gestured to her now-clean knee. When washed and cleaned, it did not look so very unpleasant. Indeed Hwenfayre felt slightly embarrassed at all the fuss over such a small thing. Adam rose and sat beside her. He helped himself to bread and cheese, gesturing for Hwenfayre to do likewise. She did so, hungrily.

'Tell me of your harp,' he asked suddenly.

'What do you want to know?' she answered through a mouthful of cheese.

'Where did you get it?' Adam answered, his expression very intense.

'It was my father's; he left it for me when he went away. He left before I was born. I never knew him. Why?'

'This friend of mine who heard you play, he described your harp in great detail, and it sounded very much like one I saw many years ago. I have wondered if it might be the same one as I saw. If so, it is a true mystery how you came to own it.'

'Why so?' Hwenfayre asked.

'It was being played by a man in a town far from here. He was a traveller, an ambassador I guess you would say, for the Children of Danan. He walked into the inn where I was playing one night. Big, he was, broad shouldered and heavy-set. He stood in the doorway and shook himself like a bear. Spray and salt scattered around him and he threw his cloak towards the barman.

'"Who's the best minstrel in these parts?" he bellowed at us all. With my usual charm and grace I stood up and bowed deeply.

'"It is I; I cannot lie." That did not impress him. He looked me up and down and snorted at me.

'"Perhaps you can learn some humility as well as some new tunes." With that, he produced the most wonderfully made harp I have ever seen. It was not big, about so wide, by so high,' Adam gestured with his hands, showing a size slightly smaller than usual for a travelling harp. 'It was made from a single piece of driftwood, bleached white by the sea and decorated with the most intricate scrollwork imaginable. And when he played, it was like no music I have known. It flowed like the tide, sweeping over me, taking me away. I begged him to teach me but he laughed, and shook his head.

'"Oh no, my young minstrel. This song is not for you. It has a destiny all its own. But I shall teach you many others. Come." He held out his hand to me and I followed him out of the inn. For the next two years I followed Feargus as he wandered far and wide across the land, singing and playing his magical harp.'

'How did you know it was magical?' asked Hwenfayre, eyes wide.

'I don't think it was actually magical, but when he played it, it seemed to take on a life of its own. He told me it had a name, but he would never tell me what it was. He'd always just say, "She'll tell you herself, one day." He always referred to it as a woman, and he would hold it gently, lovingly, as one would hold a child. I remember at night, when we were on the road, we'd sit by the fire and he'd spin the most wonderful tales about life on the sea, and how he and his people would travel by the stars, crossing and re-crossing the seas. It was a very special time for me.'

'But what does it have to do with me?' asked Hwenfayre.

'Does this tune mean anything to you?' Adam whistled a few bars of a complex melody. She felt a chill. She hugged herself tightly and stared at the minstrel. Despite her initial feelings of being able to trust this man, she found herself shaking her head.

'No,' she said. 'I don't know it.'

The tall minstrel's face fell. 'Never mind,' he said. 'It was a foolish hope anyway.'

They continued to talk for a while, and he played a few songs and sang a little. He taught her some songs and they sang them together, but all the time she could sense that he was restless and wanted to leave. All the time, Hwenfayre wanted to call him back, to tell him, to ask about her father, but something stopped her and finally she watched him stand and take his leave. He walked away without looking back.

When she went home to her mother, she told her about the strange encounter and was dismayed to see her face cloud over with the first signs of anger she had come to know so well. It was these sudden surges of strong emotion that preceded the bouts of bitterness that finally led her into the ill health that claimed her happiness and eventually her life.

'Nonsense,' she scoffed. 'A magical harp carved of driftwood? Whoever heard of such silliness? Now, be off to bed with you!'

Hwenfayre's lip trembled with the onset of tears, but her mother would not gather her in her arms to comfort her, so she sadly tucked herself into bed to listen to the sounds of her mother's slow descent into a troubled sleep.

At night Hwenfayre sometimes cried herself to sleep as she lay in her narrow cot. Frequently she would reach out and touch her bleached white harp, tracing the delicate, intricate scrollwork that adorned its surface.

When Hwenfayre's mother died, not long after the meeting with the minstrel, she started to make the jewellery that she sold in the marketplace. She rose early every morning and made her way to the wall with her harp. Every morning she played the song that she had written herself, the song that Adam had whistled.

4

It was an unnaturally hot summer, and Shanek had taken to sitting outside in casual clothes and bare feet as often as possible, much to the dismay of his father.

Leone, who was charged with his safety, took the additional issues calmly when summoned into First Counsellor Sandor's presence. 'He is First Son,' she said when told of his decision. 'It is his right to sit wherever he wishes.'

'But the extra security ...' Shanek's father, the First Counsellor, began. Rather than finish the sentence, he glared at Cadock, Commander of the Army.

Cadock in turn looked to Leone. 'Can you guarantee the First Son's safety even when he chooses to sit outside under a tree, rather than in the Counsellor's Palace?'

Leone returned her Commander's gaze. 'Yes,' she said.

'So be it then,' Cadock replied. He bowed to Sandor. 'Your son's safety is secure, First Counsellor.'

'Just like that?'

'Yes, First Counsellor, just like that.'

Sandor threw up his hands in mock defeat. 'Very well then. But on your head be it, Coerl Leone,' he said. 'You are dismissed, Commander.'

Commander Cadock saluted sharply, turned on his heel and strode from the First Counsellor's office. Behind him went the three elite fighters assigned to him as personal bodyguards.

When the Commander had left, the First Counsellor turned to Coerl Leone. He offered her a seat, which she refused with a shake of her head. Sandor eased himself into a chair carved from a single piece of tadon wood, a rare hardwood tree from the far south of the continent. It had been hand carved to his exact measurements by a Skrin Tia'k slave and modified every six months to accommodate any changes in his shape. Despite being as hard as rock, it was the most comfortable chair he had ever known. 'How are his studies going?' he asked.

'They are going well, First Counsellor,' she said.

'What does that mean?'

'He listens to the Appointed One and asks many questions. He argues frequently and is rarely satisfied with weak or inadequate answers. I feel he exasperates his teacher with his manner, First Counsellor.'

'And you?'

'I do not exasperate the Appointed One, First Counsellor,' Leone replied.

Sandor smiled. 'I did not think you would, Coerl. No, I meant, does he exasperate you?'

'No, First Counsellor.'

'Why not?'

'He is First Son. He does not exasperate me, First Counsellor.'

'Silly question, really, wasn't it?'

Coerl Leone's face was impassive. 'No, First Counsellor, it was not a silly question.'

First Counsellor Sandor nodded. 'I stand corrected, Coerl. Your loyalty to both me and my son is admirable and a true asset to the Empire. But you do remember that part of your responsibility to me is to keep me honestly and frankly apprised of Shanek's progress and activities?' Leone nodded. 'So,' continued Sandor, 'how is he going and what is he doing?'

Coerl Leone paused before answering. Whilst she believed in the Empire and loyally served its rulers, her feelings about the First Son were mixed.

His façade of ennui masked a first-rate mind. He was also showing signs of talent in the arts of battle, especially with the bolas. Yet — and this was the problem — there was something not quite right about him. It was more than his show of boredom, more than his arrogance, more even than his carefully cultivated air of thoughtless superiority. There was an air of hopelessness, almost despair, that underpinned his attitude.

'Coerl?' prompted the First Counsellor.

'I don't know, First Counsellor,' she said. 'I would almost say that he is desperately unhappy.'

'Unhappy?'

Coerl Leone frowned. 'I don't know that unhappy is the right word, First Counsellor, but he is not a happy man.'

'How about his, um, love life?'

Leone stared impassively at a point just to the right of Sandor's right shoulder. 'The First Son is well served, First Counsellor.'

'Ah,' replied Sandor. 'His reputation is well deserved?'

Leone nodded.

'How does he treat his women?'

The Coerl hesitated.

'That badly?' Sandor asked. Forty years as First Counsellor to the Thane had taught Sandor much in the art of nuance. The flicker in the eyes, the tightening of the lips, the slight straightening of her shoulders said as much as he needed to know. If Coerl Leone was surprised at his perception, she did not show it. She merely nodded.

'Are there any children yet?'

'Not that I am aware of, First Counsellor.'

'Good.' He stood. 'Thank you, Leone. As always you are a comfort and a joy. That will be all.'

Coerl Leone saluted by placing her right fist at her left hip to indicate her readiness to fight, followed by the raising of the fist to her chest, showing her willingness to die. Sandor bowed his acceptance. Leone turned and strode from his room, her sandals slapping the marble floor with a beat as regular as a drum.

The First Counsellor sank back into his chair. When he was alone, he allowed the mask of gentle calm to slide from his face. In its place was the deep sadness that he kept hidden from the world. 'Shanek,' he whispered. 'My son. What is to become of you?'

Outside the palatial ancestral home of the First Counsellor, Domovoi and Shanek sat in the cool shade of a massive spreading lonat tree. According to legend, the fruit tree from the far west of the continent had been planted by the then Thane Scyld III, in memory of a great victory. Shanek could, with a moment of thought, recall the year, some three hundred summers previous, the place of the victory and the name of the First Counsellor of the time, but he had little desire to do so.

Domovoi, the Appointed One, glared at his student with what could only be described as deferential exasperation.

'Shanek . . .' he began.

'Domovoi,' Shanek interrupted. 'We've talked about this before. As long as you are going to lecture me about the importance of my place and my duty, you may as well set me a good example by dispensing with the informality. I am First Son of the Empire. Surely you of all people should recognise the importance of correct forms of address.'

The old teacher's eyes revealed a sudden fire. He then displayed the skills developed over decades of devoted service by closing his eyes briefly, nodding in gracious submission and smiling gently.

'Of course, First Son. You make a valid point. I shall remember correct address in future.'

It was a small victory, and a disturbingly hollow one. Domovoi might be a pompous old fool, but his devotion to Shanek's family was beyond question, proven by simple acts such as this one.

'Please continue, Domovoi,' Shanek said.

'As you wish, First Son. You were asking about the place of slavery in our culture. Do you mean human slaves or the ritual slavery of the Skrin Tia'k?'

'Both. Start with human. We'll deal with the Skrinnies later.'

'Human slavery deals with two main aspects of any civilisation — cost and labour. To keep defeated foes as prisoners is a very expensive proposition, and as we only ever keep combatant foes as slaves, they are usually in excellent physical condition, ideally suited to labour. This keeps them gainfully employed, thus reducing the likelihood of rebellion that comes from the boredom so often associated with long-term imprisonment.

'It is the best use for defeated foes, non-violent criminals and debtors. And not only that,' he continued. 'As a deterrent, short- to medium-term slavery is far greater than simple imprisonment.'

'But ritual torture? The elevation of torture to an art form? What of the Royal Torturers Guild? How does that fit? What purpose does that serve?'

Domovoi frowned. 'What purpose?'

'Yes. What is the point of ritual torture, such as we had yesterday? How is the Empire of the Asan served and made better by that?'

'Surely you cannot be questioning the right of any people to punish wrongdoers?'

'Punish, yes. But ritually torture to death the friends of suspected plotters for the entertainment of the nobility?'

'That is our way. It has always been thus.'

'Oh come now, Domovoi. You can do better than that. "It has always been thus"? How feeble is that! It is not an answer, it is the last refuge of the impoverished mind in defence of the indefensible!'

Rather than answer, Domovoi observed the First Son. He was barefoot, clad in the simple clothes of a scholar, leaning against a tree in a magnificent garden kept for the enjoyment of his family alone. As with so many of the ancestral possessions of this family, there were odd customs associated with it. For example, custom dictated that no visitor was ever permitted to go barefoot within the garden. Neither could anyone not related to the family by blood ever eat any of the produce. Here, beneath this tree, which spread branches over the ceremonial meditation bower, tradition held that neither the First Counsellor nor his son could ever wear shoes of any sort. Over the centuries most of these occult laws had passed into quaint legend, to be trotted out for the amusement of whatever guest happened to be visiting at the time. Recently, however, Shanek had been showing an unhealthy obsession with these ancient customs. The Appointed One saw his duty in directing the First Son towards the future, not the past.

'You are distressed today, First Son?' Domovoi asked.

Shanek sighed. 'Yes,' he said. He closed his eyes, feeling the warmth of the sun as it shone through the leaves. The bark was rough against his back. He enjoyed the sensation almost as much as he did the feeling of the dirt on his bare feet.

'May I be permitted to know the reason, First Son?' Domovoi continued.

Shanek shrugged. 'I don't really know, Domovoi,' he said. 'But something is not right. I feel ...' he paused, seeking the right word, 'disappointed,' he said finally.

'In what?' asked Domovoi.

'I don't know. Everything.'

Domovoi frowned. 'Everything, First Son? The birds disappoint you? The trees? The earth beneath your feet?'

Shanek smiled. 'No, Domovoi. Not everything. In fact most things do not.'

'But what does?'

'I really do not know. But there's this all-pervading sense of . . .' he paused again, groping for a word, 'wrong.'

'Wrong?'

'Yes. Something, and something significant, is wrong.'

'Can you be more specific, First Son?'

'The Asan, us. We are wrong.'

Domovoi sighed. Always it came to this. He had been the Appointed One to Shanek's father and he had asked the same questions, come to the same conclusions. In between his times as Appointed One, he had taught at both of the finest locii in the Empire. Whilst there he had been exposed to the keenest minds, and with them he had wrestled with the ethical dilemmas now plaguing the First Son.

Truly, he welcomed the evidence of such a perceptive mind. It was just that he wished that just once, someone would ask something new. With the barest flicker of an eyelid, he brought his mind to order and composed himself to address Shanek's concerns.

'The issue of the ethics of slavery is one that has exercised the finest minds throughout the history of the Empire —' he began.

'And one that will always remain to vex us in our quiet moments of introspection,' Shanek completed. 'Yes, Domovoi, I have read your lecture on the subject. As it is the definitive work, it would be lax of me not to. But you did not address the core issue.'

'Which would be what?' asked Domovoi.

'How can one person own another?'

'It is not a question of ownership, but one of power.'

'No it is not,' snapped Shanek. 'Power over a person is not ownership.' He looked at Coerl Leone standing nearby. 'Leone,' he called.

'First Son,' she replied.

'Are you my slave?' he asked.

'No, First Son, I am not.'

'But I have power over you,' Shanek said.

Leone hesitated as she thought about the question. 'No, First Son, you do not,' she said finally.

Shanek stared at her. 'What?' he asked.

'You have authority over me, not power. I follow your orders willingly and accept your authority by choice. But you do not exercise power over me.'

'All right then,' Shanek conceded. 'Let's say I accept that. What is your definition of power?'

'The ability of one to decide on the life or death of another without their consent.' She regarded him levelly, her eyes boring into his with an unreadable expression. 'You could not kill me, First Son.'

Shanek tried to grin in the face of her stare, but failed. 'I'm getting better, Leone,' he said. 'It won't be long and I may well best you in the battle ring.'

'That is not what I meant, First Son,' she said.

5

When Hwenfayre went back to the wall she was not sure whether she wanted to meet Wyn or not. It was the first time she could remember going with such disquiet in her mind. Part of her keenly wanted to see him, if only for a moment, to reassure herself that he was indeed real, yet part of her was hoping that he would not be there.

When she arrived, the dawn was not far off; already the first tendrils of light were touching the skies, painting the night with the colours of morning. It was a cold morning and the wind was from the north. It was not a strong wind, but it carried with it the promise of winter. She could smell the ice and feel the chill on her skin.

She stood motionless on the wall, watching and feeling. At some stage — she could never recall doing it consciously — she uncovered her bleached white harp and started playing. The melody, as familiar to her as her own soul, yet strangely new every morning, flowed through her body, lifting her out of the mundane, freeing her from the commonplace, as it always had done. As always, her spirit drifted up and away, up with the music that her fingers drew from her father's harp. She flew freely with the birds, and then dived joyously into the waters where she swam and played with the fish. She travelled through mysterious grottoes and trailed her fingers through the swaying weed. It was a time of peace and joy for her, yet for the first time thoughts of another intruded. As she flowed with the music she sensed someone else beside her, someone else who felt the call of the sea, someone who might understand her restlessness. Every time she turned in her soul to catch a glimpse of who it might be, the sense of presence faded away, out of reach.

She reached the end of the song and reluctantly willed herself back to reality. The breeze had strengthened slightly and the swell was rising. Hwenfayre lingered; she knew that she had to return to her home soon to avoid the worst of the taunts, yet the feeling of the wind as it stroked her hair and ruffled her skirt was hard to put aside. She closed her eyes, allowing herself to lose herself again in the almost sensual feel of the wind's gentle caress.

'I thought you would have left by now.' A strong voice beside her shocked her out of her abstraction. Her eyes snapped open and she spun around to look at the Coerl. He stepped back and held up his hands. 'I mean you no harm.'

'What do you want?' she asked.

'Nothing, nothing at all. I have seen you many times up here at dawn. And I have wondered why it is that you come.'

'I come because I am safe here. The streets down there are,' she paused, 'dangerous. At times.'

'Aye, that they are. Yet standing here, alone, before the dawn, isn't that dangerous too?'

'No. Isn't your job to protect me? To keep me safe?'

The Coerl smiled. 'I suppose that it is my job to protect you. One that I enjoy. And one that I do willingly.' He hesitated and shifted awkwardly, as if troubled. On impulse, Hwenfayre reached out and touched him on the arm. Beneath her fingers his arm felt hard and strong. He straightened and looked her in the eye.

'I have never met anyone like you.'

'I would be very surprised if you had. Don't you know that I am a witch, a sea daemon? I have been known to eat babies as they sleep in their cots.'

'Yes, I have heard that,' replied the Coerl, smiling once more. 'I have always found it strange that one so small could eat so many babies and yet not seem to put on weight.'

Despite herself Hwenfayre felt a smile begin to hover on her lips. This Coerl did not seem to be quite the hard and stern man he appeared. Yet she felt uneasy, and she could put no name to her unease. She decided to ignore it.

'What is your name?' she asked.

'Niall,' he replied. 'It means "warrior" in my language.'

'And what language is that?'

'I am originally from Herath, although my father was an islander,' Niall said. 'He often told me about his life on the Sea and I am beginning to think he was more than just an islander. He often spoke of his ability to sense a coming battle or a storm on the waters. I think I inherited his fey sense of impending danger because I am always the first to know when something is coming. It has helped me in my life as a Soldier of the World. But whatever else I inherited from him, I certainly did inherit his talent for trouble. As a boy I was driven from my village. There was some problem with some missing silver. I wandered for several years, surviving as best I could. Finally I headed west. I became a soldier for the Thane and gradually worked my way up through the ranks. After a time, I tired of the Great Fastness and sought a posting near the sea. I have been here ever since.'

'Such a short tale for such a long story. I am sure that a minstrel or a bard could make much of a story such as yours, Niall,' said Hwenfayre. 'Did you meet my father?'

'Yes I did. Feargus was a strange man. He often stood on the wall, as you do. But he never played the harp; he sang.'

'What did he sing?'

'I never heard it fully; he sang low and softly, always ceasing his song when I came too close. He would never turn to me as I approached, but he always knew it was me. "Niall," he'd say, "don't you know it is rude to creep up on a man when he is concentrating?" And then he would tell me of his daughter; his child of the sea he'd call her. As far as I knew back then, he had no child. But he would describe her to me as though she were standing before him. After he left, I forgot about her.' Niall paused and looked directly at Hwenfayre, the intensity of his stare making her look away. 'When you started to clamber up the stairs to the top of the wall as a child his words came back to me. He had described you perfectly. The first time I saw you I felt that I knew you, but you were a child and I could think of no way that I would know one so young. But then, when you started to play the harp, my blood ran cold in my veins. It was the same tune that your father sang. It all came back to me, and I knew then that you were no ordinary child. So I made it my business to look out for you, to keep an eye on you. By then, however, the story of your mother's rape had spread and was widely accepted as truth, and there was nothing I could do about that.'

'Why have you never told me of this before?'

'I have tried, Hwenfayre, but you would never listen. You always ran when I came to speak to you.'

'I did, didn't I?' said Hwenfayre, smiling.

'I would like to see you smile more often, Hwenfayre. You are a woman of great beauty; it is a shame for you to hide behind a serious face so much.'

'I haven't had much reason to smile. My life has not always been exactly what I might want, despite having so doughty a protector,' Hwenfayre teased gently. To her pleasure, Niall laughed at the gibe. As she laughed with him, she took the opportunity to glance around to see if there was anything that might have been causing the strange feeling of unease that refused to leave her.

'Indeed,' replied Niall, who seemed to be unconcerned, 'I have not been as careful a protector as I might have been, but you have managed to survive despite my neglect.'

Hwenfayre laughed again. Niall laughed with her. It had been many years since Hwenfayre had laughed with another person. To the best of her memory it was the only time she had ever laughed with a grown man. They talked: he of his life by the sea in this fortified town, she of her love for beautiful things.

A peculiar feeling of wrongness swept over her again.

'Niall, is it just me, or is something about to happen?' she asked, unable to put aside the feeling any longer.

'You feel it too? I thought you might.' He looked around at the apparently peaceful scene. 'I haven't felt anything like this since I was last in battle. Maybe I should go and have a look at the wall.' He became the Coerl once again as his eyes swept the horizon. Hwenfayre suddenly felt afraid. She shivered and drew her shawl around her shoulders tightly.

'If you will excuse me, Hwenfayre.' Niall said. His eyes were hard and his face blank. 'I have to leave.'

'Can I come with you? I feel that I might be safer with you than on the streets,' she asked. Her tone, almost pleading, almost desperate, caught him off-guard. He blinked in surprise.

'If you wish. Although if my instincts are still reliable you may regret your choice. Something is wrong.' The Coerl's tone had become cold, distant. 'If you are set on coming with me put your shawl over your hair so that my men won't recognise you. Not that there is any problem but some of the men are superstitious. You know how it is.'

He stalked ahead of her, moving towards a guardsman who saluted the Coerl briskly.

'Tell me, man, is there anything amiss?' the Coerl barked.

'No, Sir. Nothing to report,' replied the guard. If he was at all surprised by either the Coerl's question or the intensity in his tone, he did not show it. He also did not so much as look at Hwenfayre.

'Stay alert, soldier. This is no time to be lax. Spread the word, ten lashes for any man not at his post.'

'Sir.' The guard continued his pacing of the wall.

Without so much as glancing in her direction the Coerl strode away from Hwenfayre. It appeared that he had forgotten her presence. However, she heard him mutter, 'Stay close, this is no time to wander off.'

Catching his mood, she only grunted in reply and hurried to walk by his side, and they walked together in silence along the wall.

The tension mounted and Hwenfayre's fear grew with every step she took. Her eye was caught by a flash of light far out at sea. She stopped and stared out towards its source, gripping Niall's arm.

'What is it?' snapped the Coerl as he turned to face her.

'I saw something out there.' She pointed. There came another flash, which lasted longer and seemed closer than the previous such flash. 'There it is again! Did you see it?'

The Coerl followed her direction. The flash came again.

'To arms! To arms!' he yelled. 'Raiders! Raiders from the Sea!' In a move that shocked her, but one she understood, he shoved her into a dark recess. 'Stay there,' he hissed.

The guards on the wall mustered quickly and the Coerl barked orders. Showing the signs of an iron discipline, the men moved to their stations and prepared themselves to face whatever was coming to their city.

The Raiders came fast, their dark warboats carrying the torches that Hwenfayre had seen. She stood in her niche, for the moment alone, mesmerised by the scene that was being played out before her. On the Sea, the Raiders' warboats swept towards the cliffs, while above them the soldiers hurried about their business, preparing their defences against the attack that was sliding inexorably towards them. Bows were strung, arrows were carried in bundles to each bowman, large cauldrons were filled with oil and fires lit underneath them. Swords were loosed in their scabbards, crossbows were cranked back and loaded, orders were shouted, armour was tightened, metal rattled against stone and metal. Somewhere in the town a baby cried and a woman screamed. Dogs started to bark and the sound of running feet grew as more and more people came out of their homes to assist in the defence of their town.

Hwenfayre watched the ordered chaos with a sense of detachment, and without consciously thinking she took out her harp and started playing.

As she played, the Raiders in their boats drew closer. The shouts of the defenders on the wall became louder and more insistent. There were torches lit and the fires under the cauldrons flickered, sending crazy shadows dancing over the wall. Hwenfayre could see the Coerl from where she stood. He was moving confidently among the men, directing, ordering, advising and correcting. Wherever he went, he left behind him men with straighter backs and steadier hands. An air of strength seemed to surround him like an aura. For the first time she felt what it was like to be inspired. Above her the lightening sky watched the unfolding drama with indifference as the Raiders prepared their assault.

The first cry of a dying man caught her by surprise.

The harsh sound shocked her into sudden awareness. The guard had taken an arrow in the chest and he fell backwards, close to where Hwenfayre hid, absently playing her harp. He screamed in agony. His face was distorted as he grabbed the shaft, his heels drumming the ground. With his last gasp he reached out a hand towards Hwenfayre and tears of pain ran down his face. He died, the whites of his eyes gleaming in the flickering red firelight.

Around her she could still hear the clamour of men shouting, of grappling hooks shot from catapults below as they rattled onto the stone battlements and of the pounding of feet as still more defenders ran to their stations. But all she could see was the face of the dead guard who lay before her, his hand still reaching out to a hope that had never come. He had been a young man, about nineteen summers, with dark hair and brown eyes. When standing he had been tall and strong, but now he seemed shrunken and somehow obscene with his contorted face and the ugly arrow shaft protruding from his chest. She noticed that he was wearing a marriage band about his wrist. A widow had been born already this day.

An anger rose within her breast that she had never experienced before. She felt that she must do something, strike back at the stupidity, the futility of what she was seeing. Other men were screaming in pain as the arrows and hooks from below found their marks. She watched in horror as one man was caught by a wickedly barbed hook and dragged screaming over the wall as the Raiders in their boats jerked the rope back. Despite her anger she felt impotent to affect the abomination before her eyes.

She kept playing her harp, her fingers weaving their complex tapestry on the strings, evoking sounds and melodies that she could not recall ever having played or heard before. Yet the music kept flowing, becoming faster and stronger, lifting her heart and assuaging her anger. She continued playing, losing touch with the reality of the screaming and the dying, becoming more and more entwined with the strains of the music that flowed from her fingers.

So lost was she in the music that she was unaware of the change in the weather. The wind started to whisper, then to wail, then to howl. Below there came the increasing sounds of breakers as waves started to surge and then to crash on the rocks. Clouds formed, piled up and then clashed together, sending great bolts of lightning tearing through the air, searing the sky. Mighty explosions of thunder rolled around the wall, drowning out the cries and screams of fighting men. Rain lashed down. The wind howled. The waves smashed with insensate fury against the rocks, and Hwenfayre played.

She continued playing as the wind and rain lashed at the wall, her fingers still eliciting the complex, flowing melody from her bleached driftwood harp. She was still playing, oblivious to the world, when the Coerl shook her by the shoulder.

'Hwenfayre,' he whispered urgently. 'Hwenfayre, you must leave the wall.'

She looked up at him. He was soaked through, his face and uniform were spattered with blood and his sword was drawn. His eyes were slightly glazed as he stared at her.

'What happened?' she asked.

'The storm,' he replied, looking over his shoulder. 'The storm happened, Hwenfayre. Didn't you see it?'

'Of course I see it. I am wet through from standing in it. What about it?'

'Hwenfayre, you must leave, now. I will explain later, but go now, you are in danger. If any of the men knew you were here . . . I am not sure what they would do, but you must leave.'

'What are you saying? I don't understand,' Hwenfayre said as he started to push her, none too gently, along the wall towards a little-used stairway.

'I will explain it all tomorrow, but you must leave quickly. And tell no one where you were this morning. If anyone asks, you left just before dawn. Now go.' He all but pushed her down the stairs and quickly stalked away. She stumbled down a few steps and then, on regaining her balance, lightly ran down the rest. Hwenfayre did not stop running until she closed her bedroom door behind her. It was only then that she allowed herself to cry.

* * *

Out at sea, the Commander stood in the prow of his vessel and stared at the storm lashing the coast. He swore quietly and fluently as he watched half his fleet being dashed against the cliffs at the base of the wall. Good men had died there this night and two people were going to pay for their deaths. One was the navigator who had assured him that at this time of the year, at this section of the Tanissan coast, storms were unheard of. The other to pay would have to wait, but her time would come. He turned away from watching the storm blow itself out and stomped back to stand beside the wheel.

'South,' he commanded. The sailor spun the wheel and the ship turned away from the shore.

They would be back; they had a job to do. The problem was that it was a mission not of his own design, and one given to him by a woman he had no reason to trust.

It had come about a season or so back, when a vessel flying not the flag of the Children but one of truce had approached the *Misty Seal*. A man had come aboard and suggested he meet with Morag, the High Priestess, to discuss 'something they could both find useful'.

The meeting was on an island that appeared on very few charts. It was an old volcano, not dissimilar to the one the Raiders claimed as their home. The High Priestess met alone with the Commander on land while their personal transports circled each other warily just offshore.

'The Danan is back in the world,' she told him. 'This will be dangerous for both our peoples.'

'How so?' the Commander asked.

'For decades we have been slowly dragging ourselves out of superstitious barbarism. The power we hold over the Sea is almost under control. Finally we can see our way clear to sharing the bounty of the Sea. It's big enough for both of us.'

'Under control? Are you saying that for all these years your people have been out of control?'

She shrugged, a carefully crafted gesture that said 'What can I do? It's beyond my ability', then she smiled a wan, little-girl smile. It was a powerful weapon that she had been using on men since she was ten. It worked for her now. 'There have always been rogue elements among the Priesthood,' she lied. 'Some who believe we should rule the whole Sea unchallenged. And this Danan who reappears every few generations is their icon, their call to arms. Whenever she comes back there is a surge of violent outbreaks.'

The Commander was visibly taken with her words. The fact that she had also allowed her robe to slip and reveal far more than decency would normally allow, something that she appeared to have overlooked in her passion to 'heal the rifts between their peoples', also distracted him. He was wavering, and the High Priestess knew it was now or never.

'What I am saying is that she has appeared in the world somewhere. And I am giving her to you. We of the Children don't need her any more. You have her.'

'We don't want her,' the Commander said.

'So kill her,' she said casually.

'It would be that easy to kill the Danan?' the Commander said doubtfully.

'It would be at this stage, yes.'

The Commander regarded her with disbelief.

The High Priestess sighed, as if suddenly realising how little he knew of their legends. 'She, whoever she is, has only just started to come into her powers. So she is young, and without training or knowledge of her true nature. As far as she is concerned, she is just a girl living in a town on the coast.'

'If we do take her, what is to stop us using her power to destroy you?'

'Two things,' she said. 'One: without training she is powerless. Two: I trust you. I am offering you this in good faith. Even with her, you know that your fleet is no match for ours anyway. I want our two peoples to live in peace. Peace takes trust and I am offering that to you.'

'And if we live in peace —' the Commander began.

'Then you can expand onto the uninhabited islands and live as peaceful traders who can raise their families in safety. Yes,' she completed.

He sat back, staring into the fire over which the High Priestess had cooked them a meal. The flames flickered and danced, sending shards of orange light over her face. In the strange, inconstant light she looked little more than a girl herself.

'You said "trust",' the Commander said. 'How can I trust you after so long an enmity between us?'

The High Priestess shrugged.

'Perhaps if you gave me some more information about this Danan,' he suggested.

'What information do you want?'

'What does she look like?'

'No one knows,' she lied, shaking her head.

'So how do you know where she is?'

Another shake of the head. 'We know, take it as fact. I am not going to tell you all our secrets.'

'I don't like this. You want my people to do your dirty work for you —' the Commander began.

'And in return,' the High Priestess interrupted, 'I am offering you peace and a future for your people.'

The Commander made a show of considering this. 'I need more information,' he said finally.

She sighed again. 'What do you want?'

'Why can't you just go and get her yourselves and be done with it? Why involve us at all?'

The High Priestess hardened her eyes as she regarded the Commander. 'I thought I'd answered that already,' she snapped. 'But since you are struggling with the idea, I'll repeat myself. On the Sea we are invulnerable, but she is on land. We have no expertise in such things, yet you do. And I would rather you did our dirty work, as you put it, because nothing must ever get back to my people about this. If it did, I would lose my credibility and all the work my mother and I have done over so many seasons would be wasted. We could be plunged back into superstition again, and I don't think you would want that.' She paused. 'If we allowed the old ways back every one of your vessels would be sunk on sight.'

The Commander held her gaze, sensing she meant the threat inherent in her words. He weighed up the potential risks of attacking a town on the Tanissan coast against the wholesale warfare she was suggesting. He nodded. 'You have a deal. We shall get this Danan for you. And you will share the Sea with us.'

'Done,' she said with hidden joy.

She was about to stand when, as an apparent afterthought, she paused. 'Oh, and one other thing. She is likely to have a harp with her. An old, weathered thing of no intrinsic value, but if you could give it to me when you kill her . . . ?' Morag left the sentence hanging as a question.

The Commander grunted in assent and the High Priestess left, having achieved all she had wanted.

6

Aldere's breath came in short gasps. The air up here was thin and the climb was hard but the view was worth the effort. He stood on the summit looking at the vista spread below him. To the north lay the Great Fastness, a vast grassland, sparsely inhabited and dotted with the remnants of the generations-long war that so dominated the sad history of this continent. It had finished hundreds of years ago, but the damage remained.

He turned to regard the east. At the foot of this mountain lay his home, the village. He had never heard it called anything but 'the village'. It lay nestled where it had for centuries, tucked away beneath this mountain beside the river that stretched from the inland plateau to the sea so far away. The still air carried some sounds upwards so that even from this height, he could hear life going on as it had for countless generations; the ringing blows of Merryk the blacksmith, as he pounded the recalcitrant metal into shape, the plaintive bleating of old Hadrill's sheep and the occasional voice raised in laughter or anger.

He let his eyes drift south, into the tamed and

civilised pasturelands of the great Asan Empire. It had always seemed to him that there was something significant about the placement of the village, just here between the mighty Empire and the wastelands that the Army of the World had created in wresting control from the Skrin Tia'k.

The sun was setting, sending shafts of golden light up through the clouds, staining the blue sky with yellows and pinks. Already a chill was seeping in and he knew that once again he had stayed too long and it was time to seek shelter. The climb down was easy enough in the light, but after dark strange things happened up here. He had seen too many things, heard too many people speak the truth about the mountain to ignore their warnings.

Seasons ago he had found a cave up here. It was small and its entrance was almost invisible to the casual observer. Each time he came up, he brought some small thing to make the cave warmer and more comfortable so that when, as often happened, he was captured by the beauty up here, his night was warm and pleasant. He took one last, long look around at the world at his feet and headed into the cave.

Inside, he wrapped himself in a heavy blanket and settled in to eat a simple meal of dried fruits and nuts before lying back amidst the furs. With the final ray of sunlight, he wondered again at the symbol carved on the wall of his sanctuary. It was clearly ancient, and corresponded to no religion or legend he knew. He'd asked every traveller who came through the village, but the stylised balance resting on a lightning bolt with the symbol for ground on one side, the symbol for water on the other, remained a mystery.

7

Hwenfayre awoke the morning after the attack curled up on her bed, still cradling her harp. Her dress was damp and her hair was a tangled mess. In her head thoughts whirled chaotically, but she felt too numb to try to make any sense of what had happened. Instead, she lit a fire in the fireplace and sat watching its flickering mysteries as her troubled mind slowly spun itself into quietude. Finally, some time after nightfall, she roused herself.

She was hungry, so she made herself a simple meal. Just as she was seated once more before the fire, there came a knock at her door. With a mixture of emotions, Hwenfayre put aside her meal and opened the door. It was Niall. He was still in uniform but the bloodstains were absent. Idly, Hwenfayre wondered if he had cleaned it himself or if he had a maid, or even if he had more than one uniform. She stood in the doorway, staring at him.

Finally he said, 'Hwenfayre? Are you all right?'

She nodded and stepped aside, motioning him to come inside. He did so, awkwardly.

'You're limping,' she observed.

'Yes, an arrow grazed me last night. It is a minor thing. Not worth concerning yourself over.'

'I wasn't concerned. I was just making an observation. Sit down, I imagine you have a great deal to tell me.'

He sat on the only chair and she sat cross-legged on the floor, her back to the fire.

'Hwenfayre,' he began. 'About last night.' He paused, frowning. 'It's difficult to know where to start. The storm, I will start with that. I have never seen a storm come up so suddenly and with such little warning. It seemed that one moment it was clear and still, and the next we were facing a gale. Didn't you think it was strange?'

'No, I hardly noticed the storm, to be honest. I was ... preoccupied.'

'I always imagined there was a lot more going on behind those lavender eyes than you revealed, but I never imagined it would be so much as to distract you from the most violent storm in years. But I digress. That storm frightened the men. It came up just at the precise moment we needed it. The Raiders had established a set of ropes to the top of the wall and they were about to start climbing. Had they made it to the top of the wall, many of our soldiers would have perished and we may not have prevailed. It was the largest fleet of Raiders seen in ten years. The men who saw the storm last night are muttering about sorcery, and I have already heard your name mentioned more than once.'

'I am no sorcerer,' Hwenfayre sighed. 'If I were, do you think I would have stayed here for so long?' She stared off into a half-imagined distance. 'It's true

I have often longed for sorcerous powers, so that I could flee these wretched walls and fly on the wind or sail with the waves. But no, all that I can do is make brooches and play the harp. And neither of those can call up a storm.' She looked intently at Niall. 'Is that why you hurried me off the wall? Did you imagine the men would look to me?'

Niall nodded gravely. 'I felt that if it were known that you were there ... well, it could have been awkward.'

Hwenfayre felt a chill as the ramifications of what Niall had just told her sank in. For years the superstitious townsfolk had made veiled accusations, but to be accused on the wall, and after such a storm ...

'Weren't the men grateful to have been spared from the battle?' she asked.

'A clean fight, even with the possibility of death, is something these men know. They face death bravely and fight hard. But sorcery. That is a very different thing. It is something they do not understand and they fear what they do not understand. They were badly frightened last night. Do not come up on the wall tomorrow morning. Not alone.'

'Niall, you are frightening me. Do you really think anyone would accuse me of being able to do such a thing?' Hwenfayre's eyes were wide.

He nodded.

'But how could anyone do that? Raise a storm, I mean?

'Hwenfayre, I am a simple soldier. I do not know of sorcery or witches. But I do know common soldiers. And you are in danger at the moment, so be very careful.' He stood to leave.

'It appears that I owe you not only an apology but also my thanks for rescuing me. Please accept them both, Niall,' said Hwenfayre, still sitting on the floor.

Niall smiled briefly and left.

Hwenfayre stayed where she was, warming herself by the dying fire, until her legs ached. Then she went to bed, her meal, still on the table where she had left it, uneaten.

The next few days passed as a dream, with little to remember them by. She woke in the mornings, went to the market, played her harp and ate a little. She did not go to the wall, she spoke to no one except the occasional customer and she saw neither Wyn nor Niall. At night she sat in silence, staring at the fire dancing its mystic dance as it consumed the logs she had bought. The cracking of the flames was the only sound she heard; all the other noises seemed to drift past her without impinging on her consciousness. She stared intently, seeing every flicker and every waver of every flame as it licked hungrily at the logs.

How long she would have been able to live like this, thinking of nothing else, she never knew, for one night she was disturbed by a heavy pounding at her door. Hwenfayre looked at the door, momentarily disoriented. What was she to do? The pounding came again and she remembered that she was expected to open the door in such situations.

Slowly and stiffly, she stood and walked to the door.

'Who is it?' she asked through the wooden door.

'Wyn,' came the gruff reply.

Hwenfayre opened the door. 'Wyn,' she asked, 'what are you doing here?'

'I,' he paused, apparently groping for words, 'I wanted to see you, to see how you were. I have not seen you for some days.'

'I am well, thank you,' she replied, unwilling to enter into a conversation that might require her to talk about the past few days.

'Good,' he said. He stood there, uncomfortable, in her doorway.

'Was there something else?' Hwenfayre asked. She put as much dismissive disdain as she could into her voice, wishing him to leave.

'Hwenfayre —' he began.

'Yes?' she interrupted.

'Hwenfayre, we need to talk. It's about the other night, on the wall. Some of the men are talking, and . . .' His voice trailed off uncertainly.

'Come inside.'

Once Wyn was inside, Hwenfayre looked up and down the street before closing and bolting her door. Wyn sat on the one chair.

'So what are these men saying?' she asked.

'Hwenfayre, they are saying dangerous things. They say that you are a witch who has power over the very elements, and that you called up the storm that drove off the Raiders. They say that you have bewitched the Coerl, that you were the mysterious woman who was with him that night on the wall.' He paused and stared intently into her lavender eyes. He stared for so long that she felt he was examining her very soul. Finally he broke off and continued. 'Hwenfayre, it has even been said that you are somehow in league with the Raiders.'

'But that is folly!' she exclaimed. 'How could they

believe that I am both in league with them and that I called up the storm that drove them off? Surely they must know that I am no sorcerer!'

'Some of the men were badly shaken by the storm. They are ready to believe anything just now. Especially now that there are stories of the Children of Danan around town.'

'The who?'

'The Sea Wanderers, the Faeries of the Wave, the Sea Dancers, the Fish-lovers. Surely you have heard tales of them?'

'Oh yes, the Sea Dancers, I have heard of them. What of them?'

'Haven't you heard the stories of how they are able to control the Sea and the mighty beasts of the deep? What of the tales of their unholy rites? How they sacrifice their children to the waters and eat their captives in rituals too black to describe. Surely you know that they are the very image of evil?' As he spoke, Wyn's eyes grew hard and piercing. He glared at her, as if daring her to disagree, or perhaps to agree.

'I have heard tales, yes. But not those. I have heard of their love for the sea, and their wondrous singing, and their beautiful ships. I have heard how they travel all their lives on the sea, never coming to land. But I have not heard any of the others.'

'Hwenfayre,' Wyn began, then paused. He had a look about him of one who has something to say, but is not sure how to. 'Hwenfayre ...' His voice was gentle. 'They do come to land.'

The following day, Hwenfayre woke early. Wyn's odd comments about the Children of Danan had played on her mind all night, leaving her sleep uneasy and fitful. He had refused to expand on his final statement and had left abruptly when she persisted.

As always, she knew when dawn was about to break, so, even before the sky began to change, to shift towards the day, she determined to greet it as she should. No matter what anyone thought, the dawn deserved to be welcomed.

When she arrived, the guards were there as usual. They walked stiffly past her, averting their eyes and muttering quietly. Hwenfayre was oblivious to their reactions. The morning was a beautiful one, and it was going to be welcomed properly.

She watched the sky gradually lighten. When the sun's edge appeared above the horizon, Hwenfayre closed her eyes to feel its warmth on her face. Almost unconsciously, she caressed the strings of her harp, forming the sounds that would welcome the morning appropriately. She played the whole song with her eyes closed, feeling the sun's warmth soothing her body and the flow of the music soothing her soul.

When the song was finished she remained still, letting the pleasure of it wash over her. It filled her with peace. It eased her fears and cleansed her mind. She felt the tensions of the past few days subside beneath the song's quiet ebb and flow. Without her being aware of it, a small smile formed on her lips. An expression of harmony and quietude slowly suffused her face as she felt the strength and overwhelming power of the sea fill her.

'You belong here.'

The deep, strong voice shocked her out of her reverie. Her eyes snapped open. She turned to see the

Coerl standing beside her, looking at her with mystery in his eyes. He smiled. It transformed his face from the hard man who commanded men into a kind man called Niall.

'You belong here, Hwenfayre,' he repeated. She nodded slowly, the feeling of peace fading slightly to be replaced by another, less recognisable feeling.

'I must go,' she said. 'I have to be in the market today.' Without a backwards look, she gathered her skirt and scampered away.

Two pairs of eyes followed her as she ran, one speculative, one unreadable.

For some reason the streets, normally dark and threatening, seemed somehow wider, lighter, almost welcoming this morning. Her heart felt light within her breast as it beat fast with the exhilaration of being alive. Happiness stole into her, planting an unexpected seed deep within her. She could not wait for it to grow and bloom.

Several days later she met with Niall at the Minstrel's Rest. As a child, Hwenfayre had seen her mother preparing herself for similar meetings with men. It had seemed to her that she spent inordinately long periods of time in doing so. There was the selection of just the right dress, which was not a problem for Hwenfayre as she had but two, and then there were the hours, it seemed, spent in applying face colours and brushing hair. Both of these activities Hwenfayre disdained. Instead, she put on her long dark blue dress, her shawl and her boots. She quickly brushed her hair. On an impulse, she picked up her harp. Hwenfayre then left her home, closing the door behind her.

It was a comfortable evening. Two friends spending a few hours together, talking, laughing, exchanging small confidences. To Hwenfayre, a new life was appearing before her. A new word entered her mind: friendship. Never before had she spent such an evening. For the first time away from the wall and the sea, she felt alive. She laughed at Niall's stories, she smiled at his smiles and she allowed herself to fall deeply into the spell of his dark, mysteriously changeable eyes.

He walked her home. They stood close together at her door. She looked up into his eyes as he smiled down at her. A strange expression crossed his face briefly. She frowned.

'What is it, Niall?' she asked.

'Nothing, dear Hwenfayre,' he replied.

Slowly, he lifted his hand and touched her gently on the cheek. At his touch, she shivered lightly. He made to remove his hand, but she quickly took it in both of her own and pressed it to her cheek. The warmth of his touch spread through her entire body, filling her with strange, unfamiliar sensations.

'I must go, dear Hwenfayre.'

He pulled his hand slowly away. As he turned to leave, she grasped hold of it again. He stopped and turned back. Their eyes locked, and suddenly she was in his arms. He held her tight as she pressed herself against his body. She felt a new warmth suffuse her.

As though he felt it too, Niall released her and stepped back. 'This cannot be, Hwenfayre. It is not right.' He held her at arm's length. 'I must go. It's late, and I have dawn duty again tomorrow.' He touched her again briefly, gently, on the cheek, and was gone.

Hwenfayre slept badly that night, awash with conflicting emotions.

She slept so badly, in fact, that she was up, dressed and on the wall even earlier than normal. She stood in the usual place, hidden in a dark niche, watching, waiting for the sun to rise. As always, she was silent, motionless. Even her breathing was slow and shallow; nothing would disturb the perfection of the sunrise.

She was so still that when Wyn walked by he seemed unaware of her presence. His eyes were hidden by the dark, but she still felt their strength as they swept over the niche where she hid. He did not pause as he walked past, but a few paces on he stopped and turned to face the sea. He stood perfectly still for a moment, then started to sing.

He sang softly, in a deep, resonant voice. As he sang, Hwenfayre's skin went cold. Her fingers trembled and her heart started to pound within her breast. The words he sang were powerful, strange, compelling. They spoke of a fierce love for the sea, for her many moods and for the myriad creatures she covered.

He sang with a passion that gave the lie to his impassive demeanour and brutish appearance.

He sang from a soul that knew and loved not only the words that he sang, but also the Sea of whom he sang.

He sang of things that Hwenfayre had hardly dared believe could be true as though he knew them to be so.

He sang the words to the song that Hwenfayre had written for herself, those many years before.

As she listened to the song, she knew that these words were the ones she would have written herself, were she but able. The words filled her with a deep longing to see and to experience in every way possible the joys and wonders that they described. She was transported in a way that she never believed possible. She gave herself over totally to the soulful sweep, the gentle flow of Wyn's singing, and lost herself in a world she hungered for.

Just as she felt she could take no more, as if she would lose herself utterly and never be able to return, Wyn stopped. He stood for a moment, looking at the eastern horizon, where the first rays of the sun were beginning to show, then turned to walk away.

As he did so, he murmured, 'You do not belong here, Hwenfayre.'

She fled without welcoming the dawn. When she arrived home she slammed the door behind her, bolted it and ran into her bedroom. She threw herself down onto her bed and lay there, still and silent, lost in her thoughts until dusk.

She pondered what she'd felt when Niall had held her, and how she had reacted to Wyn's quiet words. She had never known such a tangle of emotions. She went through the events of the past two days over and over again in her mind, yet she could not make any sense of what was happening to her.

It was finally hunger that made her move. She roused herself to prepare a meal. It was a simple meal of fruits and raw vegetables. As she picked at her food, a sudden feeling of unease swept through her. It was the same feeling she had had at the Wall with Niall, the last time the Southern Raiders had attacked. She waited, expecting the feeling to subside, but it did not. Instead it built up alarmingly. There came with it the feeling of wrongness, the feeling that something, somewhere, was not as it should be. This was unnatural; something had tampered with nature. Try as she might, she simply could not put aside these feelings. Almost against her will, she rose from her seat, unbolted the door and went outside.

The feeling of unnaturalness was even worse outside. It became a strong foreboding of disaster, a gnawing fear more than unease that threatened to swamp her, to completely overwhelm her unless she did something. But she could not think of what to do.

To alleviate her growing anxiety, she started walking. She had no aim, no direction; she walked as if in a trance. Around her the streets became nameless, formless. She walked on, seeing neither the streets nor the people who surrounded her with their normal mindless insensitivity. She walked blindly, she walked carelessly. She walked directly to the wall without knowing it.

Her reverie was broken when two strong hands took her by the shoulders and shook her slightly.

'What are you doing here, Hwenfayre?' She looked up sharply into Niall's eyes. He looked troubled, yet concerned. The shaking stopped, but he did not release her shoulders. Instead he drew her close, holding her gently against him. 'You should not be here,' he murmured into her hair. 'It is dangerous. Especially tonight. As you already know.'

'How do you know it is dangerous tonight?'

'The same way that you do. I feel it too. It is the same as before. Something is going to happen tonight. We'll be ready.' He sounded quietly confident that he would be able to deal with whatever was strange in the night. Hwenfayre was not so sure. In some way it was as if the night's strangeness seemed to revolve around Niall. She tried to tell him but the words would not come out; instead she found herself enjoying his closeness and taking comfort from his strong arms.

He released her suddenly, spinning around to face the sea. 'Here they come,' he breathed. As the words left his lips, there came a cry from the highest part of the wall: 'Raiders!'

'Stay out of trouble,' he told Hwenfayre, without turning around. 'Better yet, go home. This will be no place for a woman tonight.' He dashed off along the wall, calling as he ran, leaving Hwenfayre behind.

She stood still and silent, hugging herself tightly. As she did so, she discovered, with surprise, that she held her harp.

Around her the sounds of preparation for battle commenced. Men ran past her, oblivious to her presence in their controlled haste to ready themselves for the defence of their town. Unlike the previous time, when only she and the Coerl had been ready for the onslaught, it seemed that all the soldiers on the wall were ready. Whilst the preparations were fast, they had none of the frenetic feel that had been so evident before. She stepped back into a dark corner, where she hid out of sight, out of the way. It seemed like only a matter of moments before the cauldrons were filled and hot, the bows were all strung and the posts were all manned. An expectant hush fell over the wall as every eye was trained on the flickering torches that illuminated the black warboats as they drew ever closer.

There was a cry, and the first catapult was loosed. A fiery missile leaped from the boat. It arced high. At the peak of its flight it seemed to pause briefly as if considering its target, before hurtling downwards to the city behind the wall.

'Watch where it falls!' The Coerl's voice pierced the night and battle was joined. A hail of arrows sped down at the Raiders' boats, answered a moment later by a veritable firestorm of burning missiles fired from the catapults below.

With the first cry of alarm from the lookout, the citizenry of the town had begun their own preparations, and the fires that were started by the flaming missiles were short-lived. Both sides knew that this was only the preliminary bout, the opening gambit. Nonetheless, several people lost treasured possessions, some lost family, in this prologue to battle.

The true fight started when the grappling hooks started to replace the fireballs. With the grappling hooks came ropes, and with the ropes came climbers. Each catapult launched several hooks. As fast as the men on the walls could throw down the hooks that landed and took hold, more were quick to follow. Within minutes there were dozens of ropes connecting the warboats to the top of the wall, and on each of the ropes were several Raiders, climbing as fast as rats.

Hand-to-hand fighting followed quickly. The first wave of Raiders was soon dealt with and sent hurtling to their deaths, either bearing savage wounds from a defender's sword or simply having been pushed back as they clambered over the ramparts. The cauldrons of boiling oil were poured over the wall onto the attackers, the ropes bursting into flame as the oil flowed down. Men leaped from the ropes, only to be dashed onto the rocks below as the liquid flame raced towards them.

Yet still they came, clambering up ropes that were replaced as quickly as they could be dislodged. Despite their best efforts, the defenders on the wall were unable to stem the flow of attackers. Soon there were dozens of Raiders on the ramparts. The noise of fighting filled Hwenfayre's ears: the clash of steel on steel, the grunting of men as they strove against each other, the shouts as they ran to meet the next opponent, and over all, more chilling than all the other noises, the cries of the dying.

Hwenfayre stared at the maelstrom of violence, unable to comprehend any of it. In desperation, she summoned to her mind those memories of her life that had somehow sustained her through the pain of living as she had. She saw again the beauty of a sunrise, the majesty of a storm, the power of thundering waves, and above all there seemed to float the gentle eyes of a man whom she loved, yet could not quite recognise. As she lost herself in the magical world of her dreams, the scene before her shifted, merged, floated out of focus as she watched. She felt herself drift, as though she had left her body.

Unthinkingly, she took her harp from under her cloak and strummed it gently in stark counterpoint to the savagery around her. A sense of unreality stayed with her as she watched and played, humming softly. Nothing could touch her; she was safe, wrapped in her music, cocooned in the smoothly rippling notes that gently enfolded her. Even the cries of the dying men seemed distant, muffled. Their pain became dulled, her awareness of it diminished by her increasing detachment from reality. The only thing she was truly aware of was the sound of her song.

It rose and fell in a soothing, gentling melody, guarding her soul from the pain and death around her. It allowed her to watch as if she were outside the violence as the Raiders slowly gained purchase on the top of the wall. The complex interweaving of melody and song lent her the peaceful poise of the truly uncaring, not bothered as men whom she knew spilt their lifeblood on the stones at her feet and split the night with their agonised cries. Even through the all-consuming muse of her own music, her mind cried out in protest that this was wrong, that she did care. It did matter to her that men were dying and suffering. It should hurt her that her home was being invaded, violated, with such malice. Deep within her soul, Hwenfayre cared and suffered pain, but the music had her and would not let her go.

As she stood, eyes unfocused, unmoving except for her hands that caressed the strings of her harp and her lips that sang an unknown song, a struggle for the control of her mind and soul raged within her. A close observer might have noticed her chest heaving, as though from great exertion. Without warning, a terrible physical pain swept through her. Its sharpness, its awful poignancy, seemed to give her strength. The scene before her was overlaid with another. The two images overlapped, forming a complex vision of destruction and suffering. She struggled to make sense of the conflicting images, but in the one not before her, the one in her mind, she saw a man dying. She blinked her eyes. They focused. They saw.

Somewhere on the wall Niall lay dead. A great cry of angry defiance burst from her lips, cutting across the previously gentle song she had been singing. With a fierce anger burning in her eyes and breast, she took control of herself, driving the stupor from her mind.

A new song rippled from her harp. It was a song of strength, of passion, but above all, of love. With total control over feelings she never knew she possessed, Hwenfayre sang her song, and all around her the world went mad, as from nowhere the storm struck the town.

No longer oblivious, Hwenfayre watched as massive waves pounded the rocks below her, smashing warboats to tinder. The rain fell, a deluge, a flood from above, instantly soaking to the skin all who had not sought shelter. Lightning exploded from the suddenly cloud-filled sky. Each bolt, with unearthly precision, shattered the body of a Raider. Men from the town watched in horror as their erstwhile attackers were systematically destroyed before their very eyes by the savage power of the storm. In terror, the defenders threw down their weapons and fled the maniacal onslaught of the incomprehensible fury that rained death from the skies.

The wind screamed in concert with Hwenfayre's playing as it whipped about the wall, plucking men as they stood and hurling them to their deaths on the rocks below. It swirled around the white-haired Hwenfayre, causing her cloak to whirl and billow, her hair to stream out, a wild mane framing her face. Her lavender eyes burned with a holy fire as they stared unblinking upon the devastation she was wreaking.

One Raider, stronger than the rest, driven mad by the terror, struggled to his feet and strove towards her, axe held across his chest. Madness gleamed from his bloodshot eyes as he approached. Spittle mixed with blood and dribbled down his chin from a mouth that hung slackly open. Seeing him, Hwenfayre saw one who had brought not only destruction to her home but one of those who had killed a man she might have loved, if given a chance.

She took her hand from the strings of her harp and pointed. As if with its own life, the music continued, the harp still playing as Hwenfayre screamed a word in a language that was harsh even to her own ears. Its force struck the man, shocking him briefly back into sanity. His last sane action was to scream in abject terror as the wind leaped to Hwenfayre's bidding and plucked the Raider from his feet.

It lifted him high above the wall, holding him there, and he screamed as the last vestiges of his mind were destroyed. Then, with another thought, Hwenfayre commanded lightning from the clouds. It struck the man, illuminating him briefly. His body exploded with a blast that shook the wall to its very foundations.

Abruptly, silence fell. The storm vanished as magically as it had appeared. Hwenfayre stood alone on the wall, surrounded by the wreckage of broken men and shattered weapons. Her harp fell silent, her arms hung limply by her sides. Slowly Hwenfayre turned around, surveying what she had wrought. She stared at the bodies littering the ramparts. The faces were frozen in the snarling rictus of death, eyes wide, as if in the moment of their shocking end the men had seen something that was more terrifying than death itself.

The bodies were all washed clean of blood, and somehow this made them a more disgusting sight. Regarding their clean faces and washed bodies, Hwenfayre felt the weight of every dying moment that she had caused crash down upon her unready soul. With a heart-wrenching cry, she fell to her knees and wept, sobbing as if to wash away the horrible bloodstains that she felt taint her heart deeply.

A hand rested gently on her shoulder.

'Hwenfayre.' A strong male voice interrupted her weeping.

She turned her tear-ravaged face towards the voice. Her eyes were blurred from the tears and she could only make out a large, darkly clad man standing behind her.

'Niall?' she asked in despairing hope.

'Wyn,' came the heavy response.

'Where's Niall?' she asked, hoping that she had been wrong.

'Dead.'

The pain went through her like a sword. 'Dead?' she gasped. 'How?'

'Axe.'

The horror, the pain, the brutality that Wyn's single syllable carried was almost too much for Hwenfayre to bear. She fell face down onto the wet stones, crying out in anguish. In her heart and soul she could feel the savagery of the death blow. During her life Hwenfayre had seen men killed. She had, at times, seen men wounded by arrows, or by falls, or by accidents. But nothing compared with the hideous wounds caused by a sea-Raider's axe. The image that rose in her mind of Niall, robust and powerful, cut down in such a way, left her reeling, fearing for what was left of her mind.

She lay sobbing, yet dry-eyed. There were no more tears left for her to cry. The deep, racking sobs slowed and then stopped. The pain did not abate, but Hwenfayre was able to look up at Wyn. He stood motionless, impassive, as he stared down at her. Their eyes met. An unreadable expression flickered across Wyn's eyes, then he reached out his hand to help Hwenfayre to her feet.

She took his hand, feeling the calluses of a fighting man. He lifted her up with a strength that surprised her.

'Come, Hwenfayre. You should leave this place. It is no longer safe,' he rumbled. Numbly she nodded and followed him as he led her down the stairs and along the dark streets, back to her empty home.

As they walked, Hwenfayre was faintly aware that he never let go of her hand. She was also conscious, as though looking through a glass, of the stares of the people they passed. Their mutters, their words, went unheard. The only thing Hwenfayre was aware of was the pain.

Once inside, Wyn released her hand. Gently he guided her to a chair. She sat limply. He hunkered down in front of her, taking hold of her hand once more.

'Hwenfayre,' he said gently. 'Hwenfayre. You cannot stay here.' She stared past him, her eyes registering neither Wyn nor his words. The only indication he received that she even heard him was a slight tightening of her hand as it lay in his. 'Hwenfayre,' he said again. 'Hwenfayre, it is too dangerous for you to stay here. You must leave.'

She blinked and pulled her hand back. 'Why?'

'Don't you remember what the Coerl told you? These people are simple, superstitious. They fear what they don't understand. And what they fear, they kill. You are in great danger.' He spoke in low, earnest tones.

'But how can I leave? Where would I go?'

'Hwenfayre, you must go home. Back to the Sea, where you truly belong. Come with me.' A light of impossible hope flickered in her eyes as she stared at the man crouched before her. A small smile played about the corners of his mouth as he nodded slightly. 'It's true,' he continued, 'you do not belong here.' He stood, suddenly looming tall in front of her. 'Come. Let me take you home, my Princess of the Sea.'

Slowly, wrestling with the tumult of conflicting emotions within her, Hwenfayre reached up and took the hand he offered.

Together they vanished into the night.

8

Shanek grunted with effort as he spun away. The sun was hot on his head and sweat beaded his torso. He wore only his training kilt and his feet were bare as they scuffed the hot sands of the battle ring. Over the sound of his own laboured breathing, he heard the creak of leather armour as Coerl Leone drew back her arm for a strike at his naked back.

His momentum carried him forward, twisting to his right as he spun the bolas over his head. The ancient weapon hummed, almost in anticipation, as he regained his balance. His next move was one that he had practised in private and he was sure that Leone would have no defence.

The Coerl's blade sliced through the air. Shanek dropped to his left knee, pivoted, and spun the bolas into two overlapping circles, one horizontal, one vertical. The horizontally spinning cable wrapped around her knees, whilst the vertical one snaked around her sword arm.

'Burn it!' Leone cursed as the two bolae crashed painfully against her. But the move was not complete. Even as she started to drag her sword arm back, Shanek continued in his pivot, leaning back and throwing all his weight away from her. The sudden change of direction jerked Leone off balance. With her knees still wrapped by the heavy bolas cord, she had no option but to crash to the ground.

Still balanced, Shanek threw himself on the winded Coerl as he whipped a length of the bolas cord around her neck. Panting heavily, he grinned at her, his face close to hers.

'You're dead, Coerl Leone,' he gasped. 'Now I hold power over you.'

'No, First Son,' she said. 'You don't. And I am not dead, you are.' Her eyes looked down. Shanek followed her gaze to where she held a dagger in her left hand. It was lightly touching his groin, a hair's breadth away from the artery. He looked up into her eyes. 'Your lifeblood would be staining my uniform before you could tighten that cord, First Son,' she hissed.

'Burn me, but you're good!' shouted Shanek. He rolled off Leone and sprang to his feet. In deference to centuries of custom, he stepped out of the battle ring and bowed to his opponent.

Coerl Leone stood. Shanek was pleased to note that she was breathing heavily, her face flushed with exertion. 'That was a new move, First Son,' she said. 'You've been practising on your own again.'

Shanek nodded. 'Coerl . . .' he began.

'First Son!' the call interrupted him.

In annoyance, he looked to find the voice. He frowned as he identified Salen, a young noble who had been attempting to cultivate his friendship for several months. Shanek had considered using the ambitious man, but no one interrupted a weapons session. He turned to address Leone.

'I think that the ambitious Salen has just won a ten-year tour of the Great Fastness, hunting wyverns and keeping the Thane safe from banditry.'

Coerl Leone allowed herself a small smile. 'I think he may need some company, First Son.'

Shanek raised his eyebrows. 'Who did you have in mind?'

'Marcene and her poisonous sister should be able to keep him warm at night, First Son,' she said.

'Hmm. I hadn't thought of them.' He regarded Leone. 'Do they have any military training?'

Leone shook her head. 'No, First Son, but they're bright girls. They'll learn fast.'

Shanek laughed, half considering her idea. The two girls were becoming annoying with their importuning. A few years chasing bandits and wyverns, and maybe a few wild Skrinnies, might dampen their enthusiasm a bit. The light tread of Salen's approach broke his train of thought. Shanek slowly shifted to face the approaching noble.

'What are you doing here?' he snarled.

Salen was taken aback by the venom in the First Son's voice.

'I ... I,' he stammered.

'Well?' demanded Shanek. 'Out with it!'

'Your father sent me,' he said.

'My father? Why would he send you?'

'He didn't say, Shanek. He just told me to come here and bring you to meet with the Thane.'

Coerl Leone stiffened, her hand gripping her sword hilt. 'You will address the First Son with due respect, Salen!' she hissed.

Salen regarded the Coerl with an arrogant eye. 'Who are you to tell me how to speak?' he demanded.

'I am Coerl Leone,' she replied, her voice now a whisper.

'So?' replied Salen.

Shanek marvelled at how stupid one man could be. Surely anyone with a whit of sense could have smelled the death in the air. This fool was a careless syllable away from violent death, and he even swaggered!

Leone's anger was unlike anything he had seen in her before. It seemed that he could actually feel it, yet as he turned to look at her she appeared completely at ease. Only the slight tightness around her eyes and the way she gripped her sword gave any hint of the violence he could feel.

Salen smirked and looked to Shanek. 'Call off your bitch, Shanek,' he said. 'I am unamused by her posturing.'

The First Son was still looking at Leone as Salen spoke. Her expression did not change, but he knew what she was about to do and threw himself to the ground as her sword whistled out of its scabbard.

Salen's blood splattered the dirt around him, several heavy red drops splashing on his back. The noble was dead before he saw the sword move, but Shanek had *known* it was coming.

'It is unlike you to duck, First Son,' Leone observed as she wiped her blade. 'You should know I never miss from this distance.'

Shanek rolled over and looked up at her. 'I knew you were going to do that.'

Leone nodded. 'I thought your reflexes were good, First Son, but I must be getting sloppy if you could read my expression that easily.'

'I didn't. I just knew,' he said, still lying flat on his back.

Leone sheathed her blade and held out her hand to help him up. Shanek took it and she pulled him to his feet. 'We have been fighting together for years, First Son. You know my moves well by now.'

Shanek was unconvinced, but he nodded. He needed to think.

Coerl Leone stood beside him, waiting. Finally, he started to move away towards the changing rooms. With a gesture to the awaiting Skrinnies, Leone followed him.

Behind them, the tall, angular Skrin Tia'k slaves walked with their peculiarly lugubrious gait to clean up the mess that used to be Salen, their exoskeletal legs clicking as they moved.

Shanek received a small smattering of applause as he left the Training Arena. One or two young women called out encouragement or made other, less seemly offers. The First Son ignored them as he left, just as he also ignored the comradely greetings from other soldiers who were training. Normally, he would have stopped to talk to some, but today he was too distracted. The disappointment of his failure with the new move, the interruption, the odd sense of knowing Leone's move before time, as well as the curious summons from his father, all spun through his mind. What could his father want? It was the Thane's Week of Celebration; no one worked, not even the First Counsellor. Tradition held that it celebrated the last great victory over the Skrin Tia'k.

He stopped and looked at the three Skrinnie slaves as they carried the body off the arena, trying to imagine the gangly arthropoid creatures fighting a war that lasted for generations. They stood, usually on their hind limbs, about half as tall again as a human, with their middle limbs doing any carrying, while their forelimbs were used for any delicate work. As vassals of the Asan, their long and supple fingers were used to create art works of exceptional complexity, while their strong backs were useful for labour. A quality Skrinnie carving, especially in the rare red obsidian from the far north, would sell for a year's wages. The Skrin Tia'k slaves were strong and skilled, but usually slow to learn to follow anything but the most simple commands. It appeared that their artistic ability was innate and any slave owner who happened upon a natural artisan was suddenly wealthy. The Skrinnies were useful slaves but had been a formidable foe in a generations-long war. Shanek had trouble believing that they could ever be anything but a nuisance to the mighty Army of the World.

The historical accounts, now so old as to be almost legend, recounted that after a particularly brutal battle the humans were so impoverished by decades of losing that the Thane and the First Counsellor were barefoot, having given their shoes to the army. They also slept on the ground with the army as their fine tent had been torn up for bandages.

During the week that followed this battle, the First Counsellor showed the brilliance in warfare that had been the trademark of the Asan ever since. With a series of stunningly perceptive moves, he had outmanoeuvred the Skrinnie army, inflicting massive casualties. Each move, if legend reflected truth, seemed to fly in the face of everything they had done before, but each one caught the enemy by surprise. The carnage had been terrible, with fully eight of every ten Skrinnies killed. The entire nation was routed and the once-powerful creatures were driven into perpetual slavery.

Now, the Skrinnies were subservient and weak. Domovoi was right about one thing: the free labour provided by the Skrin Tia'k had long aided the Asan economy. By putting the captured armies of the other human peoples on the continent to work in the farms, the Asan had become wealthy beyond measure.

Now, however, the tactical genius of early First Counsellors was a thing of the legendary past. Instead of brilliance, the Asan overwhelmed their enemies by the simple weight of numbers.

Anger!

The raw emotion shot through Shanek like a spear thrust. His head snapped around, looking for the shout or the cry that must have come, but the arena was quiet. Only the normal grunts and muted clang of weapons echoed. Unconsciously, he started to whirl the bolas, the heavy spiked balls whistling as they circled his head.

The distinctive bolas whistle caused a few to stop in their practice bouts to look, puzzlement on their faces. Shanek let the bolas slow and fall to the ground.

'First Son?' asked Leone. 'Is something wrong?' Her sword was out, her eyes searching.

'No,' he said. 'No, I just thought I heard something. It's nothing.'

Coerl Leone took up her station, one pace back at Shanek's left. The rest of the Fyrd encircled them as they made their way back to the Palace of the Thane.

Outside the Training Arena, the celebrating crowds parted for them. On this the fourth day of the Celebration week, the people were free to fill the streets and enjoy a day of unbridled merrymaking. Many children owed their conception to this day of wild debauchery. Naturally, it was also a day on which many lost their lives to opportunistic crime as the various gangs took to the streets in search of easy prey.

The noise of happy revelry filled Shanek's ears as he walked within his protective shield. The normal glares of discontent that he often noticed were missing, replaced by drunken leering, the glazed stares of the drugged and the wild-eyed excitement of the young. It was another hot afternoon and the drink had been flowing freely since sunrise. The smells of stale beer, vomit and sex mingled with the normal stench of the masses to produce something special for this most special of days.

A shrill ululating squeal split the air, stilling the raucous cheerfulness as a Skrin Tia'k somewhere met its end at the hands of a mob bent on celebrating their victory in style. While the unnatural silence held, Shanek looked at the faces of the revellers around him. He saw bestial pleasure as they savoured the sounds of the death of the ancient enemy. A shock of visceral hunger ripped through him, drawing his face into a snarl. He could almost taste the blood and feel the death shudders of the slave as the knife struck again and again. He could see the angry faces of his attackers as they tore the Skrinnie's body apart. Shanek shook with the Skrinnie's pain.

'First Son!'

His eyes focused on Coerl Leone. Why was she suddenly so tall? The sky above him was glaringly bright. Why was he lying on the ground?

'What happened?' he asked. As he spoke, he felt blood trickle down his chin. He wiped it off, staring at the bright red stain on his fingers.

Leone helped him to his feet. 'You started to scream and fell down,' she said. 'We feared you had been attacked.'

Shanek felt his body, checking for wounds. Finding none, he thought back over his vision. 'Down there,' he pointed to a narrow alley. 'You will find seven men armed with knives. They have just butchered that Skrinnie we heard. I want them brought alive to me at the palace.'

Leone gestured to four of her Fyrd. They turned and jogged away, swords drawn. Shanek stalked towards the Palace, his confusion and fear rapidly changing to anger.

How dare they! He seethed. Around him the noise of the crowd seemed to dim, to be replaced by a simmering fury, the like of which he had never experienced. He was unaware of Leone and her Fyrd as they re-formed the living shield around him, he was only conscious of the hard ground beneath his feet and the rising emotion within.

His hands, gloved to protect them from the hundreds of tiny barbs that ran the length of the bolas cord, gripped the weapon. The layer of metal that prevented the barbs from catching on the gloves rasped as he alternately clenched and released his fists. By the time he reached the Palace, his fury was almost out of control. His hands, when they weren't tightly gripping his bolas, were shaking, his face was pale, and his back, still splattered with blood, was rigid. Leone had seen him angry but never anything like this.

His mood left her edgy and unsure. Normally alert for anything that might threaten his welfare, she found herself distracted and unfocused, unable to decide whether Shanek was in danger from the crowd or posed one himself. She watched his movements, trying to discern if he was about to use his weapon, and if so, on whom. Her sword drawn as she walked, she was oblivious to the trail of tiny drops of blood that followed her, evidence of the dozens of wounds Shanek had given her during their training bout. Such wounds were normal, but today he had caught her by surprise with his new move. Its combination of speed, strength and subtlety was remarkably skilful, far beyond what he had done previously.

As she followed the First Son, she tried to focus on the important things that she knew should be occupying her mind, but she kept thinking back to the time during their practice bout when Shanek had lain heavily on her. No matter how she tried to drive the memory away, the feeling of his hard body pressed against her, breathing heavily, his face close to hers, aroused in her a desire that was as intense as it was impossible. He was First Son, she a simple warrior. She had been his guard since he was a boy and he had never shown the slightest interest in her. And, if truth be told, she had never been interested in him, having watched his way with the many women who had entertained him over the years. But suddenly all that had changed; her body had betrayed her then and it threatened to do the same now.

With annoyance, she shook her head, attempting to clear the disturbing images. She hated the way her mind had reacted. It was stupid and inappropriate for her to entertain such thoughts, not to mention the fact that she had no interest at all in him. Not that way, at least.

'What is it, Leone?' Shanek asked. He stopped and turned to face her.

'Nothing, First Son,' she replied.

He stared at her, his gaze hard and unflinching. 'You're lying, Coerl,' he snapped. 'I know when you lie to me. And there is something wrong. Something you should tell me about. What is it?'

Returning his gaze, she shook her head slowly. 'There is nothing wrong you should know about, First Son.'

He continued to stare, oblivious to the gathering crowd that had paused in its merrymaking to gawk at the third most important man in the Empire. 'You are still lying,' he hissed. Coerl Leone almost stepped back in shock. His voice was harsh, brutal. It was the voice of a killer. Instinct forced her to grip the hilt of her sword. Training made her grip ease as she saw

Shanek watching her hand. A vicious sneer disfigured his face, then he spun on his heel and stalked towards the Palace.

His abrupt move almost caught the Fyrd out of position, but years of discipline meant they had formed a perfect barrier around him before he made contact with the crowd. As usual their emotionless eyes and ready swords kept the unwashed masses far enough away from nobility.

As they passed through the gates to the Palace of the Thane, the noise, the stench, even the heat seemed to fade. The tension, the anger, the confusion all drained from him as the cool quiet of the Palace replaced the madness of the Celebration.

The Palace of the Thane was a stupendous edifice. It rose like a silken mountain above Ajyne, the sprawling capital of the Asan Empire. As with everything about the Empire, the city's location was the subject of legend. It was here that the first battle against the Skrin Tia'k had taken place. Centuries earlier, Ajyne had come into being as a small collection of huts around a spring of fresh, clear water. The simple hunter–gatherer lifestyle of the people was violently disturbed by a Skrin Tia'k attack. The Skrinnies had swept across the northern plain like a flood, burning everything in their path. The legend spoke of a hunter of great skill, Ajyne, who had seen the approaching Skrinnie army and rallied his fellow villagers. According to the overblown histories, he led most of the village to safety by eluding the Skrinnies, often avoiding them by seconds. At one stage he led a few hardy souls in a lightning raid that killed the Skrinnie leader. With the death of their leader, the rest of the Skrin Tia'k army pulled back north, but several young men followed them. When the men's butchered bodies were discovered, the generations-long war began.

Shanek often wondered which particular spot in the vast city commemorated the skirmish.

He regathered his fragmented thoughts as he strode through the vast parade ground towards the main doors. Behind him, Coerl Leone, still smarting from his anger, kept pace easily, as did his Fyrd. The smooth marble covering the entire open area felt hard, unyielding and unwelcoming after the dusty training arena. His feet jangled with an odd pain with every step he took on the polished surface, making him wonder if he had sustained an injury.

Ahead, the seven steps up to the Great Gates beckoned. Each step, carved from a different rock representing the Seven Orders of Purity, was guarded with an honour guard sent from the seven provinces. The different uniforms, weapons and features of the guards showed the range of the Empire. Shanek scarcely gave them a glance as he made his way up the Seven Orders, silently reciting his lessons from Domovoi for every step. '*Granite for courage, basalt for strength, quartz for honesty, slate for compassion, agate for humility, marble for grace and obsidian for love.*'

His inexplicable anger at the death of the Skrinnie was fading, but no matter how he considered it he had known and felt things he had no right to know or feel.

He scarcely noticed the armoured guards who heaved open the massive doors with such efficiency that he did not have to break stride. Without a thought Shanek passed the wondrous entrance, gold-plated and adorned with magnificent works of art from across the Empire, and strode into the presence of the most powerful man in the Empire.

When he reached the requisite twenty paces, still blood-spattered and clad only in his training kilt, he dropped into a one-kneed crouch, bowed his head and pressed his hands, still gloved, against the polished granite floor. The metallic clink of the bolas balls rang incongruously in the silent hall.

'First Son,' the Thane's rich tones eased their way across the hall, 'thank you for your prompt attendance. I know how busy you are.'

Still bowed, Shanek stiffened at the sarcasm in the Thane's tone. Although his life was safe from the Thane's vengeance as a result of his birthright, punishment for insolence and sundry offences could still be wrought. More than one First Counsellor had carried out his office maimed.

'Stand up, Shanek,' the Thane went on. 'Your pretence at obeisance offends me.'

Shanek stood and regarded his ruler. The Thane was a vigorous man in his late forties. He had fathered eight sons and seven daughters by his eight wives. Tradition held that each of the seven provinces provided the Thane with a bride, and he was free to choose another for himself. Normally the heir would come from the chosen wife, but this Thane was himself a son of one of the provinces, so speculation was rife as to whom he would choose from his own brood to continue his line.

Thane Kasimar IV stared back at Shanek. 'First

Son,' he continued, 'Appointed One Domovoi tells me your studies are progressing well.'

Shanek prided himself on his control, but the Thane was an experienced man.

'This surprises you?' the Thane asked.

'Yes, Sir. It does,' replied Shanek. In deference to the source of their power, the Thanes eschewed formal honorifics, preferring the simple military 'Sir'.

'Why is that?' the Thane asked.

'We argue and disagree often, Sir. And ...' he paused, considering his next words carefully, 'I don't think he likes me.'

Kasimar frowned. 'Your birthright protects you from most things, Shanek First Son, but beware. Arrogant presumption is not a crime but it is not a virtue. Domovoi has served this Empire and me personally for more decades than you have drawn breath. He enjoys my favour and his skills are not to be treated lightly by anyone.'

Shanek bowed his acceptance of the rebuke.

'As it so happens,' Kasimar went on, 'you are wrong. He holds you in very high regard.' The Thane paused to accept a morsel from a waiting Skrinnie slave. 'Which is why your father and I have decided that it is time to put your training to use.'

Shanek looked across to where his father sat, half-hidden in shadows behind and to the left of the Thane's throne. He was looking up, but Shanek could not see his eyes. Shanek waited for the Thane to continue.

'Do you see this throne?' Kasimar asked.

'Yes, Sir.'

'It was carved from a single piece of red obsidian, found eight hundred years ago on the slopes of Mount Tintal. The Skrin Tia'k living there at the time brought it here and had it carved into this throne. Obsidian, you will remember, is the symbol of love, the final step unto purity. Do you think there is any significance in their gift?'

'No, Sir.'

'Really? You don't see it as a gift of love?'

'No. I don't believe the Skrinnies have ever held any love for us, and their choice of gift is more likely to be a show of their disdain.'

'How so?'

'We cannot assume that a race so different from us will either understand or accept our beliefs. They have their own and will most likely view ours with contempt. I think their choice of our symbol of love would be a deliberate show of their hate. Using our own symbols against us, Sir.'

'Are the Skrin Tia'k so subtle?'

'Without question, Sir.'

'I am glad you think so, because I am sending you on a diplomatic mission to meet with the Council of Ettan.'

Shanek's mind raced. Ettan was a subject province, one of the seven. It was far to the north, its northern border lost in the brutal foothills of the great northern mountains. The only problems that ever arose in Ettan were involved with raiding parties of bandits, escaped Skrinnies or periodic clean-ups of the various monsters that wandered down from the icy mountain peaks. Ettan's history was one of political stability. A diplomatic mission was unheard of. *What is this really about?* Shanek wondered.

He had little time for reflection, though, as the Thane continued.

'I assume you will want to take a small entourage, but not this time. You will be travelling light and fast.' He raised his head to Coerl Leone. 'You are ready to travel?'

Leone saluted. 'Yes, Sir,' she said.

'First Son,' the Thane's voice took on the cadences of formal speech, 'you are directed to travel with your Fyrd and sundry others to the province of Ettan where you will take part in the diplomatic negotiations that will take place there. You will receive all information you require whilst travelling.'

Thane Kasimar IV stood and raised a sword above his head. He gestured to the ground, indicating the strength garnered from rock, and then to the sky, whence comes rain, and then to Shanek, now ritually set apart for service unto death for the Empire. Shanek was bound beyond law to complete his mission or die trying.

To return unsuccessful was death by torment in the Arena.

9

The Sea was calm. It had stayed calm now for several days, the sun beating mercilessly down on the small, open boat. The sounds of a still Sea surrounded the man and the woman who lay side by side on the planks that separated them from the depths: the gentle lapping of the water, the light flap of the limp sail that formed a shelter over them, the distant cry of a lonely gull as it winged its way across the vast ocean.

The woman stirred slightly, groaning as she attempted to sit up. Her movement caused the boat to rock, sending small ripples over the glassy Sea. She stretched, dragging her fingers through her tangled white hair. Her skin, which had always been fair, almost to the point of being white, was reddened and burned by the sun, painful where her torn, thin shift no longer covered her.

Her companion, a large, heavy man, opened his eyes at the rocking of the boat. His face was as badly burned as the woman's, but he looked less gaunt, less exhausted. With obvious effort, he lurched to the side of the boat and reached over to pull something out of the water.

It was a bottle that had been tied to the gunwale. He handed it, still dripping, to the fair-haired woman. At first she shook her head, but at his silent, insistent offering she took it, unstoppered it and took a small sip. A tiny dribble ran down her chin, dripping onto her sunburned chest. Feeling the unexpected coolness, she wiped the drop with her finger, which she then licked carefully. With a small smile that opened up one of the surburned cracks in her bottom lip, she handed the bottle back to the man. He accepted it gravely, shook it slightly, and dropped it back into the water.

It was a scene that had been played out many times, but there were few times left when it would occur. Unless they found land soon, it was clear that both of them would die.

As he watched the young woman lie back under the makeshift shelter, the former guard shook his head slowly with deep regret. It was an ignominious end for such a woman. In the three weeks that the two of them had been together on this small boat, her nobility and strength of character had pleased and heartened him. She would need both when, if, they reached their destination.

As he thought of their destination, his eyes narrowed and his brow furrowed. Despite her dreams and obvious power, the young woman, who had already sunk back into a light, restless sleep, would not find life easy among her people. His own memories of them were not happy. He looked at her lying in the bottom of the boat, and sighed. How different she was from the frightened and unsure girl who had fled with him on that dark-omened night when she came into her power.

That night, when she stood to take his hand, he knew his life had changed irrevocably. With her decision to flee her home with him, she had not only chosen to flee a dangerous and uncertain life, she had also chosen to pursue her dreams. His knowledge of the world into which they had thrown themselves was limited, despite the tales he had told her earlier. Most of his travelling on the Sea had been as a mercenary or galley slave, not as a sailor. In truth, his job as wall guard had been the best that he had had for some years. But he had known his responsibility as soon as he had seen her heralding the morning with her song.

No matter that he had left his people behind so long ago, no matter that he had turned his back on his heritage, their shared heritage. He had a duty to those who had given him life. The Danan must be returned to her Children. He knew his own motives were unclear, even to himself, but he knew about duty. The Thane and his soldiers had taught him that much. He looked again at the young woman, barely more than a child, lying in the boat, and shook his head. What was he hoping to achieve?

It had not been easy to win the confidence of the town's mystery woman, but he was a man experienced in campaigns, and he had laid good plans. Knowing, as he believed he did, the woman's heritage, he spoke to her of the Sea. He spoke lyrically, drawing on the half-remembered tales of his childhood. His stories evoked the beauty and power of the oceans that both terrified and fascinated her young soul.

The greatness that had lain dormant within her was awakened.

But it had all gone horribly awry when the foolish Coerl, curse his stupid meddling, had interfered. He had spoken with her, filled her mind with thoughts of love and such things. He had no right to. At least he had had the decency to die at a good time, providing her with the strength she needed. Inwardly the man shuddered as he remembered how close she had come to succumbing to the treacherous lure of the harp's song as she stood watching the battle.

When the Coerl had died, the psychic shock that had run through her mind had been the catalyst to truly awaken her latent power over the mystical energies she had unwittingly unleashed. Despite the fact that the erstwhile guard had little understanding of these energies, he had heard many stories concerning them. He had faced death many times, but nothing frightened him more than those stories had.

'Wyn.' The voice was weak, hoarse and tired. It awakened him from his musings.

'What is it, Hwenfayre?' he asked gently.

'We tried, didn't we?' She stared intently at him, the strength shining from her almost glowing lavender eyes, which belied the weakness in her voice.

'Tried what, my Princess?' he responded, attempting to forestall whatever expression of defeat she was about to utter.

'Tried to reach them. Tried to get home. We did, didn't we?'

'Yes, my Princess. We tried, but we are not yet dead. We have water, there's a little food left, and while the weather holds fair we can still hope.' He reached out and stroked her tangled hair. She smiled, a small, cracked smile as she leaned into his hand.

'Wyn.'

'Yes?'

'Nothing. I just wanted to say your name once more before I die.'

'Nonsense, Hwenfayre. We are not destined to die yet.' He tried to withdraw his hand but she held it, pressing it against her cheek. He was shocked to feel how weak her grasp had become. 'You should sleep,' he suggested, easing his hand away. 'Don't try to talk too much. You need your strength.'

With a knowing look, Hwenfayre nodded slowly and sank back down onto the boards, resting her head on Wyn's guardsman's cloak that he had rolled up for her as a pillow. Once again, Wyn was struck by the tragic unfairness of it all. Hwenfayre had spent her life seeking her soul, her purpose, and within weeks of finding it, before she had any sort of chance to deal with the reality of who she was, it appeared that she would die, here, in the midst of what she loved so dearly, yet in such ignorance. Wyn knew more of the Sea and its vagaries than his young companion, and he faced it with fear.

That first night, they had run together along the back alleys of the Poor Quarter to a little-known gate that led them to an ancient stair. They followed it down to the rocky beach where Wyn had earlier hidden his small boat. When he first hid it there he had fervently hoped to let it lie and rot. The first morning he saw Hwenfayre had changed all that.

Their preparations had been, of necessity, minimal. Hwenfayre brought nothing more than her harp and some clothes. He had anticipated her decision to leave and had brought some food and water and extra cloaks.

As they sailed out of the bay below the town, Hwenfayre had watched in stunned disbelief as they passed the wrecked warboats and shattered bodies that floated in the black waters. When they finally reached open water, she turned to Wyn, tears streaming down her face. 'Did I do all of that?' she asked hollowly. In answer, all he could do was to nod gravely. She did not speak again for two days; she just sat in the bow of the boat, staring blankly ahead as if awaiting judgment.

During this time Wyn was able to reacquaint himself with his long-unused knowledge of sailing, navigation and survival on the open Sea. In truth, he was grateful for her silence, for he was too occupied with keeping them alive to answer any of the questions that she was bound to ask. By the time she had faced and quietened her personal demons, Wyn was better prepared and more confident for the flood of curiosity that had to come.

And come it did.

It started with the outpouring of anguish over the death of the Coerl. He was shocked at the intensity of her pain over Niall's death. Wyn was equally shocked at the story she told him of seeing Niall's death in a strange waking dream while she sang on the wall during the battle. Once she had cried herself dry over Niall's death, she turned with an almost disturbing pragmatism to other things.

She started with the predictable 'Who am I?', progressing to the equally predictable 'What am I?'

The former mercenary was unwilling to answer either. What he was able to tell her were the tales of their shared heritage that he had heard from his mother as a small child, sitting on her knee.

'We are of a race that long ago eschewed the land to follow the trackless wilderness of the open Sea,' he told her. 'In the very beginning of our history we were a simple farming people who lived under the heel of an oppressive Thane. A mighty hero named Morgan first challenged the Thane's armies and he led our people in revolt. We rose up and smote the forces of oppression, driving them out of the lands that we claimed as our own.

'However, the Thane did not take kindly to such a bloody nose as we had given him, and he sent against us his full might and drove us from our homes. We wandered dispossessed for a generation, across the wilderness of the borderlands, until we found ourselves by a shore. It was a lonely, windswept shore with little shelter. It was nowhere, and we were no one.' As he spoke, Wyn's words took on the cadence and flow of lines long memorised, lines that had been repeated over generations. 'The truth of our situation sank in slowly as we sat on the wet sands and looked out over the raging ocean. Our people sat in silence. Despair swept over us as our spirits sank lower.

'How long we sat there is not remembered. What is remembered is that a woman stood. She had long, tangled white hair that blew in the wind. Her lavender eyes were alight with an intensity that shone. With great passion she spoke of a love so deep, a hunger so profound, that none could refuse her words. Long she spoke, and bold were her words.

'She spoke of the Sea. She spoke of its power, its beauty. She spoke of the freedom that came from a life lived far from the land and its confinement. Her words and her passion inspired us all. We fell with a will to the task of building the boats that would take us from the dry land forever. It is not known how it was that we land-dwellers knew how to build such boats, nor how we came to be at a shore where wood might be found. But we did not think of such things at that time; we were inspired, we were alive.

'Finally the time came for us to leave the land behind. As we boarded our boats the search went out for the fair-haired woman who had so inspired us. But she was not to be found. Indeed, as the quest went on, it was discovered that no one knew from what family she came. The only thing we knew of her was her name: Danan. She had left us, but she left us her love of the Sea, her name and, most strangely, a deep understanding of our new Mistress and her ways.

'Over our history her face has reappeared. Whenever a girl-child is born with lavender eyes and white hair wild as the sea, there is rejoicing among our people, for we know that Danan has returned to us.'

At this, Hwenfayre's eyes narrowed, taking on a dangerous glint. She never told him what his words meant to her, but she insisted on hearing the tale over and over again.

Now, as she lay in the bottom of the small boat, close to death, Wyn's heart broke as he contemplated what might have been. With thoughts of lost dreams troubling his mind, the former mercenary lay down to sleep beside his dying Princess.

He was awakened by the movement of the boat. It was rocking, rocking heavily. Water slopped over the side, splashing on his face. In surprise, he sat up quickly. Beside him Hwenfayre moaned in her sleep as she rolled with the boat's motion.

It was dark, but he could easily make out the rising swell around the boat. Above him, the wind was picking up, whipping their small sail about. He reacted quickly, but without the instinct of a true seaman. The boat heaved, throwing him off his feet, and he fell down, waking Hwenfayre.

'Wyn! What is happening?' she cried.

Before the big mercenary could answer there came a solid crunch. The boat shuddered and Wyn was thrown off his feet. He crashed heavily into the gunwale, striking his head. As he slid into unconsciousness the last thing he saw was Hwenfayre's terrified eyes staring into his, her mouth open in a silent cry.

10

'Fast and light' was a literal description. Shanek had time to wash off the blood and grab a few things before he was interrupted by a knock on his door. With a snarl he wrenched it open, expecting to see Coerl Leone.

Instead he saw Caldorman Muttiah.

'We are leaving, First Son,' the ageing soldier pronounced. 'If you would come with me please.' He stepped aside and gestured for Shanek to precede him into the corridor beyond.

'Where's Leone?' Shanek snapped as he stalked out of his room.

Caldorman Muttiah followed Shanek, one pace behind and to the left. 'Coerl Leone is waiting for us outside the Palace, First Son.'

The presence of Muttiah added to Shanek's feelings of confusion. Not only was Ettan the most unlikely of provinces to need a diplomatic mission, but the Caldorman was a near-legend of the army, not the man the Thane would use for a discussion. Muttiah's methods lay just the other side of brutal. When he went into an area to put down a rebellion or drive back incursions, he left nothing behind that could breathe.

'Who is leading this mission, Muttiah?' Shanek asked.

'Diplomat Cherise.'

'Cherise? I thought he was dead.'

'Not yet, First Son.'

Shanek led Muttiah through the ornate Palace of the Counsellor. As he went servants bowed and guards saluted, but he ignored them all, pondering this development. Diplomat Cherise was as much a legend in his own way as Muttiah. He'd negotiated the Matrin Settlement, convinced the Oscran Rebels to surrender, and set up the trade agreement with Eysteinn, the continent that lay across the Gudrun Sea. To link two such disparate and important characters on one mission was perplexing at best. The only things the two had in common were their hero status and their age.

If Shanek was perplexed at the choice of personnel, he was stunned at the size of the party. Waiting outside were Coerl Leone and her Fyrd, the Fyrd under the command of Muttiah, and the men Shanek had sensed killing the Skrinnie. There were eight men, not seven, as he had thought. He hesitated when he saw them, wondering for a moment what to do with them, then shrugged. They could come along too and consider themselves lucky not to be in the Arena. Maybe when they got back to Ajyne he would consider their time to have been slavery and let them go.

His decision made, he looked again at the two Fyrds. Even given that his Fyrd was culled from the finest soldiers in the Army of the World, to be travelling into the Great Fastness with only this escort was an insult. Shanek stalked towards where Diplomat Cherise stood watching the preparations.

'Cherise!' he called. 'What is this all about?'

The elderly Diplomat broke off his conversation to bow to Shanek. 'First Son,' he said. 'The Thane has given me strict instructions to share the details of our mission with you once we are four days' march north of the city.'

Shanek seethed. A scathing retort sprang to his mind but he thought better of it. His problem was with the Thane, not this old man. Instead he nodded curtly to Cherise and turned on his heel.

The Fyrd was mounted, with Leone standing holding the reins to two horses, her own and a magnificent black stallion that Shanek presumed was to be his. Leone was watching him with a guarded expression. He nodded at her.

'Coerl,' he said curtly. 'Are you ready?'

Leone nodded. 'Yes, First Son. We are ready to ride whenever Diplomat Cherise wishes.'

'Well, I'm ready, let's go,' Shanek said. He tossed his small bag to a soldier and swung himself onto the stallion. With a clatter of hooves the horse responded to his urging and leaped forward. The Fyrd eased into formation around him as he rode out of the Palace grounds.

Ajyne was a huge, sprawling city. Most of its inhabitants had never left its environs. Many had lived their whole lives within their own sector, defined by the main roads that crossed the city. Shanek had once spent a week poring over a map, trying to discern any pattern or structure. He concluded that the city had never been planned, it had grown. With that in mind it was a simple matter to track the gradual expansion, first along the streams, and then along roads linking the streams. Over the centuries, the streams had dried up, been dammed or channelled into underground pipelines. The buildings along the ancient streams formed the unofficial boundaries between sectors.

One of Domovoi's more innovative lessons was to send Shanek out into the city dressed in peasant garb with no money or food for a month. He was accompanied by Coerl Leone and three members of the Fyrd, who were given strict instructions to intervene only if the First Son's life was in danger. At the end of the second day, Shanek was beaten and robbed of everything except his loincloth. He spent the night in a ditch, troubled by rats and disturbing dreams of sweaty, unwashed peasants, but as the sun rose he was aided by a pretty girl who took him home to meet her widowed mother.

They fed him and gave him clothes. When his wounds healed, they introduced him to Hashan, a local merchant who offered him work. For the rest of his time in the Poor Quarter, he alternated between serving in a small booth in the crowded, stinking market and acting as an enforcer for Hashan's thriving protection racket. At night, after breaking legs for Hashan, he would make his way home through the filthy alleyways to where both women awaited his arrival keenly.

He thanked them by leaving them both pregnant. After returning to the Palace, he sent a discreet messenger to their home with money and a letter allowing them to move into a prestigious area of the city, where he believed they still lived.

His memories of the Poor Quarter were therefore mixed.

Now, however, he left the Palace and headed north, through the Rich Quarter, past the fabulously beautiful Gardens of the Counsellors, to the grand Path of the Thane.

The Path was paved in pure, polished basalt, brought at unimaginable expense from the great mines on the southern coast. No one not of noble blood could set foot upon its pristine beauty. Once on the great Path, Shanek slowed to allow the rest of his entourage to catch up. He had ridden as hard as he could through the city, anger and confusion driving him. Too much had happened today to allow him to settle or focus. His mind was awash with conflicting images — his sudden knowledge of Leone's plan in the battle ring, the incomprehensible setting apart for this mission — but the one that affected him the most was his startling identification with the dying Skrin Tia'k slave. He saw the attackers through Skrinnie eyes. He felt the blades.

He had felt death.

The memory of the Skrinnie's final moments still shocked him. The pain, the anguish, the utter hopelessness of the slave's dying gasp was like an open wound in his mind. Yet somewhere, almost on an instinctive level, he revelled in the death of an enemy. The dichotomy of emotion, the raw agony of death and the sheer exultation of victory left him battered and reeling.

It was no surprise that he was unaware for several minutes that he was alone on the great Path. He reined in his horse and wheeled around, looking for the others. The rest of the party, such as it was, was still at the beginning of the Path.

Muttering a curse he pushed his mount into a gallop. The stallion, given its head, leaped forward, its hooves pounding on the basalt. Shanek realised from the powerful flow of muscle and the even drumbeat of the gallop that he had a very special horse. He was determined to enjoy the stallion's power at every opportunity.

When he arrived, the soldiers guarding the entrance to the Path saluted him.

'What's this all about?' he snapped.

'First Son,' the Coerl started.

'These officious upstarts will not allow us onto the great Path,' interrupted Caldorman Muttiah.

'Why?' asked Shanek.

'First Son,' the soldier continued, 'these men,' he indicated the men in chains, 'are not of noble blood. They may not travel the great Path of the Thane.'

'How do you know?' asked Shanek.

'First Son?' queried the Coerl.

'How do you know they are not of noble blood?'

The soldier looked perplexed.

Diplomat Cherise regarded Shanek with a quizzical eye. 'Perhaps I can help,' he suggested. 'The ancient rule of nobility, one that has fallen into disuse but has never been repealed, states that nobility can be bestowed or acknowledged by the vouchsafing of a person or persons of sufficient rank.' He turned to Shanek. 'Are you vouchsafing these persons of unknown rank, First Son?'

Shanek nodded curtly.

'Very well then,' the Diplomat continued. 'Our way is clear. Let us continue on our way.'

Caldorman Muttiah shot the Coerl a look of pure venom as he passed.

Shanek dismounted and tossed his reins to a soldier in his Fyrd. 'Lead him for me, I need to talk with these noble men,' he said with a grin. Once Muttiah and Cherise were satisfied that all was well, they set out along the Path. Shanek walked alongside the prisoners, encircled by his Fyrd.

The basalt Path took them north out of the city. It ran straight as an arrow's flight as it cut through districts. When it was built, barely a hundred years before, it followed a line ruled on a map by the then Thane, Kasimar III. So literally did the builders follow the line that it separated families who happened to live on opposite sides of the Path. As no commoner could set foot on the shiny smooth basalt, it meant that, until bridges were built, mothers had to walk for hours to go around the Path to visit their children.

Now there were guarded bridges at regular intervals over the raised Path. The armed soldiers at either end had orders to shoot to kill anyone who dropped anything onto the pristine surface. It was not uncommon for the best archers in the army to request posting on the bridges in order to practise on live targets.

Shanek's grin vanished as he turned to regard the chained men who had killed the Skrin Tia'k slave. 'You,' he snapped at the closest. 'Who are you?'

He was a small man with a heavy black beard and a sallow complexion. There was a wiry strength in his arms and he was well dressed. *Probably worked for Hashan*, thought Shanek.

The man swallowed hard. 'I am Virender, son of Tillekeratne. A merchant of the Mishtal House, First Son.'

'Merchant? What do you trade in?'

'Fine cloth, First Son.'

'Own any slaves?'

Virender nodded.

'Any Skrin Tia'k?' asked Shanek

Virender nodded again.

'The slave you butchered. One of yours?'

Virender shook his head.

'Theft, then. As well as the illegal killing of another's property.' Shanek looked at Coerl Leone. 'Death by torment, don't you think?'

The Coerl shook her head. 'Death by impaling, First Son. The law doesn't regard the death of a Skrin Tia'k slave as seriously as killing a human slave.'

'Of course, how could I forget that?' He faced Virender with an open, ingenuous look on his face. 'Well, there you are, then. Only impaling. It's your lucky day.'

The merchant had gone pale beneath his beard. His eyes were wide with terror and sweat was running down his cheeks. 'First Son, I, I . . .' he stammered.

'Was there something?' Shanek asked, all trace of lightness vanishing from his face.

'The slave —'

'It was mine,' interrupted another of the chained prisoners. Virender looked at the big man who had spoken. The expression on the merchant's face was puzzled.

Shanek ignored it. He stared at the man who spoke. 'And who are you?'

'I am Tapash, son of Hasibul,' the man intoned. Despite his chains, he carried himself with pride. Shanek regarded him closely. He was tall and deathly pale, with heavy white-blond hair pulled back into a plait that reached to his waist. Standing a head taller than those around him, he was a massive, powerfully built man.

'A Tribesman from the far north,' mused Shanek. 'You are a long way from the foothills of Ettan. What brings you to Ajyne?'

'Trade,' he said curtly.

Shanek raised his eyebrows quizzically. 'Is there anything else?' he asked softly.

Tapash shook his head. 'I would not come down here for any other reason.'

Coerl Leone dismounted. 'I think the First Son was asking if there was anything else you wanted to add to your answer,' she said.

Tapash glared at her. 'I understand his speech clearly enough, woman. I speak my mind and answer as needed.'

Leone had her sword drawn with its edge resting along Tapash's throat inside a heartbeat. 'You are addressing the First Son of the Empire. You will speak with due respect or die where you stand.'

The northern Tribesman returned Leone's gaze evenly. 'Then kill me, woman. We do not pay homage to titles. Only deeds.'

As he spoke, Coerl Leone tensed for the whiplike slash that would slice this man's head from his neck. Shanek held up his hand to stall Leone's killing slash. 'Hold, Coerl,' he said. 'I think Tapash might be useful.' He stared at the arrogant Tribesman, one of Domovoi's lessons coming to memory. 'You are dead, Tapash, son of Hasibul. There only remains the timing of your death. Coerl Leone is not easily put off and she will finish her job. But until then, you are mine.'

Tapash glared at Shanek with hatred. 'How do you, an Asan noble, know our ways?'

Shanek struck Tapash in the throat with a straight-fingered jab. The northerner went down with a gurgle, his chains clattering as he tried to raise his hands to his damaged throat. His bulk was sufficient to drag down the prisoner either side of him. Before he could draw a breath, Shanek kicked him in the chest, causing him to fall heavily back onto the basalt surface. He stood over the gasping Tapash. 'I know your ways,' he said, 'because they are facile and trivial, made for small-minded simpletons. I am unimpressed by your posturing and provincial arrogance.'

'You ... cannot ... force ... respect,' Tapash gasped. 'It ... must ... be ... earned.'

Shanek turned on his heel and walked away. 'What makes you think I would want your respect?' he snarled.

Even with an unimpeded route it took several hours to leave Ajyne. Shanek rode within his Fyrd, lost in his thoughts. His attack on the chained northern Tribesman, whilst briefly enjoyable, left him feeling

122

uncomfortable and oddly empty. Normally he would have revelled in his power, enjoying the expression of his authority, but today it lacked its appeal.

'A perfect day all round,' he muttered.

'First Son?' asked Coerl Leone.

'Nothing, Leone. It's nothing,' he said. 'No,' he corrected himself, 'ride beside me for a while, Leone. I need to talk.'

Leone kneed her horse and eased in beside him.

'Coerl,' Shanek started. 'We could have a problem before too long.'

'First Son?'

'You are a Coerl and Muttiah is a Caldorman. He outranks you, but I outrank Diplomat Cherise, and he is nominally in command. The chain of command could get a bit murky. I need to know whose orders you will obey.'

'Yours,' replied Leone without hesitation.

Shanek raised his eyebrows. 'So much for murky.'

'It is not murky at all, First Son. I received my commission to command your Fyrd from the Commander of the Army personally. His orders were simple. I have two tasks: first, to safeguard you at all times from any danger, and second, to obey your orders. The Commander outranks the Caldorman as you outrank the Diplomat.'

Shanek nodded. 'Good,' he said. 'I'm glad we've sorted that out.'

Leone nodded.

'Leone,' Shanek said, changing the subject. 'What do you know about history?'

'Only what I learned in the Military Loci, First Son.'

Shanek nodded. 'Not much, then,' he observed. 'Domovoi taught me that course when I was twelve.'

'It took me three years, First Son. I started when I was sixteen.'

'I started my education when I was three. I could read at four. By the time I was ten I was fluent in all the major languages of the Empire,' Shanek said.

'When did you start your weapons training, First Son?' Leone asked.

'You should know, Coerl. You are my only teacher.'

'I find that difficult to believe, First Son,' she commented.

'Why?'

'You are very skilled, First Son. And if you have learned all your skills in just the years I have been teaching you, and only from me, you are even better than I thought.'

'It's just us, Leone. There's no need to flatter me.'

Leone shook her head. 'You should know, First Son, that I never flatter.'

'That's true,' Shanek conceded. 'You don't.'

11

Wyn was awakened by the pain. Lying on the white sand was their little boat. One side was damaged, presumably from the reef that Wyn could see ringing the calm bay. Inside her, he could see nothing of their scant provisions; all had been lost.

He was lying face down on soft sand. It was warm; the sun was shining on his back. His head ached and his mouth was dry. With an effort, he rolled himself over, wincing as the sun struck his eyes. Through the blazing light he was able to make out a clear blue sky. The simple act of moving was enough to send waves of searing agony through every part of his body. He felt as if he had been trampled by wild horses. A groan escaped his lips as he forced himself into a sitting position.

The pain subsided after a few moments and he was able to open his eyes to look around.

He was on a small beach of white sand. Before him the Sea stretched away to a distant blue horizon. Behind him a forest of green and brown climbed up a steep mountain.

Beside him lay Hwenfayre. She looked like a rag doll, tossed carelessly aside, wet and bedraggled. He looked at her, with her white hair matted and her fair skin reddened by the sun, and, as he watched her, he loved her.

Her eyes were closed, but her cracked and swollen lips were parted slightly as she breathed shallowly. It was clear that she was asleep, not unconscious, for beneath her eyelids her eyes moved. As she stirred slightly she made small sounds. Wyn wondered what her dreams told her as she lay there. He watched her as she dreamed, but as the sun rose higher in the sky his thoughts turned to shelter.

Wyn quelled the protests from his abused body and stood. He stretched his back and stared out at the water. His attention was caught by a small object floating about twenty paces off the beach. A smile formed slowly as he recognised Hwenfayre's harp. It must have stayed in the boat until they were beached. He waded out and brought it back.

As gently as he could, he lifted his battered Princess from the sand and carried her into the cool of the forest. As he carried her, she weakly grasped the front of his salt-encrusted tunic and murmured something without opening her eyes.

Once under the cover of the forest canopy, he laid her down on a bed of soft moss. He sat down, resting his back against a tree. He watched her breathe while he pondered what to do next.

Foremost in their immediate needs was food and water. Here, Wyn felt confident for the first time since he had seen Hwenfayre. He knew forests. He had spent years marching, fighting and fleeing through them during the innumerable small ugly skirmishes that had made up the bulk of his adult life. Already his experienced eye had picked out a few berries and one or two promising gourds, and from within the many sounds of life that surrounded them, he was able to distinguish the unmistakable cheery sound of a small brook nearby.

Yet, despite their pressing need, he could not yet bear to take his eyes from Hwenfayre's sleeping face. So he sat, resting his body in the cool shade, allowing his mind to drift through his memories, pondering what might have been. Finally, the demands of his body intruded, and he reluctantly heaved himself to his feet and went to forage what he could.

He returned to find Hwenfayre still sleeping. It seemed that her dreams had calmed and she rested more peacefully.

Wyn's gathering had been successful. He had found enough food for the two of them, some herbs that had medicinal benefits, as well as a large hollow gourd in which he carried cool, clear water. Sitting beside Hwenfayre, he started grinding one of the herbs to make a soothing ointment for her sunburned skin.

He gently undressed her and applied the thick salve. As he did so, he was again surprised at how frail and delicate she was. Her thin white shift was torn and ragged, so he discarded it, wrapping her in his heavy guardsman's cloak, which she had used as a pillow. Then, confident that he had done all he could, he sat and leaned back against a tree to wait for her to awaken.

It was nearly night when she opened her eyes.

'Wyn.'

'My Princess. Did you sleep well?'

'I feel I have slept for a thousand years.' She stretched luxuriously under Wyn's cloak. Suddenly she blushed as she discovered her nakedness. Her eyes widened as she realised her situation, imagining what must have happened. 'Did you . . . ?'

'Your clothes were ruined by the sea. I tended your burns and wrapped you warmly. Yes,' Wyn replied gravely.

'Thank you, Wyn.'

'And of course I kept my eyes closed at all times.'

Hwenfayre blushed more deeply, covering her mouth with her hand. A giggle escaped. Wyn smiled back. Then they were both laughing.

A short while later, Hwenfayre and Wyn enjoyed a rudimentary meal of nuts, berries and fresh water.

'Where are we?' she asked through a mouthful of red berries, the juice dribbling down her chin.

'I have no idea, Princess,' Wyn replied. 'We are on an island. I think it is one of an archipelago. And I think we are well south of your home. Beyond that I cannot say. My navigation skills are not great.'

'And the boat?'

'Damaged when we struck the reef that surrounds this island. I fear we are trapped here. At least for the time being.'

'So, what do we do now?'

'Now, we try to find shelter for the night. After you have finished eating, of course.'

Hwenfayre grinned mischievously, like a little girl. Wyn could not help but smile back as he helped himself to some food. When they had finished their simple meal they started to look for shelter for the night.

They found a small cave. It had a narrow opening but widened out to provide sufficient floor space for them both to lie down comfortably. Wyn tossed and turned for hours, listening to the noises of the forest, worrying about what the new day would bring.

It brought a bright, fresh morning. The sky was clear and blue. He awoke to the sound of Hwenfayre singing to greet the sunrise. Her gentle, soft voice did not have the yearning sound that had characterised her singing when she stood on the wall. He looked at her as she sat cross-legged in the mouth of the cave. Her back was straight, she had discarded his cloak and was naked as she faced the morning. Her hair tumbled freely down her smooth skin. The normally wild locks caught the sun and shone, almost glowing in the early morning light. He stared, lost in thought.

She heard him stirring and stopped her song. Without turning, she put her harp down and pulled the heavy blue robe up over her shoulders from where it lay behind her.

'Good morning, my Princess,' Wyn said.

She turned her head to him and smiled. 'It is, isn't it?' she replied. Her eyes glowed with pleasure. 'What are we going to do today?' she asked.

'I think you should rest here today. Get some of your strength back. I'll scout around, look for some more food, water, maybe another place to shelter.'

Hwenfayre shifted around without standing until she was facing him. She held the robe tightly around her. 'Why do you call me Princess?' she asked, eyes intent.

'Because you are a princess.'

'Why?'

'Hwenfayre, I am not learned in the rules of our people. I am nothing more than a mercenary. I don't know why you are a princess, but you are. For some reason you have been born to be the High Priestess and Princess of the Children of Danan.' He grinned wryly. 'From what I recall of my childhood stories, your arrival could cause a few problems.'

'What sort of problems?'

'Always you ask questions that I cannot answer.' Wyn regretted his comment. She had difficulties enough without worrying about what would probably never happen. He rose to his feet. Already his trained body was recovering its strength. 'I shall go and see what I can find. Rest here, my Princess.' Without another word, he strode past her into the forest.

The sound of Hwenfayre's song followed him.

Once in the cool of the thick forest, Wyn put the image of Hwenfayre out of his mind and concentrated on the task of finding food.

It was not difficult, although he lamented the loss of his bow, for there was plentiful game. He gathered what he could as he made his way towards the stream. Once there, he saw what he had half feared, half hoped for: footprints.

They were in the soft sand beside the stream. He crouched beside them, examining them closely. His tracking skills were rusty, unused for some years, but he could easily make out that they were recent. There were three different men, running, probably hunting.

Wyn rocked back on his heels, thinking.

There were many tales of islanders, some good, others less so. The most common was that they were suspicious and wary of strangers. That did not concern Wyn. What did concern him were the rumours of human sacrifice and ritual cannibalism that sometimes surfaced. He stared at the tracks, his mind weighing up the alternatives. After a few minutes' thought, he decided to follow the tracks.

They were easy to follow, so he did not miss the blood. One of the men was injured. As Wyn continued to follow the trail, the blood traces became heavier and closer together.

It came as no surprise when he stumbled upon the body.

It was lying face down in the stream with a crossbow bolt protruding from its back. From the amount of blood that was spread over the dead man's back, it was clear that he had run in great pain. Wyn paused, considering what would make a man run so far with a bolt in his back. With effort, he pulled the bolt from the body and examined it.

It occurred to him suddenly where he had seen such a bolt before. His eyes widened in shock and he leaped to his feet. Tossing the bloodied bolt to the ground, the former mercenary turned and ran back to where his Princess rested.

As he neared the cave he slowed to a careful, silent walk. Thus it was that he heard the sounds of conversation.

He stopped to listen. Over the pounding of his heart he could discern Hwenfayre's voice. She was talking animatedly with someone who responded in tones too low for him to understand. On impulse, responding to the promptings of an instinct honed by years of danger, he left the path and crept forward, taking pains not to alert Hwenfayre to his approach.

The former mercenary experienced a moment of satisfaction that his skills had not deserted him when he saw a figure half-hidden beside the path.

It was a man clad in the leather and canvas of a Southern Raider. He held a cocked crossbow, aimed along the path. Wyn thought for a moment, considering his options. The Southern Raiders were not known for their mercy. Neither were they known for spending time talking to a beautiful young woman whom they happened across alone in a forest.

Hwenfayre laughed. The hidden man sniggered softly, an evil, chilling sound, and Wyn reacted without thought. He darted forward, moving silently through the underbrush, striking the man with a killing blow to the throat.

The Raider's eyes widened in shock, then he died, gasping, as he tried desperately to breathe through his crushed larynx. Wyn lowered the body to the ground, relieving it of a razor-sharp knife as well as the crossbow.

It was an assassin's weapon, designed to kill. Wyn tested the weight and balance of the weapon. It was a piece of quality workmanship, no footpad's tool. The knife was similar. He sheathed it carefully in his boot.

Hwenfayre laughed again. This time Wyn could hear the response of the man to whom she spoke.

'Yes indeed, my Lady. Many.'

His accent was harsh, almost guttural. It was not the voice of an islander. Rather, it was the voice of a

Southern Raider. Wyn felt the anger rise unbidden. He could almost taste it. Visions of violent death flickered through his mind as he crept forward through the underbrush towards the cave where his Princess sat, entranced by the words of an assassin.

When he could see the cave entrance, he stopped and considered. Hwenfayre sat with her back to him, facing the man who was keeping an eye on the path. He was obviously awaiting the approach of either his colleague or Wyn himself. He also was clad in the leather and canvas of a Southern Raider, but his clothes were of a better cut than those of his comrade. Wyn listened as he watched. The assassin was spinning a tale of wealth and power. As he spoke, in a low and intense voice, it became clear that he knew a great deal more of the society of the Children of Danan than he should. And he was telling Hwenfayre how she might rule the children and lead them to greatness.

Clearly the man would die; it was simply a matter of when and how. Wyn toyed with the idea of simply shooting him where he sat, but he was unfamiliar with the weapon he held, and as he only had one shot he decided not to risk it. Instead, he continued to watch, listen and await his opportunity.

Hwenfayre was leaning forward, listening carefully. As she did so, the dark blue guardsman's cloak that she was wearing slipped off her shoulder. She was so intent on what she was hearing that she did not notice, but the Southern Raider did.

His eyes widened at the sight of Hwenfayre's pale shoulder and his voice trailed away. She noticed the direction of his stare and moved to cover herself.

Wyn felt his anger rising again. He tensed, raising the assassin's crossbow almost unconsciously. Instinct took over as the mercenary squeezed the trigger. There was a dull twang as the bolt shot out, followed almost immediately by a heavy thud.

Hwenfayre screamed as the Raider slumped backwards, a crossbow bolt seeming to suddenly sprout from his chest.

Wyn leaped to his feet and bounded through the undergrowth. When he reached the cave mouth, he knelt and gently gathered the still-screaming woman in his arms. He rocked her slightly and murmured soothing sounds into her hair as she clung to him, burying her face in his chest.

After a few minutes her cries stopped. Her grip on him eased. He moved her gently away from his chest and lifted her chin. She tried to smile through her tear-ravaged face.

'It's all right now, Princess,' Wyn reassured her.

'But what happened? Who is he? Who killed him?'

'He was a Southern Raider. An assassin, most likely. And I killed him.'

'Why?'

'You do not know these men, Princess. They are hard men, killers. I do not believe he was here merely to amuse you with tales. He had a friend, an accomplice, over there in the bushes.' Wyn indicated the crossbow that he still held. 'He had this aimed at you.' It was a lie, but not one that he would lose sleep over. Hwenfayre's eyes widened at the sight of the weapon. She pushed away from him. 'My Princess,' he continued, taking hold of her hand, 'there are those who would wish you dead for the power you have. I am sorry that I left you alone.' Her hand, still resting in his, gripped tightly as he spoke.

'Wyn, there are many things that I do not understand. Why would any wish me dead? And what power do I have?'

Wyn took a deep breath. 'Princess,' he started, 'you are the living incarnation, the avatar, of Danan. You have her wildness, her passion, her face. You carry the white harp and you sing the songs of the sea. Once every generation or two Danan comes back to our people, but she has been absent for several generations, and our people have changed. We have left behind many of our old ways, and much of our old life. A new way of life has grown among the Children of Danan, and the return of the old ways in you, Princess, may not be welcomed by all.'

Hwenfayre's eyes grew wider and wider as he spoke. 'Do you think that these men may have been sent by my own people?'

'It is possible, my Princess. Power such as yours does not go unnoticed. What you unleashed on the wall would have sent mystic shock waves around the world. Once you have been found, you could well be in danger.'

'Wyn. What should I do?'

'I don't know, Hwenfayre. But we must be careful from now on. And we should leave this island as soon as we can.'

Her eyes were a mystery as she stared at him. She nodded slowly, removing her hand from his.

Wyn stood. 'But now, Princess, you must rest. You have suffered much, and you need to get your strength back.'

She gave him a small, wan smile that did not touch her eyes, then turned away from him to lie down.

Wyn stared down at the woman who had so changed his life so quickly. Lying on the sandy floor of a cave, on an island many miles from her home, wrapped in his thick blue guardsman's cloak with her back to him, she looked so vulnerable, so small. Yet her strength, her vitality continually surprised him. He had seen so many princes, so many coerls, all of them powerful, all of them now dead. But this young woman, having but recently left childhood behind, could, given a chance, shake the very foundations of the world with her awesome power. His heart ached within him as he considered the dangers that she could face, knowing as he did that he could not be beside her to protect her from the very people she sought to join. Despite her arcane power, she was a gentle soul with little protection against the guile and malice of people.

Every day the song of morning laid bare her gentleness for all the world to see. It was a song that would always reveal the heart. The soaring poignancy of Hwenfayre's voice was not to be denied, nor was it dissembled. He longed to take her in his arms, to hide her from what must come, but instead he turned to leave the cave.

During the rest of the day, he worked on making some tools with which he hoped to repair their damaged boat. By the time the sun dipped towards the clear blue horizon, Wyn was satisfied with his day's work. He had buried the three bodies — the two Raiders and the dead islander — as well as producing some rudimentary tools. The hard work helped him put aside his growing, and disturbing, feelings for the waif-like girl whom he had taken from the relative safety of home and plunged into the dangers of the untamed sea. All day, whenever he paused either to drink from the clear stream or to eat a little, he found his mind drifting back to Hwenfayre. He caught himself reliving every conversation, every time they had touched, every smile she gave him, every time she had said his name. Most disturbingly, he found himself remembering the feel of her skin as he had undressed her and wrapped her in his cloak.

As a trained fighting man he had met many women. Mostly they had been those unfortunate women who had, for whatever reason, attached themselves to garrisons and plied the oldest trade with the soldiers. He was no innocent and had availed himself of their sweet services as he had felt the need, but this girl had touched his heart in ways that he had never encountered, never known existed. Despite his hard life, his many experiences, nothing had prepared him for how this delicate, frail-seeming young woman had broken down his defences.

For years he had separated himself from any attachment, any closeness. He had built a hard shell around himself that had shielded his pain from those who would seek to touch him. The betrayals of his youth had left him damaged, but now this woman had appeared out of nowhere to drag his hidden past out into the light of day. He was not sure he could survive the pain again. His only remedy was to push his weary body as hard as he could in the hope that the pain of aching muscle and sinew would drown out other, older pains.

By the time he had made his way back to the cave where he had left Hwenfayre, it was almost dark. There was a small fire burning at the cave mouth, but she was nowhere to be seen. He experienced a moment's panic before he heard her voice calling him from the nearby stream.

After he responded, she called to him to wait at the cave mouth. She had a surprise for him. Her voice was stronger than it had been, and she sounded rested. Wyn relaxed slightly, waiting for his surprise.

It came with a rustle. 'You can turn around now,' she announced.

He did so, and was greeted by the sight of a smiling Hwenfayre, clad in new clothes. She twirled for him, displaying a grass skirt with a shirt made of fabric reclaimed from her torn shift. Her feet were bare.

With unpractised grace, she curtsied. When her head came up, a smile danced across her lips, her eyes glowed. 'So, my Prince, what do you think of your Princess? Is she not truly noble?'

Seeing her, shining with pleasure in simple clothes, showing off like a little girl, broke Wyn's heart. He could not meet her sparkling eyes. Beyond them lay a different reality. He could see the broken bodies floating in the sea after her storm had destroyed the Raiders' fleet. Instead of her smile, he saw the leer of an assassin, one sent to snuff out the vibrant life that stood before him. It was more than he could bear. Abruptly he stood and, without a word, strode past her out into the gathering darkness.

As he walked away he silently berated himself. He had always been awkward with words. He did not have the ability to say the words that needed to be said. Hwenfayre needed to hear words of gentleness, perhaps even kindness, maybe words of love? But he was just a soldier, a man of war, of violence, who had no words for a woman, not even when she needed them.

Wyn worried about Hwenfayre, how he had left her alone at night, walking away rather than telling her what he meant to say: that she was a beautiful, fragrant flower in a dangerous field. All he wanted to do was take her in his arms and whisper the right words to her, but instead he had walked away like an unfeeling beast. She needed his protection, not his criticism — for he was sure that was how she would take his departure.

He reached the beach and sat down on the sand. The waves rolled in, lapping gently in the darkness. No matter how he tried, he could not excuse his action of walking away when he should have stayed and said what he meant to say. She was a princess, but a princess in a world that would hunt her down and kill her. He spent the night on the beach, leaning against a tree that stood where the sand met the edge of the forest, staring up at the stars, listening to the waves roll up onto the sand. At some stage during the night he fell asleep. His last thoughts were that he hoped he would never be in a situation where he would face her alone, having to say the right words, for he knew he would fail and she would leave him.

The dream started as it always did: *vivid colours, loud noises, pain. Always pain. It never happened*

without pain. And running. He was running from
something. Running through a dark forest. About
his head arrows split the air, whistling past him,
never quite hitting him, never freeing him with one
sharp pain from the continual, dull, throbbing agony
that lay deep within him. He ran, fleeing, but never
outrunning his pursuers. They were always the same,
always close, never catching him, but never giving
him rest.

As he ran, the ground became less solid, turning
imperceptibly from firm earth to swamp to water,
until he was slogging through knee-deep, then waist-
deep, then chest-deep water. The arrows were now
javelins, hurled with great force by faceless men who
rode on steeds with the white spume of waves for
manes. Ahead he could just make out a Raft. It was
large, topped with a superstructure that resembled a
small town. Desperately he pushed towards the
floating village, but as hard as he thrust himself
through the water, the Raft receded from him at the
same rate. He never came close to it. People heard
his cries of anguish and gathered at the edge to cheer
him on. They called, they yelled, but all the time they
were laughing and cheering. It was a time of great
celebration; all were in bright clothes, wearing hats,
waving happily. All seemed oblivious to his pain.

Behind him the riders closed in, the wake of their
steeds rising about him. He clawed at the water as it
threatened to engulf him, but he was sinking,
drowning.

But tonight the dream was different.

As the blue-green waters closed over his head, he
saw a gentle face, lavender-eyed, framed by wild

white-blonde hair. The face smiled. The lips moved, but no sound came out. Instead, a searing pain exploded behind his eyes, sending brilliant coruscating colours splashing across his vision.

He found himself on the wall, walking the dawn watch. Behind him he heard the unmistakable rippling of a harp song. He went to turn, but he was prevented by a leering assassin carrying a crossbow. The crossbow was raised, aimed at him. As he went to attack, the assassin laughed and spun around, loosing the bolt. It struck home with a sickening wet sound. He tried to push past the assassin, but the man was too strong, picking him up and tossing him contemptuously over the wall. He fell into a darkness that swallowed him whole. Hungry rocks reached up to devour him as he tumbled screaming downwards to his death.

Wyn awoke with a start. Why had Hwenfayre appeared in his dream? What did she have to do with his exile from the Rafts? His departure, although the result of betrayal, had been his own choice. She probably hadn't even been born when he left.

He was about to rise when he heard a soft footfall. He recognised Hwenfayre from that one sound, his skills of survival returning to him. Rather than open his eyes, he feigned sleep, waiting for her.

She walked past him to stand at the water's edge. He heard her take a deep breath before starting to play.

The first rippling chords that her fingers lightly drew from the bleached white harp swept him away into another world: a world of shifting colours, of rising swells, of surging currents and untamed depths. The power of the music lifted him out of his own world, with its worries and cares, aches and pains, and transported him to a different place where life was simple, ordered by powerful, almost primal forces. It was a strange, frightening place.

The music stopped.

'Wyn.' Hwenfayre's voice was quiet, uncertain. He opened his eyes.

She was standing with her back to the sea; the water lapped around her feet, the breeze stirred her hair, rustled her grass skirt. Her eyes were still, deep and unfathomable as she gazed at him. In that moment, more than any other, he saw her as she really was: a creature of the sea, wild, beautiful and dangerous.

'Wyn,' she repeated.

'Hwenfayre,' he replied.

A smile lit up her face, the vision faded, once more she became a young woman, unsure of herself and lost, clinging to the only link she had to a life that she had left. Wyn regretted leaving her alone.

'I shall never forget how you say my name. Last night, as I lay alone, it was the thing more than any other that I feared losing. I was afraid you had left me,' she said. 'So I stayed awake as long as I could, hoping you would come to me, speaking my name as you just did, afraid that you would not, worried about you, hating you for leaving me alone, needing you.' As she spoke she cradled her harp against her breast as one would a child. 'But all the time, I think, deep down I trusted you. I knew that you would be here this morning. And here you are.'

'Here I am,' Wyn agreed solemnly. He did not trust himself to say more.

Hwenfayre stared at him. Her eyes locked onto his, briefly, then she looked away, staring into the forest behind him.

'Wyn,' she started, 'I don't understand much of what you tell me. But I see now that I must accept it as true. Wyn,' she looked back at him, 'I will never disappoint you again. I am sorry.' With that, she walked slowly back into the forest. Wyn watched her go.

He sat, not sure what to do, for some time, allowing his mind to drift.

It was mid-morning when he roused himself from his reflections. He decided it was time to fix their boat, as well as time to leave this island. Briefly he considered staying here, to explore and perhaps seek help from whoever had made this island their home, but he rejected the idea. Still in the back of his mind were those rumours of cannibalism and violence. He had brought Hwenfayre into enough danger without risking her with an uncertain welcome from unknown natives.

His boat-building skills were good, as they were for all of his people. It was a skill with which all who lived on the Sea, all the Children of Danan, were born. The lives of the Children were touched with mystery and magic at every turn. Their heritage was an arcane, mystical one. Every boy-child was trained from birth in the ways of his Mistress, the Sea, and every girl-child was taught the secrets of the denizens with whom they shared their world. It was said of the Daughters of Danan that they could bring from the Sea a meal by merely asking the fish to come forth. Wyn remembered this to be an exaggeration, yet his memories of his mother's gathering were dim. Certainly she sang often whilst fishing.

However, it was the Priestesses who aroused the most fear. Their powers over the Sea, their mystical communion with their Mistress, struck terror into the superstitious people who populated the islands and coastal towns. Much was whispered about how they were able to raise mighty beasts to do their bidding, to summon storms on still days, to cause the vessels of their enemies to stop dead in the water even when under full sail, even, it was sometimes muttered, to call down lightning from clear skies. Such stories kept the Children of Danan forever apart from other peoples.

It was of such stories that Hwenfayre was the avatar. Her eyes, her hair, marked her irrevocably. Her father, whoever he was, was wise to have left her in a town ignorant of many of the tales. Had she been born in another, more sophisticated town, she would not have seen a second summer. Her father was also wise to have bred her far from her own people at this time. The real mystery was how he knew who, and what, his daughter would be, before her birth. Normally, so the stories went, the birth of a High Priestess and Princess was a joyously unexpected event.

He thought as he worked, the hours passing quickly. As the sun dipped behind the mountain that dominated the island, the former mercenary stood back to regard his work. The boat was seaworthy once more. All it lacked was a mast and a sail. These he would fashion on the morrow.

The aches in his body were less than the previous day. His warrior's body was responding well to the labour, yet he worried about Hwenfayre. Her body was not as strong, not as used to the rigours of privation as was his, and he had not seen or heard her since she returned to the forest.

He made his way back to the cave, where he found a small fire burning. Above it was a pot, in which there bubbled a rich-smelling stew. The construction of the stand was simple and effective: more the product of years of refinement than of a few hours' trial and error. He couldn't remember bringing a cooking pot away from their wreck.

All of his trained instincts spoke to him. They sharpened his senses, alerting him to the additional footprints, the half-heard rustling in the forest, the accented voices speaking softly in the cave. Without thought, he stooped and pulled the knife from his boot. As he rose into a fighter's crouch, he tested the knife's edge with his thumb. A small drop of blood dripped to the sand.

Hwenfayre was sitting with three women, talking quietly, her back to the cave entrance as Wyn crept in, silent as a shadow.

One of the women saw him enter, knife in hand. Her eyes widened, her hand flying to her mouth. Hwenfayre, seeing this, turned quickly, half-rising as she did so. Her eyes softened when she saw Wyn. She smiled.

'Wyn,' she said. 'Put aside your weapon. These women are no danger, they have come to aid us in our plight.'

Her words were delivered with the quiet, easy flow of command. It was the voice of one accustomed to being obeyed. The soldier in Wyn sheathed his knife and stood easy before he realised he had moved. He stared at her, uncomprehending. Her smile did not waver, yet her eyes seemed to be saying more, giving him a silent plea for help.

Wyn was a simple man; the only form of protection he knew he could give her was the strength in his body. He moved to stand close beside her. The light touch she gave his arm was all the reassurance he needed. With her voice still ringing with authority, Hwenfayre introduced Wyn to the seated women.

Their names were Marran, Wellfyn and Arragone. Islander names. He stared at each of them, remaining impassive, hard. They in turn stared at him, but only Wellfyn held his eye for more than a moment. It was she who had first seen him. She measured him with her gaze and dismissed him with her eyes as insignificant, turning back to Hwenfayre.

'Please sit with us once again. Tell us more of your story.' Her voice was melodious, entrancing. It was a voice that Wyn had heard before, many years earlier, and the sound of it was enough to awaken memories long dead.

His mother glared at him, fury stalking the mind behind her blazing eyes. It seemed to the boy that she was doing this a lot more these days than she used to. At least this time he knew what he had done wrong. He knew, he had been told often enough, that to swim in these waters at this time of day was dangerous, but the water had looked so inviting, so cool after a long day's work repairing the nets in the hot sun. Declan, his best friend, had dared him, then taunted him, then finally, in the face of his persistent refusals, bet him that he could not swim under the *Two Family Raft* from one side to the other. This was not taken lightly for it was a thirty-stroke swim, and the *Two Family Raft* had the deepest draught of any of the Children's craft. He had done it before, both boys had, but in the waters of the caruda fish, in the time of the Final Song, it was a fine challenge for such a boy. He was bigger and stronger than most of his peers, which was why he was working the nets so young. Already he was eyeing enviously the men who rowed out each morning, singing the hunters' song as they left the Rafts to gather food from the ocean's bounty. Life as a child, even on the *Two Family Raft*, was beginning to pale, and he was eagerly seeking new challenges.

The bet on offer was a knife made of metal. Metal was highly prized on the Rafts of the Children, for life on the waves meant that the only metal to be had was from the landers. Trade with them was limited to certain times of the year, and much of the rest of the year was devoted to gathering such treasures as were prized by those who feared to travel the Deep. To put up against the knife, the boy had his father's hand-carved set of dice. It was a children's game, and he felt it was long past time he put such childish things aside. But it would be a shame to lose them; they were the only thing he had of his father's that he could call his own. All of his father's carvings had become greatly treasured since he died. He had been the last of the

Master Carvers to master the skill of working with the hard but brittle bone of the mighty grayfin.

The boy knew it was supposed to have been his destiny to follow the lead of his father and take on the trade of carver, but his hands were large and clumsy, better served to the spears and gaffs of the hunters than the delicate tools of the craftsman. His mother had never been happy with his decision. This, together with her grief at his father's death, had driven a wedge between them. Her anger at his many pranks and daredevil antics was merely a sign of their growing estrangement. For him, it meant that he spent less and less time with her. For her, it meant more time spent staring blankly out at the Sea, lost in memories. She stopped taking care of herself and seemed to shrivel slowly, to collapse inwards. Looking back, Wyn could now remember how his mother slowly faded out of existence, as if the death of his father, her husband, had sucked the life out of her.

He stripped off his shirt. His young body, as yet unfinished, was already showing signs of the strength that would be his when he achieved manhood. With a quick grin, he slipped over the side of the *Two Family Raft* into the cool, dark blue waters. His friend gave him a thumbs-up, then turned and scampered away to meet him on the other side.

Floating in the water, the boy took several long, deep breaths, then soundlessly disappeared beneath the surface.

Immediately, he found himself in an exciting yet terrifying world. It was a world of shifting colours, shades of inconstant light and shadow. Beneath him, the Deep called with a menacing lure. Above him, the heavy solidity of the *Two Family Raft* bulked large, ominous in its hardness, at once comforting and familiar yet also threatening in its alienness. The raft's movements were sluggish in the light swell, sending ripples away from the waterline that refracted the sunlight, casting dancing shadows on his body. He paused, watching the play of light and shadow on his skin, then with a strong kick surged beneath the black hull of his home.

As he passed underneath the hull, the light changed, and with it the world through which he moved. It was cooler, darker. The sounds were different. He heard the distant thumping of people walking about, the muffled sounds of loud conversation, a rattle, a hiss.

He drove himself on, resting his hand briefly on the wooden hull, feeling its strength, its aged reliability, its latent power. Ahead, the water lightened as he approached the other side. Beneath, he caught a glimpse of the silver silhouette of a caruda fish. It darted through the water towards him.

His heart pounded and a shock ran through his body, a heady mixture of exhilaration and fear. Even as he pushed towards the light, the old stories of hunters who had lost limbs or their very lives to the frenzied attacks of these voracious predators danced through his head. With a burst of fear-driven adrenaline, he surged upwards.

He was near the end of his strength, the surface of the water a scant stroke or two away, when he felt the first agony of the razor-sharp teeth as they tore into his leg.

The force of the attack thrust him forward, his head breaking the surface of the water. He bellowed in pain. The caruda dragged him back under, the cold water choking off his cry. His lungs filled as he tried to draw breath to cry out again. Drawing on a reserve of strength he was unaware of, he reached down to the fish, grasping it by the gills. He dug his fingers in deeply, gouging, ripping at the soft flesh. Blood swirled around him, clouding his vision. He heaved desperately at the silver predator, wrenching it away from his torn leg. There was a dull crack; the fish went limp in his hands, its jaws releasing him.

Spent, the young man floated up to the world of air. He bobbed up in a slowly expanding cloud of blood, both his and that of the dead fish still locked in his fingers. He looked up into the eyes of his mother, and then turned away. Her anger was plain.

Another set of eyes caught his. They were hard and dismissive. He knew those eyes and normally he would have looked away. It was not for him to hold the eye of one so noble, so high in station, even though they were about the same age. But today, bearing a caruda killed with his bare hands, he dared to hold her gaze.

'So. He thinks he proves his manhood. But it is such a small fish.' It was the same voice, mocking, distant, yet compelling.

Thus it was, many years later, that Wyn looked once more into the eyes of Morag, youngest daughter of the High Priestess of the Children of Danan. No matter that she called herself Wellfyn; Wyn knew those eyes.

150

Her eyes moved across his face, dismissing him. He saw no glimmer of recognition, which, given that she would have believed him dead, was not unexpected. Wyn had looked into the eyes of his enemies enough times when life and death hung on a single stroke of a sword to recognise what he saw there. This woman, whatever she called herself, did not remember him. That gave him some respite, time to consider what to do, for Morag would know exactly who, and what, sat opposite her.

But the question remained: what was she doing here?

Whatever the answer was, it clearly did not involve violence, at least not yet.

Marran, the smallest of the three, rose diffidently and went to see to the meal. Wyn watched her. She turned to him, smiling shyly. He returned her look impassively, her smile faded, her shoulders slumped slightly as she stirred the simmering stew.

'And you, Wyn. What is your part in this magical tale?' He was brought back by the mellifluous voice of Morag as she addressed him.

'I have no part in it, my Lady. I stand by Hwenfayre wherever she decides to go.'

'My Lady?' she laughed gently, clapping her hands together in glee. 'So noble. So protective of your young friend. Yet,' her eyes narrowed, the humour vanishing to be replaced by a hard glint, 'Hwenfayre tells us it was you who first recognised her song. How is that?'

'I have travelled much, my Lady. I once journeyed with one who knew something of the ways of the Children.'

'And who was that?' she asked.

'I never knew his name, my Lady. He died soon after we met. It is the way of fighting men.'

'So it is. So it is indeed.' Her tone was speculative, unconvinced. Wyn returned her stare unflinchingly, as one with nothing to hide may do. Their eyes locked for a moment, then she looked away, apparently satisfied for the time being. He steadfastly refused to look at Hwenfayre, knowing she would hear the lie and wonder at it. She would not, he was sure, dispute him, yet he could not risk allowing Morag any hint of suspicion. Were Morag to guess at his true heritage there would be no telling what she could do. The powers of the High Priestess, even one merely trained to the position rather than born to it, were daunting. And as a child Morag was, he recalled, already being spoken of as a worthy successor to her mother. The storm that had brought them to this island suddenly took on a new, frightening aspect.

Unconsciously the fighting man took hold of the haft of the knife tucked into the waistband of his pants. Quelling his own thoughts, he forced himself to listen to Hwenfayre as she continued to detail her life's journey.

Her voice had lost the cadence of command, slipping back into the simple, young woman's voice that he was used to. He relaxed slightly. Marran came back from stirring the pot.

'It is ready,' she said quietly.

Morag smiled. 'Thank you, Marran.' To Hwenfayre she added, 'Marran is the finest cook in our village. Her meals are always wondrous. Come, let us eat.' She rose with the grace of a princess, extending her hand to Hwenfayre.

Without hesitation the young woman took the proffered hand and went with Morag. Wyn stood and went with her.

Marran's stew was all Morag had promised: hot, wholesome, rich, heavy with tender meat, thick with vegetables. Wyn had not had its equal for some years. Neither, apparently, had Hwenfayre. As they ate, Arragone, the third woman, who had so far said little, told them about the island upon which they had landed so fortuitously.

It was the largest of an archipelago that consisted of seven inhabited islands and twelve smaller uninhabited islands, some of which were little more than rocks. The main source of food was obviously the ocean, but the soil on the other side of the island was rich, yielding the vegetables and herbs that so enhanced the stew.

There was little commerce with outsiders, with trading mainly limited to inter-island dealing. The islands formed a loose confederation of sorts, banding together when necessary, squabbling over the usual irritations, sharing the hardships and joys that came with island life. It was a life that had held no attraction for Wyn before, and hearing about it again still failed to entice him. There was something inherently stultifying about living in a small community bounded by ocean, yet land-bound. It was true that the islanders sailed much between the islands, but there was nothing of the explorer or adventurer in an island sailor. No, he reminded himself, it was either the open land or the open sea, not some in-between existence that lured him. He chanced a look at Hwenfayre. She looked torn: half-captivated by tales of a way of life exciting and alien to her experience, half-wondering at what this turn of events might mean.

It was as Wyn listened, not completely concentrating on the words, that a part of his mind started to warn him. There was something profoundly wrong with all this. If this was indeed Morag, how long had she been on this island? If she had not been here long, who were these other women? If they were simple islanders, as they seemed, why had they accepted her as one of their own? If they were not, then why all this elaborate façade?

If, on the other hand, Morag had been here long enough to have been accepted, then had she too put aside her heritage? Might she be an ally instead of a dangerous enemy? Wyn felt as he did when he entered battle; a strange fusion of excitement mingled with fear. His every sense was preternaturally heightened, alert to every action of these innocent-seeming women who had suddenly become opponents, subject to the full scrutiny of a man of war.

As he watched them, he started to note a few small inconsistencies. Not much. Nothing that on its own would arouse any suspicion, but when watched with a healthy paranoia, certainly enough to worry about. The way they held themselves, the way every motion was carefully balanced. It all clicked into place: these were no more islanders than he was. This was all some elaborate game Morag was playing. Wyn kept watching but kept his hand close to his dagger.

When the meal was finished it was dark outside. The night had come unnoticed, its arrival lost in stories of island life. Marran stood. Without a word, she collected the plates and utensils. Wyn watched her. As she turned to go to the nearby stream he stood too, suddenly apprehensive.

'Marran,' he said quietly. Hwenfayre stared at him, her eyes troubled. He could sense what she was troubled about but chose to ignore her pain. His instincts were screaming warnings to him. Something was very wrong here. He took a burning branch from the fire, holding it away from his face. 'It will be dark by the stream; perhaps I should go with you, to light your way.' The apparently casual way that he was holding the flame masked the fact that it placed his face in shadow, allowing him to watch not Marran, but Morag. The sudden tightening around her eyes followed by a brief nod to Marran were all the signs he needed. His decision to accompany the quiet girl was a good one.

He felt Hwenfayre's eyes on him as he walked into the darkness with Marran. The night swallowed them as they left the bright warmth of the campfire. As the darkness welcomed him, Wyn hesitated briefly, considering the wisdom of leaving Hwenfayre alone, but he continued, believing Morag would pose no physical threat to her. Any violence would be out here, away from the fire.

Around them the noises of the forest became louder, and they became interlopers in a world not their own. Wyn held the flickering torch in his left hand, near Marran, so that his night sight would improve and hers weaken. His right hand gripped the hilt of his knife. She walked carefully, her feet picking a path through fallen branches. Her breathing was rapid, coming in short, sharp breaths; her movements were jerky. Wyn slipped into a controlled calm. It was the preparation of a warrior entering battle.

The attack was fast, quiet and deadly. Had Wyn not been prepared, he would surely have died.

Two men surged from the bushes. They were armed with daggers not unlike the one Wyn held. At the first movement he dropped into a crouch. The first attacker thrust at Wyn but overbalanced as he swung at the now empty space. Wyn drove up, under the man's midriff, throwing him heavily to the ground. The man lay stunned, gasping for air.

The second, coming an instant later, went for Wyn's throat as he rose up. It was an old trick, a move an experienced fighting man would expect. Wyn's dagger slashed upwards, driving through the attacker's wrist. His eyes widened in shock, then Wyn struck him across the face with the torch in his other hand. The man fell, unconscious.

It was over before Marran's plates hit the ground.

The clatter broke the night's silence. Wyn spun on the startled woman. He stepped in close to her. 'Who were they?' he hissed. 'And what is your part in this, woman?'

She stared blankly, her eyes glazed in shock. Wyn saw the direction of her gaze. His dagger dripped blood onto the ground near the insensible man. He quickly slipped the knife into his belt. 'I don't harm women,' he assured her. 'But I need to know what is going on. And I need to know now.'

Marran nodded slowly. 'Others,' she started. 'Back there ...'

Wyn dropped the torch and dashed back to where Hwenfayre still sat waiting for him to return. As fast as he ran, it was not fast enough. He burst into the clearing in time to see Hwenfayre being carried, limp and unconscious, over the shoulder of a man dressed in the canvas and leather of a Southern Raider.

With a cry of rage, he threw himself across the intervening space at the man's unprotected back. Before he could drag the man down he was struck a powerful blow across the back of the head. He fell to the ground, dazed.

As he tried to rouse himself, a kick to the ribs drove him back down. He heard the voice of Morag once more. 'Leave him. He deserves to live, tasting his failure.' From where he lay, semi-conscious, he could just make out Morag's feet.

She crouched, then lifted his head to look into his eyes. 'Know this, Wyn: I am Morag, High Priestess of the Children of Danan. No one stands before me. No one keeps me from what I desire. I am more powerful than you can possibly imagine, little man. Live. But do not attempt to find me.' In the flickering light of the campfire her eyes glowed with an unholy power, her face a thing of dancing shadows, its angles giving her a demonic aspect. She opened her mouth and breathed on him. A red mist flowed out, enveloping him. He felt consciousness seep away.

As he sagged into insensibility, he managed to look up at the retreating back of the man carrying his Princess. 'Hwenfayre!' He was able to gasp out her name, but she did not respond.

The darkness swallowed her, leaving him alone to cry her name silently into the echoing sadness of his mind.

12

After leaving Ajyne, the party headed north along the Northern Way of the Asan. It was a wide, well-travelled route that led from the Capital through two provinces to Aphra, the provincial capital of Darkan. Ettan lay to the west of Darkan so the normal route would take them through Herath and Darkan, then along the Wesron Way to Ettan's capital, Adrastos.

Coerl Leone was envisioning two weeks on the road. As they left with little more than the hour she had boasted she needed, her Fyrd was unequipped for such a long journey. Her second priority, therefore, after Shanek's safety, was acquiring supplies. Once on the great Path, there had been no opportunity to offer the general populace a chance to help, so she had to wait until they left the city.

After checking the pack Shanek had thrown together it was clear that he was ill-equipped for any journey. All he had was one change of clothes, his bolas, three books of history and diplomacy, and the fighting kit he was wearing. She was pleased to note he had at least changed out of the lightweight training gear into a proper kit. She was displeased that he had chosen the standard gear of a common soldier, rather than the more elaborate uniform that was proper. At least she had ensured that all his gear was better quality than normal, even if he was unaware of it.

Leone was relieved that the First Son's mood had improved since talking with the prisoners. The lightning blow with which he had dropped the arrogant Tribesman was superb. It had taken her by surprise. Little wonder Tapash had no chance to dodge or even move to avoid any of its power. She was amazed that he was still alive. A blow like that would normally crush a larynx.

Another thing she was pleased about was the fading of her inappropriate feelings for the First Son. *No*, she corrected herself, *not feelings; physical responses*. And whilst a physical response to the person of the First Son was bad enough, feelings would be worse. Her body she could discipline.

As she rode behind Shanek and to his left, she kept focused by imagining attack scenarios and how she could best counter them. It was a useful training technique that she practised constantly. So far she had only had to counter one actual attack upon the person of the First Son, and her Fyrd had acquitted itself well.

The attack had occurred when Shanek had taken one of his midnight walks through the squalid Widows' Corner. Originally founded as housing for the widows of veterans killed in defence of the Thane, this place had slowly descended into abject poverty and misery. It had become a haven for criminals and opportunist slavers.

Shanek was prone to bouts of depression and anger. It was not uncommon for him to slip away from his guards at such times, wandering the dark and dangerous streets alone. Leone said she was his only teacher in martial skills, but these nocturnal adventures had contributed much to his training. As her own instructor had told her, 'There's nothing like the imminence of death to sharpen a man's reflexes'.

On this particular night, Shanek was in a black mood. He had spent a dreary day studying the financial activities of the Southern Province under the critical eye of the Reeve. By the end of the day, the First Son was seething with frustration and ready to strike out at anything.

Leone recognised the signs and allowed him to 'slip away unnoticed' while she and the Fyrd followed discreetly. The attack was fast and brutal. Seven armed thugs swarmed out of an alley, surrounding him. Despite Shanek's surprise, he had two thugs down before the Fyrd cut the rest to pieces.

'Coerl Leone!' The call snapped her out of her thoughts. It was one of Caldorman Muttiah's Fyrd.

'Yes,' answered Leone.

'The Caldorman would like to speak with you,' he replied.

Leone looked to Shanek, who nodded his approval, then followed the soldier.

'What's this about?' Leone asked.

The soldier shrugged. 'No idea, but he's in a foul mood.'

'He always is,' said Leone.

'Don't I know it,' the soldier said with a wry grin.

'You're Tanit, from Ettan, aren't you?' asked Leone.

'Yes. How did you know?'

'You're riding with the First Son. It's my job to know,' Leone said. 'Do you know what's going on up there?'

Tanit shook his head. 'Nothing as far as I know,' he said.

Leone nodded.

The Caldorman was speaking quietly with Diplomat Cherise when they rode up. He stopped speaking when he heard the horses approaching and glared at her.

'What is going on?' Caldorman Muttiah snapped.

'Caldorman?'

'Who are these commoners the First Son is dragging along?'

'They murdered a Skrin Tia'k slave during the Celebration today and the First Son wants to talk with them, Caldorman,' she replied.

'Why?' asked Cherise.

'I don't know, Diplomat,' Leone replied. She regarded the old Diplomat. If the rumours were true, he would be dead very soon. Now that she was close to him she could see the ravages of Danan Fever etched on his face. Indeed, it would not be long now.

'Well, he'd better kill them or get rid of them somehow, because we can't be burdened on this journey,' grumbled Muttiah.

Leone did not reply.

'Well?' demanded Muttiah.

'Caldorman?'

'What are you going to do about it?' he asked.

'Nothing, Caldorman,' Leone answered.

'What?' exploded Muttiah.

'I am not going to do anything about it, Caldorman. It is not my place to question or influence the First Son.'

'Humph,' Muttiah grunted. He turned to speak to Cherise again, but stopped and stared at Leone. 'What are you still doing here? Haven't you got a First Son to protect?'

Leone took this as a dismissal and rode back to her place behind Shanek.

'What did he want?' asked Shanek.

'He wanted to know who the prisoners are and why you want them, First Son.'

'He could have asked me,' Shanek observed.

'I told you,' muttered Diplomat Cherise as the two of them watched Leone back with her Fyrd. 'I told you she would not be useful in this,' he went on. 'Her loyalty to the Counsellor's line is beyond reproach.'

'So why is she here?' asked Muttiah.

'She was your job. I got the First Son. It was up to you to deal with her.'

'The Counsellor asked for her specifically, and I am not going up against Sandor. No matter what you promise.'

'So be it, then,' said Cherise.

Muttiah sighed. 'She's good, and I hate to waste good people.'

'One time I will have to tell you an old proverb about omelettes and eggs,' said Cherise.

13

He left me. It was her first thought.

'He left me.' She was unsure whether she spoke it out loud.

'Yes, he did, didn't he?' The voice at her shoulder was gentle, quiet. 'But I won't. When I say that I will stand by you and protect you, I mean it.'

'Where am I?'

'Do not fear, Hwenfayre.' The voice was melodious, flowing like the sea, calming. 'You are far from danger. Among people who will not allow any harm to come to you.'

'Who are you?'

'I am your friend. Rest now, you are still weak from your injuries.'

A soft hand rested, cool, upon her brow. At its touch, Hwenfayre became calm, her troubled mind eased. She drifted into a peaceful sleep, in which she dreamed a child's dreams of noble protectors, valiant warriors and just causes. And of men who did not leave her side.

It was light when she awoke. Her first thought was for her harp. Somewhere deep within her she knew it was dawn, and such a dawn as this deserved to be welcomed, to be greeted with the respect it warranted. She reached out to where her father's harp always lay. She sat up with a start. It was not there. Heart pounding, she took stock of her surroundings.

She was in a narrow cot. Her covering was a single blanket of a fine weave. It was soft and warm. Beneath the blanket she was naked. She was in a room with a low ceiling, and dark walls and floor. It was all of wooden planks. There was no decoration, save a single round window to her left. The room moved slightly, a gentle rocking motion. Was she on a boat?

Wrapping the blanket about herself, she stepped lightly to the window and peered out. The sea stretched away from her unbroken to the horizon. Sparkling blue, it called to her, welcoming her home. The rising sun caressed the rolling swell with gold, a seabird called soulfully, a gentle breeze teased out small whitecaps. Hwenfayre pushed open the window and breathed in deeply, taking the smells of home into her heart. She exhaled slowly. Even though the air left her, the feeling did not. She felt alive, free.

Closing her eyes, she breathed in deeply again, raising her arms above her head. The blanket fell unheeded to the floor as she drank in the rich beauty of a morning at sea. Her lungs filled with fresh air as her heart filled with joy. Unbidden, the words of her song to the morning came to her lips. Softly she sang. She sang with passion, she sang with love, she sang with power. She sang without her father's harp. It was something she had never done before; it was something she had never even considered possible.

As she sang, her eyes closed, her mind soaring, a jarring, discordant note seared across her mind: *He left me. He left me to walk in the dark with that shy islander girl.* The song died on her lips. She was suddenly cold, alone, naked. Quickly, Hwenfayre gathered up her blanket, closed the porthole and hastened back to her bed. There she lay, staring at the wooden ceiling, thinking nothing but that one thought. *He left me. Why did he leave me?*

It was dark when she finally slept.

When she awoke it was still night. The boat was quiet, the sea still. She felt more alone than she could remember. Despite having slept, she was unrested, sandy-eyed and troubled. And hungry. It occurred to her that she had not seen anyone or eaten since ... since he left. No, she would not think about that again. She had to get on, do something. At least eat something.

As she rose, she realised that she was clothed. She seemed to remember that she had been naked when she first woke up, but now she was robed in rich, warm clothes. There was a lantern flickering, hanging from the ceiling. She ran her hands uncertainly over the fine cloth of her dress. It was soft, unlike anything she had ever dreamed of wearing. Blue. It was ocean blue. But in the inconstant light of the lantern, the colours shifted, flowed like the ocean. Green, blue, indigo, bright flashes like the sun on a wavetop; it was beautiful. And the feel of the cloth on her skin as she moved was like a caress, soft hands gently easing away the pain, like Wyn's hands when he had tended her burns that first day on the island. The memory of it thrilled her. She had been conscious, but as he had soothed her she pretended to be asleep, allowing him to cleanse the hurt, to drive away the memories of what she had done, of what she had become. She knew it was wrong, she should not have let him touch her, look at her, but it had made her feel so alive, so beautiful.

He left me.

There was no escaping the confusion and pain contained within that simple sentence. With everything he had said and done for her, how had he been able to leave her? Why had he deserted her, just before... Just before what? What had happened?

With a sigh she sank back onto the bed. With her elbows on her knees, she rested her head in her hands, trying to remember, to know what had happened. She could remember that Wyn left with the shy islander, Marran, then Wellfyn handed her a piece of fruit, then nothing.

And now she was here, on a boat at sea, dressed as a princess, alone. Turmoil raged in her mind. She swept to her feet and strode to the door, dress swirling about her legs as she moved. As she put her hand to the latch, she paused. Did she know what lay beyond? What if she were truly alone?

Wyn, why did you leave me?

Hwenfayre. My name is Hwenfayre, she told herself. *I am a Child of Danan. I can do this.* Summoning her courage, she opened the door.

Outside was a passage, low-beamed, dark and narrow. To her left was a stairway, to her right another door. She went left.

The stairs were narrow and steep, leading up to the deck. She went up carefully, the smell of the sea

167

drawing her on. At the top, she stopped and looked around. She was on a two-masted ship under sail. A number of men were working. They moved quietly, tending the sails, busy at tasks she did not understand. There was a man at the wheel. Above her the moon was visible, shining softly down on a still sea. The man closest to her stopped in his task and stared. His gaze was intent, yet was not disturbing. He nodded, then gestured to the prow of the ship. Hwenfayre followed his gesture with her eyes.

Standing motionless, clad in pure white robes, was Wellfyn. As if she felt Hwenfayre's gaze upon her, she turned. In the soft glow of the moon she looked ethereal, with her long raven hair tumbling down her back. Her smile was kind. She extended a hand towards Hwenfayre, beckoning her to come forward.

Hesitantly, Hwenfayre walked to join Wellfyn in the prow. She took the woman's offered hand and stood beside her, looking out over the dark sea. 'It's beautiful, is it not?' asked Wellfyn.

'It is,' agreed Hwenfayre. 'When I lived on the land I used to welcome the morning from the wall. I thought nothing could ever be more beautiful than that. But I was wrong.'

'There is nothing like sunrise at Sea. Perhaps we should welcome the sun as it should be done on such a day.' A sailor had moved soundlessly to hand Wellfyn a harp. Hwenfayre looked at it carefully. While it was not her harp, it was very similar. The carvings on the face were not as intricate, nor was the workmanship as perfect, but it was a fine instrument nonetheless. Wellfyn released Hwenfayre's hand to take the harp. She lightly drew her fingers across the strings. They responded with a cascading ripple of sound that sent shivers down the spine. With a faraway look in her eye, Wellfyn started to play the song that welcomed the morning. It was the same song that Hwenfayre had been playing for so many years. Unconsciously, Hwenfayre started to sing along quietly with the harp.

As the words flowed from her lips there was a brief falter in the music, quickly recovered. She sang on unconcerned. It was good to finally share this moment with someone who understood. Not only understood but also joined with her, savouring the moment in song. Only after the last echoes of the harp's song had faded did she realise that it was only her voice that had welcomed in the morning. She looked at the beautiful woman standing motionless at her side. Wellfyn was staring unblinkingly at the horizon where the first rays of the sun were colouring the sky a pale pink. In her hands the harp was shaking very slightly.

The women remained silent, sharing the dawn as the sky gradually lightened. It was only when the sun had cleared the horizon that Wellfyn finally moved, turning to face Hwenfayre.

'I imagine you are hungry,' she said. 'My physician decided it would be best to let you sleep as long as you wanted. He felt it would aid in your recovery. And judging by the colour in your cheeks, he was right.' She held out her hand. 'Come.'

Her words were bright, friendly, she was smiling, but her eyes told a different story. Hwenfayre was troubled to see a hardness, an edge to her eyes that was at odds with the rest of her expression. Despite her misgivings, Hwenfayre took Wellfyn's hand, walking with her below decks to share a meal.

As they walked hand in hand the men stepped aside, bowing deeply. There was respect, honour, as well as a little fear in their expressions as the two women passed them. Behind them, the noise level increased as men started talking and calling out to each other. By the time they reached the bottom of the stairs, the deck of the ship was a rowdy, lively place.

The room where their meal was laid out was larger than the one in which Hwenfayre had awoken. The ceiling was still low, but there were two portholes that spilt more light into the room. The morning sun illuminated a large table laid with a wonderful array of food. Hwenfayre was able to identify some of the foodstuffs, but most she had never even seen before. There were fruits, meats, breads, jugs of juices, milk and pastries. Hovering along the walls of the room were a number of young girls. As the two women entered, the girls ceased talking, their eyes focused on Wellfyn. She appeared not to see them as she swept to the table. Seating herself, she gestured for Hwenfayre to do likewise as she selected some food from the platter nearest her.

Unsure, but hungry, Hwenfayre started to help herself to the sumptuous feast laid out before her. Every time she looked up or reached for something, one of the girls darted forward to fetch it for her. For a time she was content to eat, assuaging the pangs of hunger her day's sleep had left her with, but finally she was content and sat back from the table. Looking up, she saw Wellfyn watching her intently. Hwenfayre smiled weakly.

'Full?' asked Wellfyn.

'Yes, thank you. That was lovely,' she answered.

'Good. Now I imagine you have a number of questions that you would like to ask.'

Hwenfayre paused; there were so many things she needed to know. 'Who are you?' It was a start.

'My name is Morag. I am the High Priestess of the Children of Danan. You are onboard my personal transport, the *Kelpie*. We are presently on our way to rejoin the main rafts that house most of the rest of my people.'

'Why did you tell me your name was Wellfyn?'

'There are times, my dear Hwenfayre, when I must leave my people and travel abroad in the world. At such times I often need to hide myself behind a mask of anonymity. We are not a people who are always understood. Our ways seem strange to those who live on land. Often our people are the target of silly superstitions and mindless fear. So in order to protect ourselves, we sometimes conceal our true identity.'

'But I am one of your people, aren't I? Why did you need to hide yourself from me?'

Morag smiled slightly. 'There are two things there. First, it is not yet certain as to whether you are one of my people or not. There are a number of issues that need to be cleared up first.' A shock ran through Hwenfayre, shaking her to the core. Before she could comment, Morag continued. 'Then there was the man with whom you were travelling.' Hwenfayre could

171

only stare dumbly. 'He is known to us. He is not what he claimed to be. I believe he was masquerading as a simple mercenary soldier?' She raised her eyebrows inquisitively at Hwenfayre. She nodded, unable to speak. 'You are very lucky to be alive, child. The man you know as Wyn is an assassin in the pay of a people you know as the Southern Raiders.' Morag paused, picking at a morsel of fruit. She bit it appreciatively as she studied Hwenfayre. After a moment's silence, she continued. 'As you slept, you talked a little. You are concerned, vexed even, as to why he left you that night. He accompanied my Marran to the stream in order to kill her. We found her body the next morning. Do you remember how he, so kindly it seemed, fetched you your food?' After a nod, she continued. 'It appears that he poisoned your meal, which explains your unconsciousness. When he came back after killing Marran he found you unconscious. He attacked Arragone, seriously injuring her. I was able to flee and fetch some help. By the time I returned with some men, he had taken you. We pursued him for some time through the forest, finally overpowering him on the beach.'

'Did you . . . ?'

'Kill him? Yes, of course we did. He was a very dangerous man.' Morag looked deep into Hwenfayre's troubled eyes. 'So the answer to your question is: he left you to kill Marran, after poisoning you. No doubt he did so in order to deliver you to his employers.'

'But,' she struggled to find the words, 'why?'

'Money no doubt. Such men as he are easily bought.'

'But if he wanted to kill me . . .' she began. Morag held up her hand.

'He is dead,' she said in a businesslike tone. 'Put him out of your mind. You have more pressing things to consider. Specifically, who you are. This is the first time you have been fully conscious since you were poisoned, and I need some answers myself.'

'Answers to what?'

'Questions about you. Who you are, where you came from, that manner of thing.'

'But I told you everything on the island.'

'Oh, that fanciful story.' Morag sniffed disdainfully, dismissing Hwenfayre's tale. 'No, I need more. I need to know more about your father, your mother, how you came to learn that song you sang this morning.'

'I wrote the music myself, when I was fourteen. The words,' she hesitated, 'the words Wyn taught me.'

'That is impossible,' snapped Morag. All trace of friendliness vanished from her face. Her eyes glinted dangerously. 'I think that perhaps you might need to spend a little time thinking very carefully about the answers you plan to give me.' She stood abruptly, gesturing to one of the girls who hurried to collect her plate. 'We shall meet to talk again later.' She smiled once more.

With that, she turned and swept from the room.

Hwenfayre sat, too stunned to move, staring at the door that closed firmly behind the High Priestess. Her head dropped. Too many dreams had been shattered too easily and too quickly for her to deal with. All her hopes for the future lay in ruins. Her mind was not in turmoil; it seemed to have ceased to function at all. She was numb, unaware of anything around her. All she could do was pick absently at the fine cloth that covered the table.

Her whole world shrank to encompass just that small fragment of white linen. She stared, taking in the weave, the minute imperfections in the fabric. A tiny creature scuttled into view. She watched it as it moved. It was round and many-legged, moving with a mindless haste. The path it followed was random; it darted hither and yon with no apparent guiding purpose. One moment it dashed to a speck of food, the next it paused at a strand of fabric that was slightly frayed. Finally, it lost interest in the patch of linen, dashing off to the edge of the table.

'My Lady?' said a soft voice at her shoulder. She looked up quickly to see one of the girls standing beside her. 'Have you finished, my Lady?'

'Oh, yes. Thank you.' She stood to clear away her plate. 'Where would you like me to put this?'

'Oh no, my Lady. Let me.' The girl was flustered as she attempted to take the plate from Hwenfayre's hand. 'Please let me, my Lady.' She was insistent, a troubled look in her eye.

'It's all right,' Hwenfayre assured her. 'I can do this. I think I need to do something right now.' She smiled at the girl. 'So, where do I put this?'

'There's no need to worry about that,' said another voice from behind her. She turned to see a tall, older woman whom she had not seen before. 'You must forgive our ways, my Lady,' she continued, addressing Hwenfayre. 'These young girls have been chosen as Novice Priestesses, and they think that to progress they must impress the High Priestess. She has given them instructions that they are to serve you. So they are trying to do just that.' She paused to give the girl who was still attempting to take Hwenfayre's plate a short glare. 'Perhaps if you would be so kind, could you please allow them to serve you in this way . . .' She left the sentence unfinished, a brief raising of her eyebrows completing the thought.

'Of course. If you think it is important,' conceded Hwenfayre, releasing her plate.

'Thank you, my Lady.' The older woman gestured the girl away with a flick of her hand. 'My name is Alyce. I am the Priestess in charge of Novices. I am responsible for their training in the ways of our Mistress. The High Priestess has graciously granted the Novices the task of seeing to your needs. So if there is anything you wish, please be so kind as to inform either me or any of the girls.'

'So it is you I have to thank for this beautiful dress?' asked Hwenfayre.

'I trust it is acceptable, my Lady.'

'Acceptable? It is the most glorious thing I have ever worn! I love it. Thank you so much.'

During this brief exchange the Novices had unobtrusively busied themselves with the task of clearing up the remains of the breakfast. Alyce lightly touched Hwenfayre on the elbow and gestured to the door. 'Possibly you might care for a walk on deck? It has become a wonderful morning. Some fresh air is always nice after breakfast, I find. We could talk.'

On deck, the men treated the two women with similar deference to that shown Morag, but there

175

was not the eerie silence that had greeted her at sunrise. The promise of sunrise was fully fulfilled by the morning. A light breeze filled the sails, urging the ship onwards. But onwards to where?

Hwenfayre asked Alyce.

'Wherever the High Priestess directs us, my Lady. This is her personal transport and we are her chosen escort.'

'But do you know where we are going?' Hwenfayre was insistent.

'No. But I think we are heading to the *Southern Scend Raft*. It is the largest of our rafts, and it is where the High Priestess traditionally resides. She has been long away from her home, and, like us, I feel she needs to rest at home. Also,' she paused, looking around conspiratorially, 'I think there is a young man.' She winked, sharing a secret.

Hwenfayre frowned. None of what she had heard so far this day was making any sense. She knew that she was one of these people and she longed to be taken home and welcomed as one of them, to take her place in a society that would not reject and condemn her — yet the only one to even mention her heritage had questioned it. What of all the stories Wyn had told her? What of Danan, her harp, the songs, her mystical power? These had not been spoken of. She was determined to find out.

'Alyce,' she started, 'I have heard many stories about the people who live on the sea. And I was wondering if I could ask you about them.'

'Of course, my Lady.'

'That's the first thing. Why does everyone except Morag call me "my Lady"? I am no lady.'

'When we left our home rafts we were told by the High Priestess and the council that we were searching for one who had great power, who would be able to aid us in our struggle against the Raiders. We were told that when we found this person we should treat her, or him, with the utmost respect. You are the only one whom the High Priestess has chosen, and now we head home. It stands to reason that you are the one whom we sought, my Lady.'

'Yes, that does stand to reason,' mused Hwenfayre. 'But what of the legend of Danan?'

'Legend, my Lady? What legend do you mean?' asked Alyce.

'The legend of the woman who first led you — us — onto the sea, who taught you how to build the Rafts, who returns every few generations?'

'I am sorry, I know of no such legend.' She sounded genuinely regretful, yet she did not meet Hwenfayre's eye. 'We are called the Children of Danan, it is true, but only by those who do not know us. We call ourselves the Children of the Rafts.'

'But Wyn told me about her. And he told me that I ...' Her voice trailed off as Morag's words ran through her mind. What if Wyn had not told the truth? Had he been so cynical, constructing all those stories?

'Wyn? Was that the man from whom the High Priestess rescued you?' asked Alyce.

'Rescued. I suppose so, I don't know,' Hwenfayre said. There were too many things still unresolved for her to think about. Some of which she did not want to think about, not yet. 'Tell me about your life: how do you live on the sea?'

The life that Alyce told of was one of freedom, peace and uncluttered horizons. The Children of Danan, or the Children of the Rafts as Alyce referred to them, lived on large, well-constructed vessels that resembled rafts only in name. They followed the winds and currents, hunting and farming the denizens of the ocean for food and trading with any they happened across. Most trade with land-dwellers occurred as a result of meetings with the trading vessels that plied the ocean in search of far-off lands. As a result, things such as metals and wood were highly prized.

Whenever a new raft needed to be built, a landing was made on an island. This was a rare event, occasioning considerable planning, but always leading to great feasting as the islanders and the Children of the Raft met for a three-month-long celebration. During this time it was common for marriages to take place, bringing new blood to both the islands and the Rafts. Alyce's mother was born on an island and had joined the Children at one such event.

'But,' interrupted Hwenfayre, 'if islanders join the Children of the Raft, why is Morag uncertain about me being one of her people? Surely it doesn't matter whether I am or not? I can just join you, can't I?'

'With you I think it is a different matter. You see, there are divisions within our society. Most people are simple workers, living simple lives, doing the tasks that are necessary for the functioning of any society. Over them are the Sailers who guide the Rafts. The title "Sailer" was originally given only to those who actually plotted the course of the Rafts, but now it is more often given to those who fulfil the task of administering the daily life of the Rafts.

'Over the Sailers are the Navigators who in reality guide the course of the Rafts. Each raft has at least three Navigators. They meet with the fishers and hunters to discuss the movements of the fish, the flow of the currents and the like, to best guide our journeys.

'The highest level of leadership is that of the Priesthood. These are the true leaders of the Children. They are the arbiters, lawgivers and traders, and the link we have with our Mistress. It is through the Priesthood that we learn of the will of our Mistress, and through their skills that the power the Mistress lends us can be harnessed to our aid.

'I think that the High Priestess sees in you a possibility to join that august body. And that is a high honour not easily gained. Certainly no simple lander can just "join" the Priesthood. In our history, only those of pure sea-dweller descent have ever become a Priestess.'

'But ... the Danan ... my hair, my eyes ...' Her voice failed when she saw Alyce's look of sadness.

'Certainly your hair and eyes will mark you as unusual among the Children, and that will count against you. I think you should put aside these tales of Danan and the like. You should treat with suspicion anything Wyn told you; it is unlikely to be true.' She looked into the lavender eyes that were slowly filling with tears. 'I am so sorry, my Lady.'

Without a sound, Hwenfayre turned and ran across the deck back to her room, where she threw herself onto her bunk. There she lay for hours, staring again at the low ceiling, wondering where her life was taking her, where she had been, who she was. How she longed for the simplicity of her life behind the wall. Already the taunts, the gibes, the feelings of not belonging were fading, replaced by this all-consuming loneliness. She was truly alone now. Wyn had left her. Despite Morag's words, she could not bring herself to believe that he was dead. Something told her he lived. She did not even have her father's harp, or his letter.

Finally pangs of hunger roused her. And with the hunger came a new realisation. Being alone, she had to look after herself; she had done it for much of her life, she could do it again. Spending time with Wyn, even the Coerl, had dulled her, made her weak. It was up to her, and no one else, to make her way in this new life. And if that meant going with these strange people, then so be it. At least she was away from the town and was on the sea. Here at least she had a chance of discovering her destiny.

It was about sunset when she decided to leave her cabin. At the door, she paused, closed her eyes and breathed deeply. *You can do this*, she told herself. *You may not be a Child of Danan, but you are still Hwenfayre. You can do this*. Standing tall, she opened the door.

Seeing no one outside, she went up on deck. Standing in the prow was Morag, High Priestess of the Children of Danan, holding her harp, lightly fingering the strings as she hummed. Hwenfayre walked along the deck to stand behind her. As before, when the High Priestess was on deck the sailors worked silently — whether out of respect or fear, Hwenfayre could not guess.

'Hwenfayre,' said Morag without turning.

'Morag,' replied Hwenfayre.

'Sunset is a beautiful time, is it not?' asked Morag.

'Yes,' said Hwenfayre. 'But I personally prefer sunrise. There is something fresh and valuable in a new day.'

Morag nodded in agreement. 'True,' she said. 'Are you rested?'

'Yes, thank you.'

'It has been a difficult time for you, no doubt.' Abruptly, she turned around to face Hwenfayre. Her eyes were hard. 'Perhaps it would be a good time for us to resume our conversation from this morning.'

Hwenfayre nodded slowly. 'Yes,' she replied.

'I have been considering how you can best take a place among my people,' said Morag. 'And I think it would be best if you were to take your place among the Novices. I believe that Hylin would make an excellent teacher and guide to aid you in what will be a very trying time for you.' After a pause, she raised her eyebrows quizzically. 'Was there anything else?'

'No.'

'Good.' Without another word the High Priestess turned back to the sea and resumed her song.

Hylin proved to be a stern teacher. Not only was Hwenfayre expected to learn the songs of the Children of the Raft, but she also had menial jobs to perform. Her first task, however, was to move out of her own cabin and into the cabin she would share with the other Novices. They did not welcome her. This dislike was not an active thing, it was like a silent wall. They only spoke to her when necessary, and then only in clipped phrases. Her rich blue dress was taken away and replaced with a simple long white shift.

She was put to work in the galley, cleaning and chopping the vegetables. After the meals were eaten by the crew she collected the plates and helped wash them.

In between her menial tasks, there were the hours spent learning both the words and the tunes for the ancient songs of the Children of the Raft. She was given a simple harp to practise with. It was old, the strings were stretched and worn, the frame cracked and water damaged, but it had a gentle sound. Once her fingers became used to the strings, she was able to coax the flowing sounds she so longed to hear.

The other Novices learned to play by a method of gradual memorisation of the melodies and lyrics, to which were added the harp accompaniment. It was a system that annoyed Hwenfayre. She learned by ear. Once she heard a song, she could play it. It was as if each song had its own rules, its own logic, its own existence. Once she felt that existence, everything about the song followed naturally.

Her method annoyed the other Novices as well as Hylin. She was an elderly woman, grey-haired and wizened, who had been teaching Novices to play the harp for many years. As a younger woman, Hylin had been a Priestess, but her true talent lay in the area of teaching. Or so she kept telling the Novices under her tutelage.

After a few days, Hwenfayre became aware that not all of the Novices held her in the same disregard. One of the girls would occasionally smile when Hwenfayre looked her way. Whenever Hwenfayre smiled back, she became flustered and dropped her eyes. Hwenfayre decided that she had been alone for long enough, so one afternoon, after another lesson on the correct way to tune a harp, she sought this girl out.

Her name was Erin. She had seen sixteen summers, she had a voice that soared like a bird and she was an orphan. Her smile was like the sun rising on the ocean. But she smiled rarely, and then only fleetingly. When Hwenfayre spoke to her she replied softly, head bowed, refusing to meet her eye.

At first they spoke only of trivial things: the weather, the other girls, Hylin. Whenever the name of the old Teacher of Novices was mentioned, Erin would lower her voice even more and look about furtively, as if afraid. At first Hwenfayre took this to be just another example of Erin's gentleness, but after a few times she started to believe there was more to it. She decided to ask her about it.

They were on deck. The evening meal had been cleared away and the other Novices had returned to their cabin to practise and study. They stood at the railing, watching the last glimmering of the sun's rays disappear as the first twinkle of stars started to appear. The sea was calm, rolling softly with small white splashes marking their passage. Around them the sailors were going about their tasks with their usual rough good humour. One or two of the men had greeted Hwenfayre on occasion as she welcomed the dawn or farewelled the day, and as the two Novices stood together they received a couple of friendly smiles. Erin blushed and looked away each time.

'Erin,' she began, 'why do you get so nervous every time Hylin's name is mentioned?'

As before, the younger girl looked around nervously. There was no one in earshot. 'You must be careful, Hwenfayre,' she replied very softly. 'Hylin is not what you think she is.'

'What do you mean?'

Instead of replying, Erin shook her head.

'Tell me, Erin,' pressed Hwenfayre. 'What exactly is Hylin? Why are you so afraid of her?'

Erin looked up at her, naked fear in her eyes. 'I cannot tell you,' she said. 'Do not make me.'

Startled, Hwenfayre pulled back. 'What is it, Erin?'

Again, she shook her head and looked away instead of answering. Somewhere, a lonely seabird called, the sea sighed as it slid past the bows, and Hwenfayre was suddenly cold. She longed for her own harp.

Without another word, Erin turned away from the rail and went below, leaving Hwenfayre alone with the Sea. She tried to keep her mind on what Erin had not told her, knowing that this was her life and she had to learn all she could about it. She did everything she could to keep her mind busy, but no matter how hard she tried, it kept going back to Wyn.

Being here, looking out over the sea at night with the sounds of men going about their tasks behind her, brought the past flooding back. With no more than a passing thought, she was on the wall again. She could feel the gritty rock beneath her feet, smell the city below her, hear the steady, firm footsteps of Wyn as he walked the dawn watch. The memories swept over her: the gentleness of his hands, the strength in his arms, the dark mystery behind his eyes, the way he smiled at her when he thought she could not see. And the aching cry that rang through her hollow breast: *He left me*.

'Never mind her, Novice.'

The voice at her side startled her out of her reverie. She spun around to see a sailor leaning on the railing beside her, looking out at the sea. He was a tall, rangy man with long hair, bleached by the sun, which fell to his shoulders. He turned to her. His face was craggy, weather-beaten and leathery, with eyes that had seen many sunsets. After an oddly companionable silence, he sighed softly and spoke without looking at her.

'You the one they call Hwenfayre?' he asked.

She nodded.

'Thought so,' he said, and looked back out to the horizon. He said no more for a time, preferring to watch the night sky. 'Never mind young Erin,' he repeated. 'She's a nervous little thing. Always seeing what isn't there.'

'Like what?' she asked.

He shrugged. 'It's said, that Hylin is still dark at the High Priestess for her fall from position. Little Erin is nervous about her, that's all.'

Hwenfayre nodded again, watching him as he looked back out over the Sea. The other sailors had lit the running lamps, the lanterns that burned at night to alert any other ships to their presence. In the flickering light the sailor took on a different appearance. He looked older as the shadows danced across his angular face, more worn yet strangely wiser. Like all the other sailors he wore an open shirt and canvas trousers, yet he gave no indication that he felt the cold of the night. His feet were bare, toes gripping the gently heaving deck with the surety born of years of living on the open seas. From his rope-belt hung a knife, unlike any she had seen before. It was short with a wooden haft and blade that was a strange milky-blue colour.

'It's the tooth of a blaewhal,' said the sailor.

'What?' asked Hwenfayre, startled.

'My knife,' he replied. 'You seemed interested.'

'What's a blaewhal?'

He pulled the knife out from the rope-belt and hefted it, as if feeling its weight for the first time. 'The blaewhal is a hunter, a mighty fish that swims these seas hereabouts. They grow to about twenty strokes, so a big one could upset a vessel about the size of this one.' He reversed the knife and handed it to Hwenfayre, hilt first. She took it.

'It's very light,' she observed.

'Aye. It is that. But strong. Almost as strong as metal, but more brittle.'

She tested the edge with her thumb, as she had once seen Wyn do. To her surprise, a thin line of blood appeared. The blade was so sharp she had not even felt it slice smoothly through her skin. Eyes wide, she watched the blood ooze slowly from the fine cut, forming a drop on the end of her thumb. Without a word, she held her hand out over the rail and let the drop fall into the Sea. Where the blood fell it was met by a brief flash of phosphorescence.

'You know our ways,' observed the sailor. He reached out his hand and Hwenfayre gave him his knife. He hung it back at his waist. 'You'll do fine, Novice Hwenfayre. You'll do fine.' He turned to walk away, then paused and turned back. 'If anyone bothers you, anyone at all, you tell them Declan is looking out for you. That'll give them pause. Goodnight.'

And he was gone.

She stayed by the railing for a while, watching the inky black swell roll endlessly past the ship, wondering again why Wyn had left, and why the pain of this did not diminish.

The night passed slowly as she lay on her narrow cot, staring at the dark planks above her, feeling the heave of the ship, listening to the slap of the water. She shared this low cabin with four other Novices: Erin, Hagan, Sara and Maeve. As the hours crawled by, she became aware of a different sound intruding. She heard voices muttering. At first she was content to let the sounds wash over her, but then she heard her own name.

Like a wave slightly higher than the rest, her name rose briefly out of the murmur. She strained to hear more, but could not distinguish any other words.

Seized by impulse, she swung from her bed and padded to the doorway. With her hand on the latch she pressed against the door, listening for the sounds of anyone in the passage. She heard none. Slowly, carefully she eased open her door and went outside.

The conversation was coming from Morag's cabin. Hwenfayre crouched at the door, pressed her ear to the rough wood and listened.

'I tell you she's dangerous,' Alyce was saying.

'Nonsense,' said Morag. 'She's a child. And she knows nothing.'

'You are wrong, Morag,' said a deep male voice that Hwenfayre could not quite place. 'She is dangerous and keeping her here will bring trouble.'

'Trouble for whom?' asked Morag. 'She has only minimal knowledge, and there's nothing she can do without the harp anyway.'

'Are you sure about that?' asked the man.

'What do you mean?'

'The harp is little more than the channel, you know that. What if she is more than we suspect? Could she overcome that?'

'No. Not as she is,' said Alyce. 'And making sure she stays that way is my responsibility.'

'And Hylin's,' observed Morag.

'Is she under control?' asked the man.

'Usually,' said Morag.

'Not good enough, High Priestess,' said the man. 'Everything needs to be watertight if you hope to get away with such a change in the plan.'

'It was my plan, I can change it if I wish. And believe me, this could be even better than leaving her to the Raiders. Imagine what we could achieve if we can channel and control that sort of power,' she said.

'I still don't like it,' the male voice said with a hint of sullenness.

'So what do you suggest?' Morag said.

'I suggest nothing, High Priestess.'

Footsteps sounded behind her. Hwenfayre leaped to her feet and spun around. It was a sailor coming down the stairs. Heart pounding, Hwenfayre scampered back to her room.

Dangerous? she thought. *Me? Dangerous?*

188

14

The townsfolk were abuzz with excitement. Not much ever happened in this quiet little village tucked away at the edge of the Great Fastness. It nestled in the shadow of a hill, where it was bypassed by the world outside. This isolation suited most of its inhabitants, who seemed content to be left to their own devices.

Aldere, a young man of about twenty summers, walked with his mother Katya towards the open area in the middle of the village that served as both occasional meeting place and market. He held her arm gently, guiding her as she made her slightly unsteady way across the ground. Everyone they met politely ignored her uneven gait, her unkempt hair and her bleary eyes. It was after noon and she had been drinking for a while by now. They pretended not to notice, partly out of respect for what she had been, partly in pity for what had happened and partly out of shame for their own part in her tragedy.

All this Aldere knew and understood. Some of it he shared or they all thought he did. Some of the guilt was projected onto him. *You should have done something* was implicit in their eyes, but he felt no guilt for either his mother or his father. Neither was his fault.

Around them, the rest of the village was moving purposefully towards the bench set at the edge of the open area. Old Harald stood beside the bench with his liver-spotted hand resting on the shoulder of a man who was seated uncomfortably beside him. He had a simple travellers' bag at his feet and resting across his knees lay a funda, an elegant stringed instrument. Aldere stared at the beautifully carved instrument. It had a deep sounding-bowl at one end made from at least a dozen strips of different wood from all over the Empire with a long neck of tadon wood stretching as long as a man's arm to where the tuning keys sparkled in the morning sun. The strings also glinted, showing they were made of metal wire rather than the usual stretched gut.

Aldere knew very little about money or precious things, but he knew this stylish device for accompanying songs and tales was worth more than his village. He had mixed feelings about this. On the one hand he was in awe of such a piece of art, but on the other he wondered what his village could do with the money they could earn by selling it. For a moment, while his mother paused to cough, he allowed his mind to wander in such realms of fantasy — perhaps a new goat for Sylvia, the blacksmith's wife, or a healer to stay in the village for a few days at a time on a regular basis, or perhaps some new tools and building materials for the never-ending maintenance a village needed.

His mother started walking again. He stirred and walked with her, matching his gait with hers so as not to rush her. She was worse than normal this morning, but he would not judge her for her weaknesses. Life had not been kind to her. The chair he carried on his back would allow her to sit comfortably and he would sit at her feet.

Harald waited until the village settled into a sort of hushed expectation before speaking. As a young man Harald had run away to join the Army of the World. He served the Thane far to the south before being injured and returning home. The Thane still paid a small pension every season that made Harald the man with the most money in the village. This, combined with a powerful voice and his military bearing, made him the de facto head of their little community. Aldere found it interesting that Harald was always referred to as the man with the most money, never the richest man in the village.

'Friends,' he boomed. 'Today we have a visitor in our village. Yngwie,' he indicated the man at his side, 'has travelled far and brings us tales and news of the world.'

Aldere followed Harald's gesture and considered Yngwie. It was immediately obvious that he had travelled a long way. He had short red hair, fair skin that showed a light dusting of freckles across his face and the most startling green eyes. His hands wandered over the strings of the funda, drawing from them the most beautiful sounds Aldere had ever heard. Harald talked on, but Aldere did not hear any of what he said, so engaged was he on the funda. When the sound of Harald faded Yngwie started to speak.

'I have travelled from afar and come with tales of adventure and mystery, tales to scare, tales to warn, tales to instruct.' As he spoke, the lyrical flow of his words, so strangely accented, was accentuated by the skilled playing of his wondrous instrument. Aldere knew he was not listening to any normal traveller. This was a rare gift.

'This day,' Yngwie went on, 'I bring you a tale of our shared past, the great heritage of the Triumvirate.'

A shiver ran through Aldere as the whole village caught its collective breath, for 'Triumvirate' was a word whispered by the very old, and its meaning was shrouded in mystery and ignorance.

'Long ago,' Yngwie recited, 'the Hard Ones rose up to do battle against the Soft Ones. For many seasons they slaughtered and destroyed, until it was clear the Soft Ones would be wiped out. One day, when all seemed lost, three great leaders arose: one on the Sea, one on the land and one to rule over all. These great leaders had names of legend and powers beyond human understanding. The Danan, the Karanatikisa and the Chandajagat strove alongside the Soft Ones and prevailed against the Hard Ones. When their task was done they left us, but their legend lived on.

'As time went by, their true names were lost and replaced with other names. The Guardian and the Weapon are names used here in the Empire, but elsewhere they are known as Vahan the Lost and the Pivot. It matters not what they are called; their tasks remain as they have ever been. They stand guard over us and will reawaken when they are needed.'

Aldere had the sense that this was little more than an introduction, a preamble to the true tale. He was right, for when Yngwie finished he looked up and, with a smile, lifted the tempo of his playing. His voice took on the cadences of a song as he launched into a rousing ballad of ancient adventure and danger. As the ballad progressed, Aldere felt a lessening in his focus. Much of the song, he knew, was a simple story with little basis in truth and much ponderous moralising. He gave himself up to enjoying the pleasures of a skilled performer plying his art.

When Yngwie ended his songs — after several calls for old favourites, all of which he played without hesitation — he rose and bowed. Harald stood to shake his hand with tears in his eyes.

'Our thanks, Yngwie,' he said. 'You have honoured our simple village with your skills and we are very grateful.'

'Nothing shows gratitude more than food, wine and a roof for the night,' Yngwie answered.

His response, although expected, still brought a chuckle from many villagers and offers of hospitality were made by several families. Yngwie was in the process of deciding when Aldere's mother stirred.

'Nonsense,' she snorted. 'Come on, Aldere, let's go home.' She leaned heavily on his arm as he helped her to her feet. When she was upright, she rested her head on his shoulder. 'You're a good boy, Aldere,' she whispered. 'I don't know what I'd do without you.'

He patted her arm gently and lifted her chair.

On their way back home, Michaela joined them. She was about Aldere's age with skin the colour of rich chocolate, sparkling dark eyes and long black hair that she always kept tied back in a thick braid. Already past the normal marrying age, Michaela had dismissed three suitors from other villages whom Aldere knew of. She had never shown much interest in him either. They were not really close, just slightly more than acquaintances.

'What did you think of Yngwie?' she asked.

'He's very good,' Aldere said.

'No, that's not what I meant,' Michaela said. 'What did you think of the stories?'

Aldere shrugged. 'They were stories. Good stories, but just stories.'

'They weren't true?' she asked.

Aldere shook his head and her face fell.

'Of course they weren't true,' Katya said. 'That's the nature of travellers like him; they tell pretty stories and get a free feed.' She shrugged. 'It's a fair trade.'

'I suppose it is,' Michaela conceded.

'Michaela!' The call came from her father. He was standing by his cart with the normal angry expression on his face. 'It's time we left.'

'Yes, Father,' she called back. 'I'd better go,' she said, turning back to Aldere. 'I'll come by and see you both tomorrow,' she promised as she rushed away to join her father.

Aldere watched as she clambered up onto the cart. When she was seated at the reins, she smiled at him and waved. He returned the wave before taking his mother's arm again and starting the walk home. She crossly pulled her arm away from him to walk unaided.

'What are you doing?' she demanded.

'Just helping you, Mother,' he said, deliberately misconstruing her words.

'No,' she snapped. 'What are you doing ignoring that girl? She won't wait forever, you know. And wasting your time with me is not helping you.'

'She has never given me any idea that she is waiting for me, Mother,' he said.

Katya snorted derisively but continued walking. Aldere walked with her, ready to help if she stumbled.

When they arrived home, Jaya, one of the other villagers, was there waiting for them. She held a large pot of something that smelled delicious. Aldere greeted her cheerfully.

'I made too much for my family,' she explained as she held out the pot towards them. 'I thought you might like some for your meal today.'

'Thank you,' said Aldere, but his mother walked past without acknowledging the gift and closed the door firmly behind her. Aldere caught Jaya's eye and shrugged apologetically.

'Bad day?' Jaya asked kindly.

He shrugged again. 'Not so bad,' he said. 'But she's had better.'

'What is it this time?'

Aldere sighed. 'It's always the same things. Regret, grief, guilt, too much wine.'

'Is there anything I can do?' she asked.

Aldere shook his head. 'We just have to wait. And hope that time will ease the hurt,' he lied. His mother was damaged by what had happened to her, and no amount of time would make it better. How he knew this he was not sure, but know it he did. His mother would die a lonely, bitter, desperately sad woman and there was nothing he could do except help ease her suffering where he could.

He thanked Jaya again for the food and went inside.

15

Slowly the pain receded. Through a red haze the dawn broke, sending agonising shafts of light into Wyn's numb mind. He lay on his back, blinking as consciousness eased its way through the black wall of his stupefied mind.

With a groan he tried to sit up. A sharp, stabbing pain in his chest forced him to lie down again. He was unable to focus either his eyes or his mind, but there was something nagging him. Something was wrong. A warm trickle ran along his chest, slowly pooling just below his sternum. He tried to see what it was but his hand would not move.

His pain-addled mind noticed that his hands were bound tightly behind his back. The ache in his back finally registered as he went to roll over, but once again the sharp stabbing pain in his chest prevented him from doing so. Now annoyed, Wyn forced his eyes open to glare up at whatever was keeping him down.

A man glared back along the shaft of a spear. With a snarl, he snatched the spear away and roughly dragged Wyn to his feet, then, with a shove, pushed him towards the forest.

They walked for what seemed like hours, Wyn stumbling over the uneven path, his uncommunicative companion ever ready with his spear. Wyn tried to concentrate on where he was going but his mind seemed unable to focus. Instead he found himself recalling every moment of the previous day — the assassins, the dead islander, the men he killed, Morag. But mostly he kept thinking about Hwenfayre. Even as he staggered and fell, lurching unsteadily through the forest, her every expression, her eyes, her wild, untamed hair, her smile, the smell of her skin, everything about her kept coming back to him with the clarity that only love can provide.

As that word rang through his mind he stopped short, earning another spear thrust. Without thought he spun about to face his attacker, who casually clubbed him to the ground with the butt of his spear.

Love? He lay still, feigning unconsciousness to cover his confusion. To be sure, he loved his Princess, his High Priestess, the true daughter of Danan, but he knew this was more. And he also knew he had no business harbouring such feelings. Wyn was not a man given to great emotions. Love was not unknown to him, but what he felt for Hwenfayre confused him. At times he thought he would be overwhelmed by the feelings he had but did not understand.

A kick to his side roused him, and once more he was dragged to his feet. By the time they stepped out of the forest, Wyn's back was dripping blood from many wounds.

They had come to a village. As soon as they appeared, a cry went up from all who saw them. Within moments they were surrounded by happy, smiling villagers who seemed overjoyed by the return of the spear-carrying man. For the moment they were content to ignore his bleeding, semi-conscious prisoner. But that changed all too soon. The spear-carrier indicated Wyn. In response, several villagers grabbed Wyn and dragged him away, beating him as they did so.

They took him to a cage made of poles lashed together and threw him in. Then they dragged the cage along the ground until it fell heavily into a pit. Wyn lost consciousness when it hit the bottom.

It was dark when he finally came to. The cage was lying unevenly on the bottom of the pit, having landed on a large rock. He winced and tried to stand but as he did the cage lurched over, falling sideways until it lay flat. The tumble was enough to send him spiralling once more into unconsciousness.

He spent the next few days drifting in and out of consciousness, awakened by water tossed in his face to find the small meals that had been thrown down to him. He drank sparingly from the small puddles left from the water poured over him. His mind drifted, unattached, unaware of his surroundings, dimly noting the fact that his hands had been untied, distantly registering the pain in his body.

He didn't know if it was morning or afternoon when his mind found its way back to clarity. The light was dim but even. He forced his aching body to sit up, trying to focus his eyes and his brain. His back ached, his limbs were cramped and stiff but his breathing was steady and his heart was beating reassuringly.

'You are strong.' The voice was low, soft, feminine. He looked to where he could make out a woman kneeling on the ground outside his cage. 'You are strong,' she said again, 'but not wise.'

Wyn tried to speak, but nothing more than a harsh rasp escaped his cracked and swollen lips.

The woman passed a water skin through the bars towards him. He unsteadily reached out and took it, raising it to drink. His hand shook so badly that most of the cool water spilled down his chest, but he swallowed enough to wet his throat.

'Thank you,' he croaked.

'You are not welcome,' she replied. 'You should not be here at all. And you have no right to have survived this long.'

He tried to smile in reply, but merely succeeded in cracking his lips again.

'If you insist on surviving much longer you will regret it,' the woman said.

'How so?' asked Wyn.

'If you live until the night of the next moon tide, you will be sacrificed to the Sea.'

'The Sea is my mistress, lady. I do not fear her.'

'Maybe not. But you would do well to fear her servants.' She handed a bowl through the bars, withdrawing her hand quickly. 'I will bring you food again tomorrow.' She stood and turned to leave then looked back over her shoulder. 'Try to die before then.'

He didn't die that day. Instead, he waited for the woman to come back. She did so just before sunset. It had been a long, very hot day in the cage. With no shelter and no breeze in the pit, he lay exposed to the full heat of the sun as it sapped the energy from his mistreated body.

Despite his exhaustion, he heard her climb down the ladder. He did not turn his head as she padded across the pit and he did not look up as she knelt beside his cage. 'I see you did not take my advice, assassin,' she observed as she placed the bowl and flask inside the bars.

Still not moving, he replied. 'My name is Wyn. And I am no assassin, lady.'

'I do not care what your name is, but you were found near two murdered men of my tribe with the weapon of their deaths beside you.'

'I did not kill them.'

'That is not my concern,' she said.

'And what is your concern?' asked Wyn as he eased himself up into a sitting position.

'My concern is to guide you on your journey into death.'

Wyn frowned. 'I don't understand.'

'It is the belief of my people that when one dies one is beginning a great journey. It is a journey that no one should undertake ill-prepared. I am here to prepare you.'

'Your preparations are badly timed, lady,' he replied. 'I have no intention of dying yet.'

'You have no choice in the matter.'

'We'll see about that.'

'As you say, assassin.' She stood to leave. 'Until tomorrow.'

'Until tomorrow,' said Wyn. He watched her walk away, and as she put her foot on the bottom rung of the ladder he called out, 'What is your name, lady?'

'My people call me the Key, but my prisoners call me Dinah.'

'Until tomorrow then, Dinah.'

She climbed up without looking back.

The next day Wyn was feeling stronger. The day had not been so hot, as clouds had covered the sun. His wounds were beginning to heal and his mind was clearing. Also, the aching thirst had subsided, allowing him to save some of his water to drink during the day.

'Tell me of yourself,' Dinah urged.

'I am a soldier. A man who follows orders.'

'So who ordered you to kill my two fellow islanders?'

'No one, because I did not kill them.'

'But they are dead.'

'So's my father. But that doesn't mean I killed him.'

'Who did?'

'What?'

'Who did kill your father?'

'History.'

'Is that a person's name? Or is it a way of avoiding the question?'

'Neither. He was killed because he opposed the new in favour of the old. He was killed to let a new way take the place of an old way.'

'You still have not answered my question: who killed your father?'

'A young Sailer called Declan. He was a follower of a woman called Morag who wanted to rule my people. My father opposed her, and one day his boat never came back to the Raft. Declan claimed to have seen his boat taken under by a blaewhal. But blaewhals were rare at that time in that place.'

'Why was he in a boat?'

'I don't remember, but he was a Carver, so I guess he was hunting.'

'You speak in riddles, assassin. Since it appears that you have decided to live, a poor decision in my eyes, we have time. So stop talking as though I know your history. I do not even know what people you call your own.'

Wyn looked up and for the first time held her gaze. 'I am a Child of Danan,' he said.

'Ah,' she said.

'You have heard of us, then?'

'Who of those who live by the sea has not?'

'Indeed.'

'Why did you leave your people?'

'I left to seek a place in the world, since my own place had been taken from me.'

'How was it taken?'

Instead of answering, Wyn took a bite of food. He was surprised at how, after so many years, it still hurt to remember all that had happened. Slowly he chewed the tasteless morsel. By the time he had finished, Dinah was gone.

He dreamed during the night. His dreams left him sweating and cold in the morning, but he could not recall them.

Dinah was late. It was well after sunset when she climbed down the ladder with his food and water. As before she knelt by the bars to his cage, but he could tell there was something wrong.

'What's wrong?' he asked.

She shook her head and a tear trickled down her cheek. 'Nothing to concern you, assassin.'

Wyn nodded. 'I am no assassin, Dinah,' he said.

'You were telling me about finding a place in the world,' said Dinah, wiping the tear away, her voice becoming businesslike.

'After I left the Raft I sailed east. When I made land I signed on with a mercenary unit fighting a small war. I guess I wanted to fight, to somehow lose myself, maybe even die. It was an ugly little skirmish but I survived. And I learned a few things about myself. Not all of them good.' He stopped to eat, watching Dinah. She watched him back, her face impassive. He continued. 'I did that sort of thing for years. Sign up, survive, leave. But then I found myself a guard in a walled town by the Sea. I had managed to avoid the Sea up until then, but she kept calling to me. No matter how I try to avoid her, she always calls me.'

'Calls you?'

'I can't explain it, but I went to her. I signed up as a common guardsman. I'd had worse jobs. At least I had a roof over my head and regular meals. But I'd only been there for a few days when I heard the song.'

'What song?'

'The Song of the Morning. It was one of the ancient songs of my people, sung to welcome the morning. I hadn't heard it since the day I left the Raft.'

'That's something I still haven't worked out. Why exactly did you leave the Raft?'

'After my father died there was no place for me any more.'

'But surely you had a life, a family to care for?'

'My mother made it clear she did not want to have anything to do with me and I had no other family. Before my father died I was settled in what I was going to do. I was going to be a Carver, just like him. But Morag changed all that with her plans.'

'But you still haven't told me what her plans were.'

'No, I haven't.'

'I do not think you will be ready to leave this life and journey into death until you do.'

He smiled wryly. 'Sounds like the best motivation to keep my mouth shut that I've heard for many a long day.'

'So be it, then.' She left without another word.

They did not speak for a few days after that. He was unwilling to start the conversation and she seemed willing to wait him out. All the while he felt himself getting stronger; his mind was clear and he spent much of the day thinking of a way to get out of his cage. It was going to be difficult as the bars were firmly tied with stout fibres and were themselves as thick as his forearm. His food was brought to him in a wooden bowl that was taken away when he had finished, and his water came in a skin. He had no tools. For a while he tried to work at the fibres but they were coated in a resin that made them hard as rock.

The part of the day he did not spend trying to escape he spent thinking about Hwenfayre. Just the thought of her name was enough to confuse him. Perhaps it was just infatuation with a girl who needed him he tried to tell himself, something that would pass. But even as he thought it he knew it was not true. There was something about her that held him captive. It was not a simple physical attraction; he'd had enough of those to know what they were like. No, this was more. And it was not a simple case of young love; he'd had his share of that, too. He loved his Princess in a way that he had never thought himself capable of loving anyone. It was as though his recognition of his feelings in the forest had opened a floodgate of emotions that, now released, could not be held back. He tried to tell himself she was just a child, but he knew that to be a lie also. Even at seventeen she had a fire, a command about her that left him helpless. He had to find her again.

Then one day Dinah started to talk.

At first she spoke of her own people, their ways, their beliefs. Then she spoke of herself. She had no family, no lover, very few friends. Her role as guide into death gave her much grief as she watched those around her die, yet it gave her the wisdom that is found in grief. Wyn listened closely, in part out of a natural human need for company, but also to learn about his captors, perhaps to find a way to escape so that he could find Hwenfayre again.

Yet as he listened to Dinah's tale, he found himself becoming interested. For the next few days, instead of her trying to learn about him, he learned about her. She was lonely, often sad but never despairing. The guide into death for her village was a position that had been in her family for ten generations. As she was unmarried and fast approaching the end of her childbearing days, the task of selecting someone to take over from her was weighing heavily upon her mind. It was as if she needed to talk, to clear her mind, help herself think. But she never called him by name.

Slowly, as the days went by, she talked less and he talked more. He told her about his life after he left the Raft. The places he had been, the wars he had fought in, the men he had killed, the women he had met. But he could not bring himself to tell her of the woman he loved.

'But you still haven't told me about the Raft,' Dinah said one day. 'And I know,' she continued in the face of his glare, 'you keep saying you are not ready, but you only have a few days left before the time arrives for your death. The moon tide is fast approaching, and the preparations for your execution are well in hand.'

'My execution?'

'Your execution, assassin. Or had you forgotten why you are here?'

'No. But I hoped you might have.'

She shook her head slowly. 'That is not going to happen, assassin. Not given my tasks in this village.'

'How so?'

'Do you remember, some days ago, when I came to you and I was upset?'

'Yes.'

'That morning the wife of one of the men you murdered gave in to her despair and took her own life.' Dinah stared at Wyn, her eyes hard. 'She died in my arms, unprepared for the death that took her. It was all I could do to prevent the rest of her family from coming down here and taking you. I told them not to compound the suffering by making you leave unprepared as well as her. They barely heard me but they respected my wishes.'

'So you think I owe you something?'

'No. I was hoping you might respect our customs.'

'Respect the customs of a people who would condemn me to a death that I have not earned? Respect the customs of a people who plan to murder an innocent man to ease their own pain? I don't think so.'

Dinah reacted like she had been slapped. Her eyes showed shock and pain, as if betrayed. With an effort, she stood with dignity. 'Then once more we have nothing to say to each other, assassin.' She left without another word, but halfway up the ladder she looked back, which she had never done before. A coldly calculating part of Wyn's mind started to work.

'My father was Master Carver Aristide,' he began the next morning before Dinah even sat down. 'He was a respected man among his people and one who followed the old ways. For many years our people had sailed the Sea, loving her and enjoying her bounty. And every few generations Danan would come to us and teach us again the power of the Sea. She had not come for a long time when I was a boy and there were murmurings that she had deserted us. I remember listening to my father arguing with other men at night who were beginning to doubt the old ways. Our Priestesses had lost the power to control the Sea and to command her bounty. The Children of Danan were losing their way, adrift on the Sea that should have been our home. Even the Southern Raiders were becoming bold in attacking us. The High Priestess of the time was a strong woman but she had none of the old power. She ruled by fear and manipulation, using the knowledge of Sailers and hunters rather than an understanding of the Sea.

'I was just a boy but I heard enough to know that things were not as they should be. My mother taught me to read and my father had many books about the old ways. Even to a boy, being ruled by a High Priestess who had no power over the Sea seemed wrong. But this High Priestess had many followers; in fact, I remember that most people seemed to agree with her.'

'But what was she saying?'

'That it was time for the Children of Danan to move on, to put aside the old ways and take on new ways. In part I think it was because she had no powers, but there were those who had forgotten the wonder and majesty of the Sea and how she would respond to us. The High Priestess was having her way. So my father approached the Navigator of our Raft.

'Before he did this, he gave me his tools. I knew what that meant: he was not expecting to come home. The handing over of a Master's tools to his oldest son or his apprentice is supposed to be done at his retirement from the craft. As he gave them to me, he said, "Son, you are to treasure these tools and use them with pride." Then he left.

'I never saw him again. He did not come back from his meeting with the Navigator and it was two days before the lie about his fatal meeting with a blaewhal started to circulate. Naturally my mother was frantic, so she went to see the Priestess of our Raft. She spun my mother some equally thin lie about Master Carver Aristide's suitable end, about how he had gone to the Mistress he loved and served and the like.' Even though he had thought about this story so many times, it was the first time Wyn had ever told it to anyone, and he was surprised to hear his voice grow thick with emotion, to feel the burn of tears in his eyes. He forced himself to continue. 'I went to the Navigator myself, to ask him what had happened at their meeting. He was kind and friendly, expressing his sadness at the unfortunate loss of my father and how the Raft would miss the skills of such a fine Carver. But when I challenged him about his meeting with my father, he angrily denied such a meeting ever took place. Things got a little heated and I ended up hitting him. He went down like a sack of dead fish and did not get up. I panicked and ran.

'The next morning I was dragged in to answer for my actions before the Priestess of our Raft. I should have guessed there was something wrong when instead of my own Priestess, the High Priestess herself sat over me. The Navigator stood up and spun some fanciful tale about me spreading lies about him and the High Priestess. I told the truth as I knew it, foolishly including my father's worries about where the High Priestess was leading us. Up until that moment she had been listening to me like some gentle aunt, but suddenly her mood changed. She became hard and cold. When I finished, she pronounced judgment on me. I was to be stripped of my father's tools and his name. My mother and I were to be denied our position and our home on our Raft. We were made paupers, with no way of ever changing our situation.

'I stayed with my mother for a few years, eking out a living doing odd jobs until she faded away and died. Then I left.'

'And why are you going back?'

'Why do you think I am going back?'

'Aren't you?' she asked gently.

'Yes, I am,' he admitted.

'So why?'

'I found the Danan. I was taking her home when we were washed up on your island by a storm. Somehow the High Priestess knew we were here and took her away from me.'

Dinah nodded, her eyes unfathomable. 'You die tomorrow night when the tide runs at its peak.' She stood and walked to the ladder. 'Die well, Wyn,' she said without turning back.

Dinah did not return the next day. Instead Wyn was visited by a man in ceremonial garb. In one hand he held a long heavy-bladed spear, in the other he carried a sack. With a single sweeping motion of the spear he sliced open the cords holding the cage closed. When the door of the cage swung open, he tossed the sack inside, then turned and climbed out of the pit. As Wyn watched him go, he became aware of several other men, similarly garbed and armed, ringing the top of the pit. All thoughts of escape faded.

He looked at the sack. Inside there was a flask of water, a bag of fruit, some ceremonial artifacts and a small vial. The vial had a note attached to it.

Assassin,
This sack contains your requirements to
travel into death. Most are significant to our

beliefs, which I know you do not share, but this
vial is special. Take it with you as you journey
but do not make it a part of you. Remember
that the caruda fears that which it cannot see
and when you go back to your Mistress, swim
deep and swim always towards the light.

Die well, Wyn.
Dinah

Two hours after darkness fell, Wyn was dragged out
of the pit and led at spear point to a high cliff
overlooking the sea. Below him the inky water
heaved slowly. Above him the moon shone brightly.
He stood in silence with his escort of about twenty
men. They were clearly waiting for some sign, some
event that would signal the end of his life.

A sudden hissing, roaring sound erupted from the
waters below. He looked down. The water that
moments before had been calm was now boiling and
churning like a pot on a fire. The Sea was alive with
thousands of fish, each one creating a brilliant trail
of phosphorescence as it thrashed about in a frenzy.

'Assassin,' intoned one of the men behind him.
'You are to be offered to the waters in payment for
your crime. The caruda that run below come every
year when the moon tide runs. They will be your
executioners. Die well.'

The rest of the men lowered their spears and
advanced on Wyn, driving him towards the cliff
edge. As he backed away from the spear points that
glinted in the moonlight, he took the vial that Dinah
had given him. He unstoppered it, turned and dived
off the cliff.

As he fell, he stretched his arms above his head holding the unstoppered vial in one fist, being careful not to squeeze it.

He hit the water hard, the brutal impact driving the air from his body. The searing agony that swept through him burned like fire. Down he plunged, through the water that was bright with the trails of thousands of seething caruda fish. But a strange thing happened. The violence of his entry into the water had crushed the vial that Dinah had given him. As he had half expected, a thick black ink poured out, enveloping him and entirely covering the phosphorescence caused by his passing.

Instead of tearing him apart, the caruda fish were driven away from this rude black missile that plunged through them. He tore through their ranks, deeper and deeper, until he had passed right through the school. With his head pounding and his chest screaming, he turned himself upright, to swim back up, when the words in Dinah's note came to him: *swim deep and swim always towards the light.* Ignoring the pain, he looked around.

Seeing a faint glow somewhere below him, he struck out and down towards the light. The pain in his chest, the burning from his wrist, which he had almost certainly broken, and the red agony in his head threatened to overwhelm him as he thrust his protesting body on.

The light became brighter, took on shape. It was a lantern, a flame. He felt his eyes were playing tricks on him, he was almost dead, his head felt as though it was about to explode, when suddenly he broke the surface of the water.

Gasping, he pulled himself out onto a ledge, where he lay drawing the cool damp air into his aching lungs. It was a few minutes before he was able to give any heed to his surroundings.

He was in an underwater cave. The only way out was up a narrow tunnel that stretched above him. Beside him the lantern flickered, casting inconstant light on the walls. A rope attached to the top of the lantern snaked its way up the chimney. Something about this cave seemed wrong, filling him with the need to leave as soon as possible, so he dragged himself to his feet and considered the climb.

It would not be difficult, even in his aching state, so he reached up into the narrow gap and started climbing. The rock was wet, dripping with sea water. He frequently disturbed small scuttling creatures that rattled away from his groping arms as he searched for handholds, but there was little or no plant life. It was clear that this whole area was normally underwater and never received sunlight. He knew that should puzzle him but his mind was focused on the next hand or toe hold as he pushed upwards.

Finally he heaved himself out of the chimney, to lie face down and panting on a sandy beach.

'So you are both strong and wise after all.'

'Your note was not that hard to understand, Dinah,' he said, rolling over and looking up at the woman who sat cross-legged beside him.

She smiled gently, the first time he had seen her smile. It was a melancholy sort of a smile, slightly lopsided, but genuine. 'I was rather proud of the subtlety,' she said. 'I was sure no one would dare to open the gifts of the Guide, but it doesn't pay to be careless.'

'True.' He sat up, wincing as muscles protested. 'But why? I thought you believed me to be an assassin.'

'No. Not from the first time I saw you,' she disagreed. 'I have seen murderers. I have spent time with hard men, evil men, preparing them to make their journey into death. And no murderer ever spoke as you did. I decided that you had to go and find your Princess.' She reached out and smoothed his hair back from where it had fallen over his eyes. 'I always knew this cave would come in handy one day.'

Wyn frowned at her, partly in confusion at her words, partly in concern at what her gesture might mean.

As if sensing his thoughts, Dinah removed her hand and stood to pull the rope that raised the lantern. 'The cave below is only open on the nights of the moon tide. I discovered it years ago when I came down here to escape the sound of the executions above. Some peculiarity of the tide holds the water back, emptying the cavern and opening the tunnel. It fills up again soon after the moon sets and is inaccessible until next time.' She raised the lantern above her head to shine it around the beach. 'This is my special place. My father showed it to me on the day he named me his successor.' Wyn looked at the beach. It was short, maybe ten strokes across, with overhanging rocks that would shield it from above. No one on top of the cliff would ever know it was here. The black water lapped gently a few paces from where Wyn sat. Just offshore, rocking with the sea's motion, was a boat rigged for open-water sailing. Seeing the direction of his gaze, Dinah went on, 'Yes, Wyn, go. Go and seek your Princess. Save her. Save yourself.' Abruptly the lantern went out. In the sudden darkness he heard the sound of softly running feet, then, from a distance, 'Don't die, Wyn.'

And she was gone.

16

It was a good boat. Well built and well provisioned, it would serve him nicely. Within a few hours Wyn knew she was one of those boats that sailors speak of as being well behaved. She sat evenly in the water and responded smoothly to his guidance, easing over the swells comfortably, her sails swelling proudly in the breeze that bore him swiftly away from the island.

Sailing on a calm night under the moonlight gave him time to think about his strange encounter with Dinah, time to think about her words and her actions. How easily he heard her, how completely he misunderstood her every word. Why had she sent him to his death merely to offer him escape? He shook his head to clear those disturbing thoughts, only to have them replaced with thoughts that were just as disturbing.

Hwenfayre, he thought, *where are you?*

In his mind, awash as it was with confusion, it was that one thought that drove him on. Several times in the first week or so of his travels he saw inviting islands, rich with lush greenery, surrounded with sparkling waters teeming with fish, but each time he stared at an island he saw a pair of lavender eyes, wild, untamed white-blonde hair and a luminous smile.

He left the islands behind and ventured out into the open ocean. The swell deepened, lengthened and grew more powerful as if spreading its shoulders for battle. The wind freshened, carrying with it the distinctive smell of the deep ocean. Beneath the boat's keel, the water grew darker, colder and less tame. It took on the aspect of a wild thing; no longer the pet of the islanders, it became its own creature, one against whom a sailor could truly test himself in a contest as old as humanity itself. Wyn's boat seemed smaller, more fragile, more at risk as his instincts grew more wary and his senses became heightened.

Like all warriors, he relished the contest, feeling in himself the old strengths and drives reawaken. He felt more alive than he had for years with the savage joy of a life-and-death struggle filling his being. So many things he thought he had forgotten came back to him, so many skills and memories surfaced as the years he had spent away from his home sloughed off him like an old cloak. The Sea filled his mind, washing him clean once more, but Hwenfayre filled his dreams.

He slept when the Sea let him, and then only briefly, but whenever his eyes closed he could see her face, hear her voice, almost feel her skin. There were times when he was awakened suddenly, not by a shift in the wind or a change in the swell, but by the half-heard strains of a harp playing over the sea, welcoming him into the morning.

The boat was well stocked with dried fish and vegetables, and the time-proven equipment used by all the islanders to distil sea water into fresh using the sun's heat, and simple tools needed to gather food from the Sea's bounty.

Thus it was almost a disappointment when, some weeks after setting out, he sighted another sail.

It had distinctive rigging, which he felt he should recognise. He stared at it as it approached. Then it dawned on him. A shock of fear thrilled through him, galvanising him into action. One by one, he tossed the water purifier, the fishing gear, his food and his stored water overboard. He tore his clothes and pulled down his sail. Weighting it with his boots, knife and belt, he tossed it overboard as well. Then he sat down to wait while his empty boat bobbed in the light swell.

The ship altered course slightly to head directly towards him. With a speed that confirmed his first suspicions, it bore down on him. Soon he could see the white water at its bow as it tore through the swell, and hear the cries of its crew.

But, as it drew closer, the voices changed from what were unmistakably yells of bloodlust to sounds of concern.

'Ahoy!' came the cry from the ship. 'How fare you, traveller?'

'Not well,' he called back.

A coarse but good-natured laugh greeted his assertion. 'That we can see, traveller. Care for a ride?'

Wyn made a show of considering the offer. Finally he nodded. 'I think I might accept your kind offer. My afternoon's sailing has begun to bore me.'

Again a burst of laughter greeted his words. A rope was tossed to him. He caught it and made it fast to the prow of his boat. The crew above him pulled him close, then he climbed up the rope. As he reached the railing, rough hands grabbed him and hauled him aboard while other men clambered over the side to secure his boat.

'Welcome, traveller,' said a sailor. He was a huge man dressed in the leather and canvas of a Southern Raider.

Wyn thanked his early lessons of their ways. Whilst they were violent and brutal reavers of any who sailed the sea, they were committed to rescuing any who had fallen afoul of her whims. He remembered his father telling him the only way of avoiding the Raiders' violence was to be drifting and lost on the open ocean.

The massive man before him looked Wyn over carefully. 'You don't look like a castaway and there have been no storms hereabouts recently. What is your tale?' As the man spoke, the mood of the others changed perceptibly. A quiet muttering began and a number of the crew started to finger the hilts of their swords in anticipation. Wyn became aware that his life hinged on his answer.

'My last captain did not like my taste in rum,' he said. The other man frowned. 'He seemed to think,' continued Wyn, 'that his rum and mine were different, and he took it badly that I preferred his.' A smile spread across the Raider's face. 'So when I sampled his rum once too often, last night as it happened, he suggested I find myself a new boat. But as I did not have one on me at the time, he gave me one.' The smile broadened; a few chuckles were heard from the crew. 'Sadly,' Wyn continued, 'he neglected to give me anything else but the boat. I was starting to get hungry.'

'Welcome aboard the *Gretchen*,' said the Raider. 'You'll find we have no such silly rules here. What's one's is all's.' A cheer went up from the others as Wyn became one with the Southern Raiders.

The big man gave the order to alter course and the crew dispersed immediately to their various tasks. Wyn was left alone, staring at him. 'I am the Captain of this vessel,' he said. 'My name is Marek, but you can call me "Captain" or "Sir". We have only one rule aboard, and it's easy so everyone can understand it: I give the orders, you obey them.'

Wyn nodded. 'I understand, Sir.'

'I think we'll get along fine. What do they call you?'

'Wyn, Sir.'

'Wyn,' he looked up to the top of the mainmast, 'it's time for the lookout to be relieved. Go aloft.'

'Sir.'

He worked hard, but the food was good and plentiful and the rum as free as Marek had said, and the crew were pleased to have another pair of hands to share their labours. It was clear that once the Captain had accepted him, there were no doubts about him from the others. He was one of the crew immediately. A hammock was slung for him below decks, some gear was found for him and he was welcomed at the meal table. He quickly discovered that he had chosen well with his explanation about his predicament, for a brash disregard for authority was common. These were men bonded together by the harshness of their lives, their shared struggle against the Sea for existence and their paradoxical reverence for their captain.

His hammock was slung between a big islander named Sacchin and a wiry, dark-skinned man called Garth. Within a few days of joining the crew, Wyn decided Marek was a good captain. He showed a canny knack for the winds and a firm hand in commanding the men. Wyn, with his long black hair, heavy frame and fighter's stance, fitted in immediately. Most of the men had a past, so his reticence to speak of his own was not out of place.

He had a good head for heights, and the solitude that being on top of the mainmast brought appealed to him, so he found himself aloft regularly. It was about two weeks after joining the Raiders that he caught sight of a sail.

'Whereabouts?' called Marek when Wyn had bellowed his sighting.

'Port bow,' he called back, pointing.

'Come about,' ordered Marek. The helmsman responded by spinning the wheel about and the ship heeled over as it altered course to intercept the vessel.

The *Gretchen* cut through the slight swell smoothly as it made its way towards the other sail. High atop the mainmast, Wyn frowned. The ship they were chasing was not behaving like any other he had seen. Instead of fleeing at the first sight of the distinctive rigging and sail of the Raiders, it seemed to be slowly turning away, as if damaged. The crew were preparing themselves for an attack, distributing weapons, lighting the fires, shutting all hatches. Marek himself, always armed, spent the time carefully watching the other ship.

Abruptly he spun around and stared towards the other horizon, but Wyn was ahead of him.

'Sail!' he cried, pointing. A second sail had appeared on the other side of the Raiders' vessel. It came fast, rigged for speed, cutting through the water straight as an arrow towards them. Marek called orders, discerning the trap. The sailors threw down their weapons, scrambling to put about. As soon as the *Gretchen* started to turn, the first ship put aside any pretence and drove towards them. White water appeared at her bow as she trampled the waves beneath her.

Wyn felt the old thrill again, half terror, half excitement: that sharpening of the senses as imminent death approaches swiftly; that intoxicating dread of the fight mixed with the adrenaline surge of anticipation. Every nerve of his body sang as he watched the oncoming ships. Even as he did so, he readied himself for the fight, winding a leather strap around his left fist, tightening his belt for the cutlass he would soon have and tying back his hair. Then he waited for Marek's orders.

They were not long in coming. 'Any more sails?' the Captain bellowed.

'No.'

At Wyn's answer, Marek waved him down. He quickly climbed down the ropes to the deck where a cutlass was thrust into his hand. With a nod, the Mate indicated for Wyn to take his station at the port bow. He stood between Garth and Sacchin, both of whom preferred the axe to the cutlass as their weapon.

Sacchin grinned tightly at him as he arrived. 'A good day for a fight, eh, Wyn?'

Wyn looked up at the cloudless blue sky above and felt the fresh breeze on his face as he replied, 'As good a day as any to face death.'

Garth snorted a mirthless laugh. 'It's just the sort of day I would choose to die. Three months out, three to go, my lady at home about to give birth and scarce plunder in the hold. Perfect.' He gave a gap-toothed grin. 'How about you, friend Wyn? What sort of day would you choose?'

'Cold. Grey. Winter I think is the only time to die.'

Sacchin laughed, clapping him on the shoulder. 'Hah! You sound like a woman, Wyn. Next you'll be telling us there's a girl waiting somewhere. A girl of such great beauty that her smile outshines the sun, and when you left her you couldn't tell her you loved her. And now you're worried you'll die without her knowing.'

Wyn shot him a dark look, his eyes hard.

'There is!' cried Sacchin in delight. 'Hah! I knew it! The dark and silent Wyn has a woman. The man is human.'

'And you, Sacchin?' asked Wyn softly. 'Do you have a woman?'

'Me? No. I fled my home a criminal and an outcast. There's no woman left to cry over Sacchin's untimely death on the seas.'

'That death will come much sooner if you cannot hold your tongue,' growled Marek. The Captain was standing behind them, staring over Wyn's shoulder at the first of the oncoming ships. 'I want your mind on that crew over there, and on how many wives you can have lamenting their widowhood tonight.'

Sacchin nodded, the smile almost leaving his face.

A battle at sea fought under sail is a strangely slow-motion event. The ships approach each other at the behest of the wind, engaging each other in a dance of jibes and tacks that is almost ritualistic. A certain inevitability takes over as they move closer, the tension growing until it is almost unbearable. On all three ships men gripped weapons with palms grown sweaty, gave silent prayers to their various gods and waited.

'Release!' came Marek's roar and the first of the volleys from their mangonels were loosed. They shot their loads of heated metal fragments across the water. Immediately both other ships responded, loosing their own projectiles. From the ship to the starboard came red-hot sand, stinging and burning any unprotected flesh. From the ship to the port came pots of hot oil that burst in a splash of flame on the deck.

Men sprang to their tasks, some putting out flames, others reloading the mangonels while others prepared the grappling hooks. Another volley from each vessel sent more men screaming to the decks as metal, oil and sand reaped their deadly harvest. Wyn felt a harsh sting as glowing hot sand burned small holes in his shoulders. With a snarl, he brushed them off, his hand coming away bloodied. Beside him, Sacchin had experienced a similar fate, but the cheerful islander laughed out loud as another set of scars adorned his back. A bucket of water was tossed over them as a fellow crewman noticed their injuries. The water cooled the burns, but the salt stung. Wyn turned and nodded to the man, but he was away immediately, refilling his bucket.

By now the ships were close enough to see the men each would soon be trying to kill. Some men tried to disguise the true nature of a battle but Wyn always went in with the clear reality before him. He looked his opponents in the eyes, so that he could remember them. Later, he made peace. For now, he stared across the water and selected his first.

Moments later, the three ships were locked together. Each deck became a swirling mass of men and weapons as the melee engulfed them all indiscriminately. Wyn found himself backed against the railing by a swarthy sailor who fought with a sword and a dagger. All his instincts came together, blocking out everything but the fight. He thrust, parried, dodged and slashed, driving the other man back, then ran him through. There was no need to seek out another opponent; one stepped up to him as soon as the first fell. He fought until his cutlass weighed heavy on his aching arm, until his chest and shoulders were a mass of wounds and his lungs burned with every breath. The air was thick with smoke, the screams of the maimed and dying and the smell of blood.

For a moment Wyn found himself without an opponent. He stood, breathing heavily, his mind and body numb, his cutlass hanging low. Around him the struggle went on. He could see his fellow crewmembers striving, fighting against the boarders and for just a fleeting instant he wondered if he was fighting for the right side. Then he heard the guttural bellow of Sacchin as he received a ringing blow to the side of his head. The big islander staggered back, clutching at the wound, attempting to staunch the flow of blood. His axe clanged to the deck, forgotten in his pain.

Wyn's brief moment of indecision vanished as he leaped forward, shouldering aside friend and foe alike to plunge his own weapon deep into the attacker's side even as he raised his blade to finish the job on Sacchin. With a gasp, the attacker shuddered and fell to the deck. Wyn looked at Sacchin as he lay slumped at his feet. He was bleeding heavily from his head wound but he still breathed, and as Wyn looked the islander grinned back. Taking this as a good sign, Wyn turned around to face the fight that still raged.

Time ceased to have any meaning as he fought; most of his mind went cold, leaving him with his training, instincts and the fear. It was the fear that really drove him on, only the fear that made him kill, only the fear that made him ignore his many wounds, only the fear that kept him alive.

The Raiders were losing. His instincts told him that much. There were too many attackers, coming from both sides. They were too well equipped, too well trained, and he would die here. The sudden knowledge filled him with sadness. But not for himself, for her. She had power, but without anyone to help her she might never know its extent, nor would she be able to use it to save herself and her people. The anguish was overwhelming, driving him to cry out with the sudden pain. With an oath as old as Danan herself, he threw himself back into the fray; if he were going to die, then he would make them pay.

He was still fighting, driving two men backwards towards the railings, when he became distantly aware of a slowing, a quietening of the chaos around him. He paused, lowering his arms. The men, who moments ago were fighting for their lives, threw down their weapons and fled, leaving him alone. A breeze stirred his blood-soaked hair.

He turned and saw what everyone else had already seen. A squall was approaching. Where scant minutes ago there was clear sky, a black cloud was now sweeping across the sky towards them. Below it, the Sea surged, the swell rising, whitecaps showing. As he stared at the storm, all he could see was wild, white-blonde hair and sad lavender eyes. A single tear wended its way through the blood on his face. 'Hwenfayre,' he muttered.

With a rush, all the attackers who could stand were running, leaping across the narrow stretch of water, scrambling to reach their own vessels, to cut the ropes that held them tied. Desperately they hacked at the heavy ropes, knowing that their only chance of survival lay in outrunning the squall, and that they could only do alone. But they were not in time.

The squall hit them like a hammer. Instantly they were plunged into darkness, a wild sea surging all around them, rain smashing down, the ships tossed like corks. Men were thrown overboard, their dying cries swept away by the insanely shrieking wind. Wyn found himself sliding across the plunging deck towards the hungry grey waters. In desperation, he wrapped his arms around a stanchion. A wave crashed over him as if trying to tear him away from the ship. His body swung around until he was hanging over the side as the ship rose over a wave and then dove down, plunging into the sea.

His aching body was smashed against the side of the ship, driving the air from his lungs, taking the last of his strength from his arms. His grip started to loosen as he began his final plunge into the Sea, which he had deserted so many years before.

But just as his fingers despaired a strong hand clamped onto his wrist. In disbelief he looked up, into the one remaining eye of Sacchin.

The storm blew itself out as quickly as it had appeared, further adding to the fears of the crew. These were men who knew the Sea, and storms that appeared out of nowhere and then vanished just as completely were unnatural, things of superstitious awe. Marek knew this as well as any, so he gave the men no chance to gather and mutter. Instead he had them busy on the lookout for the other ships, starting repairs and cleaning the decks. Within minutes, the muttering had ceased.

The wounded, of whom there were many, were treated by a sailor with rudimentary medical skills. This explained, thought Wyn, why there were so many scars.

Sacchin had only lost his left eye, but Garth had been killed. Another widow would grieve the loss of a father for her child. For now there were things to do. His own wounds, whilst painful, were not life threatening, so he worked with the others.

The hours passed quickly, and it was nearing sunset when the lookout called.

'Sail to windward!' he bellowed.

With a curse Marek glared up at the lookout. 'How does she lie?' he called.

'Low in the water. Ill-rigged to run.'

'Come about!' called Marek. 'Rig for pursuit!'

Wyn thought this strange given the state of both the *Gretchen* and the crew manning her, but one look at Sacchin relieved his fears. The islander grinned at him.

'Better, eh, Wyn? Enough of this running. Marek knows what we need. A fight to take our minds off losing. Maybe we can end the day with some plunder.'

Wyn had to nod in agreement but as they drew closer he realised the ship they were chasing was in worse shape than they were. It was one of the vessels that had attacked them.

It was listing slightly and its sails were only partially set. Marek called the crew in.

'Men,' he said, 'most battles are won in the first moments. When you see your enemy you either think you can win or not. So even though we have taken a fair beating, they don't know that. Now we have a chance to take a ship without spilling any more blood. Any more of *our* blood, that is.' The crew chuckled, sensing treachery. 'It's simple: all we have to do is sail up to them, looking hungry for a fight, and make a lot of noise, and they'll throw in quick and easy. So wash the blood off, arm yourselves and look well. Anyone who can't stand, sit on a box and look mean.'

When they were within hailing range, Marek bellowed, 'Ahoy, the ship! Prepare to be boarded!' The crew made a brief show of defiance, but as the *Gretchen* drew closer, the cries of anger, the menacing bristling of weaponry and the loaded mangonels broke what was left of their spirit. They threw down their weapons in surrender.

When the *Gretchen* bumped alongside, the crew swarmed over the rails and claimed the vessel without a fight. The defeated men were shackled together and herded below decks to await their fate.

'Captain!' came a cry from below.

'What there?' responded Marek.

'Captain, you should see this.'

Marek, with several others in tow, stalked over to the open hatch. He peered down into the dark hold. What he saw made his face beam with pleasure. 'What have we here?' Marek said loudly. 'A hold full of plunder?' Wyn shouldered his way forward and looked down. The dark area was stacked with crates and bales. A cheer went up from the Raiders.

The defeated crew was given a simple choice; join the Raiders and sail with them or try their luck with the ocean, without a boat. They all joined up.

Thus it was that Marek, who had never lost a ship at sea, turned for home three months early with two ships instead of one, and one full of loot and a dozen or so new Raiders.

They sailed south through the part of the sea known as the Reaches where none sailed by choice. There the Sea was wild and deep, driven by harsh winds to heap up into mountainous swells. Marek never left the deck during those days, never ventured below to rest or take food. He stood by the wheel, eyes ever scouring the horizon for signs of danger.

A silence fell over the crew as they ventured further, deeper into the untamed seas. Tempers grew frayed as the days grew darker. Scuffles became common, occasionally spilling over into brawls. Two men died. One was killed in a fight; the other was thrown overboard for killing the first.

The despairing cries of the killer as they sailed away from his waving arms seemed to drive the men deeper into the darkness that had grown up around them. They became even surlier, shorter of temper and more prone to aggression. Fights became commonplace as trivial matters took on great import. Men were stabbed over food, beaten over a look or abused over a word. Even Wyn found himself falling prey to the black mood. His normally solitary and silent ways became aggressive and brusque.

It was about a week after they turned south that Marek called for the sails to be furled. Both vessels drifted, losing their way in the heavy swells. They were lashed together and Marek moved to stand amidships.

'Men!' he called. 'For most of you, we are about to go home. But for some of you this is far from home. I know the sort of thing you may have heard of us, the Southern Raiders. And in many cases it is true and well deserved. But we are not slavers. Those of you who joined our crew against their will during our voyage now have the choice. Either come with us and join us forever, or leave us. Our home is just beyond the horizon and no one who is not one with us can set foot on our homeland. So if any of you want to leave, step forward.'

A few of those who were on the captured ship stepped forward. Wyn thought about it, but he was unsure and wanted to live. Instead he stayed where he was and waited.

Marek waited until no one else moved. 'Very well,' he said. 'Blindfold these men and keep them below until we arrive.'

The home of the Southern Raiders was an island formed from the remains of an ancient volcano that had erupted with such ferocity that it formed a large bay surrounded by a high jagged ridge. Within the bay, the waters were calm and protected, and the only way in was through a narrow break in the wall.

Inside the bay was a vast shipyard. Hundreds of ships were tied up at dozens of docks or were up out of the water being repaired. All around the rugged walls that rose from the still water were dwellings perched on whatever ledge or crack that afforded any purchase.

As she sailed through the entry the *Gretchen* was met by a heavily armed vessel.

'Marek!' came the cry from the other vessel. 'You're early!'

'Aye,' he called back, 'I am, but I bring plunder and a new vessel.'

'Have you any who wish to leave?'

'I have.'

They were escorted to a dock where they tied up. The blindfolded men were led off the *Gretchen* and taken aboard another ship, which immediately set off, back out to sea.

'Where will they be taken?' Wyn asked Sacchin.

'To the first dry land they see. They'll be left there to make their own way.' Sacchin was distracted as they tied up. He was looking at the dock, scanning the people that waited there, obviously seeking someone. Suddenly his face broke into a smile and all the darkness and tension that had beset him for the past weeks fell away. He beamed as he raised his hand in greeting. Wyn followed his gaze to see a woman smiling back, her hand also raised in greeting.

'Come on, Wyn,' said Sacchin. 'Shar is here. Let's go and get drunk together.'

Sacchin, a sack over his shoulder, led Wyn down the crowded gangplank into the melee on the dock. With a bellow he shouldered his way through to catch Shar into a bearhug of heroic proportions. They kissed noisily and long, savouring the moment of meeting after months apart. Finally their lips parted and Sacchin put Shar down.

'Wyn,' he said, turning around. 'This is Shar. My woman.'

'You told me you had no woman to weep over your death at sea,' observed Wyn quietly.

Both Shar and Sacchin laughed. 'He always says that,' said Shar. 'It helps him keep his mind clear for the fight.'

Sacchin nodded.

Shar was not tall, and had long fair hair, a full figure and a ready smile. She turned her smile on Wyn. 'Be welcome,' she said. 'Come to our home and be our guest.' Although the words seemed a ritual greeting, her voice was warm and he felt welcomed.

'Surely,' he agreed.

He followed them along narrow streets that wound their way past the large harbour. Above him stretched the forbidding walls of black rock, dotted with buildings. On the landward side of the street, stalls of every kind were squeezed into any space that would hold a table. All manner of goods were on offer, but unlike most markets Wyn had been in, these merchants were quiet and polite, seeking to entice buyers with a smile and a kind word, rather than haranguing customers. He remarked on this to Sacchin.

'These are sailors, like us, on their one-year land leave. They know that next year they'll be the ones where we are. It breeds respect. And the Commander likes things peaceable.'

'The Commander?'

'The leader of the Raiders.' Sacchin looked up the cliff, gesturing towards a building perched high on the wall. 'He lives up there, although he's away at the moment.'

Wyn regarded the Commander's home. 'What's his name?'

Sacchin shrugged. 'Don't know,' he said. Noticing Wyn's frown, he continued. 'It's no secret, I just don't bother with such things. He keeps the place peaceful, we are well fed and there's plunder aplenty on the Sea.'

'His name's Garel,' said Shar. 'He was a ship's captain until he lost a leg in a battle against the Children of Danan. When he came back here he nominated for the Council. He became Commander about ten years ago.'

Sacchin grinned broadly. 'See? Why should a man bother with such things when he has a woman like this at his side?'

Wyn nodded in agreement, but his mind was picturing a mass of untamed white-blonde hair over a pair of lavender eyes. Shar's mention of the Children of Danan had reawakened his thoughts of Hwenfayre. Once more he recalled why he was here, how he had come to this place and why he had to leave. *Hwenfayre*, he thought, *where are you?*

They led him along the narrow streets then up a stairway so steep it was more like a ladder, up to a small shack set into a fracture in the cliff face.

The shack had a tiny balcony that rested on poles jutting out from the rock. Inside were two rooms: a small cooking area and a bedroom. The bedroom had the feel of a cave, with the walls and ceiling being natural rock; only the wooden floor showed that this was a home.

Wyn sat on a chair on the small balcony, looking out over the bay while Sacchin and Shar noisily renewed their acquaintance behind him in the bedroom. As he sat staring over the water, watching the movements of ships and the steady flow of people around the buildings that clung tenaciously to the rock, he thought of Hwenfayre, of the open sea and of a High Priestess who had once more taken from him.

Slowly the sun sank below the rim of the crater, plunging the home of the Raiders into darkness. The sounds of joyful coupling had long since faded, to be replaced by the contented snores of two people at peace with their world.

Wyn was awakened by a hard grip on his shoulder.

'You always snore that loud?' asked Sacchin, grinning widely.

'Always,' replied Wyn.

'Good. Come inside. Eat with us.'

Breakfast was a simple meal, soon finished. When they were done, Sacchin fixed Wyn with his one remaining eye. 'So what now for you, Wyn?'

'I don't know. What are my options?'

'Join another ship or stay here.'

'Another ship sounds good. How do I organise it?'

'Are you sure you don't want to stay here for a while? By the look of you, you've been on the move for a long time. A break might be a good idea.'

'Yes,' agreed Shar. 'Stay for a while.'

'And do what?'

'There's a lot of work to do here. Especially with storm season coming,' said Shar. 'We always need men to prepare the town.'

'Yes,' agreed Sacchin. 'Stay and put that silent strength of yours to good use.'

He shook his head. 'I must go.'

'That girl of yours?' asked Sacchin.

Wyn nodded.

Sacchin exhaled heavily, his face set in a troubled frown. 'If she meant that much to you, friend Wyn, you should not have come here.'

'How so?'

'We Raiders have a rule. If you join with us, you stay. That's why we gave every man who sailed with us a chance to leave. If you jump ship we'll hunt you down. No matter where your woman is.' Wyn stared at Sacchin, impassive. Sacchin glared back, his normal cheerful smile completely absent, his good eye hard. For a moment their gazes locked. Finally Sacchin broke away.

'My friend,' he said, looking out over the crater that had become his home, 'you place me in a dangerous position. By rights I should hand you over to the Commander right now. But,' he fingered his eye patch, 'I owe you a great debt.' He looked back at Wyn. 'If it wasn't for you, a lot more of me than my eye would be fish food right now.' He leaned back heavily in his chair, his eye never leaving Wyn's face. 'But if I help you with this, we are even. I owe you nothing more. If we meet across a sword, I will not hesitate. Understood?'

Wyn nodded. 'Understood, friend Sacchin, understood.'

'Good.' Suddenly his smile was back. 'Very good. Now let us go down to the hold and collect our share.' When Wyn looked baffled, Sacchin laughed out loud. 'What? You thought we sailed for free? No, my friend. We each get our share of the take. And since you helped us capture a whole ship, your share will not be small.' He stood. 'Smaller than mine, of course, but not small.'

The three of them made their way back down to the water's edge and along the narrow street towards a large building that was built out over the water. Their shipmates were milling around by the closed doors. They were greeted noisily as they arrived.

'Sacchin, I see you finally dragged yourself away from your bed!' Raucous laughter and ribald comments followed, which both Sacchin and Shar

238

took in good humour. Even Wyn was greeted by name, although with more reserve. He noted a number of women standing alone among the men.

'Those are the widows,' said Shar quietly, noticing the direction of Wyn's gaze. 'They are entitled to their man's full share.'

'It's only fair,' agreed Wyn.

While they waited, Sacchin explained the system. The community took six parts of ten of all plunder taken on the Sea.

'We have no resources at all here,' Sacchin told him. 'So if we want to eat anything but fish and wear anything other than seaweed, we raid.'

The captain of the vessel took one-tenth and the rest was divided between the crew, based on their length of time aboard. The present delay was over whether the ship they had brought in would be refitted or broken down for materials.

A low cheer went up when the word came that the ship would be broken up and used for materials. Sacchin explained that this meant they would get more. He didn't explain how this was so, he was just happy that it was.

It took most of the morning for all the payments to be sorted out and distributed. When he received his share Wyn was surprised at the amount. It was a great deal more than he usually earned for a few weeks' work. With their earnings, the three of them made their way to a tavern and all got happily drunk, then fell into a blissfully unaware stupor.

The next morning found them heavily hungover but somehow back in Sacchin and Shar's home. Wyn had again slept on the small balcony.

After another simple breakfast, Sacchin and Wyn went back down to the water's edge to find a ship.

They were just considering a vessel with the unlikely name of the *Peaceful Shark* when a familiar voice accosted them.

'You two! What are you doing here?' They turned to see Marek striding towards them.

'Looking for a ship, Sir,' replied Wyn.

'I'm setting sail this afternoon. I can always use good men.'

'Where are you leaving from?' asked Wyn.

Marek laughed and pointed. 'I forgot, you're new here. I always set sail from the same anchorage.' Wyn followed his gesture to see the *Gretchen* at anchor, not far off. She was swarming with men repairing the damage she had suffered from her recent battles. Most of it had already been repaired. The benefit of bringing home plunder, Wyn surmised. 'So what do you say?' Marek said.

'Where are you headed?' Wyn asked.

Marek's face lost its humour, his eyes hardening. 'Because you are new and do not know our ways I will let that pass this once. But know that is a question you never ask a captain of his own vessel.' He looked around, saw no one was listening, then lowered his voice. 'As one who knows the sea you would be familiar with the Children of Danan. Our Commander,' he jerked his head towards the house perched on the crater wall, 'has decided it is time we showed them who the masters of the seas really are. The *Gretchen* sails today to seek them out.'

At this Sacchin stepped back, fear on his face.

'Captain, that is madness! They speak to the sea. They control it!'

'No longer, Sacchin,' replied Marek. 'They have lost their way and no longer call upon the sea. Now is the time.' He fixed them both with a hard glare. 'So are you with me?'

Wyn nodded. 'Aye, Marek. I sail with you. I have unfinished business with the Children of Danan.' As he spoke, he felt Sacchin's eye upon him. He looked to see the big islander regarding him suspiciously.

Without looking away from Wyn, Sacchin said, 'I too, Marek. I will come.'

17

'The Thane thanks you for your support,' said Badghe.

He'd been saying it a lot over the past two days. After they left Ajyne, Coerl Leone went on a gathering frenzy. She sent the Fyrd out far and wide with specific targets to collect from the willing populace. Badghe was looking for warm clothing for the First Son. Fortunately Shanek was of average build and height, so finding clothes to fit was not a problem. Finding them in the right colours was the problem. The First Son had a preference for reds in all their complex variety and red dye was expensive. Not many peasants could afford red in any hue, so he and Egon had to concentrate on more well-moneyed establishments. These were becoming less common the further north they went.

The others in the Fyrd had similar tasks, some collecting food, some tents, some bedding, while others were collecting weapons. He was told that the Asan people relished the opportunity to share their worldly goods with those on the Thane's business, but on the many gathering missions he'd done, he hadn't seen much enthusiasm. He'd seen a lot of thinly disguised anger, some grudging acquiescence and even some open dissent. The last rarely endured much beyond the first killing or two.

'How much more does his Royal Firstness need, Badghe?' asked Egon.

Badghe shrugged. 'More, usually.'

'One more place, then?' Egon suggested.

Badghe nodded. 'Just one more.'

The two had been serving in the First Son's Fyrd under Coerl Leone for three years. Despite the fact that Badghe was from the Southern Province and Egon originated from Oscran, they had formed a solid friendship over the time. Badghe's burgeoning affair with Egon's sister had helped. Like most soldiers gaining promotion to Ajyne Duty, they had both moved their immediate families with them for the ten-year posting. The appointment to the First Son's Fyrd was highly sought after, usually achieved by exceptional service and skills. Badghe had earned his promotion for his uncanny skills with the bow, whilst Egon had used his native Oscran tracking abilities to good effect.

At the time, Egon was in a Fyrd guarding one of the little-used western gates to Ajyne. Bandits kidnapped the daughter of a lesser noble and fled through the gate out into the bushland. Egon was on duty and followed them. He tracked them for three days, finally catching up with them when they reached their base. They were unaware of his pursuit and he was able to enter their camp at night and rescue the girl.

Caldorman Eustaquio, who replaced the Caldorman previously in command of the western gates, was very grateful. He'd recommended Egon's appointment as he sat beside the Thane at the Arena, watching his predecessor's demise.

It was nearly dark by the time they reached what they decided would be the last house for the day. It was a small but elegant house surrounded by an immaculate garden. They walked up to the front door, their boots crunching on the pebbled pathway. They were met at the door by a massive guard. He was easily the biggest man either soldier had ever seen. With his dead-white skin, a long white ponytail that reached to his waist and intricate tribal tattoos that covered most of his torso, he was immediately identifiable as a northern Tribesman.

As Badghe approached, the guard grunted a challenge whilst drawing his sword.

'What do you want?' he snarled.

'We are soldiers of the Empire and the Thane requires the assistance of those who dwell within,' said Badghe, intoning the ritual greeting.

The Tribesman glared at the soldiers. His eyes narrowed in thought. 'Stay here,' he said. 'I'll check.'

'You'll do better than that, big man,' said Egon.

The guard snorted derisively. 'Who's going to make me?' he said as he opened the door.

As the door closed behind him, Badghe turned to Egon. 'Is it just me, or did he threaten us?'

'I think he threatened us, Badghe.'

'I am so glad you said that, Egon. Let's go and report this to the Coerl.'

The two of them grinned and went to walk away. They were three paces down the pathway when the door slammed open behind them. As one they

244

turned, and caught a brief glimpse of a huge exoskeletal form bearing down on them.

'Well, we can't wait for them,' snapped Muttiah. 'If you cannot keep your Fyrd disciplined, Leone, it's not my problem.'

Leone fumed, but there was nothing she could do. Two of her Fyrd had not returned from their task and it was time to leave. With a curt nod and a salute, she turned on her heel and stalked away, muttering to herself.

By the time she reached the Fyrd, which was packed and ready to leave, she was almost trembling with fury. She snapped a few orders at the rest of her men and they moved out.

'It's unlike Badghe,' said Shanek when Leone rode up behind him.

'And Egon,' said Leone. 'He's married. There's no way he'd just take off. Something's wrong, First Son.'

Shanek nodded. 'Do you want me to overrule Cherise and stay a while to look for them?'

Leone was glad he had not turned to face her as he spoke. If he had, he would have seen the shock plainly on her face. The First Son, asking her what she wanted? Unheard of! For a moment she was speechless.

'Leone?' Shanek asked.

'No, thank you, First Son. The Caldorman is right. The men know the rules and if they are not present, they're left behind. Once we leave, they are officially deserters and marked for execution.'

'It's a shame,' said Shanek. 'I liked Egon.'

Behind him, Leone nodded. She liked him too.

They were four days north of Ajyne, moving into the less populated areas of the Empire. So far it had been pleasant enough, with sufficient quality establishments to supply their requirements. From here things became a bit more rustic, even dangerous. Banditry was not unheard of these days, even this close to the Capital.

As if something knew of their passage, the weather took a sudden turn for the worse. Where it had been fine to hot since their departure, this morning dawned cold and windy. The clouds were low and grey, promising drizzle all day. The wind felt like it had come straight off the icy face of the Northern Escarpment from the frozen wasteland that lay beyond.

Shanek shivered in his crimson-dyed fur coat. It was a fine coat, taken from a single arox beast, which, from the richness of the fur, would have been a venerable old monster. Despite its warmth, the wretched wind cut straight through, chilling him to the bone. Not for the first time he cursed the silly whim that had led him to shave off his thick mat of black curly hair to accede to the current fashion of baldness. At least wily old Malik had had the foresight to gather a fur-lined hat to go with the coat.

Prompted by this thought, Shanek looked around at his Fyrd to find the battle-scarred veteran.

'Malik!' he called.

The soldier urged his mount forward to ride behind the First Son.

'I must thank you for this fine hat,' Shanek said, raising his voice slightly over the wind. 'I think I'd be in trouble without it.'

Behind him, Malik shot a questioning glance at his Coerl. Leone shrugged and gestured for him to reply.

'Um,' he stammered, 'it is my pleasure to serve, First Son.' When the First Son did not respond, Malik eased back into formation.

After a few hours on the road, during which time the weather deteriorated even further, Diplomat Cherise and Caldorman Muttiah called a halt. They consulted a map and Muttiah gestured at the path that ran off into the wooded region to the left. Shanek turned in his saddle and glared at Leone.

'Do you know what this is about?' he called.

Rather than attempting to shout over the howling wind, the Coerl just shrugged. Shanek hissed a curse and urged his mount forward.

'What are you doing?' he shouted at the two old men when he was close enough.

'Following the Thane's orders, First Son,' bellowed the Caldorman.

'What?' shouted Shanek.

Diplomat Cherise handed Shanek a scrolled map. Shanek snatched and unrolled it. In the Thane's handwriting were instructions to take ... *the most ancient Way of the Coerl that leads by the Shrine of Purity*. Shanek scowled.

'What nonsense is this?' he cried. 'Everyone knows the Shrine is pure myth!' He tossed the scroll back at Cherise, who caught it easily and handed it to Muttiah.

'No, First Son. This, I believe, is the Way of the Coerl.' The Diplomat indicated the overgrown track. Despite the wind, his voice carried easily. Shanek tried to suppress a shudder but failed. The Way of the Coerl had a dark history.

'How can you possibly know that?' Shanek yelled. Before the Diplomat had a chance to answer, he continued, 'This is ridiculous! We need to get out of this wind!' He didn't bother to see if they were following him, but rode on into the forest in search of shelter.

The wind seemed to die almost as soon as he crossed into the woods. Even the sound of his horse's hooves felt muted, subdued. The stallion slowed to a walk, then stopped, snorting in discomfort.

'Easy, boy,' Shanek murmured as he patted the horse's neck. 'It's just a forest.'

He straightened up and looked around. Despite what he had just said, it was unlike any forest he'd ever seen. The ground was thick with leaf litter, so thick that he couldn't see any open earth anywhere, not even on the trail he'd followed. In fact ... He looked around. What trail? In the dim light that filtered through the canopy, he couldn't see any hint of a trail. There was scarcely a trace of his horse's hooves where they had scuffed the layer of detritus.

A flicker of concern touched his mind. How could he possibly be lost so quickly? He'd only come a few strides into the forest. But which way? He urged his mount around, turning in a complete circle, but he could not see the edge of the forest, which he knew was only ten or so paces away. His concern grew, and the first glimpse of panic appeared on the fringes of his mind.

'Hey!' he called out. 'Where are you?' He strained

his ears to hear the return calls but none came. 'Hey!' he yelled.

'First Son,' said Coerl Leone calmly from behind him.

He whipped his head around to see her and his Fyrd trotting towards him on the well-defined track. Behind them he could see the edge of the forest with the road beyond, where Muttiah and Cherise were still discussing the map. The feelings of panic subsided, but in their wake they left fears that had not been there before.

'Leone,' said Shanek. 'I thought it best to find shelter in here rather than stay out there in the storm.'

The Coerl looked around. 'Yes, First Son. I'll order the Fyrd to set up camp.'

Shanek dismounted. 'Just over there,' he said. He indicated a location near the path that caught his eye. It was a round clearing about twenty paces across. He walked over to it. *Yes*, he said to himself. *This is a good spot.* Above him, the canopy stretched all the way across the clearing, providing shelter from the rain, and the denseness of the forest around it was a barrier against the wind, leaving this small area quiet and dry.

He stood and watched as the Fyrd set up camp. The tents went up in a circle around the edge of the clearing. Two men dug a firepit in the centre. Two others gathered wood. All was done without Leone or Shanek giving one order beyond Leone's simple 'Set up camp here.'

By the time the Fyrd were finished, Cherise and Muttiah had completed their discussion. Surrounded by Muttiah's Fyrd, they joined Shanek in the clearing.

Muttiah looked with approval at the efficient way Shanek's Fyrd had established camp. He nodded at Leone. She saluted in acknowledgement of his silent praise. The Caldorman gestured to his own men and they started to set up alongside the rest.

When a fire was going and the evening meal was being served, Muttiah eased himself down alongside Shanek.

'Good location, First Son,' he grunted. 'Defensible. Sheltered. Good size.' He looked at Shanek with approval. 'Like it.'

'That's more than I can say for your plan,' said Shanek.

'My plan, First Son?' asked Muttiah.

'This ridiculous idea of yours to find the Shrine of Purity,' snapped Shanek.

'It isn't my plan, First Son. You read the direction from the Thane.'

Shanek sneered at the old Caldorman. 'How stupid do you think I am?' he asked.

'First Son?' asked Muttiah.

'I don't know what you think you are doing,' snapped Shanek, 'but it isn't going to work.'

'First Son, I'm confused. I am only following the Thane's direction. You saw the message.'

'You really do think I am stupid,' Shanek said softly.

'Not at all, First Son, I have great respect for your intelligence,' said Muttiah.

Shanek watched the old Caldorman closely. He had been trained in the nuances of communication for years and knew when someone was lying. There was no doubt that the Caldorman was holding something back but the First Son was unsure whether it was a deliberate lie, or simply something he was not yet permitted to reveal. He decided to wait until Cherise told him the full details of the Thane's orders before doing anything.

'Not enough respect, I think, Caldorman,' hissed Shanek. 'We'll talk about this later.' He walked away, leaving Muttiah to watch him and wonder how much of the plan he knew.

It wasn't much, Shanek had to concede. All he knew for certain was that whoever had written on the map, it had not been the Thane. One of the many skills that Shanek had been taught over the years was the art of handwriting. He had studied thousands of examples of writing and knew the Thane's hand intimately. What few people knew was that Kasimar IV had a history much more colourful than even his public image revealed. When he was seventeen he had had a close encounter with an arox kid. It bit him on the hand, severing a tendon in his little finger. The loss of movement gave his writing a characteristic drag on the downstroke that even after years of practice was discernible to the expert. This writing, although a good copy, was not the Thane's.

Shanek had to wonder if Muttiah and Cherise knew of the forgery or were ignorant. Or perhaps they were actively involved.

'Leone!' he called. The Coerl's uncomplicated worldview was often a valuable counterpoint to his own, more complex way. On hearing him, she stopped speaking with a soldier and looked around. 'Walk with me,' Shanek said.

251

Pausing only to buckle on her sword and grab a burning torch, Coerl Leone followed Shanek as he strode out of the clearing.

'Tell me about the Way of the Coerl,' Shanek instructed when they were about twenty paces from the camp.

'It is an old legend, First Son,' began Leone. 'We learned about it in our final year of officer training at the Loci.'

'How old?' interrupted Shanek.

'Almost as old as the Empire itself,' said Leone. 'It was supposed to have been a secret way through a forest. The legend tells of a battle between —'

'Wait,' interrupted Shanek again, holding up his hand. 'Listen. Can you hear it?'

Leone listened. 'A stream?' she suggested.

'Yes, over there,' Shanek pointed. He walked off the path towards the cheerful sound of running water. Leone followed as the First Son of the Empire picked his way through the undergrowth.

The stream was a glittering ribbon that threaded its way between the dark and brooding boles of the ancient trees. Despite the canopy cover above them, the joyful flow of water seemed to sparkle as if in the starlight that probably still shone somewhere beyond this forest. There was a narrow strip of thick grass on either side of the stream that was just wide enough to sit on, if they sat on opposite sides. Shanek stepped over the water and sat down. He gestured for Leone to do likewise.

She examined the area carefully before seating herself with her sword drawn on the ground close to her right hand and her back to a tree. As she did so,

Shanek allowed himself the luxury of regarding her closely. She was taller than he, and probably heavier, although there was not an ounce of excess fat on her. Her musculature was spectacular, but rather than lending her a hard look, it gave her a stunningly beautiful physique. Whilst he had enjoyed looking at her physical beauty for the years she had been his instructor and protector, he had never given much thought to the fact that this beauty had a life apart from him. He wondered if she had a lover at the moment. Was she married? He doubted it.

'Leone,' he started. 'Tell me about yourself.'

'Myself, First Son?'

She was used to his ways, his mercurial mind and its habit of shifting focus. It was characteristic of his arrogance, this habit of following his own way with no thought of what others might want. Even his demand that she tell him about the Way of the Coerl was indicative. He certainly knew more than she did, but he wanted her to tell him what she knew, probably, she thought, so that he could demonstrate his greater knowledge.

'Yes. Tell me about Leone, the woman.'

'Of course, First Son,' she replied. 'I am six and one-quarter measures tall and weigh —'

'No, not that. Tell me about you,' he interrupted. He watched her in the dim light, surprised and oddly pleased to see her confused and discomfited. 'Where were you born? Do you have any brothers or sisters? A lover perhaps?'

'I was born in the Southern Province —'

'Ahh,' interrupted Shanek. 'Badghe was from there, wasn't he?'

'Yes, he was, First Son.'

Shanek frowned as a thought occurred to him. 'How is it I know that about him but not about you?'

'You are given the personal information about every soldier in your Fyrd for approval. I was appointed to command the Fyrd before you achieved the age of responsibility.'

Shanek nodded. 'Very well. So, if I were to be given your information, what would it say?'

'I was born in the Southern Province to Misca and Petran, of Gernier. Misca, my father, was a cobbler, and Petran, my mother, worked as a baker's maid. I was the middle child of five, with two older brothers and two younger sisters. When I had seen nine summers, there was a fire in my district. I had run away from home again, and my whole family perished in the blaze. The Coerl of the Fyrd assigned to protect the area from looting found me in the ashes and took me home. He and his wife cared for me and when I was twelve sent me to the Military Loci. When I completed my training I was sent to Ajyne to join officer training. When I finished there I served under Caldorman Muttiah for a while in Oscran. After that, the Caldorman recommended me for the position I now hold.'

'And your life outside the army? Friends, lovers?'

Leone shook her head. 'No, First Son.'

'No, you don't have any, or no, you are not going to tell me?'

'No, I am not going to tell you.'

Shanek leaned back, allowing himself to sink into the cool soft grass. He stared up at the dark canopy. 'That is a very serious risk, Leone, you know that.'

Leone smiled. 'I know, Shanek, but I think you brought me here for a reason. And threatening me is not part of it.'

'Shanek?' he asked without moving. 'You've never called me that before.'

'True, Shanek. But you've never sat me by a stream in a forest before either.'

'And you think that permits you to ignore years of training and put aside the formality that our positions and the law demand?'

'Yes.'

'I like you, Leone.'

'Thank you, Shanek.'

'But you don't like me much, do you?'

'No. Not much.'

'Why not?'

'You are arrogant, rude and cruel. You do not care for your people and you treat those around you badly. You are also the most intelligent and gifted man I have ever known and you take it all for granted. You act as if it's your right to be the way you are. And I have seen enough good people suffer to know that gifts like yours are rare and to be treasured, not wasted so carelessly.' As she spoke, Leone felt like she was listening to someone else. The words flowed easily, each one ending her life, but she could not stop them. They tumbled out, condemning her, betraying her every secret thought as though with a life of their own. When she finished, she was panting, flushed with exhaustion, fear gripping her. *What have I done?* she cried silently. Across the stream, Shanek did not move. She waited for him to speak, but he remained silent.

'First Son?' she asked tentatively.

'Not Shanek?' he asked the canopy overhead.

'No, First Son. I offer my life for the affront I have given you. I offer no explanation for my unforgivable behaviour. Please take my worthless life now.'

'Oh, sit down, Leone. You've said it yourself: I couldn't kill you.'

She was seated before she wondered how he knew she had stood up. His eyes had never left the canopy above. He remained silent, as if listening to the forest.

'Tell me about the Way of the Coerl, Leone,' he said.

'Legend says that after defeat in the Skrin Tia'k wars, a small band of soldiers was chased into a nearby forest. They hid for several weeks while the Skrin Tia'k hunted for them. Every time they came close, one of the soldiers volunteered to lead them away from the others. Finally there were only two soldiers left. As the Skrinnies closed in, the two soldiers ran in opposite directions. The Coerl, Samba I think her name was, went to the left and Tintal went right. Each time the Skrinnies had attacked, some of their number had been killed, so by this time there were only three left. One chased the Coerl and the other two went after Tintal. Nothing is known of his fate, so presumably he was killed, but Samba escaped.

'She ran until she was exhausted and fell into a stream. When the Skrinnie found her, it picked her up and carried her to a nearby clearing and started to torture her. When it started to cut her skin, she woke up and attacked it.' Leone paused. 'The story gets a bit odd at this stage. She somehow spoke to the ground and it rose up and engulfed the Skrinnie where it stood.

'Its screams were so loud that other Skrinnies heard and came through the forest to help. Samba fled deep into the forest. Wherever she put her feet, the earth turned to mud and trapped any Skrin Tia'k who stood in the same place. Her path through the woods was marked by screaming, dying Skrin Tia'k warriors. When no more came after her, she stopped and went back to the last one. It was trapped in the mud, screaming in pain. She took pity on its pain and attempted to release it, but every time she touched it its pain increased. Finally it died and Samba wept in sorrow. She built a shrine around its upright body and spent six years contemplating what she had learned in the forest. When she came out, she proclaimed the Laws of Purity as we have them today.'

'That doesn't explain why the Way of the Coerl has the dark reputation it has today,' said Shanek.

'Ever since then, no one has ever found the forest or the shrine, or the path she made in the forest. It is said that anyone who does will be sent mad by the power that is still in the ground.'

'And yet,' Shanek said quietly, 'Diplomat Cherise thinks we are currently on the Way of the Coerl.'

'Yes, First Son,' Leone replied.

'No other comments, Coerl?' Shanek prompted.

'No, First Son.'

'I am disappointed, Coerl Leone,' Shanek went on. 'Here we are, sitting together beside a romantic stream, we've shared a moment, I haven't killed you and yet you have nothing to say.'

Leone held her silence.

'Diplomat Cherise is wrong, Coerl Leone,' Shanek said. 'We are no more on the Way of the Coerl than on the Great Path.'

'Diplomat Cherise believes we are, First Son.'

'Diplomat Cherise believes in myths and legends. And you, Coerl Leone, what do you believe?'

'I believe that every civilisation has its myths, and this is one of ours.'

'No substance to the myth, then?'

'No, First Son.'

'That's a shame,' he said. 'I enjoyed that one. As myths go, it's good. Our society has a strange view of myths, you know, Coerl.'

'How so, First Son?' Leone asked, interested now.

'So much of our history, our way of living, is determined by ancient myths and legends, yet we tend to discount most of their substance.' He stood up. 'Remind me one day to tell you the one about the Danan.'

Leone scrambled to her feet.

Abruptly, Shanek dived across the stream, cannoning into her. His sudden impact threw her off balance, driving her heavily back into the tree, then they crashed onto the ground. The air whooshed out of her lungs, leaving her winded. As they fell, an arrow buzzed through the air. It went straight through where Leone had been standing seconds earlier.

Before Leone could regain her breath, Shanek rolled off her and dashed into the woods. She heaved herself back to her feet and went after him. Already, she could hear the whistle of his bolas.

Not in the forest, Shanek, she thought. *It will tangle.*

A thud, followed by the crash of a falling body, suggested that Shanek's skill with the weapon was as good as he thought it was. By the time she caught up with him, he was choking the life out of the would-be assassin with the barbed cord.

'No, First Son,' she cried. 'Leave him alive!'

He released the cord, allowing the man to fall unconscious to the ground. 'Good call, Leone,' he said. 'We need to talk to this one.' He stepped aside to reveal the man. 'Recognise him?' he asked.

It was Tapash, the Tribesman.

Coerl Leone stared. The big northern Tribesman was breathing shallowly. His throat was badly torn by the wicked little barbs on the bolas cord, but the windpipe was not opened, nor were any of the major blood vessels in his neck. Either Shanek was very lucky or his skills were finally becoming instinctive. Until now his emotions had tended to override his control.

She struggled to keep her own emotions under control. The past few minutes had been the most terrifying of her life. Not only had she acted the cheap slut with the First Son of the Empire, flirting with him and calling him by name, but she had insulted and denigrated him. Then, to compound her confusion, rather than taking her life, as he had every right to do, he had saved it, at cost to his own. Never had she known such inner turmoil. Even the day she found her family dead in the ashes of their own home had been less confusing than this. At least then she had known what to feel. Anger was so much easier to understand than this complex man to whom her life now belonged. Until the moment he had not taken her life, she merely served him out of duty; now she owed her life to him twice over.

The most ironic thing was that she only half meant the things she said.

What came over me? she asked herself. *What possibly possessed me to say those things?*

Regarding the wounded man, Coerl Leone found something definite to hang her feelings on. Anger, welcome in its simplicity, welled up in her. *He tried to kill Shanek! Or me?* The arrow was coming at her. *Is he just a bad shot?*

No, the arrow was aimed at Shanek. He came towards me and it went over him. Leone shook her head. Had the First Son just dodged the arrow, it would have killed her instead. Tapash had aimed it so that he would have got one of them.

Shanek dragged Tapash to his feet. 'So, Tribesman, you made your move.' He pulled him close, so that their faces almost touched. 'But you missed, *shlapan*!' he hissed.

Leone did not recognise the word, but from Tapash's reaction she presumed it was a curse in his own language.

'*Tipanch ne argan tishnare!*' he snarled.

Shanek laughed and threw him back to the ground. 'Is that the best you can do?' Contemptuously he kicked Tapash in the stomach, causing the man to double over, gasping in pain. Shanek crouched beside him. 'Now, let's have a look at this weapon you managed to find,' he said calmly. He picked up the weapon. 'I recognise this,' he said as he examined the bow. 'It belongs to one of my Fyrd.' He tossed it to Leone, who caught it easily.

The feel of the riser against her hand was all she needed. She'd know that wood, that finely carved tracery anywhere. 'It's Dushyan's,' she said.

Shanek kicked Tapash again. 'I know Dushyan well. He only shares his bed with two people, his wife and that bow. He calls it his widow-maker. Most think he's being brutal, but he's referring to his own wife as the widow. He spends more time with this weapon than with her. Even when he's on leave.'

When Tapash did not respond, Shanek leaned over and dragged him back to his feet. 'Where did you get that bow?' he shouted into Tapash's pale, bloodstained face.

Tapash gurgled, blood trickling down his cheek. 'I found it,' he mumbled.

'Burn you!' shouted Shanek. 'Your life is mine! You will answer me true or you will die here and now.'

'Then kill me, First Son of the Empire,' Tapash slurred. 'I owe you nothing.'

With a curse, Shanek shoved the Tribesman against a tree. 'Coerl,' he snapped, 'bring that back to camp!'

Leone heaved the Tribesman over her shoulder and followed Shanek. Anger, the need for violence, the burning desire for revenge: all much simpler, cleaner emotions, Leone thought, as Tapash's blood stained her uniform. They were so much easier to deal with than the confusion of the emotions she had been experiencing earlier.

Ahead, Shanek crashed through the undergrowth in fury, muttering and cursing to himself. Leone wished she were close enough to hear what he was saying.

What came over me? she asked herself again. *What was I thinking? How could I say that to the First Son?*

Shanek stopped abruptly. He turned to face her. In the darkness, she could just make out the pale gleam of the whites of his eyes. 'Coerl Leone,' he said softly. 'I just remembered that you offered me your life a moment ago.'

Now it comes, she realised. Allowing Tapash to slide off her shoulder, she stood straight and drew her sword. With the ritual movements required of a Coerl, she reversed it and handed it to the First Son. He took it, the cold steel sliding across her hand, leaving a fine mark that oozed blood.

'Leone,' Shanek said.

He paused, and Leone noticed he had not used her title. *So he strips me of my title first. It's fair. I deserve to die in shame.* The pause continued. She realised he intended her to respond.

'Yes, First Son?'

'I hold your life in my hand right now, don't I?'

'Yes, First Son.'

'Is this power?'

'Yes, First Son. This is power.' She was never prouder of her control than at that moment. *Get it done, you burned bastard!*

'If I were the arrogant, cruel, burned bastard you consider me to be, I would kill you now, having stripped you of your title. I would leave you here to bleed to death in this dark forest and no one would ever mourn you.' He looked up.

Even in the dark she could feel the intensity of his gaze, and in that moment she knew hope. 'That is true, Shanek,' she said.

He nodded. 'I deserved that,' he conceded. 'Leone, until tonight I never realised how much I have come to value your good opinion of me. To hear you say what you did has wounded me more deeply than I care to admit. I want you to promise me something.'

'Anything, Shanek.'

'If I let you live, will you promise to give me another chance to win your respect?'

'Yes, First Son.'

They walked into the clearing side by side. Leone threw Tapash down beside the campfire and retreated into the shadows. Shanek stepped forward, the fire casting a ruddy glow across his face.

'Why were we not challenged as we entered?' he snarled.

Muttiah sprang to his feet. He gestured to one of his Fyrd, indicating that he should go and check. Cherise also stood, his focus on Shanek.

'First Son, what happened?' he asked.

'This happened.' Shanek indicated Tapash, lying at Leone's feet.

'Your prisoner? What about him?'

Shanek looked to his own Fyrd. 'You,' he said. 'Harin. Go check on the prisoners.'

Harin leaped to obey and disappeared into the dark. Shanek stared at Muttiah. In the flickering, inconstant light of the fire, Leone saw darkness and danger in Shanek that she had never truly believed to be there. He burned from within with a power and danger that both repelled and chilled her. In that moment, after the strange events by the stream, her view of him changed forever.

'Muttiah,' Shanek hissed. 'You have some explaining to do.'

'How so, First Son?' Caldorman Muttiah, First Caldorman to the Commander of the Army, returned the glare of Shanek, First Son of the Empire, with arrogant confidence.

'How is it that while under your personal responsibility, a chained prisoner escaped, killed his guards and made off with a weapon? He followed the Coerl and tried to kill her.'

'The Coerl?' asked Cherise. 'Why her?'

'Good question, Diplomat,' said Shanek. 'I've been asking that myself.'

'Probably because ...' began Muttiah. 'How do you know he killed the guards?' he asked.

'The bow he carried. He couldn't get it from the owner without killing him. And you still haven't told me why we were not challenged when we arrived.'

Caldorman Muttiah fixed Coerl Leone with a hard glare. 'Perhaps because the First Son's Fyrd is not as good as we are led to believe.'

Leone bristled and reached for her sword, but Shanek laid a restraining hand on her arm. 'No, Coerl,' he said, still looking at Muttiah. 'Perhaps the Caldorman is right. Perhaps,' he shifted his gaze to her, 'we should send one of our men out to find the guards.'

Leone released her grip on her sword, allowing it to slide back into the scabbard. She gestured to

Ekaterina, indicating that she go and check the guards. As Ekaterina leaped to her feet, Harin strode back into the circle of light cast by the campfire.

'First Son,' he declared. 'The prisoners are all dead.'

'And the guards?' asked Shanek.

Harin simply nodded; no words were needed.

'How can this be?' asked Cherise.

Shanek gave no answer, he just stared at Harin. 'Dushyan and Lyaksandra? Both?'

'Yes, First Son.'

'And the prisoners? Still in chains?'

'Yes, First Son.'

Muttiah suddenly roared an inarticulate bellow of rage. Before anyone could react, he took up his axe and launched a brutal attack on the semi-conscious Tapash. He had landed three savage blows, striking Tapash's head from his shoulders and nearly cleaving the dead body in two by the time Leone could draw her sword. Blood spattered the ground, sizzled in the fire.

Shanek spun his bolas over his head and released it, wrapping the Caldorman with the metal cable around his body, causing him to drop the axe.

Muttiah wrestled against the constricting cable, all the while roaring and cursing. Shanek gave the older man a roundhouse kick to the chest, sending him staggering backwards off balance. When he reached the log he'd been sitting on, he tripped and fell heavily. He continued to struggle against the cable, the barbs scraping against his armour and opening nasty little wounds on exposed flesh. His inchoate cries of rage continued unabated until Shanek kicked him solidly in the side of the head.

The First Son looked down at the old man with an unreadable expression. Coerl Leone watched the whole scene aghast. She had just seen the third most powerful man on the continent attack and kick the third most senior man in the army into unconsciousness.

'Coerl Leone!' called Ekaterina.

Leone spun around to see Ekaterina enter the campsite. 'The guards?' she asked.

Ekaterina shook her head. 'All four dead. Shot in the back.' She held up four arrows. Even in the inconstant firelight, Leone identified Dushyan's fletching. Along with Badghe, he was the finest archer in the army, and like most good archers he made his arrows to suit his own style. A sudden thought occurred to her.

'Diplomat Cherise,' she said. 'How many of Caldorman Muttiah's Fyrd were on duty tonight?'

The Diplomat shook his head. 'I don't know, Coerl,' he said.

She gave Ekaterina a quizzical look. The soldier shook her head. *That's eight I've lost today*, Leone thought. 'What tribe was Tapash?' she asked.

Ekaterina frowned. 'I don't know, Coerl, but Gerhay would know.'

'Ask him.'

Ekaterina went to seek out Gerhay. Most of the Fyrd had gathered around the prisoners, checking for evidence of how Tapash was able to escape his chains and kill the two guards without anyone noticing.

Gerhay was half-Ettan. Brought up in the Ettan wilderness, his knowledge of the various tribes who wandered the northern wastelands was considerable.

He lacked the colouring of the far north, favouring his Oscrae father. He had brown hair, green eyes and a darker complexion. He took one look at Tapash and spat on the ground.

'It's Basharii,' he snarled. 'The worst scum of the lot.'

'How so?' asked Leone.

Gerhay squatted beside the damaged body. 'See this,' he indicated a tattoo visible on the torso. It would normally have been hidden, but Muttiah's frenzied attack had damaged the leather to reveal it. 'It's an arox. They hunt them for sport and breed them as weapons. This one,' he indicated Tapash, 'was a torturer. He'd breed the arox for viciousness and feed unwelcome guests to it.' Gerhay stood. 'Remind me to thank the Caldorman when he comes to. He's made the world a better place.'

'Thanks, Gerhay,' muttered Leone. The Ettan saluted and went back to the rest of the Fyrd. Leone was wondering what a Basharii Tribesman would have been doing with a trader in Ajyne.

And what burned ill-luck had brought him here, now?

Another thought occurred to her, one that sent a chill through her body. What if it was not luck?

18

Hwenfayre hummed quietly to herself. Another day of learning the words of songs she knew as well as if she'd written them. After a morning of music training, there were pots to clean and fish to gut. Then an afternoon of history and traditions lessons before the evening meal. Despite the tedium and drudgery, she found she was beginning to enjoy herself.

After overhearing the conversation about herself that night, she had decided to revel in her danger. Hylin was a teacher who demanded absolute attention and complete belief. No questions or debate were permitted. Whilst Hylin had cowed the other Novices with her sharp tongue and stern glare, Hwenfayre chose to ignore the steely gaze and snapped responses. Instead she drew on the tales that Wyn had told her to question everything the old Mistress of Novices taught. As well as the tales, she paid attention to the words of the songs. Most of them were simple songs about the Sea and her ways, but some spoke of devotion to a Mistress, of summoning power, of commanding the forces of the ocean's might.

Whenever she asked about the meanings of these songs Hylin would fix her with her best icy stare and give one of two responses. She would either declare, 'Novice, the meaning of that song is not permitted to anyone who has not achieved the rank of Priestess' or 'Novice, you speak of things you clearly do not understand'.

It became a game for Hwenfayre to keep a record of how often Hylin used each response. Today it was two priestesses and three not understands. It had been a good day. She had managed to soundly irritate old Hylin and at the same time Erin had given her one or two suspicious, yet calculating looks. At the end of the class she walked beside Hwenfayre, giving her a sidelong glance.

'What is it?' Hwenfayre asked innocently.

'Why do you bait Hylin so?' she asked.

Hwenfayre paused before answering, in part to consider what to tell her, but in part to allow a sailor to pass by. No matter what she was going to tell her new friend, she was sure she did not want it to be heard by a sailor.

'I am not convinced,' she started, 'that Hylin is telling us everything. I cannot help but think there is more to being a Priestess than just overseeing justice and singing a few songs at ceremonies.'

Erin's eyes widened as if in shock. 'What do you mean?'

'I'm not sure,' she said, watching Erin closely. 'But I think there's more. I think there's something they're not telling us.' Erin's response, neither too shocked, nor too comfortable, told Hwenfayre that she had

269

chosen wisely. If she were to be dangerous to Morag she would need allies.

The other girls who shared her room, Maeve, Hagan and Sara, were also on her list as possible allies, but they were proving less open to her ideas. Late at night, as she and Erin talked about the songs and stories they had practised during the day, the three girls lay silent, perhaps listening, perhaps sleeping. But they never raised a dissenting voice when Hwenfayre questioned the Teacher of Novices, unlike so many of the others.

In some ways it was like being back home. She was the outsider, the different one. Everyone knew her even though she did not know all of them. People she did not know would nod and refer to her by name, then fall silent as she walked by, watching, always watching. But there were differences. There she was denigrated, here she was feared.

It took her several days to realise the difference, but once she did, it was clear. The looks she received were not dismissive; they were nervous and quickly ended. The older members of the crew were the most afraid. It was they who most quickly averted their eyes or refused to look at her. Any who were about Morag's age or younger seemed less afraid but even they gave the impression of nervousness around her.

It was subtle, and she was not always sure that she was seeing what she thought she was seeing, but for all of her life she had been on the receiving end of stares and looks, so she was accustomed to it. In fact there were times she could recall when it seemed that she went for days without talking to anyone, but she was better at reading looks than she was at understanding conversation.

Every day she started her morning by slipping from her narrow bunk and creeping up on deck to greet the dawn. She took her harp, not her own which she still could not find, but the Novice harp she had been given. It had a harsh, scratchy tone and it was cracked, but it was better than no harp at all. Most mornings she met the High Priestess at the prow. Since the day when Morag had so finally extinguished her hopes, Hwenfayre had hardly spoken with her. Some mornings Morag acknowledged the Novice, but most she did not. Even so, Hwenfayre was sure that the High Priestess was becoming more uneasy about her presence every day.

One morning, when the south wind was bitter and clouds were scudding across the sky, Hwenfayre stood at the prow of the ship, softly singing a welcome to the morning. It was a song that she rarely sang; it spoke of melancholy, a quiet sadness that sometimes settled deep within her. She stood staring at the grey Sea, watching the slow swell as it eased across the water, her fingers unconsciously caressing the strings. Unbidden, the words of the song came to her lips and she sang of the pain, the longing that sometimes flooded her soul. As she sang, the waves of sorrow that swept across her were almost too much to bear.

Her eyes closed as she sang, her fingers faultlessly flowing over the strings. She lost herself in the song, allowing her spirit to soar. The sadness, the deep aching sorrow that had threatened to overwhelm her, faded as the song took her. A gentle peace beckoned her from somewhere; she could almost taste it as she reached out with her spirit.

'What are you doing, girl!' The words cut across her thoughts; the hard slap cut across her face. Her fleeting moment of peace was dashed. With a cry, her hand went to where her cheek stung from the blow. Her eyes snapped open and she spun to stare at the High Priestess. Almost unnoticed, her borrowed harp slipped from her grasp and fell into the sea.

A sudden rage boiled within her, seizing her with a violence she had never before felt, and she took a short step towards Morag. The High Priestess stepped back at Hwenfayre's unexpected fury.

For a moment the two of them stared at each other, neither moving.

Morag was the first to move. Regaining her composure in the face of Hwenfayre's blazing eyes, she stepped up to stand so close their noses almost touched. 'Don't you ever play that song again!' she hissed. 'You have no idea what you are playing with.'

'Do you?' asked Hwenfayre. She did not flinch under the High Priestess's anger. Startled by her response, Morag blinked and hesitated. Hwenfayre seized the initiative. 'If what Hylin is teaching us is any indication, you have no idea yourself of what power lies in these songs,' she said, so quietly that no one but Morag could hear.

The High Priestess narrowed her eyes dangerously. 'You are a child, Hwenfayre. And you do not know everything, not by half,' she snapped. 'Do not presume to instruct me in the ways of the Rafts.'

'I think someone should,' muttered Hwenfayre as she went to move past Morag. But as she did, the High Priestess grabbed her arm and dragged her in close again.

'Be very careful, child,' she hissed. 'People have died for much less.'

'Then kill me,' said Hwenfayre, looking Morag in the eye.

'We shall see, Hwenfayre,' said Morag, pushing her away. 'We shall see.'

Hwenfayre watched her stalk away, her anger subsiding as quickly as it had arisen, leaving her feeling empty and strangely unsatisfied. She had not felt like this since the day she first met Wyn. That day, too, she had meant to greet the dawn but failed. But unlike that day, today she had been prevented by malice.

It was something she knew she would not forget.

Morag went below after speaking briefly with one of the sailors. Hwenfayre continued to watch the High Priestess as she disappeared down the companionway. So it was that she did not notice Declan's approach.

'Are you sure you want to do this, Novice?' he asked quietly.

Startled, Hwenfayre spun around to face Declan. Briefly her anger flared again, but she forced it down when she saw Declan's kind expression. 'Do what?' she asked.

The sailor nodded towards where the High Priestess had disappeared below decks. 'The High Priestess Morag is not to be trifled with, Novice Hwenfayre,' he said. 'She is the leader of our people and has much power.'

Hwenfayre snorted dismissively. 'Power? She hardly knows what her own songs mean.'

'Not all power is mystical, Novice,' he gently chided. 'There is a great deal of power in commanding a people feared throughout the world. It may be that we do not live up to your dreams of a magical race who can conjure up storms and monsters at will, but we are not so lightly dismissed by those who share the Sea with us.'

'How so?'

Declan smiled as he looked away, out over the Sea. 'We have been sailing these waters since before most histories began. As a people we know more of the vagaries and mysteries of her ways than any other ever has. Even in a simple battle on the water we would defeat any enemy, with or without mystical help. And that is assuming these songs you sing are what you think they are.'

Hwenfayre nodded. 'But I have seen what these songs can do.'

Declan allowed a fleeting smile. 'Do not underestimate the Sea and her ability to surprise even the most experienced sailors. I have seen many strange things that most men would describe as sorcery.' He turned away from her to stare out at the open waters around them. 'The Sea is vast and dangerous and it can turn on you like a caruda, but it cannot be commanded. Not by the High Priestess, not by any man, nor,' he turned back to look at her, 'by you. Be very careful, Novice. You seem a nice girl; it would be a shame to see you end up as fish food.' With a nod and a half-smile, he turned and walked away.

It was hard for Hwenfayre to concentrate on her lessons, her mind constantly replaying the two conversations. Whilst the High Priestess had startled and angered her, it was Declan's quietly understated threats that unnerved her. There was something far more terrifying in his simple statements than in the harsh blustering of Morag.

With her mind wandering, it was not surprising that she missed most of what Hylin was talking about. But towards the end of the morning's lesson the old Mistress of Novices hummed a few bars of a song. There was something about the melody that caught Hwenfayre's attention. With a start she realised it was the song she had tried to sing that morning. When she looked at Hylin she found her teacher staring back at her with a calculating look in her eye. Their eyes met and Hylin nodded slightly and stopped humming.

At the end of the lesson, Hylin gestured for Hwenfayre to stay behind. Normally this would have meant a scolding, so the other girls scampered quickly past her. When they were alone Hylin closed the door.

'I hear you managed to annoy the High Priestess again, Novice,' she said without preamble.

Hwenfayre nodded.

'Normally I would not recommend that as a wise course of action,' Hylin went on. 'But there are times when, with care, it can be, um,' she paused, searching for the right word, 'profitable.'

Hwenfayre's eyes widened at her choice of word. 'Profitable?' she asked. 'How so?'

Instead of responding, Hylin stepped aside and ushered Hwenfayre out. 'I will see you tomorrow,

275

Novice,' she said. 'When we will be learning a new song. A song without words.' Hwenfayre went through the door, but paused at Hylin's final words. 'By the way,' she said, 'there are many songs that can be sung without a harp and still retain their power.'

Hwenfayre spent the day considering what Hylin had said. During her few moments of rest in between her tasks, she hummed the tunes she would normally play on a harp. It was strange but not altogether unpleasant. On a number of occasions as she hummed, she noticed her fellow Novices staring at her as if half-recognising the tune. Only Erin held her eye long enough to look surprised.

It took several days of this quiet practice before she felt confident enough to greet the dawn without a harp. She felt the lack of her morning welcome keenly, but believed it was worth the sacrifice, especially when the morning was so magnificent. Even as she dressed for the day, the soft pre-dawn light washed over her from the porthole. She hurried up on deck, every nerve tingling.

As before, the crew was working quietly, indicating that the High Priestess was also on deck. Hwenfayre smiled to herself, thinking how appropriate it would be for Morag to be present when she sang this song.

The High Priestess was standing alone in the prow of the ship, staring out at the slowly brightening sky. Gently, almost absently, Morag fingered the strings of her harp as she watched another dawn at sea. As Hwenfayre walked silently to stand behind her, Morag started to sing the song to greet the morning. The rich and beautiful sounds washed over

Hwenfayre, filling her soul with the simple joy of being alive and on the water.

The music took her as she listened to the High Priestess's soaring, rich voice. Despite herself and her reasons for being there, it lifted her above the simple and led her away to a time and place in her mind where she was free of all distractions, free to think and be herself. She felt herself being drawn back, back to where she first came alive, to that time and place where she most loved this music and felt its magic. Back to the time she first met Wyn.

She remembered his stories, his strong, callused hands, his frightening strength, but most of all she remembered his timeless eyes. The way he could stare at her and seem not to see her but someone else, someone who she wanted to be but could not be. The way he had so gently undressed her and eased her pain with his hard but kind hands. The way he spoke of the Sea with such longing and love.

The way he left her.

Abruptly the peace left her soul and pain jolted her back to the here and now. Back to the High Priestess. Back to the reasons she stood alone at dawn. But as she stood, remembering, the song in her heart changed. Instead of the peaceful, uplifting greeting song she had planned, a different song came to her. A song of great anger, of pain and loss, came to her lips. She sang words she barely knew, words she had sung only once before.

The song poured from her heart and her soul, bearing all the hurt, all the confusion that she felt. Dimly she heard the High Priestess stop her own song, but nothing could stop the storm of passion that had been building in her for so long. Feelings she could barely contain rang through her voice as she sang, calling to the Sea as she had done only once before, on that terrible night when Niall had been taken by a Raider's axe.

With a detached, dispassionate eye, she watched as the Sea changed from the gently rolling, kindly blue friend to a harsh, grey malevolent beast, preparing to strike with fury. Above her, heavy black clouds formed from nowhere, a wind sprang up from the breeze, whipping the sails into a frenzy. With cries of terror, the crew tried to lash down the hatches and prepare the ship for the storm that had come at her bidding.

Still detached, Hwenfayre watched as she sang. She watched the frantic efforts of the crew. She watched Declan as he strove to drag the High Priestess away from her precarious position in the prow of the plunging ship. She watched the waves surge and heave about her. She watched the clouds heap and swirl. But, most of all, she watched the blind terror grow in the eyes of the High Priestess.

Their eyes met as Morag allowed herself to be hustled away. Her voice had a hysterical edge to it as she cried out, 'Stop this now! You don't know what you are doing!'

But Hwenfayre knew exactly what she was doing as she turned back to face the raging waters. Without changing the passion in her voice, she formed an image of Wyn in her mind and sent the storm to hunt him down. Within moments, the violent squall passed and the Sea calmed. The storm had not ended; it had merely moved on, seeking a new target.

If Wyn still lived, he would remember her when this storm fell on him.

She was not sure what she had expected to happen as a result of her experiment, but she was unprepared for the utter normality that followed. The rest of the day passed as if she had not summoned a squall out of a perfectly calm sea. No one mentioned the storm, the song or the High Priestess. Hylin taught the Novices a song that Priestesses sang at wedding ceremonies, Alyce instructed them about cloud formations and Declan was too busy to speak to her.

It was as if nothing had happened.

By the end of the day, Hwenfayre was beginning to wonder if Declan had been right when he had told her that the Sea had simply done something strange that had caught them by surprise. But the look on the High Priestess's face kept coming back to her. There had been more in her fear than concern about a simple unexpected squall.

That night as she lay in her bed she felt the pain of guilt. Her mind would not let her rest as she tossed and turned. Images of Wyn, of Niall, of her mother danced in front of her, taunting her and deriding her for her impulsive act of violence. She knew, even as she did it, that such a storm was dangerous, and sending it after someone was an act she would regret. To add to her confusion, she had only Morag's word that Wyn was dead, and that he was not what he seemed. What if Morag were lying? What if everything she said was a lie? Hwenfayre remembered Wyn again. She drove herself through every memory she had of the man who had taken her away from the place of her birth. Nothing in what

279

she remembered could make her believe that he was a brutal assassin. Yet he had left her.

But what if that, too, was a lie? What if her memory were wrong?

It was very late when a cold sweat overtook her. What if these were not the people she thought they were? Who were these people she had joined? Did she really know anything about them? Their legends were different from what she had been told, their ways were not what she had been expecting, and they did not recognise her, as Wyn had said they must.

She must know the truth, must discover who was lying. Only then could she truly know who she was and if her destiny lay here or elsewhere.

So she started to tell the stories Wyn had told her. She spoke, not caring whether any listened; it was for herself that she did this. As she spoke, retelling the great stories she had heard but once, yet which felt as much a part of her as her eyes, a decision stole into her mind. She would join this people whether they wanted her or not. Hwenfayre would become one with the Children of the Raft, ever mindful of how she came here, always seeking the truth.

And the days passed into weeks as they sailed upon the endless Sea. Each day she attended to her tasks dutifully; watching, listening and learning all she could about the strange people she had joined. At night, as she lay on her bed, she told the stories to the silent Novices who shared her cabin. As she worked at her menial tasks, she told the stories. During her lessons, she asked questions about the stories. And every day she greeted the dawn with song.

It was a cold, overcast day, the wind whipping the grey Sea into short, steep waves, when Hwenfayre learned the truth. She greeted the morning as usual, singing into the wind. She still keenly missed the gentle sounds of the harp, but she persevered and was beginning to love the song for itself. As usual the High Priestess had sung the same song, and as usual, she had ignored Hwenfayre. Even Declan had been less friendly of late as if her continuing defiance of Morag were troubling him.

After singing, Hwenfayre went below for another breakfast during which she told the tale of how the Children of Danan first left the land behind for the strange delights of life on the Sea. Then it was time for lessons with Hylin.

'Good morning, Novices,' the old teacher greeted her charges. 'Today we are going to learn one of the great songs of our past. It is a song of power and mystery. It is not one we trifle with, nor is it a song to be underestimated. We sing it only at times of great need and peril for it is a song of the Ancient Ways.'

Hwenfayre looked up from her practice harp sharply but Hylin was steadfastly looking away from her. She looked around the room to find the other Novices were also showing interest. Erin, in particular, was staring at Hylin with rapt attention, absently fingering her harp.

Hylin continued, 'This is a song that is not usually taught so early in a Novice's training, but I have been hearing a lot of talk about the old ways recently and I have become a little nostalgic.' She chanced a glance at Hwenfayre. Their eyes met and a flicker of understanding passed between them. 'Let us begin,' the old teacher went on briskly, taking up her own harp.

Within seconds Hwenfayre recognised the song. It was the one she had sung on the ship to summon the storm. Hylin stopped playing after a few bars. She looked up, placing her hands on the strings to still their sound.

'This song is one of the first that the Children learned when we took to the Sea. It is used to call a storm that can be sent after an enemy, but it is rarely used because it is so dangerous.' She paused and looked straight at Hwenfayre. Their eyes met again, but this time Hylin held her gaze for so long that the other Novices turned to see. Hwenfayre suddenly found herself the centre of attention. 'It can only be used by one who has true power,' Hylin continued without shifting her gaze. 'And then only by a Priestess who has a harp made of driftwood. Only one person can ever summon a storm without such a harp.'

'Hylin!' the High Priestess's voice cut across the room. She was standing in the doorway, her eyes flashing with anger.

Hylin stood slowly and put her harp down carefully. 'Yes, High Priestess?' she said, raising her eyebrows. 'Is there a problem?'

Morag stood still, breathing heavily as she sought to keep her anger under control. 'Could I see you outside please, Hylin?'

'Of course.' As she walked to the door, Hylin turned back to the silent Novices. 'Continue practising the song from yesterday, Novices. I shan't be long.'

But Hylin did not come back.

The Novices sat in silence, not quite sure how to respond. After a few moments they started to talk quietly among themselves. The main topic of discussion was Hwenfayre. For a while she sat alone, not saying anything, hardly hearing the hum of conversation around her. It was only when Erin addressed her directly that she snapped out of her reverie.

'Hwenfayre,' she said. 'What did she mean by that?'

'By what?' asked Hwenfayre.

'What she said about only one person. Who did she mean?'

'Danan,' put in Maeve. 'She meant Danan, didn't she, Hwenfayre?'

Hwenfayre nodded. 'Yes, she did. Only Danan can raise such a storm.'

'But Danan is dead, isn't she?' asked Maire, another Novice.

'Yes, the original one is,' said Hagan. 'But she comes back to us every few generations, doesn't she, Hwenfayre? That's what you've been telling us with all those stories, isn't it?'

'What stories?' asked Novice Nicole.

But before anyone could answer, Alyce came in. 'Novices,' she said, 'I am going to be continuing your training for a while.'

'Where's Hylin?' asked Erin.

'Hylin is ...' she paused, thinking of the right words, 'presently indisposed.'

'When will she be back?' asked Hagan.

Alyce fixed the girl with a steely stare. 'Let us continue with your lesson, shall we?' And the lesson continued, but there was a sullenness to the Novices that irritated the normally even-tempered Alyce.

The weather that had threatened in the morning became a storm later that afternoon. All the Novices were safely below decks, while above them the sailors strove to keep the ship from damage upon the heaving sea. Hwenfayre sat beside the porthole in her room, watching the waves as they surged beneath her, sending the ship plunging violently one moment then climbing precipitously the next. She was lost in her own thoughts; thoughts of Wyn, of Niall, of Morag and of Hylin's strange choice that morning. *Why that song? And why today?*

And what of this storm? Is it entirely natural?

Unable to rest, even while watching the sea, Hwenfayre stood and made her way to the door.

'Where are you going?' asked Erin.

Hwenfayre shrugged. 'Up on deck,' she said. 'I can't rest down here. I need some air.'

'But it's dangerous,' said Maeve.

Again Hwenfayre shrugged. She felt beyond caring. If the Sea wanted to take her, so be it.

On deck the storm defied comprehension. The wind shrieked like a rabid animal, tearing at the shrouds, ripping the sails to tatters. All around them the waters heaved and plunged, tossing the ship like a cork. Men screamed and bellowed as they battled with the madly plunging vessel. Hwenfayre clung to the railing, feeling the wind tear at her clothes and hair. The waves crashed over the ship, soaking her to the skin and leaving her shivering and shaking. She gasped with shock as the icy cold of the Sea bit deeply.

A high-pitched cry of horror cut through the

insanity of the wind. Hwenfayre turned to see Hylin sliding across the deck as the ship started to descend into a deep trough. She watched in disbelief as the aged Teacher of Novices tried in vain to find a handhold, her hands scrabbling desperately on the deck planking. With a despairing cry, Hylin slid past the stanchions, then out over the side.

Hwenfayre screamed as Hylin fell out of sight. Her cry attracted the attention of Declan who was fighting with a shroud. He looked up and followed her staring gaze to where Hylin hung, grasping the railing with one hand. She dangled helplessly above the furious Sea while Declan worked his way to her, forcing himself against waves and wind that seemed to be actively opposing him.

As he came close enough to reach out and help her, a wave crashed across him, throwing him to the deck. With a wail, Hylin's grip failed and she disappeared into the Sea. Disbelieving, Hwenfayre stared at where Hylin had been, as if by watching she might somehow bring her back. But Hylin was gone; the Sea had taken her.

Declan rose up against the surging Sea and looked back towards the mainmast. There the High Priestess stood, wrapped against the elements in a magnificent blaewhal fur cloak. She nodded to Declan, a small smile hovering about her lips. He nodded, almost imperceptibly, a pleased look on his face, and then turned to go back to his work. As he did, he caught sight of Hwenfayre watching him. The expression on his face changed to one of sadness. It changed so quickly and so completely that Hwenfayre was unsure whether it had even happened.

Hwenfayre turned to regard the High Priestess. Unlike Declan, Morag made no attempt to hide her pleasure at Hylin's death. When their eyes met, Morag smiled and nodded at Hwenfayre. Her smile seemed pleasant, but her eyes were hard. The message was clear, the threat made and understood. Hwenfayre knew she was on notice for her life.

Perhaps it was that sense, perhaps it was the knowledge that she had been betrayed again. Or perhaps it was the violence of the storm making her reckless. Whatever it was, she threw back her hair and walked towards the High Priestess.

Morag watched as she made her way across the heaving deck. Waves crashed around and over her, the wind tore at her clothes and hair, but her stride was steady. She was not consciously aware of what she was going to do; even years later she was unable to say why she moved on Morag at that time. But she fixed her eyes on the High Priestess, ignoring the insane storm all around her and the deck heaving beneath her feet.

As she walked, the words of a song started to form in her mind: a song of great power, a song of great anger, a song she had never sung. But before she could utter a word, a powerful arm seized her, pinning her arms to her sides. A knife was pressed against her throat.

'I tried to warn you, Novice,' hissed Declan into her ear. 'But no, you were too smart for that. I told you there were many types of power.'

'What are you saying?' cried Hwenfayre.

'I have been ordered to kill you but I am going to give you a chance. If you are what you seem to be, I am saving your life. If not, we are all fools and I am the captain of fools.'

He picked her up and carried her towards the same place where Hylin had vanished into the raging Sea. Realising what he intended, Hwenfayre screamed and started to pound her fists against his body. The sailor seemed not to notice her struggles as he inexorably took her to the edge. When he reached the side of the ship he stopped.

'Any last words, Princess?' he asked. Instead of replying, Hwenfayre lashed at his face with her fingernails, leaving two bloody slashes down his cheek. With a roar of pain and anger, Declan heaved her over the side.

19

'Aldere!' called his mother. 'Aldere! Where are you?'

'I'm here, Mother,' he replied.

'Where have you been all day?' she snapped.

'I was with Silvia during the morning. Her goats were poorly and I helped her tend them. This afternoon I was with Merryk, helping him fix his bellows.'

'It's time you got yourself a trade, boy,' Katya grumbled. 'You're old enough.' She fixed him with a hard stare. 'You were old enough ten summers ago.'

Aldere sighed. It was going to be one of those evenings. He stood, stirring the pot that hung suspended over the fire. A delicious aroma of vegetables and lamb rose up from the bubbling surface. The lamb was a gift from Silvia, and Merryk's wife had given Aldere some vegetables from her garden. It always seemed to work that way: he had no trade and his mother had no skills with either garden or needle, yet they were never hungry or cold.

As he stirred the stew he added a pinch of a herb he found growing high on the mountain that soared above their village. It gave their meals a subtle flavour and seemed to ease his mother's need for the drink. Whenever he went up there, he brought back a pouchful. Just a few leaves would usually be enough for him and his mother, but he could easily trade it for whatever they needed. All of the women in the village would take as much as they could get.

'Did you have a good day today, Mother?' asked Aldere.

She snorted in derision. 'And how exactly am I supposed to have a good day?'

'I don't know, did you talk to anyone?'

She snorted again. 'Talk? Who is going to talk to me?'

'Yesmah, she's always nice to me. Why don't you visit her? I'm sure she'd be nice.'

Instead of answering, Katya broke the seal on a new flask of wine. Aldere sighed. Sometimes she'd wait until he'd served dinner, but not always.

He put his mother to bed when there was still a mouthful left in the flask. Once he had poured such a mouthful out, but she'd remembered it and there was unpleasantness in the morning. Now he just stoppered the flask and left it beside her bed. As he tucked her in, he kissed her gently on the forehead.

'Goodnight, Mother,' he whispered. 'I hope tomorrow is better.' She lay still, her mouth open slackly, snoring quietly. 'I'll talk to Yesmah myself,' he said. 'I'm sure she'd like to spend some time with you.'

'I'm sorry, Aldere,' Yesmah said the next morning. 'But I'm just too busy today. Maybe tomorrow.'

Aldere nodded. 'Maybe tomorrow, then. Goodbye.'

It had been like this since his father died. No one wanted to spend any time with his mother. They were always very polite, but ... Always the 'but'. They were either too busy, or not quite well, or something. Every village had to have one but it was hard to be the one's son sometimes.

It hadn't always been like this, or so he'd heard. When she was young, his mother had been a beauty. Her long, jet-black hair, sparkling blue eyes and soft skin had made her the most sought-after girl in the village. But the lovely Katya, the pride of the village, married a Tribesman. No one spoke his name any more. He got her pregnant, then left. Everyone thought he'd deserted her forever, but he came back a year after Aldere was born. He came back with treasures from afar, or so the story went. They were deliriously happy for about six summers before the event that changed all their lives forever.

Aldere's father was climbing the mountain as he often did. He always said that it helped clear his mind and cure the need to travel, being so high above the world. *Looking down on life gives you perspective*, he'd say. *Take the large view of things, my son.*

Aldere and his mother were carrying lunch up the mountain to share with him when they heard an odd clicking sound. As one, they turned to see a Skrin Tia'k standing behind them.

Skrin Tia'k were rarely seen this side of the Great Fastness. Everyone knew that the arthropoid creatures still roamed the grasslands freely, but south of the river they were unwelcome. If caught, they faced either lifelong slavery or death at the hands of whatever mob felt bloodthirsty enough to attack. Given their status as defeated and enslaved enemies, they enjoyed no protection whatever from any human agency.

Katya screamed and fled down the hill, in her terror running very close to the Skrinnie. It stood impassively watching her. Aldere, a sturdy boy, watched the huge creature lower itself to its four walking limbs. The two of them stared at each other for a long moment as if summing up an opponent. Abruptly the Skrinnie leaped backwards, uttering a high-pitched scream that had Aldere's ears ringing for days afterwards. It raised itself onto its rear two legs and spread its other four limbs wide.

To Aldere's stunned amazement, massive translucent wings erupted from its sides between the first and second sets of limbs. They unravelled to a wingspan of at least twenty paces, in lurid pinks and greens. The Skrinnie's head also grew, opening up to reveal huge red eyes that were set above a suddenly savage-fanged mouth. Horns sprouted from the back of its head and its second set of limbs took on the appearance of weapons. The tone of the squeal shifted, becoming modulated, ululating. Aldere was transfixed, unable to move. The Skrin Tia'k sprang forward, mouth agape, attack limbs flailing.

Aldere's father never stood a chance as he threw himself into the Skrin Tia'k's body.

'Run, son!' he screamed.

Aldere never forgot that he ran without a moment's hesitation. He sprinted past his bloodied father and never stopped to look back, even when he heard the screams end.

Katya started drinking soon after. Aldere watched his mother become a fat, bitter, ugly woman who cried herself to sleep every night when she went to bed sober. He noted that the nights she spent racked with guilt and tears gradually became fewer and fewer as she drank more and more. Many times he tried to explain to her that it was not her fault, but it only made her guilt worse to know that he could accept this while she could not.

Another thing that puzzled and saddened Aldere was that no one ever believed him when he described the change in the Skrin Tia'k.

'Nonsense,' they would all scoff. The Skrinnies could not do what he described. Such a thing had never been seen or recorded. He must have been imagining it; he was only a small child; the fear made the Skrinnie seem different. The explanations were as predictable as they were banal. Aldere knew what he'd seen and what he'd seen made the Great Wars between humans and Skrinnies believable.

It was only a year later that he discovered the cave and saw the sign carved into the rock.

20

The Commander put down his telescope, disappointed again.

They'd been hunting the Children for weeks without so much as a hint of a sail. Even in this new ship, the *Misty Seal*, the finest vessel he had ever commanded, he'd had no luck. It was important that they find them, far more important than any of his crew realised. It would not be far off the mark to say that lives depended on this mission. A great many lives, and one of them his.

He considered calling for a course change, but he'd done that so many times in this fruitless search that he despaired of making any more. They'd swept the deep Reaches without luck. Now they were venturing further north into the Stragglers, the island region where the Southern Raiders had first made their reputation. He had been part of that reputation.

Even though his was a name not commonly known, his face and ship were recognised and feared throughout the Stragglers. He had cut a swathe through these islands, preying without mercy on both land settlements and any ships foolish enough to stray into his territory. His exploits of pillage and rapine during fifteen years were enough to attract the attention of the Officers' Council of the Southern Raiders. When he lost a leg in an unwise battle with the Children of Danan, he decided to put his sailing days behind him.

A seat on the Council was easy enough to buy. After his fifteen years of sailing and raiding he had a sizeable fortune put aside. At first he'd been regarded as little more than a thug to be tolerated by the other Officers. But he was an astute captain and knew the ways of men, understanding the uses of power and skilled in goading others to do his bidding. In a short time he built himself a new reputation.

In less time than it took to become a Southern Raider, he became an Officer. The respect he had earned as a captain quickly grew as an Officer. However, being an Officer had its responsibilities as well as its privileges and he soon learned the burden that all the Officers carried. He learned of the future facing the Southern Raiders.

The plan that had ultimately led to his being here, on a ship again after so long, with this damnable wooden leg, was his. As would be the sole blame if it went wrong.

Damn that treacherous bitch! he raged inwardly. He'd already lost a lot of good men through her schemes, and now, thanks to her obsessive need for secrecy, he did not even know what he was looking for.

In frustration he turned away from the railing and noticed a crewman standing nearby.

'What is it?' he asked.

'Sir,' the crewman started. 'Sir, wreckage.'

'Whereabouts?'

'On the starboard bow, Sir.'

Pleased to have something else to think about, the Commander turned and stomped across the deck to consider the wreckage. It was a small boat, more abandoned and battered than wrecked, but timber floating in the sea was not to be wasted, whatever form it came in, so he ordered it to be brought aboard.

'What do you think, Commander?' asked one of the other crewmen as it came on board.

'Islander,' he grunted in reply. 'Northern Straggler, I'd say.' He shrugged. 'Could be useful as timber, or as a bay tender.'

'Not what we're after then, Sir,' the crewman continued.

The Commander shook his head and gave an order for it to be stowed away. He turned, in part to hide his frustration, but also to return to his post in the stern of the ship. As with most who spend their lives on water, the simple contemplation of the sea would often ease his mind and help him think. And he needed to think, to try and find some way out of this trap he had made for himself.

Before he could even reach the stern railing, an old, querulous voice interrupted him.

'A boat? Is that all we have?'

The Commander stopped. Without bothering to turn around he said, 'Yes, Officer Manno, a boat.'

'Is it a big boat?' the old man asked.

The Commander sighed. 'No, Officer Manno, a very small boat.'

'Probably not the boat that contains the legendary Danan, then?'

Biting back a number of colourful responses he would have normally used in the face of such sarcasm, the Commander answered through gritted teeth. 'Probably not, no, Officer Manno.'

Behind him he heard the old man bang his walking stick firmly on the deck. 'You will face me when I speak to you, Commander!' Officer Manno hissed.

The Commander turned slowly to regard the wizened old man who stood hunched before him. Officer Manno was the oldest Officer on the Council. He had been sailing and raiding these waters before the Commander was born, and even though the Commander now outranked the old man, he knew he owed him respect that went beyond mere rank. The aged Officer glared up at the Commander with eyes that glittered with rage.

'How dare you speak to me with your back to me!' Manno said. 'Do not forget that it was my casting vote that won you that position you hold! I will not be treated disrespectfully!'

'I apologise, Officer Manno.'

'And don't apologise!' he snapped back. 'Come with me to my cabin; we need to talk.' Without waiting to see if he was being followed, Manno shuffled towards his cabin.

Inside it was cramped, as cabins usually are. Manno sat on a stool with his back against a wall, staring at the door as the Commander entered. He nodded, indicating the younger man should sit on the bunk.

'Talk to me,' the old man said without preamble.

'What do you want to hear?'

'Just talk.'

He shrugged, leaning back. 'It was such a simple plan, really,' he started.

'Always the worst kind,' Manno grunted. The Commander grinned in agreement. 'Never trust a simple plan,' he continued. 'They will always blow up in your face.'

'This one hasn't yet,' commented the Commander.

Manno snorted in amusement. 'Hasn't it?'

'No. But it is becoming ugly.'

'What do we need to rescue it?' asked Manno.

'At this stage I don't know.'

'What's the worst that can happen?'

'The Southern Raiders cease to exist. Hundreds of women and children starve to death and the seas belong to Morag, the High Priestess of the Children.'

Officer Manno nodded. 'It's important to keep the objectives firmly in mind,' he said.

'You think I've forgotten!' snapped the Commander. He surged to his feet, towering over Manno, glaring again at the old man.

'No, I don't,' he said, looking up at the Commander. 'But you have been showing signs of losing hope. And with what's at stake here, despair is not a luxury you can allow yourself.' He paused as the younger man took a number of deep breaths then sat back down. 'If the plan has gone awry it is up to you to either fix it or make a new one.'

'I thought I'd done that.'

'What? With this so-called raid? This hunting mission? What of the great massing of the fleet? No one believes that. Everyone believes you have some plan, some way of outsmarting the Children, because everyone knows they cannot be defeated on the Sea.'

'But they can be!' declared the Commander, once again surging to his feet. 'I know it!'

'Do you?' Manno asked quietly. 'All you have is the word of a woman who has proved herself treacherous. And she comes from a long line of treacherous women. Ask yourself why you kept the original plan quiet.'

'You know why I kept it quiet. We knew we couldn't really trust Morag.'

'And you came out here, with almost the whole fleet, on a hunt that everyone knows cannot succeed!'

The Commander nodded, his face showing near-despair. Officer Manno pointed at him with a steady finger. 'Again you indulge yourself!' he snapped. 'The stakes are high and you must take control, first of yourself, then of our destiny.'

It had been such a long time since anyone had dared to speak so bluntly to him that for a moment the Commander was taken aback. He stared at Officer Manno and blinked slowly. The silence between them was punctuated by the sounds of the crew from outside. Finally, the Commander shook his head, a small smile forming on his lips.

'Got any ideas?' he asked.

Manno slowly shook his head.

'So we're stuck with my plan, then?' the Commander said.

'So it seems,' agreed Manno. 'For now, at least.'

'Commander! Commander, you must see this!'

'Hold that thought,' the Commander said as he opened the door. 'This shouldn't take long.' But what he saw coming towards his ship took Officer Manno's words from his mind.

21

Soaked with sweat, Declan cried out and sat bolt upright. For a moment he stared at the bulkhead, too stunned to think about what had woken him up. He sat still as the dream that had awakened him slowly resurfaced. When he realised what it was, the cold sweats came again. His eyes widened and his heart started to race.

Beside him, High Priestess Morag stirred. 'What is it, Declan?' she asked drowsily.

'She's alive,' he breathed.

'What?' she asked. 'Who's alive?'

'Hwenfayre,' he said.

Morag sat up, all traces of drowsiness vanishing. 'She's what?'

'She's alive,' Declan repeated.

The High Priestess slid out of bed, wrapping a sheet around her shoulders. Without a word she walked over to the porthole and stared out at the night sky. Declan watched her, waiting for her response. Her hair tumbled down her slender back. At her shoulder the sheet revealed skin, untouched by years at sea, that was smooth and creamy white in the soft moonlight. She turned slightly. The gentle light softened her strong profile, revealing traces of the happy, cheerful young girl with whom he had first fallen in love so long ago.

'Are you sure?' she asked. Declan nodded. She pursed her lips thoughtfully. 'Interesting,' she observed. 'I wonder how she survived.'

'If we were right about her, the Sea itself could have saved her.'

'Of course we were right,' Morag snapped. 'There is no other explanation for her.'

Declan shrugged. 'Much of the old lore has been lost. Maybe there's more we don't know.'

Morag nodded. 'Perhaps we were a bit hasty in killing Feargus. He could have had more to tell us.'

'Unlikely,' disagreed Declan. 'If he'd known anything else he'd have told us.'

A savage grin marred Morag's face. 'True,' she agreed. 'He told us all he knew.'

'But we still don't know how she ended up in that town,' Declan said.

Morag nodded again. 'That still troubles me. As does Wyn. How did he find her?'

'Why didn't you kill him?'

Morag shrugged. 'I thought I'd leave it to the islanders,' she said dismissively. 'They can dream up the most interesting ways of dealing with murderers.'

'Did he survive?' asked Declan.

Morag shook her head. 'The islanders are reliable when it comes to killing people.'

'And we left enough bodies for them to find.'

'Killing the girl was a masterstroke,' Morag said. 'No one can resist a pretty dead body when it comes to a murder.'

Declan's answering grin was wolf-like in the moonlight. 'Wyn was better than I thought he would be. I had to go back later to kill her but she was still so shocked it was easy.'

Morag was breathing heavily, remembering the night when she had snatched the avatar of Danan herself from the clumsy hands of her self-appointed protector. The thrill of that unexpected chance still gave her a shudder of excitement that left her flushed and trembling. She had been so sure that she could turn the Danan to her own devices that she had put aside the original plan of killing her. But the Danan had proved obdurate, leaving her with no choice but to order Declan to slit her throat and give her lifeless body to the Sea. Looking at Declan, she allowed the sheet to fall to the floor, leaving her naked in the silver light. And the Danan was still alive.

No matter, she thought. *I held her once, I can do it again.*

Later, as they lay beside each other, spent and weary, Morag lifted herself up on one elbow and looked down at her lover. 'Where is she now?' she asked.

Declan's eyes clouded over as he focused inwards, seeking Hwenfayre. After a few moments, he snapped back into reality. 'On a ship. South of here.'

'How far?'

'A few days' sailing.'

'What sort of ship?'

'Big. Well armed. Dangerous.'

'How could she possibly have gotten so far away?'

Declan shook his head. 'I don't know, but the Sea has its strange ways.'

Morag frowned, then got up. 'Let's go get some more ships and kill her.'

Declan let her get to the door before reminding her of her nudity. She turned and laughed throatily. 'You don't think the Navigator would appreciate me like this?'

Declan shook his head. 'He's not young any more. I don't know if his heart would take the excitement.'

She dressed in her white High Priestess robes while Declan watched her. 'I'll be back after I've given the Navigator his new course,' she said. 'And when I return we can talk again about what we will do once we have finally put the Danan and her untamed ways behind us.'

In the morning, after she had greeted the dawn with the beautiful harp carved from a single piece of driftwood, Morag stared out over the gently rolling ocean, remembering the day, so long ago, when she had first stepped on this dangerous path.

'Attend me, Morag,' the High Priestess directed. Sulkily, Morag obeyed her mother. Making sure her mother saw how slowly she obeyed her, Morag made her way to stand beside her. Anwyn, High Priestess of the Children of the Rafts, watched her recalcitrant daughter.

So much to learn, she thought. *And so little time to learn it in.* 'Morag,' she said. 'It is time for you to start to learn about the true uses of power.' Morag's eyes brightened at her mother's words. Her mother smiled at the display of hunger. *She'll do nicely,* she thought. 'Come with me, child,' she said.

Anwyn took her daughter to the window. 'Look out there and tell me what you see.'

Morag looked out at the *Two Family Raft*. It was a large raft, the largest of any the Children sailed. This day, the second after the Festival of the Winds, was a busy one. The decks needed to be cleared of all the assorted detritus that had accumulated over the Season of Storms in preparation for the Harvest Season. Everywhere she looked, people were scurrying about like the crabs that so often found their way onto the Rafts. Men called, women laughed, children squealed and ran as all did their part to prepare the Raft. Overhead the massive sails flapped in the light breeze while men clambered over the rigging, completing the checks and repairing whatever damage the winds had caused.

The sheer energy of the Raft nearly overwhelmed her, as it usually did. Morag would often spend hours sitting by this very window just watching those around her. Those she would one day rule.

Behind her she heard her mother stir impatiently as she awaited her answer.

'I see people. Many people, the Raft, the preparation for the Harvest Season.'

'What do you know about these people?' Anwyn asked.

'They are the Children of Danan. They are preparing for the Harvest Season.'

'Is that all you know?'

Morag frowned, not knowing what her mother meant.

'Do you know what they want? What are their

dreams, their hopes? What are they looking for in their lives?'

'How can I possibly know that, Mother?'

'By listening, by watching. But most importantly by understanding that everyone wants basically the same thing.'

'What is that?'

'Security. We all need to know that tomorrow is not frightening, that tonight we can sleep in comfort and wake up in the morning with the world as we left it. And as leader your job will be to give these people that peace of mind.'

'How is that possible?'

'There are many ways. But the simplest is to give them a dream, a hope, something that will fill their minds with the knowledge that all is well.'

'How can you give people a dream?'

'By telling them.'

'But don't we already have a dream?'

'You mean the legend of Danan?'

'Yes, Mother.'

'A dangerous dream. A very troubling legend.'

'How so?'

'It is a dream of great power, of someone coming to save us. But we do not need saving. We rule the seas. None dare challenge our right to come and go as we see fit. It is time for us to set aside the outmoded ways and make our own destiny.'

'But isn't Danan more than just a legend? What of the old stories and the songs of power?'

Anwyn allowed herself a tight smile. 'She doesn't have to be more than a legend. We have the opportunity to free our people from the restraints of the ancient ways.'

'How?'

'Do you see those two boys over there?' Anwyn pointed. 'What do you know of them?'

Morag looked to where her mother was indicating. She saw two boys whom she knew slightly. They were firm friends those two, inseparable since they had been infants together. The bigger, darker of the two was a Carver's son while the slighter, fairer was an orphan. Secretly Morag had noticed the Carver's son more often, keeping a few quiet dreams about him to herself. He had a dark and brooding quality to him that she found interesting, whereas the other she had already dismissed.

'What of them?' Morag asked.

'They are the key to the future of the Children of the Rafts.'

'How so?'

'There is one other in the legend of Danan; a man who is not well known to those outside the Priesthood. The Finder always comes before Danan returns. It is his arrival that always heralds the coming of Danan.'

'And they are ... ?'

Anwyn nodded. 'One of them is the Finder, I am sure.'

'Why have I never heard of him before?'

Anwyn took Morag's arm and led her away from the window. She sat down at her desk, indicating for her daughter to sit near her. 'For many years now, the High Priestesses have been preparing the Children for the day when we can step out from the shadow of the past and make our own way. The first stage was to take some of the ancient texts off the training schedule of the Novices. Then the more explicit teachings of Danan were removed from the Novice training, so that she was reduced to a figure of legend rather than a real person.'

'Why, Mother?'

'Haven't you learned anything?' she snapped. 'If Danan comes back she will be High Priestess and Princess. The whole structure of our society will be changed. We have spent far too long building our lives to have some mythical figure float in and take all that away. She will drag us back into howling mystical barbarism! We have evolved beyond that sort of nonsense.'

Morag considered that. 'So what do those two boys have to do with me?' she asked.

Anwyn smiled at the perception behind the question. 'You have a task, daughter. It involves those two. One we need, and one we need to dispose of.' Morag's heart leaped as she imagined what was to come, but she was disappointed, briefly, as her mother outlined the plan for her daughter's future. However, as she listened she came to appreciate the necessity.

Now, as she looked at the coming dawn, she thought about the man who shared both her vision and her bed, and she was satisfied. In her hands, the harp she had taken from Hwenfayre stilled as the final chords died. She had come a long way and done many things, but finally success was within her grasp. The Danan and her harp were separated, the harp was in her hands and the Finder was in her thrall.

The harp. Thinking about it reminded Morag of her failure to elicit anything from the instrument beyond what she could from an ordinary harp. She had long believed it would make any Priestess as powerful as the Danan herself, but now she was not so sure. Doubt had crept into her plans. Could she have gotten it wrong? Was there more to the harp than she knew?

She shook her head, as much to clear her mind of troubling thoughts as to feel the soft flow of hair across the skin of her back. Morag had many weapons at her disposal, but her physical beauty was one of her most powerful and she used it well. A slow smile formed on her perfect lips as she contemplated how easily Declan had fallen for her. And how easy he was to keep where she needed him.

Her mother's original plan had been effective in weaning the people away from a mythical hope and leading them towards self-sufficiency, but it had involved simply killing the Danan when Declan had found her. Morag had elevated the plan to a new level. Once the Danan had evaded the Raiders' clumsy attacks, she was adrift, a child alone and rudderless. Morag had tried to provide that rudder and tame her. The Danan dead was one thing, but the Danan tame and under Morag's control was something else entirely. However, the child had proven stronger than she appeared. Not only had she resisted her teaching, she had also survived the Sea alone. She had to die this time.

They had to find Hwenfayre again and kill her. Then it would be time to deal with the incompetent Southern Raiders. Not only could they not kill a child, they even thought they could mass their fleet without her knowing about it.

At no stage did it enter her mind that she also had been unable to kill Hwenfayre — twice.

22

'That's it?' shouted Shanek. 'That's the great mission the Thane sent me on, on pain of death by torment?'

Cherise lowered his eyes. 'Yes, First Son, that is the mission the Thane set us.'

'Us?' Shanek cried. 'Us? Are you set apart? Are you bound beyond law?'

'No, First Son. I am simply commanded,' conceded Cherise.

'And you,' Shanek whirled on Muttiah, 'are you set apart?'

The Caldorman shook his head. 'No, First Son. Only you have that honour.'

'Honour?' Shanek almost shrieked. 'Honour? I am set apart beyond law to negotiate a—' he shook the scroll in his hand, 'a sheep-trading agreement!' In disgust, he hurled the offensive document to the leaf-littered ground.

The men were standing a distance away from the two Fyrds: far enough for Shanek to feel unhindered, yet not far enough to feel unsafe. Not that these two old men could pose any threat to him.

Certainly not after the way they had dealt with Tapash.

When he and Leone dragged the barely conscious Tribesman back into the campsite, their reactions had been instructive. Cherise was shocked, but not at the presence of Tapash, and Muttiah was angry. Neither was surprised that the Tribesman had escaped, somehow found a bow and shot at Leone. The subsequent discovery that the rest of the prisoners had their throats cut, along with two of Shanek's Fyrd who were guarding them, also did not surprise the old men. Muttiah's feigned rage at the discovery, followed by his convenient killing of Tapash, only served to confirm Shanek's first impression. The two of them were involved somehow, or at the very least aware. There was, as he had first thought, a great deal more to this than sheep.

Caldorman Muttiah stooped to pick up the Thane's directive. He handed it back to Shanek. The First Son simply stared at it.

'What makes you think I would want to read that again?' he snapped.

'The Thane insisted that you carry the document and read it more than once,' said Cherise. 'He said that you would need to contemplate it in order to appreciate his instructions.'

His curiosity piqued, Shanek took the scroll. It was short and written in Matrin script. The flowing, elegant style of the penmanship was not that of the Thane, but was done by Shanek's father, Sandor, over the seal of the Thane. And yet it was badly written. It was clumsy and wordy, most unlike either his father or the Thane. In addition, the joint issue of the decree made it even more significant, and all the more odd, given the prosaic nature of the mission.

'Tell me, Cherise,' asked Shanek. 'Do the Ettans even breed sheep?'

'No, First Son.'

'That's what I thought. So why does the Thane want a sheep-trading agreement with them?'

'We breed sheep, First Son,' said Cherise.

Shanek grunted in reply and waved the Diplomat away.

Why, he wondered, *would the Thane ask my father to write this in Matrin?*

He remained where he was, studying the document while the two old heroes of the Asan Empire made their way back to the waiting Fyrds. So engrossed was he that he did not hear them break camp and mount up. Neither did he notice when Coerl Leone rode up to his side and addressed him.

'First Son?' she said.

He ignored her. Leone waited while Shanek quietly muttered to himself. After a few minutes he looked up.

'Ah, Coerl,' he said. 'Are we ready to go?'

'Yes, First Son.'

'Good.' He swung himself onto the back of his stallion. 'Let's sort out these wretched sheep.'

'Sheep, First Son?' asked Leone.

Shanek laughed. 'Yes, Coerl, sheep. We go, under pain of death by torment, to negotiate a sheep-trading agreement with the sheep-deprived people of Ettan.' He did not need to turn around to know that Leone nodded slowly, accepting the orders with her usual aplomb. *She's probably already accepted that it is for the good of the Empire,* he thought.

They rode through the forest for the rest of the day. There was little need for conversation so they were free to think. Leone spent most of the day watching Shanek, wondering what he was thinking. She saw anew his confident, easy seat as he rode. She pondered his ability with the bolas, how he had managed to bring down a running target at night in a forest. His surprise attack on the Caldorman was as skilled as it was brutal. He was trained and he practised hard, yet he had brought down and could have killed one of the best fighters in the army. Where had this skill come from? It was rare in his family, despite their centuries-long association with war. The family of the First Counsellor was known for its brilliance and tactical genius, but not its skill with arms.

She could not recall the night without remembering the startling vision of the two disparate sides of him. The revelation of his feelings about her, coupled with the darkness she saw in him by the campfire, was confusing. Yet, if the legends about his family were true, she should not be surprised by his complexity. One is not the sole hereditary heir to the most powerful family in existence without some inheritance.

It was the mystical aspects to his heritage that troubled her. During her time as Coerl of the First Son's Fyrd, she had read widely about the history of the First Family of the Empire. It was written that in times past they had commanded great mystical powers in battle that had been the cornerstone of the

Asan victories. Over the past few centuries, this power had waned, and no one had an explanation, or seemed particularly interested in finding one. Now such mysticism was consigned by most to the ignominy that such fanciful myths deserved.

For his part, Shanek was vexed by two questions: why was the message written in Matrin, and why sheep? He was under no illusions that there was more to this than negotiating some trade agreement, but why sheep? Why not something that Ettan either had or needed? It was obviously a front, a blind to the real mission, but it was too obvious. The Thane was a subtle man, and Sandor was the one to whom he went for advice. Neither would be so clumsy. So what was it about?

The key, he felt sure, was the language. He knew from his studies that Matrin was a beautiful, flowing language, suited to poets and orators. Many in the Hall of Counsellors gave their speeches in Matrin. It was also a strangely quirky language, full of unexpected and subtle twists of meaning, gradations of nuance. It was the language of scholars.

He gave up thinking about this early in the afternoon. It would come to him, he was sure.

Putting aside the Thane's missive, Shanek was free to contemplate the forest around him. The trees were evergreens, not uncommon so far south, but he expected to come into the deciduous forests soon. The cool of the morning had reminded him that they were heading north into the winter. It would be harsh, especially as the summer in Ajyne was so hot this year. He smiled as a thought occurred to him.

'Cherise,' he called. The Diplomat turned. 'Are you still sure this is the Way of the Coerl?'

'That was the information I received, First Son,' Cherise replied.

'I don't see many petrified Skrin Tia'k lining our way,' Shanek commented.

'That is only one version of the tale, First Son,' said Cherise.

'Oh? Tell me yours and I'll tell you mine,' said Shanek, grinning.

Behind him Leone stifled a smile. It was unlike the First Son to be funny. Diplomat Cherise did not seem to appreciate the humour. He urged his horse forward. Muttiah came with him as he made his way out through the protective ring of his Fyrd to join Shanek within his Fyrd. When the Diplomat was riding beside Shanek, the Caldorman's Fyrd formed a ring around the outside of the First Son's Fyrd.

'Legend tells us, First Son,' began Cherise, 'that Coerl Samba led an attack team into this forest in pursuit of a raiding party of Skrin Tia'k. Her team was assembled from the outpost town named Fyrd. She took the twenty best fighters and trackers she could find and pursued the Skrinnies for ten days before they gained the sanctuary of this forest.'

'Why?' asked Shanek.

'First Son?'

'Why was she chasing them?'

Cherise looked confused. 'They were a Skrin Tia'k raiding party, First Son.'

'Yes, I got that, but why pursue them for so long? What had they done?'

'They had sacked a small village,' muttered Muttiah. 'It was a day's ride from Fyrd, and Samba, whose other name incidentally was Coerl, was assigned to its defence. She had failed in her duty to the people. Hunting down the Skrinnies was the least she could do.'

Shanek fixed Muttiah with a hard glare. 'I can see that would sound a chord with you, Muttiah, seeing that you have had recent experience in failure. You do remember that six of my Fyrd are dead because of your laxity, I trust?' Shanek felt anger surge unexpectedly within him. It was as if he had suddenly realised that six soldiers whom he knew had died, and Muttiah was as responsible as Tapash. He wrenched his horse around to face the Caldorman. 'You!' he cried. 'You failed those soldiers! You were personally responsible and you failed!' Shanek was screaming in rage. 'And you have the audacity to speak to me!'

Caldorman Muttiah was visibly shocked by the sudden outburst. He stared at Shanek as if unwilling to believe the transformation that had so abruptly taken place. He went to speak, but as he drew in breath Shanek shot him a glare of such unfettered rage that he faltered and felt the words slide away.

'You will not speak to me unless I command it!' screamed Shanek. 'You are unworthy of your rank!' He looked around at his Fyrd, his rage now completely out of control. 'You, Malik, come here!'

The veteran eased his horse out of formation and approached Shanek.

'You are now Coerl of that Fyrd,' Shanek shouted. 'And your first mission is to make sure he,' Shanek pointed at Muttiah, 'is kept away from me.'

Malik saluted and wheeled his horse around to face Muttiah.

'Caldorman, if you would come with me . . .' Coerl Malik said. Dumbstruck, Muttiah followed Malik.

Shanek did not watch as the newly promoted Coerl took the Caldorman away and rearranged his Fyrd into a tight, guarding formation, leaving the Diplomat, the First Son, and his former Coerl within a circle of only eleven soldiers. Instead, Shanek turned his focus back to Cherise, his rage fading with every step the Caldorman took away from him.

'Continue with your tale,' he commanded the Diplomat.

'Samba pursued the Skrin Tia'k raiding party into this forest,' Cherise continued smoothly. 'She discovered that our ancient enemy is not suited to such a dense forest. They were slowed by the undergrowth and easier to track. She and her party caught them easily and cut them to pieces.'

'I prefer your story, Leone,' Shanek observed.

'Mine isn't finished, First Son,' said Cherise.

'Good.'

'After killing the Skrin Tia'k, Samba went to return home but found herself lost. It was as if the forest itself had changed. Her trackers were as lost as she, and they wandered aimlessly for several days before happening upon a path.

'They followed the path, quite unaware that it was leading them deeper into the forest rather than back home.'

'Oh, come on, Diplomat. She had the best trackers available and you are trying to tell me that they couldn't tell north from south?'

'In here, First Son,' Cherise indicated the heavy canopy, 'it's not surprising.'

'What direction are we heading now?' Shanek asked.

'North,' replied Cherise.

'How do you know?'

'We have a map, First Son.'

'Hmmm. I'll let that one pass for now. Go on.'

'One night, as they made camp, they were attacked by a beast they had never encountered before. It was unlike any of the monsters that inhabit this region: it was bipedal and upright.' The Diplomat's voice slipped into the cadence rhythm of recitation. 'With great fangs and mighty claws it rent the soldiers asunder. Samba fled with the six surviving members of her party, deeper into the forest. The beast hounded them for days, gradually killing them one by one until only Samba herself was left alive. Finally, her strength spent and her will gone, she stood to face her tormentor. After the pursuit the only weapon left to her was her bolas. She awaited her death as the beast crashed through the forest towards her.

'When it burst into the clearing she had chosen for her final resting place, it raised itself to its full height and went to fall upon her. In the fleeting moments before the vast creature rended her utterly, Samba was granted insight. All of the Way of Purity was made clear and she cried aloud in anguish that she would not be able to share the truths. Her cry startled the beast and it dropped to the ground before her. To her surprise, it spoke to her in a language she did not know she could speak.

'She never revealed what she and the beast spoke

of, but it spared her life and led her to a stream where she rested. While she regained her strength, the beast, whom she called Morrigan, taught her many things concerning the Way of Purity. When Samba was fully recovered the beast took her to the Shrine of Purity, where she found solace for her guilt. She threw herself down on the ground before the Shrine and slept. When she awoke, Morrigan was gone. With a light heart and a clear eye, she left the forest by the path, only to discover that she had been gone from this world for six years.

'No one has ever found the Shrine or encountered Morrigan since.'

'What did Morrigan look like?' asked Leone.

Cherise frowned. 'The only descriptions I have read suggest that it looked like an enormous horned sheep with fangs and claws.'

'Burn me!' cried Shanek. 'A sheep! Of course! How dense could I be?' He laughed out loud, a chilling, harsh sound. 'Thank you for a wonderful story. You may go and join Muttiah.' The Diplomat bowed slightly and urged his horse into a trot as he left the First Son.

'A great big sheep,' muttered Shanek, watching Cherise go. 'I liked the story until then. And I'll wager the Thane himself made sure Cherise was fed that little morsel of information.'

'First Son?' asked Leone.

'We'll talk about it later, Coerl,' he said. 'I need to think now.'

For the rest of the day he rode in silence, lost in his thoughts as the group continued north through the gloomy forest.

After dinner that night he sat cross-legged by the fire, reading the scroll. *Matrin and sheep*, he mused. *Matrin is said to have mystical origins.* Despite himself, he laughed out loud. *Perhaps it was delivered to us by an enormous fanged sheep!*

'First Son?' asked Leone.

Ever since their encounter by the stream, Shanek felt slightly embarrassed around the Coerl. He had revealed too much to her, and she had paid too much attention for him to be comfortable. She kept looking at him in a different way. Before they had talked, she had been aloof and loyal. Now she acted as if she liked him. Whilst it was nice, on one level it was also annoying. He wanted things to be as they were.

It was odd but this apparent fondness she had inexplicably developed for him seemed to reduce her slightly in his eyes. Before, she was self-contained and strong, she needed no one's approval. Now it was different. He knew what it was about, but he didn't have the time to ponder it; he was busy with this document.

'It's this,' he said to Leone, holding it up for her. 'It's written in Matrin and I know there's more to it. But I can't work it out.'

Leone looked up. Seeing the Diplomat talking with Muttiah, out of earshot, she frowned. 'First Son, why do you think there is more to it?'

'Leone, use your intelligence! I am First Son. Cherise is the most distinguished Diplomat in the Empire, and Muttiah is a Caldorman. Do you honestly believe for a moment we three would be sent to the most stable province on the continent to negotiate a sheep-trading agreement?'

320

'No,' said Leone.

'Good. So what's it all about?'

Leone shook her head.

'Can you read Matrin?' Shanek asked.

She shook her head again.

'Didn't think so,' he muttered. 'Think! Why Matrin?' He lay back on the leaf-covered ground, staring up at the canopy. An idea came to him slowly. 'Burn me,' he whispered. 'Sheep. Burned, stinking sheep.' He lifted the scroll up and unrolled it. How could he have missed it?

Matrin was not only the language of poets and scholars, it was also the language of mystics. 'Leone,' he said without taking his eyes off the words, 'get a quill and parchment. I want you to write down some words for me.'

While she was gone, Shanek re-read the instructions, only this time, instead of being irritated by the occasionally clumsy wording, he took note of the words and phrases that made it clumsy.

'Write these down. Each one on a separate line,' he said when Leone sat beside him. 'Sheep. Make all haste. Freely negotiate with all care. Sheep movement. Missing no small thing. Peaceableness. Your Thane gives all his noble caring. Sheep caring. Fiery chase of fleeing sheep.' The list went on, each oddity in the command adding to the message that Shanek was sure his father was sending him. 'Show me that,' he said when Leone reached the end. Leone gave him her parchment. Shanek took it and read it. 'Father, you are a sly old fox. But I am your equal,' he muttered. 'Now I can translate these into arcane Matrin and read the real mission.'

Leone watched as he concentrated. She saw his expression change from smug self-satisfaction to perplexity to wide-eyed shock. 'This can't be right,' he whispered.

He scrambled to his feet. Leone leaped up, her sword appearing as if by magic in her hand. 'What is it, First Son?' she asked.

Shanek did not speak. He looked about, his eyes wild, his breathing fast and shallow. Leone watched him closely, alert for any hint of the bursts of anger that he was prone to, but after only a moment or two he calmed himself.

'Well, well,' he said. 'This could be interesting.'

23

'Sail to starboard!'

Wyn heard the cry and inwardly tensed again. Even though they had been hunting the Children for weeks, they had had no luck. Every time they changed course to intercept yet another ship, he wondered. Would this be the time he had to betray someone?

When he signed on with Marek again he did not think beyond finding the Children, joining them, then finding Hwenfayre. Always that, the need to find her, the aching, gnawing need. It was a nagging feeling that had become a part of how he faced every day, like an old wound that never healed. She was his waking thought, his constant companion, her face the last thing he saw before falling asleep. Always, though, he shied away from the truth: that he loved her. He loved her with a passion, with a depth that frightened him with its intensity. It also frightened him that his love was all he had to offer her. He was a coarse, rude man with no subtlety, no grace and little intelligence.

Hwenfayre, he thought for the thousandth time, *where are you? I will find you,* he promised himself again.

But will you want me? Will you want to be with me, now that you have found your home? How can I love you, a Princess? Even as he thought it again, the prosaic cliché of his situation did not fail to make him smile at his foolishness. Here he was, a scarred veteran of too many battles, hopelessly in love with a beautiful young princess. He had laughed out loud at more than one badly written tale about his own situation. He was firmly trapped in his own tragic story and he knew he would continue to search for her, wherever that took him.

The first ship they sighted was an islander cutter. It saw them and tried to run, but the *Gretchen* was a fast fighting ship. They chased the cutter down and prepared to sink her. Just as they readied their weaponry, a new crewmember tried to prevent Marek from giving the order to fire. He desperately pleaded with the Captain, crying out that the ship belonged to his family. Marek coldly ran the man through with his cutlass then opened fire.

They left the cutter burned to the waterline with all hands dead.

As a soldier, Wyn had been witness and at times party to many acts of violence, even brutality, but nothing had ever shocked him the way that senseless destruction had. They were seeking the Children, and this cutter had no plunder and no connection to their prey. Marek ordered its destruction, first for pleasure, then as vengeance on a dead Raider who had dared challenge his orders. All the sailor had wanted was for his family to be spared.

Wyn wanted Marek to put aside his whole mission.

But such thoughts were a distraction, and by the look of the sails, the vessel approaching them would need his full attention. It was a warship.

'What do you think?' asked Sacchin.

Wyn shrugged. 'Mainland,' he suggested. 'One of the Southern states, maybe Oscran.'

Sacchin grunted in agreement. 'Is it after us?'

'Hope not,' said Wyn.

As if in answer, Marek called for full sail and a change of course. They were going to run. Normally no Southern Raider vessel would turn and run from a warship from any of the kingdoms, but Marek's decision only served to emphasise his focus on his mission.

The warship was fast but the *Gretchen* was faster and they left it in their wake with ease. They continued to head generally north into the more populated regions. Within a few days they would find themselves in the normal shipping lanes where the ships of Tanissan would be patrolling their southern coastline for protection from just such a Raider vessel as the *Gretchen*. As they were travelling alone, it could be a nervous or even dangerous time. Wyn could remember times when, as a young man, he sailed these seas on ships from various of the southern kingdoms. He had seen action battling vessels just like the *Gretchen*. Usually they hunted in packs in this part of the Sea, so as a single Raider ship they would need to be careful.

He was still unsure as to what exactly Marek had in mind. There was no way he could possibly hope to do any damage to a Raft, even if he could locate one. Wyn's recollection of the *Two Family Raft*, even allowing for his youthful memory, was one of a vast floating city surrounded by up to fifteen fast attack ships. The whole Raider fleet that he had seen would be hard put to cause a Raft any serious problems. Even so, the Rafts rarely ventured out of the deep western ocean. To find any of the Rafts could take years if they did not want to be found, and if Hwenfayre were helping them they would not only be protected by distance and fast attack ships, the Sea herself would hide them.

He stared out at the featureless horizon that bordered a calm sea. It worried him when she was this calm. He often felt she was waiting, or resting to gather her strength. The long, powerful swell eased past the keel as it made its way to the wild open waters of the south. Somewhere down there a storm would be brewing. There, the forces of tide and wind would whip up these seemingly gentle rolls into the brutal steep waves that could crush a ship or flood a Raft. In his mind he could conjure up the images: the smell of the ice, the feel of the wind-driven slivers as they cut through leather and flesh. With ease, he could transform this placid, kindly blue water into the howling beast that still haunted his dreams.

It had been many years since the storm had almost destroyed the *Two Family Raft* and killed so many, but the pain and terror remained with him. He knew it always would. In his quiet moments he liked to tell himself that he had left his home because of the High Priestess and her schemes, but in truth he had left because of fear.

After his father died, he and Declan existed in a kind of lost haze for a while, unsure of their place and confused about their lives. Declan had been his friend forever. He was an orphan and Wyn's family had taken him in, given him a name and a home. Wyn's father was a good man who loved both boys well, teaching them the skills and ways they would need. But when he died and Wyn's mother collapsed in on herself, they both felt they had been cast aside to drift aimlessly.

They would talk endlessly, comparing dreams and goals, hopes and plans. Wyn found himself looking away, further from the home he felt he'd lost. His eye drifted to the land, the enticement of adventure and discovery. Declan's eye stayed closer, but he was looking up, thinking of leaving behind his humble beginnings.

At first it was a simple dream of leaving the *Two Family Raft* and joining another Raft where he could start again. Declan as the *de facto* son of a respected Carver had status, but Declan the friend of the dissolute Wyn was once again an orphan, of no note and of little value. Declan started to plot, to plan and to scheme. They were little things to begin with: ingratiating himself with the Raft's Navigator, greeting the Priestess whenever she passed; nothing to cause concern. But one lazy afternoon late in the Migrating Season, he told Wyn the news that turned their lives upside down.

They were sitting in the shade of a damaged sail they should have been repairing. Wyn had stolen a cask of ale and they were over halfway through it, leaning on a storage crate, watching the day drift by.

'I'm leaving here,' Declan said.

'What?' asked Wyn. 'Where?'

'I've been accepted into the Learning.'

'What?' asked Wyn again. 'The Learning? Why?'

'I'm going to train to become a Navigator,' said Declan. 'I'm leaving for the *Learning Raft* tomorrow.'

'But that's not possible!' exclaimed Wyn. 'No one gets into Navigator training without a sponsor. Who'd sponsor you?'

'Our Navigator.'

'Our Navigator? But he doesn't even know your name.'

'He does now.'

'So this is what all that grovelling and sliming up was all about. This is what you wanted all along!'

'No, it isn't, but I'll take it.'

'But how can you? You know what my father thought about the Learning.'

'Yes I do, but I don't agree. He was wrong.'

'He was not wrong!' barked Wyn. 'He knew what was happening. And you know how they treated him!'

'Nobody did anything to him!' shouted Declan. 'He was eaten by a blaewhal.'

Wyn stood abruptly and went to leave. Declan scrambled to his feet to follow him.

'Wyn, wait!' he said. 'I'm sorry, my friend.' Wyn paused without turning. 'Look,' Declan went on, 'I know how you feel about the Learning. How they're leaving behind the old ways and how you don't like where they are leading us, but what if you're wrong? What if they are right and it's time for the Children to move into a new way of life?'

'What if I'm right?'

'How better to keep an eye on what they're doing? From the inside!'

Wyn did not respond.

'I know you don't like this but can't you at least be pleased for me?'

'No.' Wyn started to walk away but Declan grabbed his shoulder to hold him back. Instinctively Wyn shrugged his grip off.

'Wait, Wyn.' Declan grasped his arm more forcibly.

Perhaps it was the ale, perhaps it was pent-up resentment over his father's death, perhaps it was the heat of the day, but, whatever it was, it made Wyn suddenly see red. He spun around and grabbed Declan by the shirt. His powerful muscles bunched as he heaved his friend off his feet. With a snarl of rage he tossed him away.

Declan landed awkwardly, falling as his ankle gave way beneath him. His head hit the deck with a shockingly loud sound and he lay still. Wyn took a step towards him, but stopped in horror as he saw the blood start to pool behind his friend's motionless head. He sank to his knees and cried out, 'Somebody help me!'

Declan did not leave to join the Learning the next day, nor the next. He lay still, drifting in and out of consciousness for three weeks as the *Two Family Raft* made its way north. It was nearly the Season of Storms and they followed the schools of fish away from the fierce southern weather. They had to wait a few days for the Healers to arrive from the nearest Raft. With them came Morag, the daughter of the High Priestess.

She had spent time on their Raft before and Wyn had noticed her. He had always felt she thought well of him. How wrong he had been was made clear as soon as she saw him.

Her glare was colder than the southern wind. She walked up to him and stood silently staring.

'I wonder why you are still here,' she hissed. 'You should know by now that you are not welcome. Not even among your own people. Think about that.' She turned and swept away.

Morag stayed for three weeks, visiting Declan every day, sitting by his bed, wiping his brow and talking to him. It seemed she never stopped talking, except when Wyn entered the room. She would fall silent and stare at him until he left feeling hurt, angry and impotent.

When Declan was well enough to leave the Raft, he went with Morag back to the *Kelpie*. Wyn had not seen him since then.

The delay while they waited for a Healer to arrive had proved deadly, as the *Two Family Raft* was caught too far south when the Season of Storms started. Wyn could remember very little of the actual storm that howled out of the southern polar regions to smash into the *Two Family Raft*. Unusually, the storm gave plenty of warning of what was going to happen. One thing he could remember was the immense black thunderhead that towered over the horizon. The old Sailers sniffed the wind and frowned. There were shaking heads and furrowed brows as they watched the storm bear down on them.

It struck just before dawn.

By the time the sun broke through, the largest, most populated Raft the Children had ever built was badly damaged and listing. Hundreds floated dead on the heaving waters. Not even the fast attack ships had been able to outrun the ravening wind. Only five of the fleet had survived. These few now scoured the waters, seeking the living.

Wyn was dragged from the sea's grasp a scant hour before sunset after hours of the most acute terror he had imagined possible. Every moment in the water he spent looking over his shoulder expecting another monster wave to come and drive him into the black depths below him. For the first time in his life, Wyn experienced the deep fear that leaves scars on a man's soul. Even as he lay shivering and gasping on the deck of the ship, he knew that he would never be the same again.

24

Shanek awoke to the sounds and smells of a world at peace. Birds, the first he had heard for several days, twittered and whistled in the canopy above him, and the campsite was filling with the delicious aroma of cooking. He lay staring at the luxuriant greenery above him, watching as it drifted from black to grey as the sun's light penetrated the dense mat of foliage. Even the normally strident voices of the soldiers were hushed as they went about their business. It was one of those days that made him glad to be alive.

The First Son of the Empire felt a gentle peace suffuse him as he eased himself into wakefulness. It was an experience he had never known before, and for a brief, fleeting moment he forgot how far away he was from Ajyne. The simple pleasure of the forest, the company of his soldiers, the feeling of the ground beneath him were all as new joys to him. Faded from his mind were the sophisticated and increasingly jaded pleasures of the city.

All thoughts of the Army of the World, the Empire of the Asan and the treachery his father warned him of in his message were far from his thoughts as he lay on the ground. Beneath him even the slightly uneven earth digging into his back felt good. He revelled in the sensation.

A thought occurred to him. *Why Matrin?* There were several other languages he knew, some of which were even more arcane. And it would not be hard to hide messages in any of them. He rolled over and pulled the document out of his pack. Unrolling it, he noticed a mark he had not seen before.

He squinted at it. It was not a smudge, nor was it a random, incidental mark. It was a complex drawing. In the diffuse light of the morning, his eyes seemed to be playing tricks on him. The convoluted marks within the drawing whirled, shifting before his eyes.

Even as it writhed across the page, Shanek began to recognise the handiwork of Bedi.

'You old trickster,' gasped Shanek. 'How did you manage to get to a secret document sent from the Thane and the First Counsellor to the First Son?' He shook his head. No matter how impossible it seemed, he would not put it past Bedi. Not after all he'd seen.

Shanek lay back, staring once more up into the canopy, remembering the first time he had met old Bedi. It was during the month he'd spent in the Poor Quarter. Bedi was a soothsayer who plied his charlatanry on the side of a road near one of Hashan's stalls. Shanek was instructed to move the old beggar along. At first Bedi nodded and smiled. He started to gather his paltry belongings, then stopped.

'Shanek?' he asked, looking up at the First Son.

Shanek nodded.

'You are more than just another of Hashan's thugs, aren't you?' When Shanek shook his head, Bedi sat down again and unpacked.

'Hey!' said Shanek. 'I told you to move on!'

'I know,' said Bedi. Shanek went to kick the old man but hesitated. Bedi fixed him with a gaze that seemed to hold more than just an old man's fear. 'A coin, Sir? A single coin for an old man?' Bedi said.

'What? You want me to pay you for moving?'

'No, Sir. It is just a small recompense for a day's lost trade.'

Shanek snorted. 'Trade? You're nothing more than a charlatan, a trickster. You deserve to starve. Now be off.' He aimed a well-timed kick at Bedi. It caught him just below the ribs and sent him sprawling on the ground, amid his scant belongings.

The old man lay gasping in the wreckage of his livelihood. He looked up at Shanek. 'Just a coin, Sir. One coin.'

The First Son sneered and stalked away. As he did so, he fingered the coin in his pocket. It was his last. It was a shiny new coin, untarnished, unused to the rigours of human trade. Rolling it through his fingers, he caressed its surface. It reminded him of the skin of a girl he had taken. Her name escaped him. His throat went dry as he remembered. He missed the Palace, the clean clothes, the servants, the riches. He missed people taking note whenever he spoke, he missed being important. But now he was reduced to thinking about a coin.

He snorted derisively at his own thoughts. It was a coin, to be spent, used, traded. He put it back into his pouch, comforted by its solid weight against his leg. As he walked, he thought about what the coin would buy him. Maybe some food, maybe a night's lodging, maybe an hour with one of the local ladies. The women waiting for him at the hovel he currently referred to as home seemed far away. Only a few weeks here in the Poor Quarter and his view of the world had changed. These people he was being trained to lead, they were thugs, beneath his contempt. They scuttled about their meaningless lives, begging for a coin.

Pathetic! he thought, fingering the coin again.

He knew that Hashan was expecting him but he couldn't face any more of his empty posturings, so he went to a tavern. He took out his coin and spun it on the table before him.

He caught the eye of the ample serving woman. 'Wine,' he said curtly. She hesitated until he gestured at the coin, still spinning, shining, glinting on the table. The sooty orange light from the flickering torches reflected off its surface, staining it, defiling its purity. The woman nodded and scurried away. She left the coin rattling as it spun to a stop.

When she came back, she left his drink on the table, ignoring the coin with a wink. Perhaps she would want different payment later, Shanek mused. He raised the battered metal flask to his lips and drank deeply.

'Faugh!' He spat the wine onto the table. 'What is this?' he roared. The wine was foul. His stomach heaved. He lurched to his feet, snatching up his coin as he went. 'Barman! You will die for this! Poisoning me!' He staggered across the room towards the startled barman. His eyes became blurred and unfocused as he tried to reach the bar. Around him the room swum and spun, tilting until the floor leaped upwards and smashed into his face.

Stunned, he lay motionless for a moment, stomach heaving and head spinning. His breath came in short, rattling gasps and sweat poured off his body. He was burning. With a grunting effort he pushed himself to his feet, leaning on his sword, which he could not remember drawing. The room had not slowed in its sickening motion.

He stood with his own vomit staining his dirty tunic. He couldn't remember vomiting. The room slowly stopped its crazy spinning. A few moments later he felt able to stand without support. Then his ability to walk returned. He took a few staggering steps towards the staring barman.

'Poison.' He croaked. 'You tried to poison me. You die for this.'

'No. No. Sir. Not poison. Only our finest do we serve for you. Only our finest.' He was babbling, almost incoherent in fear. Normally such naked fear would have brought Shanek some satisfaction, but all he could do was concentrate on staying upright. Somehow the barman managed to move out from behind the bar and dart to the table where Shanek's unfinished tankard rested. With his heart in his eyes, the barman raised it to his lips and drained it to the last drop.

'You see, Sir? No poison. Surely you are unwell, Sir. Allow me to fetch a healer to you.' Around the tavern a few chuckles were quietly beginning. As the still First Son lurched around to face his mockers, he once more lost balance and crashed to the floor. The chuckles built to a storm of laughter. The room swam again as the laughter rose to a crescendo that threatened to swamp his battered senses. Somehow Shanek clambered back to his feet and weaved his way outside.

The First Son of the Empire slept with the rats in an alley. It rained during the night and he awoke in mud, with cockroaches on his face and refuse as a pillow. His waking thought was for clean water and good food. The water trickling by his pounding head looked clean enough so he lapped at it like a dog. Immediately he spat it from his mouth and tried to leap to his feet. The leap was more like a lurch and startled the ragged man near him. The man looked at Shanek pityingly, re-fastened his breeches and limped away.

Food. The thought was loud in Shanek's fuddled brain. So he left his alley, his evening's resting place, and went in search of what his body needed. Around him the normal routine of life continued. Women and children walked the streets, men laughed and bargained, dogs whined, and above him the sun glowed brightly. Too brightly. He shaded his eyes from the stabbing glare and staggered on.

Food. He walked through the baking morning sun. Already the heat was drying the overnight rain, turning the mud to dust. Food. He must have food. Following his nose to a baker, he lurched against the door. He was a big man, and the door was old and poorly made. He crashed through it and found himself once again sprawled on the floor. He fumbled in his pocket for his last coin. With a shaking hand he offered it as he lay on the ground to the big woman with flour on her face.

'Bread,' he asked, his voice no more than a whispering scrape of sound. He proffered the coin again.

'Well, now. If it's bread ye'll be after, it'll cost ye more than that poor coin there. Here take this old crust and be off with ye.' She tossed him an old hard loaf-end and took up a broom. Beating him soundly, the large, heavy woman drove Shanek out into the street. The coin he had offered her slipped through his fingers. Glinting in the sunlight, it fell and rolled until it slowed and spun on its axis as it lost energy. With a metallic rattle it rocked crazily until it lay next to him on the cobbles. He grunted and picked it up.

'Well, little coin, it seems no one wants you.' He shoved the shiny coin back into his pocket.

Shanek staggered off down the dusty street, gnawing on the old crust. So intent was he on his hunger that he had nearly finished it before he even looked at it. One look and he hurled it to the ground in disgust and his stomach heaved. He retched dryly from his empty stomach as he watched the cockroach-infested loaf squirming in the dirt. He shuddered as he tried not to think of how many of the insects he had already eaten. Falling to his knees, dry retching, he could almost feel the 'roaches scuttling about in his gut. How long he stayed there, retching, coughing, gasping in the gutter, the sun beating on his neck, he couldn't say. At some stage he passed out. He drifted in and out of consciousness for most of the day, his mind tortured by images of cockroaches and fat women with brooms. When the cool of the evening brushed over him, he stirred and roused himself. The pains had gone, his stomach no longer rebelled, but the memories persisted. How could some bad wine and bread have made him so unwell? At the time he gave no thought to Bedi or the possibility that there was more to his illness than simple stomach problems. That thought came later.

Bedi was back in the market next morning. Shanek had slept badly, again in the street, as he could not face going home. As he passed the old man, he tossed the coin into the begging bowl.

The beggar grinned a crooked grin and pocketed it. 'I knew there was hope for you, Servant of the World. Sit down here in the dirt with a charlatan.' Despite his irritation, Shanek sat before the old man and began to listen. It was almost an hour before he realised he was speaking in Matrin. Thus commenced a daily ritual that lasted until the time came for Shanek to leave the poor streets. Every morning he would sit with Bedi and discuss the history of the Asan Empire, or the Empire of the World, as Bedi insisted on calling it.

The First Son had received an exquisite education. All the finest minds from across the Empire instructed him in all that was known. He studied under great philosophers, mathematicians, scientists and generals. There was no matter too small or too arcane that he was not expected to master in his quest to fulfil his duty to the Empire.

The history he learned from his teachers was a rich and bloody tale of massive conquest as the Army of the World carved their way across the continent.

They were irresistible, led by the uncanny brilliance of the hereditary First Counsellors. Many times Shanek cried out in surprise as he read about a seemingly impossible manoeuvre that extricated the Empire's forces from destruction. No one ever mentioned it, and most flatly denied it, but Shanek often wondered if the First Counsellors had access to some knowledge that gave them understanding beyond the normal human ken.

He even asked his father, once. Sandor gazed at his only child in bewilderment. 'How can you ask such a thing, Shanek?' he said. 'If I had any supernatural advantage, don't you think I would have shared it with you? No, my son, we First Counsellors are trained and skilled, not magical.'

The history that Bedi spoke of, however, was more than this. He told tales of mighty magics and mystical forces. In this history, the First Counsellors had a different title. Bedi called them Servants of the World, and he insisted on using this title when addressing Shanek.

'You have a heritage, Servant of the World,' he would say. 'It is a heritage, not a role. You are the guardian of the world. You can hear him, you can know him and he will need you.'

'He?' asked Shanek. 'Who is this?'

Bedi smiled his irritating, smug grin and would not answer. He only ever said, 'One day, Servant, one day. You will know.'

Years later, Shanek, First Son of the Empire, Servant of the World, lay on the ground under a canopy of leaves that softened the sun's glare to a subtle green glow, looking at a mystical sigil that swirled and shifted. 'Bedi,' he whispered. 'What have you left for me to discover?'

Even after a whole day pondering the strange sigil, Shanek was no closer to discerning what Bedi had left for him. He was not even sure any more whether it was the soothsayer's work. The bizarre swirling stopped after a few minutes, leaving a highly stylised picture of a set of balance scales. It was a design that looked vaguely familiar to Shanek, but try as he might he could not remember where he had seen it before.

After the evening meal, Shanek sat staring into the fire with a cup of water in his hands. Diplomat Cherise came and sat beside him.

'First Son,' he said. 'You have been very distracted today. Is anything troubling you?'

Shanek looked at the Diplomat. In his fascination with the mystical symbol left on the document, he had almost forgotten the message his father had hidden in the script. If there was treachery in Ajyne, so much that Sandor and Kasimar had felt it necessary to send him away on a spurious mission, then surely Cherise was above suspicion. He regarded the aged face, ravaged by the last stages of Danan fever, and made a decision.

'Cherise,' he said, 'are you aware of the contents of the Thane's command?'

'Yes, First Son. I have read it.'

'Did you happen to translate it from Matrin into symbolic Matrin?'

'No, First Son. My symbolic Matrin is not what it should be.'

341

'You know that the symbols have numerous meanings depending on the context?'

'Yes, First Son.'

'When I read the command I felt it was badly worded. Clumsy, overwritten. So I took all the words and phrases that were unnecessary and translated them into symbolic Matrin. Then I read them vertically, as ancient Matrin is traditionally written.'

Diplomat Cherise gave every appearance of listening politely, but he was too intent, too focused. He disguised it well, but Shanek recognised the signs. Cherise was expecting something. *Are you involved?* Shanek wondered.

'Did you discover anything?' asked Cherise.

Shanek feigned a wry smile. 'My father and the Thane have played a joke on us I fear, Diplomat.' To give himself a moment to think, Shanek took a sip of his drink. 'Whilst the sheep-trading agreement is real, it is written to hide a very funny joke at the Ettans' expense.' As he spoke, Shanek watched the Diplomat closely. Relief, well-hidden, but present, flooded the old man's features. 'Is there any truth in the rumour that Ettans are uniformly stupid?'

Cherise smiled. 'No, First Son, the Ettan people are most hospitable and kind, but the jokes about them are funny.'

Shanek laughed easily, apparently sharing a pleasant moment, but inwardly his mind was racing. *You* are *involved, burn you! How much do you know? Why are you here?*

Across the fire, Leone watched them closely. Shanek had not spoken a word to her for two days, not since he had read something in the document.

342

She did not know what he had found but she knew it was not a joke about Ettans. His silence worried her. It was not normal for him, and it usually led to an outburst of some kind, usually a sudden surge of sexual activity. Out here in this oddly quiet forest, she wondered what form his response would take. Her first thought was some sort of violence against Caldorman Muttiah. The First Son's responses to the aged warrior had been growing increasingly hostile over the past few days.

A cry shattered the evening quiet. Leone leaped to her feet, sword drawn. The other soldiers also sprang up, looking towards the sound. They paused, as if waiting for Leone's direction, and another cry split the night. It was a cry of agony. There was no need for spoken orders; Leone's look and curt gesture was all the soldiers needed.

Even as they hurried to the aid of their comrade, the sounds of a large animal cut across the cries of pain.

'Arox,' someone hissed. Leone muffled a curse. The large predator often hunted in packs, sometimes numbering up to ten. With the losses to her Fyrd, their numbers were not enough to fight off a large pack of arox beasts. Coming to a hard decision, she stopped running.

'Hold!' she bellowed. 'Regroup by the campfire!' The cries of pain ceased, replaced by the sickening crunching of bones as the arox started to feed. 'Regroup!' Leone called again.

It was testament to the superb training of the Fyrds that they obeyed Leone's command without hesitation. Once they were back she and Malik had them ring the campsite, facing outwards. Within the defensive ring were Muttiah and Cherise. Shanek insisted on standing beside Leone.

The noise of the arox feeding faded as it finished its ghastly meal.

'How many are there?' a nervous voice asked.

'Three,' said Shanek without thinking. He gestured to his left, 'One there, one there,' pointing to the right, 'and the one eating Ashfaq.'

Leone waved a soldier to reinforce the left and another to the right. It was as well she did, for no sooner had they taken up their positions than two aroxii plunged out of the undergrowth.

No amount of planning or training can ever prepare even the hardiest soldier for their first sight of a charging arox. A full-grown beast can stand as high as a man at the shoulder. Their porcine features, fangs and large curving tusks are usually enough to send a shiver through anyone, but when they charge they utter a loud squeal that is as painfully penetrating as it is incongruous. They attack with their tusks, seeking to disembowel their victim, and with their fearsome front claws, not unlike the raking attack of a large cat. Covered in thick fur, they are normally found in the northern wastes, and the ones that drift south are often enraged by the heat.

The arox on Shanek's left crashed into a soldier, taking her to the ground. Her cry of pain was quickly cut off as the arox ripped her open with a single sweep of its tusks. With blood and entrails dangling about its snout, it turned to the nearest soldier and squealed as it lashed out with its right paw. The soldier had fast reactions and threw himself back so that the claws just raked across his chest, leaving four bloody trails slashed through his armour. He fell back screaming. The arox lowered its head and, standing over the fallen woman, regarded the others who were circling around it with swords outstretched. It shook its massive head and charged into the ring of waiting steel.

The arox to Shanek's right approached more cautiously, almost as if sizing up its opponents. It walked slowly out of the bushes and stared at the waiting soldiers. Shanek tensed. The noise of the other arox tearing at the soldiers to his left seemed to fade as he focused on the one nearer him. The whistle of the bolas attracted the arox's attention, and it turned a baleful glare upon the First Son. Leone stepped up, edging ahead of Shanek.

She raised her sword and faced the arox. 'Stay back, First Son,' she whispered.

The arox shifted its gaze to Leone, then looked back, straight at Shanek. For a moment their eyes locked, neither able nor willing to break the contact. Leone, aware that her movement did not distract it, took a step forward and away from Shanek.

With breathtaking speed the arox charged. Leone recognised instantly that Shanek was in danger and dropped to her knee, swiping her sword at the arox's leg as it thundered past her. The blade cut deep, severing nerve and sinew, causing the beast to stumble. Shanek moved quickly to attack from the opposite side and used the manoeuvre he tried on Leone in the Training Arena. He swung his bolas so that one ball spun towards the uninjured foreleg, while the other went to the head.

The arox was already staggering to the left, and when Shanek dragged back on the bolas cord, jerking the right leg outwards and the head down to the right, there was a loud crack. The beast squealed in agony as its leg snapped. It fell heavily, thrashing its hind legs, attempting to gore anything that came within range of its tusks.

Shanek let go of the cord and drew his sword. He darted in and drove his blade deep into the arox's back, just beside the spine. Thick red blood spurted out, drenching Shanek's arm as the arox stiffened.

'First Son!' called Leone.

Shanek dragged his sword out of the dead arox. 'I'm fine, Leone.' He looked wryly at his blood-soaked clothes. 'A bit wet and sticky but uninjured. None of the blood's mine.'

'Stand clear, First Son,' she said. 'These things are hard to kill. It may not be dead yet.'

'It's dead,' he said. 'Trust me.'

Leone nodded and turned her attention to where the other arox was battling for its life. It was clear that it had wreaked havoc upon the Fyrds. Several soldiers lay dead or badly injured, but the beast was in its death throes. Before she could take two paces towards it, it shuddered and fell, bleeding from dozens of wounds.

Silence descended, punctuated only by the groans of the dying. Leone knelt to examine a wounded member of her Fyrd. It was Ekaterina. She was lying still, her eyes unfocused, as she felt her lifeblood flow out of the gaping wound in her chest. The arox had torn her open with its tusks, revealing shattered ribs and slashed lungs. Her breathing was short and shallow, and the gurgling in her throat told Leone that she was close to death.

The Coerl held Ekaterina's hand. It was cold and clammy with no strength in the grasp. 'You are dying, Ekaterina,' Leone told her. 'You fought well and the arox is dead. The First Son is safe and uninjured.'

'Coerl,' Ekaterina gasped. 'Tell the First Son I am sorry.'

'Sorry for what, Ekaterina?'

'I will not be able to aid him in his mission.'

'True, Ekaterina, you won't, but dying here has aided him. If you had fled and lived, he would have died,' she said. 'You die a good soldier. Your Coerl is proud of you.'

A faint smile eased its way past the agony. 'Thank you, Coerl,' Ekaterina said with her last breath.

Around Leone the dying continued, as it would for a number of days. Even with the cursory look she had given the others, it was clear that most of the injured would die. She closed her eyes and bowed her head over Ekaterina's body, silently reciting the Warriors' Way of Purity.

The courage to stand, the strength to fight
The honesty to fear, the compassion to serve
The humility to obey, the grace to die
The love to command, the Warriors' way to purity
The service of the world demands
The peace of the world repays

That done, she stood up and started thinking about the burials.

347

'How many dead?' asked Shanek from behind her.

'Four, First Son,' she replied without turning. 'And two more from Malik's Fyrd.'

'Will any survive?'

'Of the injured, First Son? No.' He did not reply, but she heard him murmuring the Warriors' Way of Purity as he walked away. She sighed, took a deep breath and buried the pain away. 'Harin, Akash!' she called.

The two men trotted over to her. 'Coerl,' Harin said.

'We need to put our dead to Rest,' she said. 'Too many have fallen without proper honour. Akash, take Gayathri and find Ashfaq's body. Harin, put together a burial party. I'll officiate.' The two men saluted and went about their tasks.

The formal Resting of a Soldier of the World was a solemn yet simple process. First the body is ceremonially cleansed in clean earth, then it is laid face down on the ground while the Warriors' Way of Purity is recited by all gathered. The senior officers responsible for their safety then apologise for their failure and the body is buried seven measures deep.

Leone watched impassively while the bodies of her four dead soldiers were cleansed in the dirt of this burned forest. She stood nearly motionless during the recitation; only her lips were moving as she muttered the Way. Malik stood beside her, facing his first Resting as Coerl.

After the Way was finished and the graves dug, Leone and Malik stepped forward. The gathered soldiers murmured in surprise as Shanek stepped up beside them.

'We, those set aside to protect those gathered here,' intoned the three, 'seek forgiveness from those left alive. We failed in our duty to these who Rest, and stand guilty of their deaths. We seek the forgiveness of those who Rest here, and vow to give our best to those who remain.' The three stepped back, and the remaining soldiers covered the bodies of their fallen comrades.

When the graves were covered and the final farewells said, Shanek walked away from the Fyrds. He made his way towards Caldorman Muttiah.

'A word, Caldorman,' he muttered. With a curt gesture, he called Muttiah aside, into the darkness of the forest.

When they were alone in the dark, Shanek waited in silence.

'A good ceremony, First Son. The Fyrds were moved and gratified by your decision to take part,' the Caldorman said.

'Tell me, Caldorman, who is the senior soldier in this group?' Shanek hissed.

Muttiah stiffened as he realised Shanek's intention. 'I am, First Son,' he said.

'So who exactly is responsible for the safety of every soldier here?'

'I am, First Son,' Muttiah conceded. His eyes widened suddenly, the whites gleaming obscenely in the darkness as Shanek's dagger found its mark. The First Son felt the Caldorman's final heartbeat tremble through the handle of his knife.

'Lie here without Rest,' Shanek muttered. He knelt and took the Caldorman's dagger of rank. The Thane's Needle was a poignard more than a dagger.

Long and thin, its blade was designed for stabbing rather than slashing or cutting. Every Coerl received their own Needle as part of the promotion ceremony. 'You don't deserve to die with this,' Shanek snarled. As he went to walk away, he paused and spat on the old man's face. He turned from the body and looked back through the trees at the glimmer of light from the campfire. Around him the forest was quiet. None of the normal sounds of scurrying or rustling reached his ears. The muted sounds of conversation filtered through the trees. He had committed cold-blooded murder here and nothing was different. No one had challenged him. No one had watched the old soldier draw his last breath. No one cared. Shanek was troubled, not by the direction of his thoughts, but by their existence. He had killed before, often for less reason than this, but he stood still with blood dripping from his unsheathed dagger and wondered what his latest murder meant. Domovoi had once told him that every killing left a mark on the killer and nothing could ever remove that mark. When pressed, the Appointed One had admitted that he had never killed anyone, so Shanek gave him a slave to kill. He refused to kill her; instead he took her home and freed her.

Why am I thinking about that now? Shanek wondered. He shook his head, sheathed his dagger and strode back towards the fire.

When he entered the circle of light around the campfire, every pair of eyes turned to watch him.

'Muttiah has decided to leave us and seek Purity,' Shanek lied.

Cherise frowned. 'That is a surprise, First Son. He never mentioned this desire to me.'

'What can I say?' Shanek shrugged. 'The decision is always a personal one and it obviously came on the Caldorman suddenly.' He sat down and looked around. Hofie handed him a steaming mug of jerva. He took it and drained it. 'I have decided to promote Coerl Leone to Caldorman,' he said after wiping his mouth on his sleeve. With disgust he tasted Muttiah's blood.

'I see,' the Diplomat said. 'But Leone . . . ?'

'Leone is the senior soldier here now that Muttiah has deserted, so I am granting her a field promotion.'

'But —' Cherise started.

'But nothing, old man!' Shanek shouted. He surged to his feet. 'You dare to question my decision?'

'No, First Son. Of course not. My apologies,' he muttered.

'Now, go away, Diplomat, I need to consult with the Caldorman.' Shanek waved a dismissal at Cherise and sat down again. The Diplomat bowed and shuffled away. The First Son beckoned to Leone. She had been watching the exchange and was ready for the summons.

'Caldorman Leone,' Shanek said. 'I like the sound of that.'

'So do I, First Son. Thank you.'

Shanek looked away. 'You deserve it. Certainly a lot more than that ancient dodderer did.'

'And what shall I do with his body, First Son?' whispered Leone.

Shanek whipped his head around. 'What?' he demanded.

'His body, First Son. Did you really intend for him to lie without Rest?'

'Yes,' he snapped.

'Very well, First Son.'

'How did you know?' Shanek asked.

'I didn't, First Son, but when I saw you and the Caldorman leave together, I guessed.'

Shanek laughed. 'Burn me, you're good, Caldorman Leone.' Leone bowed her head in acceptance of the compliment, pleased that the discipline of the Fyrd had held. No one believed the First Son's story for a moment, but equally no one would dare challenge him. No with her around, they wouldn't.

The map that the Diplomat was following indicated that they were finally coming to the border of the forest. After so long under the dark canopy, they were all looking forward to seeing the sun again, but as they moved towards the edge of the forest Shanek grew increasingly tense and distracted. His horse had developed a slight limp and rather than swap horses and risk his stallion to someone else's care, he decided to walk him. The dense undergrowth and narrowness of the trail had limited them to a walking pace anyway, so his decision did not slow their progress. Beneath his bare feet, the leaf litter was soft and oddly comforting. The border of the forest was visible when Shanek realised with a start what was making him nervous. They were being hunted! The third arox! He'd forgotten it in the events of the previous night!

'Leone!' he called.

'First Son?' she asked.

'Have we anyone on patrol over there?' He gestured to the right.

'Yes, First Son. Harin.'

'Send someone out to check on him. Preferably someone good with a lance or polearm of some sort.'

Leone saluted and turned to give the necessary orders. Gayathri urged her horse off the trail and plunged into the bushes.

Leone watched her go, then turned back to Shanek.

'First Son,' she started. 'Was there a reason for your orders?'

Shanek stared at Leone, then remembered that as Caldorman she had the right to request the reason for orders, after she had obeyed them of course.

'The third arox. I think it's tracking us,' he said.

Leone's eyes widened as she realised that she too had forgotten about it. 'And the polearm, First Son?'

'It will keep it at bay long enough to call for help,' Shanek said. 'I think it's already taken Harin.'

He caught Leone's look of puzzlement before she looked away. He wasn't surprised; *he* was puzzled by his intense feelings of *knowing* things that he should not know. It started with the time he had sensed her move in the Training Arena and had continued ever since. It was as if he could *feel* Harin's blood seeping into the ground, the powerful arox claws gouging the soft earth and the fear of Harin's horse as she trotted away from her rider's dead body. This time, instead of dismissing the feelings, he decided to concentrate on them. He closed his eyes and focused on the arox.

Angry, hungry. The beast was a powerful creature, full of rage and base instincts. He was dominated by the overwhelming need to

353

kill, to tear, to eat. He was hunting the whole
party, picking them off one at a time.

Scent! Another comes! Low, get low. Hide.
A call!

It was a harsh, shrill and incomprehensible cry, but
the arox sensed the emotion in it.

When did I call out? wondered Shanek.

The arox hid, watching as a human on a horse
trotted past. She paused, also hearing the call.
Another rider came into view. The arox beast's
anger rose as it sensed another kill being taken
away. The new rider stopped beside the first
and spoke to her animatedly. The beast could
not understand her words through the arox's
ears, but when she looked directly into the
beast's eyes and drew her sword, he felt the
threat.

With a squeal of rage, he leaped out of the
bushes and hurled himself onto the rider and
horse.

Leone looked out into the forest, watching Gayathri
ride away. She was the best with the bardiche. The
weapon's length, together with the vicious, curved
axe blade, might give her an advantage should she
encounter an arox. Leone was troubled. Shanek was
beginning to scare her. These odd flashes of insight
he'd been having were disturbing, not only for their
existence, but for their uncanny accuracy. The way
he had dived across the stream. How had he known

that Tapash had fired an arrow? Unless the Tribesman was so far away that his shot was in the air that long, in which case he was the best archer to ever live, or Shanek had known he was about to fire. How could he know before the arrow was released? What about the aroxii last night? He knew how many, where they were and what they were doing. How was that possible?

'Gayathri!' Shanek screamed. 'Look out!'

Something inside Leone responded without thought. She was urging her horse through the undergrowth before she realised what she was doing. Gayathri was moving carefully and she was startled when her Caldorman galloped up behind her.

'Be careful!' shouted Leone. 'There!' She gestured at what the soldier had taken as an old log half-hidden under a bush. The arox squealed as it surged up and leaped at Leone.

Both women were trained and experienced warriors, and despite being surprised by the sudden attack they were able to react with the split-second responses of experts. Gayathri swung her bardiche with a smooth round-arm action. It sliced across the arox's side, opening up a deep gash, slicing through to the ribs. As solid as the blow was, it was not sufficient to slow the huge beast's momentum. It crashed heavily into Leone's horse, opening its throat with a savage swipe. The horse collapsed under the sudden weight and went down squealing. It broke a foreleg as the arox landed, the sickening crack echoing through the forest. Leone was thrown off, her sword spinning out of her hand. She lay winded as the arox turned towards her.

The arox's squeal faded to a deep throaty purr. With its own blood streaming down its matted fur and pooling at its feet, the arox slowly moved towards Leone. Gayathri yelled and swung her bardiche downwards with every ounce of strength she possessed, but it smashed onto the beast's spine and bounced off, sending a brutal jarring along its length. The arox whipped its head around and squealed at her, then resumed its approach on Leone.

She gasped as she urgently tried to get air back into her lungs, but as she went to stand her ankle gave way. It was broken from the fall. She collapsed back onto the ground. The arox was so close she could smell its breath, the rotten, foul stench of the carnivore. Its fanged mouth slavered, dripping blood from an earlier kill. For the first time Leone knew terror. Frantically she scrabbled at the leaves, trying to pull herself along the ground. She edged away, but the arox reached out and sank its claws into her leg.

Leone screamed as she was dragged back towards the arox. With the strength of desperation, she kicked and thrashed, raining blows from her uninjured leg onto its head, but she may as well have been kicking a tree for all the effect this had. When the beast had dragged her close enough, it retracted its claws and stepped forward. All of its weight rested on her broken ankle. She felt she would pass out from the agony as it stepped on her other leg and started to move towards her head. Seeing her death in the eyes that drew closer, she launched a frenzied attack, pounding at its massive head with both of her fists. Almost casually, it turned slightly and took her arm in its mouth. White-hot agony shot through

Leone as the powerful jaws slowly closed, the fangs tearing through muscle and bone. In horror, she lay helpless as the arox eased itself down on top of her and bit off her arm.

She struggled to breathe as the huge mass crushed her. Her head rang with lack of air. The last thing she remembered seeing before she consigned her life to the Rest was her arm disappearing down the beast's throat.

Shanek fell to his knees, retching as the taste of Leone's blood stung his throat.

'First Son!' called Malik. 'Are you all right?'

'Get everyone out there, right now!' he gestured to where Leone lay. 'The arox. Go!'

The shock of what he had just experienced left him exhausted and dazed. He lay on his back feeling Leone's agony simultaneously with the arox's relish at eating her flesh, as well as its annoyance at being pounded by Gayathri. The bizarre combination of images and sensations threatened his grasp on sanity. He groaned and writhed in pain as he lay, feeling Leone's lifeblood pour out onto the soft earth.

Unconsciousness was a welcome guest, bringing a gentle release.

Shanek came to under a clear, bright sky. The sun shone down benignly and nearby a river meandered past, bubbling over rocks. For a moment he lay comfortably, revelling in the feeling of sunshine on his face. The sound of voices intruded on his pleasure.

'Will she live?'

'I don't think so.'

'Are there any of her Fyrd still alive?'

'Just me and Hofie and Gayathri.'

'So it's just the two, then. You're the Coerl of our Fyrd.'

'I keep forgetting that.'

Shanek stirred. 'Where's Leone?' he asked.

Malik leaped to his feet. 'First Son,' he said. 'Leone is over there.'

Shanek lurched unsteadily to his feet. Leone was lying on a makeshift litter. She was grey. Her right arm was heavily bandaged, but that could not disguise the fact that half her upper arm was gone. Blood seeped through the wrappings, mostly torn blankets, that covered most of her body. Her breathing was shallow and sweat beaded her face. As Shanek approached, a member of Malik's Fyrd stood.

'First Son,' she said. 'I am Myandra. I have some training in medical care.'

'How is she?' he asked.

'She will die soon, First Son,' Myandra said. 'Caldorman Leone has lost too much blood and the shock of losing her arm will kill her.'

Shanek nodded. 'Keep her warm. We wait here until she is gone.'

Myandra saluted.

Rather than sit and watch her die, Shanek walked away to regard the surroundings. The campsite was beside a river that ran slowly along the base of a range of hills that stretched away to the east and the west. To the east they turned south, seeming to merge with the forest, and to the west they gradually reduced, leading into a plain. The forest ended about fifty paces away from the river. To the north lay the Great Fastness, its grasses waving and rippling in the wind. The hills that rose from the other side of the river were covered in low bushes. They looked lush and inviting.

Hunt!
No, we must not, not yet.
There is more to do.

Thoughts that were not his own rang in his mind. Shanek's recent experience with the arox beast gave him pause to think. This was a voice, not an instinct. Someone intelligent was out there.

He looked back to where Leone lay dying. His emotions were in more turmoil than he was used to. He knew that he could not simply sit and watch her die, and this gave him a perfect excuse to leave.

He thought about taking an escort but decided against it. There were too few of his Fyrd left alive, and he did not trust the members of Muttiah's old command. Briefly he toyed with the thought of letting Cherise know what he was planning to do, but he could not see any point. The old Diplomat was not his keeper, and the First Son did not answer to him. He waited until Cherise was deep in conversation with Malik, and slipped away.

The river was shallow. His feet tingled with the icy chill as he made his way across. As soon as he stepped onto the opposite bank, he felt as if a weight had been lifted from his shoulders. He stopped and breathed in the clean, crisp air with relish. Without looking back, he started walking up the hill.

It was late afternoon by the time he reached the summit. The sun had already dropped behind the hill, leaving the forest in darkness, but Shanek stood atop the hill and watched the sun dip beneath the horizon. To the north, the Great Fastness shone gold in the last rays of the day. Beyond the grassland, he could just make out the first of the volcanoes that dotted the Arc Mountains. From the reddish glow that was visible against the darkening sky, it was clear that some were becoming active again. He wondered why.

A movement on the slope below caught his eye. He strained to make out what it was. As he looked, he froze. Skrin Tia'k. A knot of about ten was making its way up towards him. From the way they were moving, it did not look as if they were a war knot, although Asan knowledge of wild Skrinnies was limited, so it was possible they were unaware of the camp.

Shanek looked back towards the campsite. They had a fire burning, making it impossible to miss. He regarded the Skrinnie knot. They were moving fast. Out here, alone, armed only with a bolas, he could not hope to survive in a fight. Could he make it down to the camp before the Skrinnies? Not a chance, he realised. The arthropoid creatures could move with astonishing speed, even through undergrowth. He could never outrun them now, and if he tried they would cut him down before he came within earshot of the camp.

Could he draw them away from the camp and elude them somehow? He crouched behind a bush, pondering.

Hungry! We are hungry.

The thought, as powerful as it was unexpected, shot through Shanek, almost making him cry out loud. In the deepening gloom Shanek smiled. It was just like the arox; he could hear the Skrinnies!

Spread out, find the beast.

Shanek listened to the thoughts in his head, able to track where every Skrinnie was. He needed to take them down the slope, away from the camp. Their voices, somehow different, somehow all the same, spoke in his head. He could understand their clicking, sense where they were.

There! It is there! It runs! Come, nestlings, we feed on beast tonight.

All the nestlings followed, their powerful legs carrying them over bushes, past rocks in pursuit of the beast that enslaved so many.

Gone! It hides. There; you, there; you, look there; you, go to that bush; you, go to that shadow. All have places to look. We will find it.

No; it is not here; nor here; nor here. It eludes. Sound! There!

Freeze it! The beast eludes. It flees.

But it flees down.

Yes, down, beast. Go down to the flatland. Go down to where the nesters wait.

Noise! There! Hunt!

A bolas! It hunts us! There!

The nestlings ran as one to the sound of the bolas, the ancient enemy of their kind. Long

*have the beasts fought us with their feeble
weapons. Their pointed steel that scrapes our
shells, their sharp flying sticks that rattle off
us, we scorn them. But a bolas! It tangles, it
breaks, it brings us down!*

Hunt the beast!

Where is it? It eludes! Hunt!

Shanek dodged the Skrinnies as they pursued him.
He waited to hear where they went, then went the
other way. He hid where they were not looking, he
ran as they searched. In the exhilaration of the chase,
he did not have time to ponder what he was learning,
but he knew he would remember it all.

By the time he reached the flatland, the Skrinnie
knot was looking for him a hundred paces to his
right. He almost laughed out loud as he listened to
their increasingly angry clicking.

No wonder you lost, he thought.

With a final look back to check that none of the
knot was searching his way, he jogged to the west.
He had travelled so far west on the slope that it
would be easier to go around the hill and back to the
river than to go back up and over.

It would have worked, but he got careless. He
heard a warning in his head, but thinking it was still
the Skrinnies he ignored it.

The arrow took him high in the chest, punching
through just under his collarbone. The impact spun
him around, throwing him to the ground.

Twelve horses were coming towards him.

Where'd they come from? he thought as he faded
into unconsciousness.

* * *

'What do we have here, then? A pretty boy?'

Shanek coughed and spluttered as water was thrown onto his face. His shoulder ached, but the arrow was gone. His eyes were covered and his hands were tied behind his back.

'A pretty boy? Way out here in the Fastness?' the voice went on. Shanek recognised the accent as Ettan, but not that of a city dweller. *Probably a Tribesman*, he reasoned.

'Just kill him, Ejaj,' another voice called. 'The knot will be back soon.'

Shanek was lying on the ground. Rather than focusing on listening to the loud chatter all around him, he concentrated on listening to his mind.

Twelve men. No, four were women. A bound figure lying on the ground with a bloodied shoulder. Conversation. Fear, worried looks around. The horses are restive, snorting and tossing their heads. Skrin Tia'k are close. One woman draws a sword. The big man, apparently in charge, nods. No words pass between the two of them. She swings at the bound figure.

Shanek rolled aside as the sword drove into the ground. He heard the woman hiss in annoyance. She drew back and took another swing. Shanek watched her with his mind, leaving his dodge until the last possible moment. The sword thrummed in protest as it slammed once more into the dirt.

The chatter around him died.

363

'What the . . . ?' started the big leader. He was cut off by Shanek's well-timed and powerful kick that smashed unerringly into his groin. He went down clutching himself, groaning in pain.

Shanek scrambled to his feet. Still blindfolded he spun around to face the armed woman.

'Want to try again?' he snarled.

Her eyes widened and she thrust at him. It was a clumsy thrust that he easily avoided by turning aside. As she stumbled past him, he tripped her. She fell heavily. While she was down and the rest were watching dumbfounded, he knelt beside her and, with his uninjured left hand, snatched her dagger from its sheath and cut his bonds.

He toyed with the idea of removing his blindfold, but rejected it. Behind him a man reacted faster than his fellows and drew his sword. Shanek swivelled, dropped to one knee and hurled the dagger. The man gurgled and went down when the hilt thudded into his forehead. Still kneeling, Shanek placed both his hands on the ground in front of him and threw his feet out backwards, catching the woman behind him as she clambered to her feet. She grunted and went down again, her sword falling out of her hand.

Shanek picked up the sword and whipped it around to rest on the throat of the leader who was slowly regaining his breath.

'I don't like your attitude,' Shanek hissed. 'Call off your rabble or I gut you like the pig you are.'

The man was pale with pain and shock. His eyes still watered but he was able to stare at Shanek.

'Who are you?' he whispered.

'Shanek.'

'Shanek,' the leader started, starting to rise.

'I never said you could stand up,' Shanek said, exerting a little more pressure on the man's throat. He sank back to the ground.

'Had we known you were blind we would never have shot you,' the leader went on.

Shanek tore off his blindfold. 'Who said I was blind?'

'But to fight as you do, blindfolded ...'

Shanek smiled coldly. 'You are not the best fighters I have faced. I could take you left-handed and blindfolded.'

'You are not even left-handed?'

'No. But you shot me.'

'Burn it!' cursed the leader. 'Shanek, would you like to join us?'

Shanek pondered the offer. With Leone dying, most of his Fyrd gone and the mission, such as it was, in tatters, he had no reason to stay here. And yet there was his father's message; if there was treachery in Ajyne, what chance did he have if he went home? Even so, he could not simply desert the soldiers he'd left behind.

'What do you offer me if I do?' he asked finally.

'Freedom. The sky for a roof, the earth for a bed, all the Skrinnies you can kill, all the wealth you can carry.'

'I have something to do, otherwise your offer is interesting.'

Ejaj regarded Shanek carefully. 'This something you have to do, does it involve the knot we saw earlier?'

Shanek nodded.

'They went over the hill a while ago, after they'd given up on you.'

'How long was I out?'

'Hour, maybe two.'

'Where am I?'

'Not far from where you fell.'

'I have to go,' Shanek said. He turned and looked around. The hill was not far away, but it would be quicker to head directly to the river and follow it back to the camp. With a muttered, 'Purity go with you,' he started to jog away.

They parted and allowed him to leave, but before he had gone a hundred paces, he heard hoofbeats behind him.

'Hey,' called Ejaj.

Shanek turned his head.

'You'd be quicker on a horse.'

By the time they arrived at the campsite, he knew it was too late. The Skrin Tia'k knot had managed to overwhelm the entire Fyrd. There were bodies strewn about, all bearing the heavy slash marks characteristic of wild Skrinnies.

'Burn it!' cried Shanek. He leaped off his horse and ran to where Leone had been. There was a lot of blood and a woman's body so badly hacked it was completely unidentifiable. A wave of tangled emotions swept through him. He fell to his knees and stared up at the sky. *So much death. And such a waste!* A cry of anger, mingled with a sense of loss, tore from his throat. It echoed back from the hills around, a faint, mocking sound. 'Where are you, you monsters?' he screamed, surging to his feet. 'All the Skrinnies I can kill, you said,' he yelled at Ejaj. 'There aren't enough out there for me!'

25

The Commander stared in disbelief at the sight that greeted him. In all his years at sea, he had never seen anything like it. Around him the crew assembled, all equally fascinated although he was already hearing the expected mutterings. Despite their deeply pragmatic lifestyle, most Raiders carried with them the superstitions common amongst seamen and this was enough to make even the most hardened man shudder.

It was a woman. She was lying unconscious on a large piece of bleached driftwood, her long white hair trailing in the water. Her dress was tattered and her skin burned by the sun. Clearly she was either dead or near death.

But whilst finding a woman drifting in the sea was strange enough, having her escorted by a force of blaewhals was utterly alien. The blaewhal was carnivorous and wild, known for randomly attacking ships and taking unwary men from small boats. Even as they watched, the lead blaewhal nudged the wood towards the ship. An eerie silence fell over the crew as every eye watched the floating wood sliding across the water. It made an audible *thud* as it bumped against the hull.

No one stirred. The wood bumped again as the ship rolled in the gentle swell.

Suddenly the lead blaewhal surged forward, raising its ugly head, uttering its unmistakeable warbling cry as it thrashed at the water. It seemed to be about to attack the *Misty Seal*, but it stopped short, subsiding a mere couple of strokes from the hull, sliding under the surface. Three others followed the leader, and the *Misty Seal* shuddered as they bumped and scraped their way under the hull.

This was clearly a signal, as the rest of the force closed in around the ship, nudging and bumping until it heaved and surged under the assault. The silence that had seized the crew ended as men started to mutter, their eyes becoming wild.

'Bring her onboard,' murmured Officer Manno. He had quietly made his way to stand beside the Commander. His words were pitched so that none but the Commander could hear him.

The Commander nodded. 'Bring her onboard,' he ordered, raising his voice.

Grateful to have some direction, several crewmen moved to obey him. 'And bring the driftwood, too,' he added as an afterthought.

He watched as his crew prepared to bring the woman aboard. First a number of men clambered over the side with ropes. These they tied to the driftwood. Then a sling was lowered and arranged under the woman. This last was done very carefully by two men who slowly slid into the water, keeping a nervous eye on the blaewhals. They, it seemed, were also content to watch.

Once the ropes and sling were all in place, the woman and her makeshift raft were hauled onboard. As she was being lifted out of the water, she stirred and her eyes flickered open.

'At least she's alive,' muttered Officer Manno.

'Hmmm,' agreed the Commander. 'But who is she?'

'And what is she doing out here?' continued Officer Manno. 'And why is she being protected by the most voracious hunters in the sea?'

'I was trying not to think about that,' answered the Commander. 'Doctor,' he called as he turned away. 'Call me when she's awake. I want to talk to this hwenfayre.'

It was nearly dark before the ship's doctor sent word to the Commander that the strange woman from the sea was awake and alert enough to talk. She lay in the *Misty Seal*'s makeshift medical room, her eyes open and staring. When the Commander came in, his large frame filling the doorway, she started, then subsided as he approached her.

Unsure of what to say, he stood awkwardly beside her bed, looking at her. She was young, maybe nineteen summers, with long white hair and strange violet eyes that shone and dimmed in a heartbeat. Her skin, although sun-reddened, would be fair. Clad now in the rough canvas and leather of a Southern Raider, she seemed frail and small, but as he regarded her he became aware of a strength in her, more so when he realised she was returning his gaze. For the first time in more years than he could remember, he actually felt embarrassed by her frank stare.

'Do I know you?' she asked suddenly.

'No,' he said. 'I don't think so.'

'Oh,' she replied. 'From the way you were staring at me, I was sure you knew me.'

Her accent was unlike any he had heard. It was a mixture of islander, seafarer and mainlander. He was intrigued. He sat on a small stool beside her bed. 'Tell me about yourself, hwenfayre.'

Her eyes widened in shock and she sat up abruptly. 'What did you call me?' she asked.

'Hwenfayre,' he said. 'It is an old islander word, meaning "child of the sea". I thought it was an appropriate name. Why do you ask?'

She lay back down again, her shock diminishing. 'It's nothing,' she said. 'I have heard the word before, that's all.'

'You're an islander, then?'

Hwenfayre shook her head. 'Mainland,' she said. 'I think,' she added.

'You think?'

'Often.'

The Commander laughed. 'No, that's not what I meant,' he started.

'I know,' she said. 'What I meant was that I am not sure any more where I am from.'

'That would explain your chosen method of transport then,' the Commander said.

Hwenfayre frowned. 'What do you mean?'

He explained how they had found her. From her look of disbelief, it was clear that she was unaware of it, and was as mystified as he was.

'So, where am I?' she asked.

'You are on the vessel *Misty Seal*, under my command.'

'And who are you?'

'I am called the Commander.'

'No name?'

He shook his head. 'Not any more,' he replied. 'I command the people commonly called the Southern Raiders, and — ah, I see you have heard of us,' he said, smiling tightly at her immediate response.

Instead of answering, Hwenfayre tried to push herself away from the big man sitting by her bedside. Finding her back to the wall, she started to force herself up, getting as far away from the Commander as possible.

Hwenfayre could not speak; all she could see was images of smashed and broken ships and men, broken by the might of a storm that she had called down on them. But even as she watched the scene replaying in her mind, she could not escape the thought that came suddenly crashing in on her.

I tried to kill Wyn!

No matter that she did not even know whether he was alive or dead. No matter that at the time she'd believed he had left her. The fact remained that she had deliberately summoned a storm and sent it after him. *How could I have done that? What kind of person am I?*

Misunderstanding, the Commander tried to placate her. 'There's no need to be afraid,' he said. 'As a hwenfayre, one who has been lost at sea, you have nothing to fear from us. We are your brothers on the water.'

'I'm not afraid of you,' she said.

'Good,' he said, relaxing again. He frowned. 'What are you afraid of?' he asked. She shook her head. 'You're not afraid, or you're not telling me?'

Again she shook her head.

'Perhaps you can remember your name?'

Sensing the irony, Hwenfayre shook her head once more. 'What was that word, the one you called me?'

'Hwenfayre?'

She nodded. 'I like that word. Call me that.'

'A strange name for a mysterious woman. Very well, Hwenfayre it is.' He stood to leave. 'When you are feeling stronger come up on deck and talk with me. I have missed female company and I think you could have some interesting things to tell me.'

'I doubt that.'

The Commander smiled, a strange, wan sort of smile. 'Let me be the judge of that. At least you will distract me.' He turned and walked from the room, his wooden leg pounding heavily on the deck.

Hwenfayre slept uneasily in the narrow cot. All night her mind was tortured with images of destruction and murder, of betrayal and lies, and of Wyn. How could she have so quickly forgotten him? How could she have been so easily swayed by the deceits of Morag? The more she tossed and turned, the more convinced she became the liar had been Morag, not Wyn. The murder of Hylin, the ignorance of the Novices, the duplicity of Declan all told her who to trust. But beyond everything was the simple fact that she did indeed have the power to summon a storm. She had done it twice that she could remember: once to kill hundreds of Southern Raiders, and once to kill Wyn.

At times her mind turned to the period she had spent alone in the Sea after Declan had tossed her into the storm. At first she had felt terror, then a strange resignation to her death. As the waves crashed over her and the *Kelpie* sailed unheedingly away, she gave herself up to the cold and the violent water. She was driven deep below the surface into the darkness, where the water seemed calm. It seemed that she stayed alive much longer than she should have been able to, but a warmth suffused her and she felt herself rising to the surface. As she rose, she thought she was just floating, but as the light returned she chanced a look down to see a dark shape beneath her, lifting her.

When her head broke the surface of the water, she felt a thrill of naked fear, what Wyn had called a grue, as she realised she had not simply floated up, but had been lifted up by a blaewhal. The huge predator had positioned itself beneath her dangling feet and swum up to where she was able to breathe again, and when she found a piece of driftwood, it dived into the waiting dark of deep water. Scarcely able to think in her fear, she scrambled up onto the driftwood and lay shivering with far more than just the chill of the water.

And yet ... No. She dismissed the thought as quickly as it had come to her. But she could not escape the thought that, while she lay on the calming Sea, she could sense the presence of the big fish, and others like it, swimming beneath her.

Now, as she lay safe and warm in a bed, she remembered seeing more blaewhals as she drifted and wondered whether she did, in truth, simply drift.

If she were the Danan, could she not call the beasts of the deep to her aid? And if she could, what manner of being did that make her?

By the time the dawn touched the tops of the waves, she had left her bed, tormented by her own guilt, self-loathing and doubts. No wonder Morag wanted to kill her! She was indeed dangerous, and perhaps, for all Morag's lies, the High Priestess was right.

26

On his way back to Ajyne, Diplomat Cherise stopped at a small but elegant house surrounded by an immaculate garden. As he led his horse wearily along the pebbled pathway he nodded a greeting to the huge Tribesman standing guard at the front door.

'Urtane,' Cherise said. 'It is a pleasure to see you again.'

'Cherise,' the Tribesman grunted in reply. 'I hope you're not here scavenging like the last visitors we had.'

'Badghe and Egon were not missed for long,' Cherise said softly. He leaned against his horse and coughed harshly. 'Burn this fever!' he muttered. 'Could you let Maru know I am here?' he asked.

'Maru is away,' Urtane said.

Cherise nodded. 'Ys, then?'

'Ys is here, Cherise.'

'Good.' Diplomat Cherise went to walk inside but paused at the door. 'Bring that inside, Urtane,' he said, indicating the body on the litter behind the horse. 'I'll need it later.'

Inside, the house was beautifully appointed with exquisite works of art from the northern regions. On the floor were tribal rugs, Ettan tapestries hung on the walls, and set into purpose-made niches was a fortune in Skrin Tia'k carvings in rare blue ebony and obsidian. Cherise, accustomed as he was to luxury, was astonished at the wealth on display. Each carving was worth a year's wages for a skilled tradesman.

He stood in an antechamber. In front of a door carved from a single plank of a tadon tree stood a beautiful woman. She was small and delicate, with fair skin, long, thick, white-blonde hair and the most startling violet eyes. She smiled at Cherise.

'Diplomat,' she said in a low, vibrant voice, 'how nice to see you again.'

'Danan,' the Diplomat bowed. 'You are as lovely as ever.'

The woman laughed. 'I wish you wouldn't call me that. You know it's not my name, or my title.'

'It should be, Andrine, it should be.'

Andrine shook her head and wagged a finger at him. 'You are a cheeky man, Cherise. I don't know why Maru puts up with you.'

Cherise bowed again. 'Nor do I, Danan, nor do I.'

The door behind Andrine opened. 'Yes you do, you old fraud,' boomed a powerful voice.

'Ys, what a pleasure.' Cherise beamed.

Ys was even bigger than Urtane. He filled the doorway, top to bottom and side to side. His massively muscled torso was wreathed in intricate tattoos of battle scenes and stylised images of weaponry. 'Come in, come in, Fraud. Tell me about the success of our plans.'

Cherise followed Ys through the doorway, taking care not to stand on his unbound hair as it swept the floor.

'I see you have trimmed your hair again, Ys,' Cherise observed.

Ys boomed with laughter as he swept it up and sat heavily in a throne-like chair. He indicated another, similarly sized chair. Cherise bowed and sat while Ys began plaiting his hair.

'Yes, Fraud, I had to trim it again. One of my pets attacked my braids the other day.' He looked up, 'And besides, Andrine hates it when she trips over my hair.'

Cherise turned at a skittering sound. A small Skrin Tia'k scuttled across the floor, carrying a tray.

'Thank you,' the Diplomat said, taking a glass. He sniffed at the rich aroma that rose from the warmed liquid. 'Ah, my favourite. No one can make hot radfire like the Skrin Tia'k.'

The Skrin Tia'k clicked and Diplomat Cherise bowed his head to listen.

'Of course you may convey my thanks to your nestling,' he said. The Skrin Tia'k clicked again and scuttled to Ys, who accepted the other glass, and then it hurried out.

'So, tell me,' prompted Ys. 'How did you manage to get Tapash near enough?'

'It wasn't easy but Shanek helped.'

'Unlike the First Bastard to be helpful,' Ys grumbled.

'The first plan was for Muttiah to fit Tapash into his Fyrd under some pretext, but Shanek decided to bring some slaves along, probably to kill them for fun later. It was simple enough to slip Tapash in. No one paid any attention to a Tribesman among a group of Ajyne merchants.'

Ys chuckled. 'Love the arrogance of the Asan. It gets me every time. And no one even noticed?'

Cherise sipped his drink again. 'Not a murmur.'

'I take it the aroxii were effective.'

'Your aroxii were perfect. Please pass my compliments on to the trainer. Sadly, the handler was killed by Shanek.'

Ys grumbled in distaste. 'Burn it,' he said. 'I liked Tapash. He was married to Andrine's cousin. She won't be happy.'

'And you met the knot by the river?'

Cherise nodded. 'They were waiting for us.'

'All dead?'

'No, not all,' said Cherise.

'What?' bellowed Ys, rising from his chair.

Cherise held up a pacifying hand. 'Some were taken by the nestlings and I kept one alive for corroboration. That way there'll be someone to back up my story.'

Ys calmed and sank back into his seat. 'Hmmm. Good plan.' He scratched his chin thoughtfully. 'And the one you kept. Is he reliable?'

'She is most reliable, and she will be believed, trust me.'

'And Shanek? He is dead?'

'Oh, yes. Most definitely dead.'

'You've seen his body?'

Cherise barked a sudden, harsh laugh. 'You've seen what the Skrin Tia'k leave behind. I saw bits of lots of bodies. But no one escaped, believe me.'

378

Ys frowned. 'I don't like this. He was supposed to have been killed by either Tapash or the aroxii. You were supposed to bring me his body!' he bellowed.

Cherise waited until Ys calmed again. 'I know that, Ys, but as you appreciate, the First Son was a very skilled fighter. He was hard to kill.'

'You'd better be right about this, Cherise. This plan will all fall apart if he is still alive.'

Diplomat Cherise sighed. Ys was intelligent and articulate but he worried too much. 'You have already killed the Weapon, years ago, right?' Ys nodded. 'Without that, they were doomed anyway. The others are useful, but . . .' he let his voice trail away, allowing Ys to complete the sentence for himself.

'You and I have never agreed on that point,' Ys objected. 'I've read the histories too. Any one of them alone is a threat. That's why we need to eliminate them all.'

'And the Danan?'

Ys frowned. 'Still missing.'

27

Hwenfayre stood at the bow of the *Misty Seal*, watching the sun rise. They were sailing north and west under full sail. The Commander wanted to get somewhere in a hurry, that much was clear. Despite the yearning that grew by the moment within her breast, Hwenfayre refused to let herself sing, so she just watched and listened. It was a pleasure to hear the sailors go about their business, laughing and cursing, singing and talking about their women. After the eerie silence of the High Priestess's ship, their rough bluster was soothing. So caught up was she in the joys of a morning at sea, that she failed to hear the quiet shuffle of an old man coming to join her.

'Beautiful, isn't it?' Hwenfayre spun around to see a bent-over man leaning on a stick beside her. He cast a gap-toothed grin at her as he lit his pipe. 'I often come out here at dawn. Even after a life at sea, there is still nothing like dawn in the prow of a ship under sail.' He puffed on his pipe, sending blue smoke wreathing his head. 'The Commander tells me you won't tell him your name.' Hwenfayre narrowed her eyes, staring at the man in his halo of smoke. He shrugged.

'Doesn't matter much. Most of us have several names. It can be very useful from time to time. At the moment, mine's Manno. It's served me well for a long time now. But your new one will cause a few problems, you know.'

'How so?'

'Hwenfayre,' he said, as if trying it out, testing the sound. 'It's an old, old word. Not many use it as a name. Bad-omened, you see.'

Hwenfayre said nothing; she just stared at Manno.

'The rather unconventional nature of your arrival will not help. Sailors are a superstitious lot and you do not seem to be like us. It is said that a child of the Sea will always betray you. She belongs to the Sea, and the Sea will always hold her close. We honour the hwenfayres and will harbour them, but we never truly trust them. Now we of the Raiders, we love the Sea too. But she never owns us the way she owns the Children.' As he spoke, he watched her closely. When he mentioned the Children, he raised his eyes to meet hers. She returned his steady gaze frankly. He nodded. 'I thought as much,' he said. 'No one aboard knows the legends of the Danan as I do, so it is unlikely anyone will guess. But be careful. And don't, whatever you do, sing anything.' With a friendly wave of his pipe, he shuffled away, leaving Hwenfayre confused and troubled. Who was this man, and how could he know who, what, she was?

She had always considered the Southern Raiders to be little more than pirates, thugs who plundered the Sea, but perhaps there was more to them. As she watched Manno make his unsteady way away from her, she saw him nod to the Commander who was standing amidships. The Commander nodded back and listened as the old man spoke quietly to him. It was not a long conversation, but twice during it the Commander looked up at her. When they were done, Manno went below decks and the Commander made his way towards her.

'Good morning, Hwenfayre,' he said.

'Commander.'

'My old friend Officer Manno tells me you are a very interesting woman.'

'We've hardly met,' she replied. 'I think he is exaggerating.'

The Commander shook his head. 'Unlikely,' he disagreed. 'Officer Manno does not exaggerate. No, he thinks you are interesting. And he was very keen that we talk.'

Hwenfayre shrugged, feigning disinterest as she continued to stare out at the rising sun. Beside her the Commander waited for a few minutes, then he was called away by a crewman to see to something. He gave a brief grunt and left without a word.

Despite what Officer Manno had said, none of the crew seemed at all concerned by her choice of name. They were friendly and welcoming, seemingly unconcerned by the manner of her arrival, which was also at odds with what Manno had said earlier. They greeted her cheerfully by name and showed neither fear nor lack of ease around her. So much so that she quickly found herself enjoying their rough and ready fellowship.

It was only after a few days that the Commander attempted to make conversation again.

She was standing alone in the prow of the *Misty Seal*, watching the waves and sky. They were still in deep ocean so the swell was long and powerful, the water dark and cold. Occasionally she caught glimpses of streamlined dark shapes sliding beneath the hull and each time she felt a tremor of half-fear, half-excitement as she imagined their world. There was something about the deep ocean that sang to her like no other part of the Sea ever had. While she lived in the town, the coastal waters had raged and thundered on the rocks, showing their wrath at being stopped by the cliffs. On the small boat with Wyn she had experienced the joy of the open Sea with no sign of land so the waters could roll and tumble freely. Out here, deep and unfettered, the Sea took on its true life. The Sea could breathe and surge as she felt fit; nothing here could challenge her might or tame her passion. Here she could gather her strength and prepare herself for whatever might come.

At last Hwenfayre could feel what it was to be a child of the Sea. It was as if she were somehow larger and more powerful. Here, now, the Sea could truly sing to her, call to her and summon her home. Hwenfayre revelled in the glorious wonder of it all, completely unaware that others were noticing her.

'You named yourself well, Child of the Sea,' commented the Commander. He had quietly made his way up behind her to stand and watch. 'I've been on the water all my life, but I have never met anyone who loves her as much as you.'

'What do you mean?' she asked, startled by his approach.

'When I see you standing here, it is like watching someone coming home,' he said, staring at her. 'Who are you?'

Hwenfayre smiled. 'As you called me, I am Hwenfayre.'

He shook his head. 'I don't think so. You came from somewhere. You had a mother and a father, I am sure of it. But where are they now? And how did you come to be here? Now?'

There was something in his emphasis on that last word that made her turn to face him. 'What is so special about now?'

The Commander shrugged and stared out at the horizon. 'Now is a strange time,' he said.

'Tell me why.'

The Commander smiled sadly and shook his head. 'No. Tell me about yourself.'

She looked at him closely, seeing for the first time the sadness in his face, the deep pain in his eyes, the weariness in his stance. Something about him touched her. 'What do you really want to know?' she asked.

'Where are you from?'

She stared again at where the Sea met the sky, the line of the horizon clean and flat, wondering what to say. 'I don't even know the name of my home town,' she started. 'And I don't think I could find it again. It was on the coast on top of a high cliff. There was a wall built high above the rocks. I used to stand on the wall and just watch the waves crash against them. Sometimes I would imagine throwing myself off the wall into the water. I would wonder how it would feel, whether I would die, and if it would hurt. But I never did.'

'Strange thoughts for a young girl.'

'Not really. I was very lonely.'

'Your parents?'

'For much of my childhood I thought I was the result of rape. A Southern Raider, during an attack. But later my mother told me I wasn't. I had a father, but he left us before I was born. Sometimes I think I prefer the first story to the truth.'

'What do you know about your father?'

'Nothing, really. A name. A letter he left me.'

'What people was he?'

She shrugged. 'I don't know,' she lied.

'Your mother?'

'A local. After my father left she never married. She became very bitter and I think she blamed me, so I grew up alone.'

The Commander looked away at the Sea, lost in thought. Finally he nodded. 'Some evil things have been done in the past by my people,' he said softly.

'In the past?' Hwenfayre asked. 'Since when have the Southern Raiders become peaceful traders?'

Instead of replying, he gestured out towards the open Sea. 'Who with?' he asked.

'You could try talking with the people you meet, rather than killing them and sinking their ships,' Hwenfayre countered.

'We very rarely sink ships,' the Commander replied mildly. 'We need them. So we take them.'

'Why? Is building them beyond you?' snapped Hwenfayre.

She was surprised to see the Commander smile. 'Yes, as a matter of fact,' he said, 'it is.'

'It's not that hard,' Hwenfayre said. 'People have been doing it for centuries.'

'With what?'

'Wood, obviously.'

'Obviously.' He turned away from his consideration of the open Sea all around them and looked her in the eye. 'Do you see any trees around here that we can build ships out of?'

The simplicity of his answer made Hwenfayre blink in surprise. 'But surely . . .' she started.

'Surely we can build our ships from the trees of our homeland?' he finished for her. 'But we do not have a homeland. We live on the open sea.' A call from a crewman caused him to turn his head abruptly. Seeing that it was something that needed his attention, he gave a curt nod and limped away leaving Hwenfayre to her thoughts.

She thought mainly about the other people she knew who lived on the open Sea, the people she still believed were her own, the people who had abandoned her. Why was it that everyone who seemed to care for her eventually abandoned her? Was it her? Or was this how life really is? How long until these people abandoned her as well?

And when they did, where would she go then?

28

He scarcely spoke to her on the long journey back through the forest. At first she believed that he was too shocked and lost in his own thoughts to speak, but after they left the gloom and passed into the sunshine again she wasn't so sure.

Why pass by several fine places to stay and come here to this small, if elegant, house? It couldn't be money; she was still in uniform, so she could request accommodation anywhere. Perhaps he was concerned about the possibility of treachery; that could explain it. However, if that was the case, why ignore the Army outposts?

Her litter bumped and scraped over the pebbled pathway before it stopped, presumably near the entrance of the house. She was strapped into her litter and could not turn to see anything ahead.

'Urtane,' Cherise had said. 'It is a pleasure to see you again.'

'Cherise,' the Tribesman grunted in reply. 'I hope you're not here scavenging like the last visitors we had.'

An Ettan accent! Another Tribesman? Leone thought.

Cherise said something so quietly that she could not make out the words, before coughing harshly. 'Could you let Maru know I am here?' he asked.

'Maru is away,' the Ettan voice had answered.

'Ys, then?'

'Ys is here, Cherise.'

'Good,' said Cherise. She heard him take several steps across a wooden floor. 'Bring that inside, Urtane,' he said. 'I'll need it later.'

She heard more footsteps and then a door opened and closed. Heavy feet approached her. On impulse she closed her eyes and lay still.

'You're a pretty one then, aren't you?' the Ettan voice asked. She felt the slick smoothness of a knife against her skin as the man cut her bonds. To complete the illusion of unconsciousness, she allowed herself to slump, sliding down the upright litter. A powerful hand grabbed her and hefted her up, over his shoulder. The man made no sound as he lifted her, nor was there any indication that she was a burden to him. Years of training and experience meant that, even in her present state, she was assessing him as a possible adversary.

Right-handed, tall, very strong, she thought. It was a chill evening, yet his chest was bare. *A northerner.* The smell of strong herbs assailed her nostrils as she dangled over his back. *A Tribesman, no question.*

He carried her up the stairs and through the door. As they entered, she heard a woman laugh.

'... wouldn't call me that,' she was saying. 'You know it's not my name, or my title.'

'It should be, Andrine,' replied Cherise, 'it should be.'

'You are a cheeky man, Cherise,' replied Andrine. 'I don't know why Maru puts up with you.'

'Nor do I, Danan, nor do I,' replied Cherise.

A door opened. 'Yes you do, you old fraud,' boomed a powerful voice.

'Ys, what a pleasure,' said Cherise.

The man called Urtane carried her through another door before she could hear any more. *All Tribesmen,* she thought. *Danan? Where have I heard that name before?*

She did not have time to ponder the answer as she was thrown roughly down onto a bed or couch of some sort. The pain from her injuries shot through her like a lance. Before she could stifle it, a groan escaped her lips. Urtane heard the sound.

'Awake are we, pretty?' he rumbled. A rough hand shook her. More agony drove another sound from her. Some water was dashed into her face. She coughed and gasped, opening her eyes.

Urtane was even bigger than she had imagined. His muscled chest was covered in tattoos and his leering face bore the scars of either ritual initiation or brutal torture. One look into the dead-blue eyes and she decided on the latter.

'Cherise told me to bring you inside but he didn't say what I was supposed to do with you,' he said. 'What can we do?' he said. As he spoke his hand gripped one of her breasts and squeezed. She gasped at the pain. 'Good size,' he commented, squeezing again. 'And firm. I like it.' He started to undo her tunic but gave up after a few fumbling attempts.

Abandoning any effort at subtlety, he ripped the tunic off. He gazed at her chest, now only lightly covered by a cotton undershirt. This also went the way of the tunic. 'Nice,' he commented.

Leone lay still, but with her uninjured left hand she was slowly searching for the long narrow dagger that was hidden in a sheath under her hip. Urtane started to pull at her greaves, lifting them up to tear at the skirt beneath. His actions gave her the cover she needed to unsheathe the poignard without his noticing.

He was just about to rip off the last of her clothes when she whipped the poignard up to rest against his throat, its tip trembling slightly with the pulse that ran through his jugular. Leone rose to a sitting position. Urtane stayed crouched beside her.

'I never have sex on the first date,' she hissed. 'And I don't like you anyway.'

She stood slowly, keeping the point of the blade against his throat. He swallowed, the movement causing the point to draw a drop of blood.

'Danan's blood!' Urtane gasped. 'What a woman!'

'More of a woman than you can handle,' she snapped.

'I can see that,' Urtane agreed. 'What's your name, fighting woman?'

'Leone,' she snapped. 'Caldorman Leone, to you.'

'I guessed Coerl, from the Needle,' Urtane said.

'Sit down,' Leone ordered, easing the point of her Needle into his neck a bit more. He sat down quickly as more blood trickled down his neck. With the Needle steadily pointed at his face, she glanced around. Seeing some rope close by, she kicked it across the floor to him. 'Tie your left hand to your right foot,' she ordered.

Urtane's eyes widened, but one look at her bruised face and hard expression was enough. He complied.

When he was finished, Leone quickly stepped in close and dealt him a ringing blow to the side of the head with the hilt of the Thane's Needle. It was not enough to render him unconscious, but it stunned him long enough for her to tie his right hand to his left foot. She stood up quickly, but as she did, the sudden exertion sent her head spinning. With a startled cry, she lost her balance and crashed to the floor.

When Leone came to, she realised she was dressed and lying on a bed. She was not bound, but pain still racked her body. Slowly she opened her eyes, focusing on her surroundings. Standing over her were Diplomat Cherise, a huge Tribesman and an exquisitely beautiful woman with white-blonde hair and the most startling violet eyes.

'It's about time you woke up,' grumbled the big Tribesman. 'That's a very nasty blade you carry, woman. That little nick was almost enough to kill Urtane. If we'd been a few minutes later, he'd have bled to death. That's almost enough reason for you to die, right there.'

Leone went to answer, but the Tribesman grabbed the stump of her right arm and squeezed it savagely. She screamed.

'Ys,' murmured Cherise. 'Remember the state we found her in. I imagine she was merely defending herself.' He looked at Leone, a kindly smile softening his avuncular features. 'Isn't that right, Leone?'

Through the red haze of pain she managed to nod.

'There,' said Cherise, 'that's all right then.'

'My uniform?' Leone croaked.

The small woman frowned and shook her head. 'I'm afraid Urtane spoiled it, and what with all the bloodstains ...' She let her voice trail off.

Leone was surprised at how the news cut. For all her adult life that uniform had been her anchor, her source of security. It had given her a place in the world, a meaning to her life, and now, with it gone, destroyed by the twin events of her own brutal wounding and the attack by Urtane, she did not know how to feel. She wondered at the numbness she felt.

'I have given you some of my clothes,' the woman went on. 'I had to modify them but they look well enough on you.'

Leone looked down. She was wearing a long dress with a tight bodice. On her feet were sandals over thick stockings. Her eyes went to the wreck that was her right arm. The arox had taken it from just above the elbow, leaving her with little more than a useless stump. The sleeve of the dress lay limply on the bed beside her. The pain of looking at the empty sleeve was far worse than the physical pain of her injuries.

'Perhaps we should leave Leone to rest,' suggested Cherise. He ushered them away and closed the door behind them, leaving Leone alone.

She lay awake for a long time, listening to muffled conversations and the normal sounds of a house at night. There were a few odd sounds, skittering and clicking from time to time, but she finally drifted into a dream-filled sleep.

She woke up some time after dawn, ravenously hungry and parched with thirst. With a grunt of pain, she swung her legs off the bed and lurched unsteadily to her feet. She stood still while the room slowed its crazy spinning. Once she was sure where the door was, she carefully made her way towards it.

It was not locked and she opened it. It led out into a corridor. From her left came the sounds of conversation, from her right wafted the smells of cooking. She chose the right. As she walked, the rustle of her skirt, the way it flowed about her legs, the unaccustomed feel of the bodice disconcerted her. It was years since she had worn anything so overtly feminine. That was not to say she had no skirts or feminine clothes of her own, but she rarely had opportunity to wear them, and none was so rich or, as she looked down, revealing. The Ettan woman was not so well endowed that she had need of much covering. Leone realised that she was almost overflowing the resewn bodice. Self-consciously she tugged at the material, attempting a more appropriate arrangement.

The kitchen was a warm, busy place where the cook and her several assistants and two Skrin Tia'k slaves worked on preparing a large breakfast. Leone stood at the door waiting to be noticed. The small Skrinnie swivelled its head towards her and clicked. The larger one turned, saw her and clicked also. They went back to their work, clicking busily. After a few minutes the cook looked up.

'Who are you, then?' she snapped.

'Leone,' Leone replied. 'I am a guest here. I was wondering if I could have something to eat.'

'A guest, eh? That's not what Urtane told us,' she laughed. The others chuckled as well. 'Come on in then,' she said. 'Sit over there, I've got some warm oats and fresh bread.' She frowned. 'From the look of you, you could use some meat and eggs too.'

Leone sat where she was bade and a young girl hurried to fix her a breakfast. It was hot and wholesome, and after she had washed it down with two mugs of steaming jerva she felt human again.

'The Thane thanks you,' she said automatically.

The response was not what she was expecting.

'I certainly hope not!' the cook shrieked in laughter. 'Not around here, at least!'

The two Skrinnies clicked rapidly at each other, while the rest of the servants either busied themselves with their work or looked away nervously. Leone was a leader and a trained observer of responses, and she was troubled by what she saw. This was a house that had set itself apart from the Empire, a place of treachery, but not everyone here was a willing traitor, which spoke of coercion and threats.

Leone's military training took over as she pushed aside her plate. Instead of seeing a kitchen, she saw a potential battle arena. The cook's assistants she dismissed as threats, they were mostly young girls or old women, but the cook herself looked oddly out of place. She was a big, strong woman with not an ounce of excess fat on her, unlike the traditional view of cooks. Leone watched her closely. She had strong hands and the way she used her knife was military, not domestic, Leone realised with a start.

What is going on here? she wondered.

She did not get much time to consider what it was as Diplomat Cherise came into the kitchen. 'Ah, there you are, Leone,' he exclaimed. 'And looking well this morning. Excellent!'

Leone nodded as she stood.

'Are you up to travelling?' he went on.

'Yes, Diplomat. I think so.'

'Good.'

Outside, two horses were saddled and waiting. The pretty Ettan Tribeswoman was standing by.

'Good travelling, Diplomat,' she said. 'And,' she turned to Leone, 'I trust you will accept our apologies for the disgraceful behaviour of Urtane. He will be dismissed from our service as soon as he is recovered.'

Leone nodded curtly. 'My thanks for the clothes,' she said.

Andrine gave her a cheerful smile. 'They look much better on you than me. At least you can fill a bodice.' To Leone's surprise, her cheeks flamed.

Cherise laughed as he clambered up onto his horse. 'Now, Andrine, don't embarrass Leone,' he chided. 'She is still a Caldorman in the Army of the World.'

Andrine's smile faded. 'Indeed she is, Diplomat. Indeed she is.'

Leone swung up onto her horse, feeling the imbalance of her lost arm as she did so. She tried to fight down the pang of anguish but failed, and tears sprang unbidden to her eyes. To cover the rush of emotion she spurred her horse on as soon as she was set in the saddle.

It was a good horse and it took to the gallop with pleasure. 'Come, Diplomat,' she called as she sped past him. 'Ajyne awaits.'

29

The ship they were chasing was fast, but the *Gretchen* was slightly faster. Assuming the ships had captains of equal skill, it was just a matter of time. Marek had greatly impressed Wyn with his skills as a captain during the three-day pursuit. He had never let the vessel out of sight and despite the obvious skills of the other captain, he had matched him move for move.

It was the time Wyn had dreaded throughout this whole voyage, the time they caught a ship of the Children. He had worried about how he would feel once they had a ship of his people in their sights, but he found himself strangely detached.

'What do you think, Wyn?' asked Sacchin. 'Tonight we catch her?'

Wyn nodded. 'About an hour before sunset.'

Sacchin agreed. 'That's the talk. Should make for an interesting night, don't you think?'

Wyn shook his head. 'No, a very unpleasant night. They won't give in easily.'

'Hope not,' grinned the big Raider. 'It's been a long time coming.'

They were wrong. It was just after midday when the vessel they were chasing slowed and came about. Marek had not expected this but his crew was ready for the fight anyway. The mangonels were loaded, the fires burning and the men armed.

As the ships closed, Wyn saw what he had hoped not to see. Standing in the prow was a woman. She was clad in the long robe of a Priestess and she bore a harp. Brandishing it like a weapon, she held it aloft and screamed a challenge at the approaching *Gretchen*.

'This is not good,' muttered Sacchin. 'Do you know what this means?'

Wyn nodded. 'I know.'

'So much for the Children's vulnerability.'

'This is what I have been told by the Commander,' said Marek from behind them. He was staring at the Priestess with a strange half-smile. 'The Children still bluster and posture but they have lost their power over the Sea. Normally a display like that is enough to scare off most attackers. But today we're going to test their threats.' He turned to call an order. 'Ready the mangonels!' he called. The two ships approached; Marek waited. 'Fire!' he bellowed.

The mangonels groaned and thrummed as they released their lethal load of red-hot metal. On the Children's ship men screamed.

'Reload!'

'Fire!'

Men died. Fires started.

The two ships closed to attack distance. Raiders swung from ropes across the intervening water, landing on the deck with swords and knives ready for the bloodletting. They swarmed over the defending crew with brutal efficiency, cutting men down, driving them back.

Wyn ignored the battle on the main deck, concentrating instead on the Priestess still standing in the prow playing her harp. She was watching the swarming melee in disbelief, as if seeing such a thing for the first time. So distracted was she that she failed to notice Wyn approach her.

'Put the harp down, Priestess,' he said.

Her eyes widened in shock as she took in his size and his sword. But her fear did not overwhelm her; instead she continued playing. She looked up at Wyn, a small smile forming.

'Do you know this song?' she asked calmly as she changed the tune.

Wyn frowned as he listened. It was familiar, one he had heard a long time ago. Suddenly it came back to him and he raised his sword to threaten the Priestess. 'Don't do this, Priestess,' he said. 'Our vessels are too close together. Neither will survive this.'

'So you do recognise the song. I thought you would, Wyn. I remember telling you about it.' She placed her hand on the strings, stilling their song.

He stopped in shock, his sword wavering. 'Audra?' he asked uncertainly.

'You remember me,' she said, smiling. A particularly loud scream of pain from the wild scene behind him made Wyn suddenly remember what was going on. He raised his sword again.

'I still can't let you sing that song,' he said.

'No. I am sorry, Wyn. I won't allow you to interfere with what is happening.'

'Even if it means we both die?'

'Even if everyone on both ships perishes. I cannot let the Southern Raiders take this vessel.' She lowered her head briefly to place her hand on the strings, preparing to play once more. Wyn took a step forward, close enough to rest the point of his sword on the harp. Audra's head snapped up in surprise. 'Would you kill me? One of your own people?'

Wyn did not answer; he let his hard stare do the talking for him. He knew his eyes could be intimidating, for he had stared down opponents before. Audra held his eye, but all the while her fingers caressed the strings, summoning disaster upon them all.

'I warned you, Audra,' said Wyn harshly. 'If you do not stop playing I will have to make you.'

She raised her chin defiantly. 'Then you will have to force me. For the Raiders will not prevail here.'

As he looked at a woman whom he had known when they were both children, he knew he could not simply kill her. The answer was simple when he thought about it. With a quick flick of his wrist, he slashed at the strings of the harp. There was a single despairing tone, like a sigh, and the strings parted. Audra screamed in anger. She wrenched the harp away from Wyn's sword and threw it at him. He stepped aside easily, watching the ruined instrument spin past him. But as he did so, his sword point shifted.

Audra lunged, throwing herself at him, her hands outstretched to gouge at his eyes. Her sudden movement surprised him and he reacted instinctively, swinging his sword around to face the threat. She gasped in pained shock as the blade slid easily into her. He stood watching in disbelief as she slowly sank to her knees, her blood staining both her robes and the deck.

Audra died.

As if this were some kind of signal, the fight seemed to go out of the rest of the crew. Within minutes they were subdued and the Raiders took possession of the ship.

The *Merial* was a trim ship. She was fast, sat well in the water, if a little low for Wyn's taste, but she had a cargo hold full of valuable items. There were spices, fine silks, raw timber, grain and seed and even a small cache of gemstones. But even more interesting, there was a prisoner.

He was chained to the wall inside a small room deep in the hold. From the look of him he had been there for some time. When he was dragged out of his cell to face Marek, the prisoner cringed in the sunlight. The surviving crew of the *Merial* were hustled below to await Marek's pleasure, while the Raiders gathered around to watch the outcome of this meeting.

'So,' said Marek. 'An enemy of our enemy. By rights, a friend of ours. What say you? Friend of the Southern Raiders or not?'

The man dragged himself up to his full height to look Marek boldly in the eye. 'I am Nolin, Navigator of the First Rank. A Child of Danan.' A strange half-smile crossed his face. 'And yes, I am a friend to the Southern Raiders.'

'A Navigator, eh?' said Marek. 'Never met a Navigator before. I hear they are highly regarded among the Children.'

Nolin nodded. 'We are indeed.'

'So I find myself asking why one so highly regarded would be so badly treated by his own people.'

At this, Nolin laughed out loud. 'Ask away, Captain. But I will not tell any but your Commander.'

At his insolence, Marek surged forward, sweeping his sword from its scabbard. It came to rest lightly, touching the Navigator's throat. 'I command here,' he hissed.

Nolin did not waver or flinch as he stared back along the glinting steel. 'I am not referring to this vessel, Captain,' he said. 'And I meant no disrespect. Anyone who can run down and take the *Merial* is worthy of regard. I meant the man who calls himself Commander. The leader of your people.'

Marek calmed himself, resheathing his sword. 'What do you know of the Commander?' he asked.

The Navigator shook his head. 'Why wouldn't I know of him? He sails our Sea.'

'And that is why you will lose it,' said Marek. The Raiders murmured their agreement. 'It is this arrogance that will cost you dearly. It is no longer your realm.'

'How little you know,' responded Nolin. 'And I will tell your Commander some of what you do not yet know when I meet him at the next moon by the Wrested Archipelago.' He paused, eyebrows raised, as he regarded Marek. 'Those are your orders, aren't they? To "scour the seas in search of the Children" before "meeting at the second moon by the Wrested Archipelago to mount the final campaign against the Children"?'

Marek's face was a study of conflicting emotions: part fury, part surprise, part burning curiosity. Instead of replying, he merely nodded for the Navigator to continue.

'There are things afoot within the Children that your Commander needs to know about, and it is because of my desire to tell him that I found myself in my recent predicament.'

Marek looked beyond the Navigator to seek out a face in his own crew. 'Wyn,' he called.

Wyn stepped forward. 'Captain?'

'That Priestess you killed. What was it she said?'

Ignoring the Navigator's hard stare, Wyn focused on Marek. 'She said she was willing to sacrifice both vessels and all hands to prevent our capturing the *Merial*.'

'I guess that shows us how keen she was for you not to tell us what you know,' the Captain said to Nolin.

The Navigator smiled. 'It's nice to be needed,' he said.

'Speaking of being needed,' said Marek. 'I assume you know where the Wrested Archipelago is?'

Nolin grinned as he nodded.

'Sacchin?' called Marek.

'Yes, Captain,' said the big islander as he stepped forward.

'How do you feel about having a Navigator, First Rank, as a First Officer?'

'Sounds good, Sir.'

'Good. You now command the *Merial*. Select enough men for a skeleton crew and take this Navigator to the Wrested Archipelago as fast as you can sail.'

Sacchin's grin was like the sun rising. He turned to Wyn. 'What do you say, friend Wyn? Care for a sail under a one-eyed islander?'

'Any day, friend Sacchin.'

With a skeleton crew and a Navigator of the First Rank at the helm, the *Merial*, relieved of her cargo, fairly flew over the water. They sprang away from the *Gretchen* like a hungry caruda, leaving a creaming wake behind them. Sacchin's grin did not fade for three days.

Nolin was a man of almost supernatural skill. He could, it seemed, read the water. He never missed a gust, never caught a squall. At his hands, the *Merial* seemed to come alive, eager to do his bidding, keen to please him. Wyn had forgotten how skilled the Navigators were, how little he really knew about the Sea and sailing her. Similarly, the rest of the crew, hardy seamen and experienced sailors all, seemed almost in awe of Nolin. By the end of the first day, they hung off his every word, nodding sagely at his merest utterance, as keen as the *Merial* to do his every whim. It became the most harmonious vessel Wyn had ever known.

They had been underway for six days before Wyn found himself on watch alone with Nolin. It was the midnight watch on a perfect night. The stars were brilliant, glittering gems embedded in the velvet of the infinite sky, shining down on a placid sea. They stood on the quiet deck, comfortable in the silence of the night. Behind them the only other awake crewman onboard stood at the tiller, holding steady the southerly course that would take them to the Wrested Archipelago.

'I've been watching you, Wyn,' Nolin said. 'You don't like me, do you?'

'Not particularly,' Wyn replied.

'Why not?'

Wyn shrugged, partly to deflect the question, partly to hide his discomfort. He had never met Nolin, but his memories of the arrogant Navigators who directed the Rafts were not kind. He knew he blamed them for taking his only real friend away from him, all the time knowing how pointless his blame was.

'We have never met, I know,' said Nolin. 'But I have a perfect memory for faces, and you remind me of someone.'

'That's not my problem.'

'No it isn't. But I have a feeling that you could become mine.'

'How so?'

'I don't know.'

Wyn grunted, turning away from him slightly, indicating the end of the conversation, but Nolin was persistent.

'Indulge me,' he said. 'Tell me where you are from. Perhaps our paths have crossed somehow.'

'Not likely. You have that perfect memory, remember?'

'That's what I was meaning. There is something about you. Talk to me, I crave conversation.'

Wyn shook his head. 'Talk to yourself if you need conversation.'

'Very well then,' agreed Nolin. 'But remember you asked me to.' He grasped the railing with both hands and leaned far out over the edge, staring deep into the black water. 'My people, the Children of Danan, are an ancient and noble people. We are steeped in mystery and power, some would say lost in it. For millennia we ruled the waters unchallenged. Our love for the Sea, our ability to summon her to aid us, was legendary.

'But for all our history, there was also fact. We really could call upon the might of the Sea and She would answer us. Of course, this made us terrifying opponents in battle. None could ever defeat us, for we could call down mighty storms upon their puny fleets.' He stood up, laughing quietly. 'Sometimes I think I should have been a bard,' he said. 'Without even trying I slip into the language of the bard. But our history is the subject of many stories. Most of them are even true.'

'You weren't particularly terrifying opponents for us the other day,' observed Wyn.

'And there you point out the reason why I was in chains,' said Nolin. 'Whilst our power over the Sea remains considerable, many of her ways are lost to us now. We have forsaken our old ways and turned our backs on the ancient teachings.'

'That was silly,' said Wyn.

'Silly,' Nolin mused. 'What a quaint way to describe the utter destruction of an ancient civilisation. Silly.' He fell silent and gazed out at the waters again. 'No, it wasn't silly. It was evil and malicious.'

'Now who's being quaint?'

'How else would you describe the deliberate and calculated dismantling of a whole culture over two generations by a mother and daughter who had eyes only for themselves and their own power?'

'And how would you describe the culture that let them?'

Nolin's head snapped around to stare at Wyn. 'You are no ordinary sailor, Wyn. That I know.' He turned back once more to contemplate the Sea. 'But you are right. We all stand condemned with Anwyn and her bitch whelp, Morag. They led us, true. But we followed them blindly to our destruction. And now we are so weakened by their wretched ideas that we cannot even defeat one lone Raider ship.'

'And why has that led to you being in chains?'

'Ah, that.'

'Yes, that.'

'There is a certain amount of shame in that, I must admit. You know that we of the Children know just about everything that happens in our realm.'

'I thought we had already decided it wasn't your realm any more.'

'Your fine Captain may have decided that, but I think it is far from actually decided. No, we may not have all our powers, but in our knowledge of the Sea we are still unequalled. We would eventually win any conflict on the waters; do not be misled on that score. But it would take time and cost many lives. I wanted to avoid that.'

'How so?'

Nolin looked at Wyn through narrowed eyes. 'I feel I can trust you, Wyn. I don't know how I know this, or why it is true. But true it is. So consider this: if I know Marek's orders, don't you think the High Priestess does too? And if I know that the whole Raider fleet will be gathering at the Wrested Archipelago, where do you think our whole fleet of attack ships will be waiting?'

30

It was cold on top of this mountain. No matter what the season was, it was always cold up here. Aldere knew why, he'd always known why, just as he'd always known that it was guilt that drove his mother to drink and bitterness. He understood why the village shunned the two of them, just as he understood why the world seemed to pass the village by.

Understanding lent him forgiveness. Despite the years of abuse and neglect he'd suffered at the hands of everyone he knew, he bore them no malice as he understood their reasons. He watched their lives and wondered why it was that no one else seemed to see or understand what he did. So much suffering, so much unnecessary alienation happened because those around him missed the obvious.

It took him longer to accept this than it had taken him to accept their treatment of his mother. She was drunk already. She had started drinking after lunch and was now snoring contentedly in her favourite chair in front of the fire that would smoulder all night. He knew she would be safe and warm until the morning.

Aldere felt no guilt about climbing up here, leaving her alone. On days like this his presence would just inflame her to guilty anger, and it pained him to see her like that. No, it was better for him to be away today, and up here he was free to think and to enjoy the world. He stood atop the mountain and looked down on the vista. The Great Fastness, the river, the village, the mighty volcanoes away in the distance, all were as they should be.

He frowned. There was another volcano alive today. There was something wrong about that. It was not its time to erupt. Again, he did not know how he knew, he just knew. As he concentrated, he realised that the wrongness was serious.

This should not be!

The thought ripped through him with a shocking intensity. It left him dazed and dizzy. Panting, he discovered he had fallen. He couldn't remember falling. Aldere lifted himself up onto his elbows and stared at the volcano in the distance. As he did, an anger built within him. It rose from deep, down beneath his conscious mind, from somewhere base, somewhere primeval. It took hold of his emotions, leaving his mind cold and calculating. He saw the volcano, he felt its anger at being awoken from its slumber before its time.

I know, friend, he thought. *Let me help.*

Aldere sank his hands into the soil and sent his anger through the ground. As it surged away from him he was left with only the cold, hard knowledge that he had done right.

The volcano eased its rumblings and stopped, falling back into welcome slumber. Aldere sank exhausted onto the ground, where he slept until morning.

Aldere awoke the next day feeling refreshed and well with all traces of yesterday's anger gone. He stood and surveyed the world. All was well. Except ... He sniffed. That smell wasn't right. Fire? He looked down. No fire in the village that wasn't supposed to be there.

He looked out to the Great Fastness. There it was. He watched the fire for a few minutes, but he had his suspicions about it long before he stopped watching. He knew that fires did not move like that. This one was heading directly towards the village.

Without thought he started running. He ran down the mountain as fast as he could, leaping over rocks and dodging trees in his headlong flight. By the time he reached the village, everyone was out with buckets of water or blankets to drive back the flames. He could hear the flames, feel the heat on his face as he continued running towards the river.

Merryk was there, shouting orders, directing the efforts to hold back the flames. Despite the width of the river at this point, the intense heat and sheer ferocity of the fire made it clear that soon it would jump the barrier and engulf the village.

Aldere stood for a moment, watching the wall of leaping, writhing fire. Like the volcano yesterday, this was wrong. It was not a natural fire. He stared into its heart, slowly seeing what no one else could. This was not a fire, it was a creature! This wall of fire was alive!

With a hoarse cry, Aldere strode towards the river. He glared in fury at the beast that threatened his home.

'No!' he screamed. 'This is not for you! Go back!' Impossibly, the fire flinched at his commands. Aldere stepped into the water and raised his arms above his head. 'I said go back!' he cried. The flame hissed in reply and surged to the very edge of the river. Aldere felt the hair on his head start to singe with the heat. He looked down at the water that swirled about his feet. An incredible idea came to him. He lowered his arms and sank to his knees. 'Go,' he murmured to the river. 'Rise and go.' To the shock and horror of everyone watching, the river rose from its bed and hurled itself at the fires.

Aldere stood in the suddenly dry riverbed, watching as the flames turned the water into a vast cloud of steam that wreathed about him like a cloak. Slowly the heat faded and the fire guttered and died with a gasp. He turned to see the people of the village staring at him, unable to move.

The strange tableau was held for a few silent minutes as the steam writhed and swirled about Aldere, then with a mutter, the villagers turned as one and walked away.

31

Morag stood in the prow of the *Kelpie*. Before her, the Sea reached out to an uncluttered horizon. Beneath her, the vessel gently heaved as it cut through the low swell. To either side, the white water generated by the *Kelpie*'s wake danced away merrily like a stream on the ocean's depths. Behind her came the greater part of the Children's fleet of fast attack boats. Hundreds of them stretched for miles across the Sea's face. She doubted whether a larger, finer fleet had ever been assembled.

And they are mine to command! she exulted. The thought of what she was heading to do filled her with a delicious sense of power. In a few days her fleet would fall upon the pride of the Southern Raiders like a school of ravening caruda fish. They would tear them apart like a rotting corpse and leave wreckage strewn for all to see. None would ever challenge her again.

Luxuriating in such beautiful thoughts, she closed her eyes. She felt the wind, cold from the south, as it cut through her robe setting her shivering. The taste of the spray was sharp, salt crusting slightly on her face. Hovering on the very edge of the air was the tingling, elusive scent of the ice. It had been too long since she had ventured so far south and she had missed the thrill that only the fear of ice could bring.

Too rarely had she been able to revel in the inexpressible joy of terror. There was nothing to compare with the rushing surge that came with facing death on the Sea. Life for her was tedium, the endless round of petty squabbles and meaningless decisions. It seemed that no one could ever deal with their own lives. They all needed her to mediate, to adjudicate, to decide for them. Her only escape was the *Kelpie*. It was hers to do with as she saw fit. She sailed where she wanted, did what she wanted. But her moments of freedom were all too short. Too soon she was called back from the wide ocean, back into the drudgery of administering a fractious people.

Not today. There was no calling her back now. This time she would sweep down upon her enemies and nothing would stop her. She caressed the weathered face of Hwenfayre's harp, feeling the intricate tracery of carving. The power it gave her, the freedom that came from its unrivalled voice was intoxicating. With just a few chords she could control the very Sea beneath her.

Or she would soon, with more practice.

That galled her more than anything. The fact that an uneducated child brought up on land could have used this wonderful device with such ease when she, the High Priestess, could still barely raise a breeze and ruffle a calm Sea drove her to anger. But soon it would all be hers. Despite what her mother had tried to tell her, Morag knew the power was still there. And soon she, and only she, would wield it. No matter what kind of ship Hwenfayre was on, this fleet would crush them underfoot, sending Hwenfayre back to the Sea she claimed to love.

'It's as well the Raiders are such poor killers, is it not, High Priestess?'

Morag smiled. Without either opening her eyes or turning from the wind, she replied. 'Indeed it is, Declan, my love.'

'If it weren't for their incompetence you would not have that harp, would you?'

'True. And that fact alone makes up for having to deal with them in the first place.'

'What would you have done if they had managed to kill her?'

At that Morag opened her eyes and turned to face Declan. 'Rejoiced,' she said simply. 'And thanked them for the pretty harp.'

Declan smiled. 'And they would have handed it over.'

'They would have indeed. Idiots.'

'I still wonder, Morag, why kidnap her at all? You could have left her on that island. The Raiders had found her. They would have killed her,' Declan said.

'The Danan dead is one thing. The Danan under my control would be so much better,' Morag said.

'And now she is neither,' Declan observed.

'True,' Morag conceded. 'But without her harp she is powerless.'

'Another thing I have wondered about; was the plan yours or your mother's?'

A cold, predatory smile crossed the High Priestess's face. The intrigues, the plotting also made her life bearable. And none more so than the long-term plot she had devised to deal with this dangerous child. 'Mother's at the start. But mine at the end.'

Declan raised his eyebrows quizzically.

'She started it, but the business end was me.'

Declan frowned, still not understanding.

'Mother was the one who first started to remove the Danan from the teaching of the young. As soon as she recognised you two for what you were, she knew the Danan was close. My task was to separate the figures of legend. That was you, my love, and your friend Wyn. You two are as much a part of the legend of the Danan as Hwenfayre is. You both had roles to play. You, as Finder, were able to locate her, no matter how well Feargus hid her from us. Wyn, the Protector, was easily driven from us, so that he never learned of his role. It was much easier than we'd hoped. With the two figures of legend separated and under control we were well underway. But the masterstroke was mine. Mother would never have considered involving the Southern Raiders, but they were easily duped.'

Morag had become carried away by the thrill of her plan, so that when she turned away from Declan to consider the Sea she missed the sudden change in him. His normally passive face flickered suddenly into anger, before relaxing back to normal. But left in the anger's wake was a coldness that had never been there before.

Morag continued, blithely unaware. 'Mother believed that simply removing the Danan from the people's consciousness would be enough. But she had to be physically removed as well. Enough people would remember her if she reappeared, so she had to disappear. And that's where the Raiders were so useful. They hunted her down, thanks to you telling them where she was, lover.'

'And yet Wyn still managed to find her, despite your best efforts,' Declan reminded her.

Morag still did not turn from her contemplation of the Sea. 'He did,' she conceded. 'That I still don't understand, but it meant nothing in the end. You saw that storm Hwenfayre sent after him. He would never have survived. She did our work for us.'

'Something the Raiders did not,' Declan said.

Morag nodded. 'How they let her escape that town I'll never know, but their clumsiness drove her straight to me.'

'And we dealt with her,' muttered Declan.

'Yes, we did. Although I imagine the Raiders could be confused about what happened to the men who followed her to that island.'

'They might think we killed them,' suggested Declan.

Morag shrugged. 'It won't matter what they think when we get to the Wrested Archipelago.'

'No, it won't,' agreed Declan.

'Not with our fleet awaiting them. And me with this harp.'

'Indeed,' said Declan.

Morag smiled again, believing the two of them to be in agreement, as they always had been.

The fleet had not been hard to assemble. The Children had been on attack readiness for months, ever since Declan had located Hwenfayre, although they did not know that that was the reason. Morag had told them that the time had come for the final showdown with the Southern Raiders. Those weren't the words she used, of course. She spoke with impassioned fire about the viciousness and casual brutality of the Reavers of the Sea, how they had terrorised the peaceful Children of the Raft for long enough. She implored, she exhorted and she goaded her people into a raging wave of righteous vengeance. It took her quite a while. She knew that her attack fleet would need her personal appeal, rather than the usual messages relayed mystically through the Priestesses.

And now that joy was close to being complete. She had the Finder, she had the harp and the Southern Raiders were soon to be crushed forever. Not long now before the Sea would be hers to rule and to command. Morag, High Priestess of the Children of the Raft, turned again to survey her realm. She lost herself in the wonder of all that was soon to be hers, unchallenged and unshared. She was so full of this joy that she did not hear Declan walk away. She did not hear his muttering nor sense his anger. She would not have understood if she had.

'High Priestess!'

The call interrupted her reverie. She spun around, eyes flashing in anger. 'What?' she snapped.

The seaman cringed visibly under her glare. 'We have news, High Priestess.'

'Well?'

'Nolin, the Navigator.'

'I haven't the time or the patience for riddles, man. Tell me what you are trying not to tell me.'

'Priestess Audra is attacked, most likely dead. Nolin is probably captured.'

Morag turned away, looking out at the distant horizon. 'By whom?' she asked.

'A Raider vessel, High Priestess.'

'Do we know which one?'

'No, High Priestess. Priestess Audra's harp was destroyed before she could finish her message.'

'Was there anything else in her message?'

'Only that she knew the man who attacked her. He knew the significance of the harp and destroyed it.'

Morag frowned. 'Who could that have been, I wonder?' She fixed the seaman with a hard gaze. 'What do we know about the *Merial*? And the ship that attacked her?'

'The *Merial* is one of our fastest, High Priestess. And the Raider ship was a warship of some kind, fast and heavily armed.'

'So it's war, then,' she said. 'Good.'

32

The city of Ajyne squatted like a sleeping bear amid the vast fields of waving wheat. Leone stared down at the Capital from atop the Mount of the Thane. Diplomat Cherise rode on ahead, unmindful of her, as he had been since leaving the house of the Tribesmen. He never mentioned the attempted rape or her near killing of Urtane. Neither did he explain how he came to know them.

Now, as they neared the Capital, she found herself becoming concerned about what was going to happen. She looked down at herself. Dressed in the borrowed clothes of a Tribeswoman, her right arm taken by an arox beast, and riding on a borrowed horse, the only thing about her that said Caldorman was the Thane's Needle that hung at her hip.

Her fears were realised when they were challenged at the gate.

'Diplomat Cherise and Caldorman Leone,' the Diplomat said evenly. 'Returning from the north with vital news for the Thane's ears only.'

'Diplomat Cherise is dead of Danan fever,' the guard assured Cherise.

'Oh, I see,' Cherise murmured.

The guard dismissed Cherise and turned his attention to Leone. 'I know of a *Coerl* Leone,' he sneered. 'But there is no Caldorman of that name.'

'I was granted a field promotion by the First Son himself,' interjected Leone.

The guard shot her a hard glare. 'If you are going to impersonate an officer, lady, at least steal a uniform first.'

Rage built within Leone. Instinctively she went to whip her sword out, but only succeeded in unbalancing herself as the stump of her right arm flailed across her body. The guard saw her suddenly sway uncomfortably in her saddle. He roared with laughter.

'As Caldorman I am giving you a direct order,' said Leone in a low, controlled voice. 'Stand down!'

'You should have stolen an arm as well as a uniform, Caldorman!' he bellowed, eliciting laughter from the other soldiers.

Her rage changed to fury. Without thinking, she dropped her left hand and pulled out her Needle. A controlled flick of arm and wrist sent it flickering unerringly across the intervening space to bury itself between the offensive guard's eyes. For a moment, he stood, shocked into silence, then he sank dead to the ground.

'Anyone else?' Caldorman Leone called. 'Anyone want to challenge my rank?'

Her challenge was greeted by the rustle of arrows drawn from quivers, followed by the simultaneous creaking of a dozen bows being drawn back.

'Get off your horse, woman. Whoever you are,' came a voice from by the gate. It was deep and drawling, with a Southern Province accent. Leone could not remember any Coerl from the Southern Province. He stepped out into the sun. 'Who are you?' he demanded.

Leone regarded the man. He was tall, but not exceptionally so, angular with long, brawny arms and a shock of auburn hair. He returned her gaze with an even intensity that unsettled her.

'My name is Leone,' she replied. 'Caldorman Leone. I am travelling with Diplomat Cherise, returning from an important mission for the Thane.'

The Coerl waved a negligent dismissal. 'Yes, yes,' he said, 'I heard all the "vital news" stuff. Any proof?'

Leone frowned. 'Proof? Since when do travellers need proof to enter the Empire's capital?'

'Since they make wild claims about their identities, claim an audience with the Thane and,' he paused to look down, 'kill the Thane's soldiers.' He frowned as he looked down at the dead soldier. With a grunt of surprise, he stooped and dragged the Needle out of the dead man's head. He held it up to examine it closely. 'And with a stolen weapon, too, I might add.'

Leone sighed. 'It is not stolen, it was handed to me personally by the Thane on my promotion to Coerl.'

'Really?' the Coerl said with feigned surprise. 'If that's the case, you would know what it is called and what inscription is traditionally hidden beneath the binding of the hilt.'

'It's a Thane's Needle and beneath the binding is inscribed the Seven Steps unto Purity.'

The Coerl nodded. 'That's true but hardly clinching proof.' He turned to the bowmen. 'Stand down and arrest them on charges of murder, impersonation and, um, looking at me in a nasty way.' He walked away, dismissing Leone and Cherise from his mind.

The soldiers swarmed around them and took them into the guardhouse. Cherise and Leone were searched and thrown into the small cells built by the gate for just such a purpose. Leone sat down on the single hard cot that ran along the full length of her cell. She stared at the opposite wall, a mere arm's length away. By the light of the single slit window she could just read some of the names of those held here before her. It was a litany of anonymity. These were names of people from all over the Empire who had fallen foul of idiot Coerls like the one she'd just met. She read down the list, then stopped short when she read her own name.

Leone. captured. forgotten.

How long ago was that? she wondered. Who were you, you who shared both my name and my cell? Will your fate be my fate?

As she had discovered when Shanek fell on her in the Training Arena all that time ago, her mind and emotions were less easy to discipline than her body. She lay down on the cot and stared at the ceiling, her mind awash with fears and imaginings.

Night fell but sleep would not come. She heard Diplomat Cherise in the next cell as he muttered to himself. 'Diplomat!' she called.

'Caldorman,' he replied.

'How are you?' she asked.

'I am well. You?'

'I'm fine, but . . .' Her voice trailed away; she was uncertain how to phrase the question that was on her mind.

'But what?' prompted the Diplomat.

'Why didn't you say anything at the gate?' she asked.

'It wouldn't have achieved anything.'

'You could have protested or something.'

'You remember how the Coerl took your Needle?'

'Yes,' she replied, her latest humiliation still a fresh scar.

'Why did he do that, do you think?'

'They are valuable. He probably thinks I stole it.'

'No, Caldorman, think. If he believed that, he would have ordered us killed, but he didn't. He took the Needle for a reason. As you know, every Needle is individually made, with distinctive markings. I think he half-believed your story and took your Needle to verify it.'

'Why do you think he believed my story?' Leone was intrigued.

'You're a very impressive woman, Caldorman Leone. You carry yourself like a leader, you speak expecting to be obeyed, and do you have any idea how hard it is to throw one of those Needles?'

'It's easy enough,' she said.

Cherise snorted with laughter. 'There speaks one trained for years in every weapon known. The Needle is designed as a close-quarters thrusting weapon. It's an assassin's tool, yet you threw it, left-

handed, like a perfectly balanced throwing dagger.'
He paused. 'That throw alone was almost proof
enough. The guards all knew it.'

'How can you say that?'

'What is the penalty for killing a member of the
Thane's Army?'

'Death,' she replied.

'Are you dead?'

'No.'

'What is the penalty for disobeying the order of a
Caldorman?' he asked.

'The Caldorman has the right to strike the soldier
dead where he stands.'

'You see,' the Diplomat went on. 'Everything you
did spoke the proof of your claims. The Coerl knew
that but he had to check first.' Leone heard Cherise
lie down on his cot. 'It won't be long now,' he said
confidently.

He was right. Just after the changing of the night
guard, their cells were unlocked and the doors
thrown open. In the flickering torchlight Leone
could just make out a figure standing in the open
doorway.

'Coerl Leone,' the figure said. 'The Thane wishes
to see you.'

She scrambled to her feet and followed the figure
out. The Coerl from earlier stood in the dimly lit
corridor. He held out a Thane's Needle in one hand.

'Yours, I believe, Caldorman Leone,' he said.

Leone took the weapon and sheathed it. 'Yes,' she
said. 'It is mine.'

The Diplomat was standing behind the Coerl with
a faint smile on his lips.

'You were right, Diplomat Cherise,' she said.

'You really should trust me, Caldorman Leone,' he chided.

They were led to their horses and escorted through the night to the Thane's Palace, where, even though it was just past dawn, they were ushered into an antechamber. Leone was ordered to wait while the Diplomat went in first.

While he was gone, Leone stood staring at the door. Inside she was a mess of conflicting fears and emotions. Although she was confident she had done nothing wrong, the facts were damning and it could all come down to what the Diplomat said about the events.

Who were those people in the house? And why did he visit them?

The door opened. A guard motioned her forward.

Leone strode in, her sandals slapping on the marble floor. At the prescribed seven paces before the throne, she dropped to one knee and went to make the ritual salute, which was usually done with the right arm. She hesitated, unsure of what to do.

'Get up, woman,' Kasimar IV snapped.

Leone scrambled to her feet.

'Tell me everything that happened,' the Thane commanded.

Acutely aware that she had not washed for three days, that she was wearing a bodice that barely covered her and that she was the one who was individually responsible to the Thane for the personal safety of the First Son of the Empire, Leone realised there was only one way this meeting could end. In an act of personal courage unparalleled in her life so far, she told the Thane everything that had happened since they had left Ajyne.

When she finished, she looked the Thane squarely in the face, awaiting the inevitable.

'Let me summarise events,' said the Thane. 'You left here with two Fyrds, a senior soldier, a senior Diplomat, the First Son of the Empire and several prisoners, whom you arrested and took with you for reasons not fully understood, correct so far?'

Leone nodded.

'You left to undertake a mission given personally by me to the First Son that was of vital importance to the Empire. How am I doing, accurate?'

Leone nodded again.

'You leave the normal route to follow some agenda of your own that you have not fully explained here, and whilst in the forest manage to lose most of the Fyrds, the prisoners, one of whom took a shot at you, the Caldorman and your arm. You also claim that the First Son read some mystical message in his orders that spoke of treachery.' As the Thane spoke, Leone felt the first stirrings of grave misgivings. The path through the forest was the Diplomat's idea, not hers! Why had he lied? One look at the Thane's face told her that no matter what she said now, her fate was already decided.

All her adult life, Leone had prided herself on her ability to keep her face impassive, and it did not let her down now. She stared at the Thane as he continued.

'Once you led the remnants of your party out of the forest, you were attacked by a warrior knot of wild Skrin Tia'k and it was only the quick thinking of the Diplomat that saved your lives.' Kasimar IV sat back on his throne and regarded Leone with hard eyes. 'Not an impressive record, is it?'

Leone shook her head. 'No, Sir. It is not.'

He held out his hand. 'Your Needle,' he commanded.

Leone pulled the poignard from its sheath and took the seven steps to the throne. Reversing it, she handed it to the Thane. He took it and stood up.

'You are a disgrace to your uniform,' he said. 'You have failed in your sworn duty to protect the First Son and you have brought dishonour to your teachers. Your shame is to be unending.' With a quick, savage motion, he slashed her face with the Needle, laying her cheek open to the bone. 'I dismiss you from service.' He slashed again, opening her other cheek. 'I condemn you to lifelong poverty and ridicule. Never will your shame be expunged. Get out of my sight!'

With blood coursing down her face, she bowed, turned on her heel and walked out of the throne room. Her blood left a spreading stain on the marble. As she passed through the doorway she heard the Thane bellow for slaves to clean his floor.

33

The Commander was nervous.

It was not obvious, but everyone knew it. And it affected everyone. The *Misty Seal* was normally a tight, harmonious ship but it became a nervous ship. Things started to go wrong: rigging parted, sails tore, tempers frayed, and then a man died. There was no reason for him to die, no excuse. But he died, his blood staining the deck where he fell. And no amount of scrubbing could wash it away. It remained as a stark reminder of wrong.

But it was not that nor the fact that the crew was unsettled that made the Commander nervous. Nor was it the several days of clear skies and fair winds that had him on edge.

In fact, there were only two men onboard who knew why he was so nervous, and they stood in the bow talking in low, earnest tones.

'It's been weeks, Manno,' the Commander said.

'It's a big sea, Commander,' Officer Manno replied evenly.

'Not that big.'

'It doesn't bother you that in all this time we have not seen one single ship of the Children?'

Officer Manno stared out at the horizon without answering. He dug his pipe out of his pouch, filled and lit it before answering. 'Yes, it bothers me, Commander. But not for the same reason it bothers you.'

'Oh? And why does it bother you?'

'It bothers me because it is getting dangerously close to the Season of the Winds. And I fear you will not turn for the Archipelago before it is too late.'

'Too late?' exclaimed the Commander. 'It is already too late! Where can they all be? I fear a trap, but I do not know why, or how. And the longer we stay out here, the more that fear becomes real. That is why I am staying out here. To find them.'

'I know, but it cannot go on for much longer.'

'Do you have any idea how important this is?'

'No I don't. And I have been wondering why we are out here, sailing around in circles.'

Both Officer Manno and the Commander turned, startled at the unexpected interruption. Hwenfayre stood nearby, uncertain, but curious.

'Why are we out here?' she repeated.

Officer Manno shot the Commander a hard glare. 'I think you had better deal with this,' he said. 'I have things to do.' He shuffled away without acknowledging Hwenfayre. The Commander watched him leave with a strangely relieved look in his eyes. When Officer Manno was out of earshot, he gestured for her to come and stand by him.

'Look out there,' he said, indicating the Sea with a wave of his arm. 'What do you see?'

She looked away, savouring the beauty and wonder that was the Sea. 'I see beauty. I see a mighty, untamed wildness that sings to my soul. I see mystery and love, peace and terror. What do you see?'

The Commander smiled. 'I see the Sea, vast, bountiful and dangerous. But I also see the Children of the Raft.'

Misunderstanding, Hwenfayre spun around. 'Where?' she asked, her eyes wide.

'Not literally,' the Commander said. 'But wherever I look they sail across my view.'

'How so?'

'Hwenfayre, I know so little of you,' said the Commander. 'You came to us like a creature out of legend. There is nothing even slightly normal about you. Officer Manno believes you to be mystical, did you know that?'

She shook her head, half fearing what he would say next.

'Yes. He says you are a legend come to life, an offering from the Sea herself. You have even bewitched my crew. I believe old Kelsy made that dress for you.'

Hwenfayre blushed. 'Yes, he's so sweet. He said it wasn't right that I should wear a man's clothes. So he made me this out of some cloth he says was a part of his last payment.'

'He was saving that for his own daughter,' the Commander said. 'We took it from a trading ship, along with some wood and woollen cloth.'

Hwenfayre turned to look at him. 'Took?' she asked.

'Traded, actually,' he said.

'Traded? For what?'

'Don't jump to conclusions, but we had some people from their home town. They were happy to have them back.'

'Are you slave traders as well as Raiders and assassins?'

'I asked you not to jump to conclusions.' He frowned. 'And why assassins? We have never been assassins.'

'Just something I heard,' said Hwenfayre. 'You were about to tell me why we are out here.'

'A year or so ago,' he started, 'I met with Morag, the High Priestess of the Children of the Raft. Ah,' he said, seeing her sudden start, 'I see you have heard of her.' Hwenfayre nodded, not trusting herself to speak. 'She is a nasty piece of work, that woman. We met to discuss peace between our peoples. For too long we of the Southern Raiders have lived meagre lives, scraping an existence out of piracy and violence. Our families live on an extinct volcano that encloses a deep bay far to the west of here. It is little more than a rocky cliff that rears above the deep ocean. It is cold and bleak and nothing grows there. During the Season of the Winds many die from the cold and the brutal winds. But every year we increase. Our numbers grow, we have more mouths to feed and house. More children to care for and too many wives who become widows whenever a ship comes home. We are at breaking point. If we cannot find somewhere else to live, we will fall apart as a people. We will be scattered to the tides and cease to exist.'

'Tell me why this is a bad thing.'

She was shocked at the sudden flare of naked fury that disfigured the Commander's face. For a moment she feared he would strike her but his rage faded almost as quickly as it came.

'I forget,' he said. 'You do not know us or our ways, and your views of us are coloured by stories you have heard.'

'And things I have seen,' added Hwenfayre.

The Commander nodded. 'And things you have seen,' he conceded. 'I cannot deny there are violent and brutal things in our past. I will not attempt to evade or excuse our history. But I do wish to escape from it and create a better future for our children.'

'How?'

'That was what the meeting with Morag was about. For decades, the Children have harried us on the Sea and driven us off any island we have tried to settle. For years we tried to meet, to reason, to somehow try and share the bounty of the Sea, but they would not listen. And then suddenly she arranged to meet with me.

'Of course I agreed. We met and she told me of an ancient legend of her people. She said that the avatar of a godlike woman in their past, the Danan, had returned. This Danan, she said, would bring with her vast, wild power that would incite the rogue elements of her priesthood to great acts of violence against us. We are only too well aware of what the Children can do with the Sea already, but with this new, wild power threatening, we would be doomed.

'Then she offered me a trade. She would give me this Danan in exchange for freedom to expand into the uninhabited islands far to the east. All we had to do was find her and keep her. Kill her if we wanted, but for proof of our side of the bargain she wanted the harp the woman would bear.'

'The harp?' asked Hwenfayre. 'Why?'

'She did not say.'

'How were you supposed to find this woman?'

'Morag told us which town she lived in. She had a man called a Finder who could track her mystically. So we attacked this town. But she never told us how much power this woman had, and she raised a storm like no one had ever seen. It wrecked our fleet. She fled in a small boat. Fortunately the vessel that held this mystical tracker survived the storm and followed her to an island.'

'What happened then?'

'That twice-damned bitch Morag betrayed us and killed my men. She murdered them and took this Danan for herself. By her treachery she sank my ships, killed hundreds of my finest men and left us vulnerable to utter destruction.'

'But Morag didn't kill the men at the town, this Danan person did that, surely?'

'True,' conceded the Commander. 'But only because we attacked her home. She is not really to blame. She simply defended herself in the only way she knew. If Morag had not sent us there, she would probably have lived out her life in blissful ignorance of her destiny.'

'What are you going to do now?'

'The only thing left. I have sent the rest of my fleet out with instructions to engage and sink every ship of the Children they encounter.'

'But if they have this Danan, how can you hope to succeed?'

'Hwenfayre, my people are going to be destroyed! What choice do I have?'

Hwenfayre stared out at the Sea, lost in thought. 'I don't know,' she said finally. 'But I can't accept all-out war. You will lose and Morag will win. No matter what else happens, that much I am sure of.'

'Don't be too sure,' said the Commander. 'We may not have the powers of the Children, but we have some fine seamen and they are fighting for their homes. We will not be too easy a target.'

Hwenfayre stared at him. She was torn between her past hatred of this people and what they had done to her and her home, and a strange desire to laugh in his face and taunt him for not seeing what was so clear. How could he not have recognised her for what she was? Manno had, and it seemed he had all but told his Commander. And yet he still did not see her.

34

The hardest thing, Leone thought, was the hunger.
She could deal with the leers, the comments, the
unseemly suggestions, even the occasional attack,
but the hunger was the worst. Even sleeping on the
ground was easy enough; the weather was still mild.
Come winter, she'd have to reassess her situation. As
she thought these things she realised how completely
she had accepted her lot. This was her new life
and she had to adapt.

Still, the hunger was hard to take.

One thing she had always taken for granted as a
Soldier of the World was food. When in barracks she
was always fed well, and when on the road she could
easily acquire anything she needed. Now she had to
beg, steal or somehow earn her meals. After begging
and stealing a few, she knew that it was more than
simple conditioning that made her reject this as
wrong. She saw the others, here in the Widows'
Quarter, and knew that she was better off than most,
even with her borrowed dress and one arm. She had
her health, she was big and strong and she was
skilled in any weapon. It would be easy for her to

take whatever she wanted, but these people were no challenge, it was no contest. It would be simple theft, taking advantage of people worse off than her. That left her with earning a meal. By the end of the first month or so, she had worked out enough of her situation to assess her saleable skills.

She was a woman, and that gave her the oldest way that all women had to make money. She dismissed that out of hand. She'd starve first.

Her army training, she discovered, opened many doors. Most obviously, she was deadly with any weapon; even left-handed she could best any of the common thugs she'd come across so far. The first one who had tried his luck with her left a rusted dagger behind, and got away with a lot more bruising than he'd anticipated. With some polishing and sharpening on a stone, the dagger revealed itself to be a quality piece of steel. The next thug left a sword; the one after that offered her money which she took.

Now she had a new choice. Her skills were becoming known, and a second-rate standover thug offered her work as an enforcer. Had the offer come when she was hungry, she might have taken it, but now, with a purse of coins and food in her stomach, she was able to say no.

Refusing closed one door, but it did not apparently open any others. The money ran out after a new dress and a few meals, so she was back where she started.

One thing was different, she realised, looking down at her dress. Before the Ettan woman loaned her a dress, Leone had rarely worn one. Her clothing consisted almost entirely of three uniforms — battle fatigues, special cold-weather issue and a best dress uniform worn on ceremonial occasions. She'd had some civilian clothes but wore them so rarely that she had trouble remembering what they were. It was a conversation with a woman selling clothes in the market that changed her mind.

'Army, eh?' the woman asked.

'Why do you say that?' asked Leone.

The woman grinned a gap-toothed smile. 'You're big, you stand like a fighter, you're looking at men's clothes and you wear that dress like you're afraid it'll fall off,' she said. 'Not that it's likely to, not with those holding it up,' she added, with a pointed glance at Leone's chest.

Leone glared at her, daring her to continue.

'And that's the point, isn't it?' the woman commented, returning the glare evenly. 'That stare will not achieve what you want it to around here. You were an officer, right?'

Leone nodded.

'Thought so. Around here that will frighten young girls and dogs. Boys will laugh at you and men will take it as a challenge. And if you dress like a man, they'll feel the need to meet your challenge.' She rummaged around in a pile of dresses, pulling one out. 'Here, try this one,' she said, offering Leone a modest, high-necked dress in green. 'The colour will suit your eyes nicely and if you let your hair out, it'll help to hide those scars a bit.'

'My eyes?' asked Leone.

'Burn me!' the woman burst out with a smile. 'How long were you in the army, girl?'

'All my life,' Leone conceded.

'I think you need a lot more than a new dress, child.'

Until the moment when the Thane had stripped her of everything, her life had been one of duty, honour and obedience. Now she was confronted with the anarchy of poverty and fear. Even when she was in battle she had not sensed so much fear. It seemed that everyone was afraid here in the Widows' Quarter.

When it was first established, all those centuries ago, the Quarter had been well presented and well cared for, but as the years and the Thanes went by, it fell into the disarray that it presently endured. Once the Thane's soldiers stopped their regular patrols, the thugs and enforcers moved in, setting up the kind of underbelly culture from which most large cities suffered. Like most who did not live there, Leone had dismissed it as not her problem, but now she was faced with it daily.

At first she tried to ignore the violence and thuggery, but it did not take long for them to wear her down. All her life she had lived in service to the Empire and she had taken that to mean following the Thane's orders as given to her through the chain of command. Now, as she watched people suffer around her, she realised that the Army of the World served more than one purpose. Not only did it protect the Empire from threats without, it also protected from within. It was not an epiphany but it saved her life, not in the physical sense, but truly, nonetheless.

Military training is a powerful thing. Not only was she, even with one arm, a physical match for any of the thugs she met but her tactical skills gave her an awareness that few could even begin to grasp. With years of training and experience at her behest, she planned her campaign.

First, logistics. She needed a base of operations, a supply source, money and weaponry.

Weaponry was the easiest; she already had the dagger and sword. A chance encounter solved the other logistical issues in a most unexpected way.

She was standing at the end of one of the small markets that dotted the Widows' Quarter, waiting for the prices to drop as they always did at the end of the day. There was little left in her purse and she had waited as long as she could before spending the last coins. Leone intended they would be well spent.

A man she knew brushed past her. Her eyes narrowed as she watched him shoulder his way through the thinning crowd. Arden was a bully-boy. Big, strong and lumbering, with a mind that would be hard put to outwit a log, he enjoyed bluster and used his strength to take whatever he wanted. Leone's eyes took in the scenario, assessing possible risks, weighing up options and determining possible attack scenes. In a flash of insight, she saw Arden's target. He was making his hulking way towards a young man who was bartering with a stallholder. As she watched, it became clear that it was no young man, he was a boy, tall for his age, but with the gangling awkwardness of a growth spurt.

Without thought, Leone slid through the crowd, easing her way past conversations, slipping between small groups, until she was within easy sword's reach of the boy. Her superior skills meant that she arrived just heartbeats after Arden, and was a pace behind him, to his right.

Arden unsheathed a dagger and went to stab the boy but froze as a razor-sharp blade caressed his throat.

'Put it away, Arden,' Leone hissed. When he hesitated, she slid the blade lightly over his skin, drawing out a thin line of blood. 'I said, put it away,' she repeated.

Arden thrust the blade back into its sheath. 'I know you, don't I?' he snarled.

Leone took her blade away, resheathing it. 'Yes,' she said, seeming to take her eyes off Arden.

He turned and, seeing her apparent lack of attention, took a clumsy swing at her. Leone's attention was only apparently elsewhere, as Arden discovered when she easily dodged his wild swing. He staggered past her, unbalanced by his miss, and Leone helped him to the ground with a well-placed shove with her foot.

Roaring with anger, Arden surged to his feet, only to be confronted by Leone's sword, pointing steadily at his eyes.

'Stay on the ground where you belong, Arden,' she said softly. 'Unless you want to bleed, of course.'

He slumped back to the dirt, his eyes never shifting from the point of Leone's blade. 'What do you want?' he snapped.

Leone frowned. 'Nothing. I just stopped you killing a defenceless boy.'

'Kill? I was never going to kill him, just cut him a bit,' Arden protested.

'Why?' Leone asked.

'His money,' Arden said.

Leone snorted derisively. 'Not today. Get up and get out of here,' she said, sheathing her sword. Arden started to move, but Leone recognised the signs and kicked him back down again. 'If you're going to try to fight me, think again. I could kill you before you got to your knees.'

Arden glared at her but lurched to his feet without menace. She watched him leave through hard eyes. When he was out of sight, Leone turned to speak to the boy.

'You all right?' she asked.

He nodded. 'Why did you do that?' he asked.

She paused, unsure of the answer. 'Because I could,' she said finally.

The boy frowned, then shook his head. 'I've got to go,' he said.

Leone nodded. He turned and scampered off through the nearly empty market.

Why did I do that? she wondered. *He wasn't threatening me. I still don't even know the boy's name.*

'You're new,' said a voice at her shoulder. She whirled around, whipping her dagger out and holding it at the throat of the speaker before he could blink. He was a well-dressed man of middle years, portly, with greying hair and a long, carefully tended beard. His eyes were wide with fear as he regarded the shining blade.

'Not that new,' said Leone. 'Who are you?'

'My name is Zatopek. I am a merchant from the Southern Province.'

'Zatopek isn't a Southern Province name,' she observed, not removing her blade.

'No, my parents were from Herath.'

'What do you want?'

'I could use someone of your skills and courage,' Zatopek said.

Leone shook her head and put her dagger away. 'Not interested,' she said.

'But you don't know what I want,' Zatopek protested.

'I think I do,' she said.

'Will you at least come to my home to share a meal and let me tell you?'

Leone thought about the offer. By the look of him he ate well and he already knew she would not take any job offer. *Why not?* She shrugged.

'Fine,' she said. 'Lead the way.'

Zatopek's home was on the edge of the Widows' Quarter, far enough out of the way to escape most of the beggars, but close enough to smell them. It was a modest home, but one that displayed the taste of the owner. Leone looked closely at the quality of the workmanship, then reassessed Zatopek. He was a man of considerable means. This house would have cost her several years' wages.

'Please enter my home and be welcome,' he said as he opened the door for her. His words had the intonation of ritual greeting. On impulse Leone replied in the formal, ritualistic way used by Shanek on entering the house of an important dignitary.

'May the Ways of Purity meet within your walls,' she said.

Zatopek smiled. 'I knew you were an educated woman,' he said. 'Please, come in.'

Inside, the house was a study in understated magnificence. Everything was of the finest quality, tasteful and elegant. Leone looked around, checking for any indication of hidden guards and defensible positions. She found none.

Zatopek led her through the entry hall into a library that opened out onto a small garden in a courtyard that would have been invisible from the street. A fish splashed happily in a pond that was set just off centre. Across the courtyard, Leone could see windows that looked down over the garden. Lights were glowing in two niches. It was a scene of tranquil beauty.

A discreet cough brought her back to the reason she was here. She turned to see Zatopek seated in a comfortable chair. He gestured for Leone to sit in its mate.

'I see you like my humble home,' he said without a hint of irony.

'It is beautiful,' she said.

'Not only are you an educated woman,' he observed. 'You are also a woman of discernment.'

Leone sat still, wondering where this was going, acutely aware that the chair he had given her had its back to the courtyard. The space between her shoulder blades twitched uncomfortably.

'And,' he went on, 'you have military training.'

'What makes you say that?' she asked, dismayed at how obvious it must be.

Zatopek wagged an admonitory finger at her. 'Don't be shy. It makes you a very attractive prospect.'

She stiffened.

Zatopek saw the response and hurried to reassure her. 'Oh, no,' he said. 'Nothing like that, nothing like that at all. No, I want to hire you.'

'I've already told you no,' she replied.

'But you said no to an offer I hadn't even made.'

'Make your offer.'

'After we share that meal I promised you,' he said. The door opened and a servant entered with a tray holding two drinks. 'An extra guest for tonight, Mayenne,' Zatopek said, taking a glass.

'Very good,' Mayenne said. She turned to Leone. 'Are there any dietary requirements you need me to allow for?' she asked. Her voice was soft and gentle, betraying only a hint of a Matrin accent.

Leone shook her head. 'I'm hungry,' she said. 'I'll eat anything.' She accepted the drink Mayenne offered her.

Mayenne bowed and left the room.

When the door was closed, Zatopek fixed Leone with a questioning gaze. 'Tell me about yourself,' he asked.

Leone shook her head.

'Very well then, I'll tell you about me,' he went on. He sat back and steepled his fingers, staring up at the ceiling. 'As I've said, my parents were from Herath. They were moderately successful merchants, trading mainly in cloth and exotic spices. Herath is not exactly the cultural centre of the Empire, so they moved, when I was about ten summers old, to the Southern Province. They were more successful there, dealing with the Children of Danan when they deigned to come to shore, and with other travellers. When I was about sixteen, they made a very bad deal with a rogue Child.

443

'Somehow she managed to convince them that an old harp was worth a fortune. They sold all they had and bought it, convinced that it had magical powers. It didn't. She cheated them badly and they lost everything, or so they thought.

'For about a year they wallowed in self-pity and poverty, before a Skrin Tia'k slave saw them carrying that wretched harp through the market on their way to their little stall and tried to steal it. In the course of the altercation, a Fyrd came to their aid and recognised the slave as an escapee.

'The owner was so happy to have his slave back that he gave my parents a rich reward, enough to set themselves up again as merchants. It took them a few years but they regained their wealth. By the time I took over the business, they were happy to retire rich.' He paused to sip his drink.

'For a while I was happy with their business, but for some reason I couldn't get the harp out of my mind, so I took it to the harbour. I went to the first Children's ship I saw and spoke to the Captain. When he saw it he offered me his ship for it. I traded on the spot.

'The ship was laden with rare blaewhal carvings, spices and some of the most beautiful artworks I have ever seen.' He gestured around the room. 'It made me as rich as you see here.'

Leone looked again at the room, taking in the elegance and simple beauty in every corner. As a woman who had spent most of the past several years in and out of the palaces and homes of the richest, most powerful members of the greatest empire the world had ever seen, she felt she knew about wealth.

Yet here, in this simple house on the edge of the Widows' Quarter, she saw some of the most beautiful things imaginable. Leone looked back at Zatopek.

'That harp?' she asked. 'What was so special about it?'

Zatopek shrugged. 'I have looked into the legends of the Children and harps do tend to figure in many of them. This one was old, made of wood so old it was bleached white. The best legend they have is the one about the Danan and her magical harp.' He shrugged and took a sip of his drink before going on. 'I imagine the Captain thought he was getting his hands on an ancient harp of legend. He wasn't, of course, but at the time I knew nothing about the Danan and harps, I just wanted money. Since then, I have learned more about the harps of the Children. The Captain swindled himself, which I still think was poetic justice considering how badly his fellow Child had swindled my parents.'

Leone took a deep swallow of her drink. It was, she imagined, an expensive wine, but to her it was cool and tasted good. 'So why do you live here?' she asked. 'With this kind of wealth you could live anywhere in the Empire.'

Zatopek's face darkened. 'I have my reasons,' he said.

Leone regarded him impassively, aware that silence can be the most effective question of all. Zatopek returned her gaze and waited her out. How long the silence would have lasted, Leone could not tell, for it was interrupted by Mayenne's entrance.

'Dinner is ready,' she said.

445

As they stood, Leone was reminded of the document Shanek had struggled with. On impulse she paused and faced the woman.

'Mayenne,' she said, 'in Matrin, is there any significance attached to the word for sheep?'

Mayenne's face showed shock, followed by an odd mixture of fear and suspicion. She shot Zatopek a questioning glance but Leone was unable to see his response.

'Yes, there is, Kind Lady,' Mayenne started, using the ancient Matrin honorific. 'The Matrin symbol is often translated as "sheep" but it can also signify any kind of owned creature, sometimes even slaves. It's the case with many Matrin symbols,' she went on, her voice becoming animated. 'The most common confusion is the symbol that gave the Empire its name.'

Leone frowned. 'In what way?' she asked.

'It's nearly always translated "world", but it also means "earth" or even "dirt".' A smile lit her face. 'I like to think that the mighty Empire of the World is actually the Empire of the Dirt.'

Leone laughed at the image of the Thane boldly holding court over dirt. Mayenne joined in, her laughter rich and gleeful. Zatopek chuckled as he urged Leone into the dining room.

The meal laid before them was simple and satisfying. It consisted of roasted meats, vegetables and thick, piquant sauces. There was a selection of fine wines to accompany the dishes with a tasty selection of fruits to follow. Leone ate with relish and gusto, enjoying it as much as she had any meal she could remember.

By the time she pushed aside her plate, she could eat no more. She stifled a hearty belch of satisfaction. Zatopek pretended not to notice.

'You set a good table, Zatopek,' Leone said.

'Thank you, Leone,' he replied. 'My cooks are very good.' He leaned back slightly to allow Mayenne to take his plate. 'Thank you,' he murmured. Mayenne smiled.

Leone watched the brief interplay and wondered at their relationship. It wouldn't be the first time, she reasoned. And Mayenne was a handsome woman.

Zatopek sat back and regarded Leone. 'Now to business,' he said. 'I want to offer you a job.'

'I've already said no,' said Leone.

'I know, but you said no before you knew what it was.'

Leone shrugged.

'I do not want you as an enforcer or a hired thug, if that's what you were thinking. No, you have more talents than that. You are an intelligent, educated woman, Leone. As well as that, you clearly have some military training. I would think you were an officer. And then, when you lost your arm, you were either discharged or left of your own accord. Either way, you aren't a soldier any more.'

Leone glared at him, the pain of her shaming still sharp.

Zatopek considered her response. 'Not of your own accord, then,' he said. 'I am guessing you bear little love for the Empire.'

Leone shook her head, confident that he would misinterpret it. She meant that he was wrong, but most people would interpret it as agreement, that she

447

did not love the Empire. It still surprised her that despite the Thane's shaming of her and stripping her of her life, she bore neither him nor the Empire any malice. If the truth were told, she agreed with his action. She had failed, and the hereditary line of Counsellors, dating back to the first days of the Empire, was broken because of her. No, the Thane had been justified, and in fact she regarded his actions as merciful. She had expected death by torment.

Zatopek nodded. 'I thought as much,' he said. 'I am usually a good judge of character.' He leaned forward, his expression intense. 'The world is changing, Leone, and it's time for those of us with means to be a part of it.'

'What do you mean?' asked Leone.

'I think you know what I mean, Leone. I want you to join me and others like me.'

'Exactly what do you want from me, Zatopek?'

'Our forces are spread far and wide across the Empire. We need as many trained soldiers as we can get. They need training and organising; we need officers.'

Leone sat back, thinking. She knew her face was unreadable when she wanted it to be, so she was confident that Zatopek would have no idea that her mind was whirling with possibilities. First among them was the thought that if she were to join this rebellion, she would be in the perfect place to learn of their plans, maybe even help direct them into ruin. Despite Zatopek's assumption, she still believed in the Empire, and she bore a great deal of love for aspects of it.

'I need to think about it,' she said finally.

'Of course you do,' agreed Zatopek. 'Can I offer you a place to sleep tonight?'

Leone nodded. 'Yes, that would be nice. It's been a while since I slept in a bed.'

Mayenne, who had been standing silently in the shadows by the doorway, led her upstairs to a comfortable bedroom. She lit a lamp and showed her in. There was a large bed, a wash basin, a wardrobe, a mirror and a bookshelf.

'I hope you sleep well, Leone,' Mayenne said. She turned to go.

'Mayenne,' said Leone, 'that Matrin word for sheep I asked you about earlier?'

'Yes, Leone?'

'If someone was negotiating a treaty and it was about sheep, could the word have any other meanings?'

Mayenne shrugged. 'It could. If the treaty was well worded, it could refer to the Skrin Tia'k.'

Leone nodded. 'Thank you,' she said. 'Goodnight.'

Mayenne nodded and left the room.

Leone looked around. The room was not overly large, but certainly larger than any room she'd ever had to herself. She opened the wardrobe and found it full of beautiful clothes. With a smile, she undressed and pulled out a dress. She held it in front of her and stood in front of the mirror. It was so beautiful it took her breath away.

It was a slow process, but she tried on every item of clothing in the wardrobe. Most of them were too small, but those that fitted were gorgeous. She even

449

found some sleeping clothes in her size. When she eased herself between the thick blankets, she was wearing a silk nightdress that had probably cost a month's wages for an artisan.

She lay for hours staring at the ceiling, thinking and planning. Many times she silently berated herself for not spending more time during her training on ways of infiltrating an enemy camp and methods of covert sabotage.

It had not escaped her notice that Mayenne had not called her 'Kind Lady' when showing her to the room, but Leone. The change in address most likely meant that she believed Leone to have joined them. She wondered if Zatopek would be so easy to deceive.

35

The Wrested Archipelago was a dismal, storm-lashed collection of ten small islands. They were all that remained of a once-mighty mountain range that thrust itself proudly above the Sea, challenging her might and power. For aeons they stood rearing over the waves that crashed, seemingly impotent, against them. But time is an implacable foe and the mighty mountains were slowly worn down to this collection of jagged rocky outcrops.

For centuries these islands belonged, as did all such things, to the Children of Danan. They mined the crags for gold and iron, which they traded with islanders for wood and cloth. During Wind Season, they left and headed north, taking their goods, leaving behind only debris to be blown away.

One of the Commander's greatest moments was when he led a raiding fleet against the archipelago. With cunning and skill, he ambushed the Children's work fleet as they left at the beginning of Wind Season. He attacked them with speed and brutality, sinking most of their ships and taking what was left for his own. In a move that surprised everyone, he left behind a small garrison on the largest of the islands. They built a small barracks and stayed through the Wind Season until Harvest Season. During this time the Raiders battened down inside their new home, building siege weaponry and designing tactics so that when the Children next came to mine the archipelago they would find it occupied and defended. The Children were driven back when they arrived and the Raiders claimed the rich source of minerals as their own. For the first time, the Raiders had wrested something from the Children.

Over the following years, the Raiders who stayed eked out a harsh existence on the barren rocks. Their families came and joined them, more buildings grew like limpets on the sterile rock and children were born there. For them it was all they knew and they learned to love the untamed, wild beauty of the southern seas. For the first time, the Southern Raiders produced poets and artists. After years of piracy and violence being the only things they had to offer the rest of the world, they now had art and raw materials.

Still, nothing grew there and during the Wind Season it was pitiless, but somehow it had become a home to them. For the rest of the Raiders, it took on iconic status, a new place, a symbol of the Commander's vision. Many took it as hope, but some saw it as folly. It had taken the Commander years and all of his persuasive skills to move the Southern Raiders to where they could follow him in his plan. The fact that he had succeeded was testament to his tenacity as much as to his foresight.

But none of that really mattered to Sacchin who skippered the *Merial* towards the Wrested Archipelago, nor to Nolin, who navigated. They drove the ship over the waves at breakneck speed.

Wyn, even after having been away from the Sea for years, could smell the ice and feel the change of season as the winds swung. They were drifting around to a southerly direction, bringing with them the harsh tang of old ice and cold green water. To be heading south as these winds started was folly. Everyone onboard knew it and was getting nervous.

But Wyn had experienced and survived such a storm as only the far south in Wind Season could throw up, and he was far beyond mere nervousness. With every hour, every stroke they travelled south, he could feel the fear building within him. He had known real fear, that deep terror that few men ever felt, as he had clung for hours to a broken spar in a brutal storm and he knew he would not survive again. He also knew that Sacchin would not turn the *Merial* around, even if Nolin let him.

They both had their own reasons for braving the folly of the far south in the Wind Season, and neither would turn aside. The Raiders must be warned about the waiting Children's fleet or they would be wiped from the face of the waters.

So they sped south, watching as the sleeping monster stirred, brooding on the surging terror that was about to descend upon anyone foolish enough to get in its way.

'How much further?' Sacchin asked Nolin.

'You should know,' the Navigator replied. 'They are your islands.'

Sacchin laughed. It was the first time laughter had been heard for two days, and it sounded strained. 'I've never been there,' he replied. 'I've heard about them, of course, but ...' his voice trailed off.

Nolin nodded. 'I have been there. Once. And I have no desire to go back. They're unattractive, to say the least.' He suddenly looked up, his eyes becoming unfocused as he sniffed the air. A frown crossed his face as he looked to the south. 'That's not good,' he muttered.

Sacchin watched as he made a minute course change and ordered a shift in one of the sails. 'What's the problem?' he asked.

'Storm coming,' Nolin replied.

'How can you tell?'

'Smell. A wind shift brought the smell of ice. Couldn't you smell it?'

'No,' replied Sacchin.

'I did,' said Wyn. He had been standing by the railing, ostensibly tending a shroud, but all the while listening.

Nolin regarded Wyn through slitted eyes. 'You're no lander, are you?'

Wyn flicked Sacchin a glance, knowing how he would react. 'No.'

Sacchin's eyes widened as realisation slowly dawned. 'You're one of the Children, aren't you?'

Wyn nodded.

'What are you doing here?'

'Going home,' Wyn replied.

454

Sacchin frowned, not understanding. 'But the Children have no home.'

'They have the Sea,' murmured Nolin. 'But I don't think that's what he meant, is it, Wyn?'

'No.'

Sacchin's frown deepened. 'That girl?' he said. 'You're going home to her?'

Wyn nodded.

'She's one of the Children?'

Wyn nodded again.

'So that's why you signed up on this voyage in the first place, isn't it? You were planning on betraying us all along! You said there was a girl, but you never said she was one of the Children!'

There was nothing that Wyn could do but nod again.

Sacchin's normally genial and open face changed, suffused with rage, into something almost unrecognisable. 'I invited you into my home! I trusted you!'

Wyn was about to say something when Nolin interrupted.

'This girl, is she a Priestess?' he asked.

Wyn shrugged. 'In a fashion.'

'You have been away a long time, Wyn,' observed Nolin. 'To have forgotten our ways so completely. No one is a Priestess "in a fashion".'

'You don't know her,' muttered Wyn, unwilling to be drawn.

'If she is a Priestess, I assure you I do. As Navigator of the First Rank I have met them all.'

'You haven't met her yet. But I think you will.'

'Again, you intrigue me,' said Nolin. Wyn watched him closely, allowing the Navigator to consider what he had just been told. Abruptly, his eyes snapped wide as a thought occurred to him. 'Just who is this girl?'

'Her name is Hwenfayre,' said Wyn. 'Blonde, lavender-eyed. Sings very well. Nice harp.'

'Do you know what you are saying?' asked Nolin.

Wyn held the Navigator's eye as he nodded slowly. 'I know exactly what I am saying, and when I last saw her Morag had her.'

'Morag?'

'Yes. Morag, High Priestess of the Children of Danan.'

'This is very bad,' said Nolin. 'Very bad indeed. Does Morag know what she is?'

Wyn nodded. 'I think so, yes.'

'What about Hwenfayre herself? What does she know?'

'More than Morag does, I think.'

'That's unlikely,' disagreed Nolin. 'For all her faults, Morag is a scholar of rare ability. And one of the most brilliant, if devious, minds I've ever known. No, she knows exactly what is happening around her.'

'So what is happening?' asked Sacchin. 'I don't understand any of this. What does this traitor's girlfriend have to do with anything?'

'Best you don't know too much,' said Nolin. 'But Wyn here is a very dangerous man, and he has very dangerous friends.'

'I already know how dangerous he is. I've seen him in a fight.'

'Not that sort of danger,' said Nolin. He looked at Wyn, his eyes hard. 'I think we should find your Commander,' he continued, without looking away from Wyn. 'With your permission, Sacchin,' he said.

Sacchin nodded, a troubling thought growing within him.

'More sail,' bellowed Nolin. He took the wheel again and made yet another slight course adjustment and the *Merial* seemed to gather even more speed.

36

Shanek scratched at his beard as he stared out over the Great Fastness. The itch was a part of him now; he didn't feel right without it. The ever-present wind whipped his long black hair over his face. Annoyed, he pushed it back.

This burned wind! he thought. *It always blows out here.* Of all the various things he'd had to put up with, this wretched wind was the worst.

Recently it was bringing with it the scents and tastes of volcanic ash. Another mountain had blown its guts out. That made six in the last two months. The range marking the northern edge of the Great Fastness glowed with the angry red of lava. Every night it tinged the sky, casting an eerie light over this most lonely of places.

'Shanek!' called Ejaj. 'See anything?'

Shanek shook his head. 'They've made it to the mountains by now. They're gone.'

'There'll be more tomorrow.'

'There'd better be,' Shanek muttered. Even after months of slaughter, his hunger for more Skrinnies to kill was unquenched.

'Leave it, Shanek,' said Ananda. 'Let's make camp. That knot had enough to keep us busy for a week, just counting it all. So what if three got away?'

Shanek whipped around to fix the woman with a glare.

'I know, I know,' she said. '"The monsters didn't let any of mine escape, why should I?"'

She returned his glare. 'Don't you ever get tired of the same line?'

He shook his head and returned to his contemplation of the grassland. 'Never,' he muttered.

After the discovery of the massacre, Shanek's memory went hazy. It was as if a portion of his life disappeared, leaving only flickering remnants that haunted his sleepless nights. He caught images of hunting down Skrinnies and slaughtering them to the last one, of long hunts deep into the grasslands, of seemingly endless pursuits across miles of flat plains, but mostly he remembered the sights, sounds and smells of hundreds of dead Skrin Tia'k.

He'd learned much: Skrin Tia'k tired quickly if pursued uphill; they were afraid of the bolas; they ate rarely, but voraciously; and his mysterious ability to hear and know them was somehow linked to the ground. When riding or even wearing boots, he could hear nothing. When barefoot, he knew where his enemy was and what they were doing.

His feet grew leathery and hard as he ran across the plains in pursuit of the ancient enemy of his people. At first, none of the others with him questioned his hunting; they seemed to accept his need for vengeance. But as the days melted into weeks, then to months, they became reticent. The first to broach it was Ejaj.

'Shanek,' he said one night, 'I think it is time we put aside just hunting Skrinnies. Don't get me wrong,' he added hastily at Shanek's glare, 'I enjoy killing the monsters as much as anyone else, but we are bandits, not a forward-scouting Fyrd for the Thane.'

Shanek continued to glare, silently challenging the older man. Ejaj was a leader and he knew what Shanek was doing. *So it comes to this,* Shanek thought.

Ejaj continued. 'We are heading back south tomorrow, back to where the pickings are easier.' He paused, looking at the rest of the troop for support. 'And richer.'

Shanek, too, was a leader, and a better one than Ejaj. He knew what drove people like this ragtag bunch. 'It's money you want, is it?' he said quietly in the tone his Leadership Tutor had drilled him in. He knew it was a tone people heard and heeded. 'I'll show you more money than you can carry.'

'Skrinnies never carry anything valuable,' Ejaj said. 'Everyone knows it. That's why we've never bothered hunting them before.'

Shanek grinned a cold, hard smile. 'You've just never known where to look.'

Ananda snorted. 'I've lived all my life out here and you say I don't know where to look! What would you know?'

'Give me tomorrow. If I don't lead you to a rich take, we'll all go south and take the easy road.'

Ejaj narrowed his eyes. 'You're good, Shanek, I'll warrant, but you don't know the Fastness like we do.'

'How many have you lost since I joined you?' asked Shanek.

'No one,' admitted Ejaj. 'I said you're good. The best tactical man I've ever met, but you still don't know the Fastness or the Skrinnies like us.'

'Is that a no, then?' asked Shanek.

'That's a no, Shanek.'

'Fine. I'll go alone. Wait for me by the Weeping Outpost tomorrow night. I'll join you there and show you what you're missing.'

Dotted across the Great Fastness were hundreds of ruined keeps, castles and defensive outposts left over from the great wars. They provided shelter and haven for people like Ejaj's band. The one Shanek referred to was little more than a tumble of stones, but a peculiarity of its structure meant it acted as a moisture trap for the winds. Every night as the air cooled, moisture trickled down the stones like tears, collecting in a small hollow.

'It's been good to know you, Shanek, but if you're planning to hunt a knot alone, we'll be travelling south, the day after tomorrow, without you.'

Shanek's eyes hardened. 'We'll see.'

Later, when the sounds of contented snoring were all that broke the silence of the night, Shanek rolled out of his bed. The ground was quiet, nothing moved close by. He rested his hands lightly on the dirt, feeling the ancient pain of battle that still lingered.

Still not knowing what he did or how he did it, he made sure everyone was asleep, even, he noted with annoyance, the sentry. On silent feet he padded out into the night. Knowing the exact location of every rock, root and dip meant that he could confidently run across this land even in total darkness.

He ran until he sensed the now familiar presence of a Skrin Tia'k knot. It was a hunting party carrying nothing. He ignored it and continued north.

His confidence was based on the fact that he had sensed many more knots than the ones he had hunted. So far he'd only been interested in warrior knots or hunting knots. The trade knots he'd left alone, but they were out here.

He found one just after dawn. It was not a large one, only four nestlings, but they carried a fortune in diamonds and beautifully carved ebony. They were travelling west and would come across his path within the hour. He could sense no hunters and they were careless. Shanek 'watched' them for a while. They were spread out, with a younger one lagging behind a bit. That would be his first target. He settled in to wait.

The sun was already hot by the time they arrived. He watched the first three pass him. They were unaware of Shanek's presence.

The lagging Skrin Tia'k wandered along, completely ignorant. Shanek waited until it had passed and then stepped out. The distinctive sound of the bolas alerted it, but too late. Its head snapped cleanly off when the heavy metal ball smashed through the exoskeleton at the base of its neck.

The sounds alerted the others but Shanek was ready for them. They split up to find him; he hid.

462

Knowing exactly where they were and what they were doing enabled him to pick them off one by one. Each time the bolas sang its deadly song, he could feel the fear in the remaining Skrin Tia'k increase.

The last one left of the knot, the one carrying the largest bag of goods, decided to run from its hunter. It turned away from where Shanek lay in wait and fled northwards. Shanek stood, his bolas whirling above his head, and called out to it.

'Hey, monster! Stand and fight, coward!'

The Skrin Tia'k slowed, then stopped and turned back to him. It raised itself on its rearmost legs and clicked at him. Shanek listened, aware that the Skrinnie believed that he could not understand it.

Beast, it clicked, *I hear you. You hunt us and we die. But the time comes when we shall hunt you. You will not kill us then. We have taken your Guardian and your Weapon.*

While it clicked, Shanek slowly moved closer until, just as the Skrinnie finished, he was in range. It lowered itself to the ground and Shanek released the bolas.

The weapon flew across the intervening space with a whistle and the cord caught the Skrinnie around the neck. With a squeal, the Skrin Tia'k clutched at the barbed cable but the metal balls spun around and smashed into its face. It clattered to the ground and lay still.

'He'll be here,' Ananda said.

'No, he won't,' said Raol. 'He's either long gone or Skrinnie food by now.'

Shanek listened to them as he lay behind the wall of the Weeping Outpost. It had been a hard run but he'd made it here before them. He was sure the selection of treasure he'd brought was enough to whet their appetite.

When they rounded the wall, he was leaning back counting diamonds.

Ejaj relinquished all semblance of command after that. Shanek became their leader and he drove them hard. They had no way of knowing it, but he was training them as a Fyrd. He taught them to use the bolas, he taught them battle strategies and he taught them field communications. At first they resisted, preferring their own tested ways of fighting, but after a few easy wins they took to Shanek's ways with a passion.

Shanek was initially pleased with their willingness, but it faded as he realised that their passion was for the ease of victory, not the point of the wins. They simply enjoyed winning, they saw no purpose in their winning. Neither, if it came down to it, did he. Time had eased the burden of his guilt, and he hunted Skrin Tia'k because he could. They were a defeated enemy, defeated centuries ago, and his personal vengeance had lost its sweet flavour. Despite that, he *knew*, at a visceral level, that the Skrin Tia'k still posed a threat and that hunting them was *right*, somehow. It troubled him both that he knew and that he did not know how he knew. No matter that he had grown up with ritual torture and casual brutality, the simple hunting and slaughter of Skrinnies should not feel so right. All his training and his beliefs led him to reject living his life by feelings. Feelings are unreliable, they change too quickly, they can be inflamed and lead to irrational actions, yet ... He sighed. That was the problem: he was doing the right thing, he knew it, but how could this be right?

37

The sun was barely over the horizon and ice was forming on the ground. Shanek was standing watch, looking north into the wind screaming across the Fastness, feeling for the presence of any knots.

'Even the monsters stay at home on days like this,' he muttered.

'That they do, Shanek,' said Ananda.

He had been distantly aware of her presence but had dismissed it. She was no Skrin Tia'k. He grunted in response.

'What do you see that we don't, Shanek?' she asked.

'Nothing,' he said.

'We all know that's not true,' she said. 'There's something about you that's odd.'

'Thanks for that,' he said wryly. He was aware of her attraction to him but chose to ignore it.

'I didn't mean it that way,' she continued hesitantly. 'It's ... you're not like us. You're ... I don't know ...'

Shanek suddenly sensed something. Holding up his hand to stop Ananda speaking, he focused inwards.

Someone is coming. Not Skrin Tia'k, people. A large company of people. Coming from the south. He turned around to look. Nothing visible, yet.

'Ananda, go and wake Ejaj and the rest. I think we're going to have some company.'

She took one look at his face and ran.

Shanek focused on the approaching people. There were one hundred and nine horses, all bearing a rider. They were all armed but there was no malice in their approach. They were peaceful.

He listened.

I still think this is a bad idea, Maru.

I don't care what you think; if these are half as good as the rumours, we'll do well.

But if they aren't?

Then we turn around and go home.

Ejaj isn't known for being friendly.

It's not Ejaj's troop any more. It's this new one, this Shanek. He's supposed to be the brains of the outfit.

Where did you get your information, Maru? No one's been out here for months.

Never you mind, Bartin. I hear things.

'So do I, Maru,' whispered Shanek. 'And I want to know where you get your information too.' He intensified his attention on the small, wiry man on the lead horse, the man named Maru.

He was fair-skinned with white-blond hair. A Tribesman! Shanek remembered all too clearly the last Tribesman, Tapash, whom he had killed. Did this one have tattoos too? Shanek could not see. Was he the only Tribesman? No, about a third of the company was from the northern reaches of Ettan.

Shanek probed deeper, seeking treachery.

There it is, Shanek realised. A group within a group.

Ejaj jogged up. 'You wanted to see me?'

'There's a company coming,' Shanek said. 'I think they want to join us.'

Ejaj nodded. 'Good. The more men we have, the more Skrinnies we can hunt. The richer we all get.'

Shanek grunted in agreement. 'I don't think we want to trust them completely.' He stared into the south. 'Wake everyone up, let's greet our visitors.'

When Maru and his company rode up to the ruined keep known as Mischa's Outpost, they were greeted by a lone man standing about twenty paces away from the base of the keep.

'Greetings,' the man called. 'You choose a cold morning to visit.'

'We're looking for Shanek,' replied Maru.

'Oh? Why is that?'

'We've heard he's making a lot of money and we like money.' Maru turned to his men. 'Don't we, boys?'

The company behind him roared in agreement.

Shanek regarded Maru carefully. He was wrapped against the bitter wind, but his long bone-white hair was uncovered and blew freely, wreathing his head in an outlandish white halo. The man was a liar and a thief, but he was also very intelligent. A plotter and a schemer.

'What tribe?' Shanek asked abruptly.

If Maru was taken aback by the sudden change of subject he did not show it. 'No tribe, not any more,' he said. 'Just a free man making his way in a violent world.'

'For a man who has renounced his tribe you bring a lot of your old tribe with you,' Shanek observed mildly.

Maru laughed. 'I can't help it if others feel the same way, can I?'

'No, that's true, Maru,' agreed Shanek. 'Be welcome at our fire, and may you find Purity.'

And so Shanek's company went from twelve to one hundred and twenty-one. The rest of his troop poured out from their hiding places and greeted the new members. Shanek watched Maru carefully. The man was surprised that Shanek knew his name, as he was at the size of the troop he had just joined. The First Son of the Empire needed neither extensive training, years of practice nor mystical assistance to know the Tribesman was already thinking of taking over the operation.

Wait your turn, Maru, thought Shanek.

38

'Bring me my harp, girl,' said the High Priestess. She was standing alone in the prow, watching the sun rise. Erin, nervous at being so close to Morag, scurried to obey. The Novices were rostered to serve the High Priestess and, every time her turn came, Erin panicked. It was not that the High Priestess had ever been unpleasant or threatening, it was just that she radiated power. There was something about her that frightened the timid girl.

She was well aware that many things frightened her, but Morag was different. Her casual disregard for the feelings of others, her almost callous treatment of Hylin as well as the way she seemed unconcerned by the death of Hwenfayre made the young Novice more than afraid. She found herself becoming increasingly angry.

It was an unfamiliar feeling for Erin. She was comfortable with feeling fear, helplessness was normal, but anger was new and she was unsure what to do with it. She considered talking to Sara or Maeve, but they had never been kind to her or understood her gentle nature. The only person who had ever really spent time with her had been Hwenfayre.

As she gathered the beautiful bleached driftwood harp from the High Priestess's cabin she was startled by a voice.

'Be careful with that, Novice.'

Erin looked up, the harp slipping in her grasp. Hurriedly she clasped it to her chest as she looked to who had spoken.

Declan was slouched in a chair, partially in shadow. He did not move as he spoke. 'That harp is worth more than your life, Novice Erin,' he observed. 'Worth more than any of our lives in fact.'

Not knowing what to say, Erin nodded.

'You have no idea what I am talking about, do you?' he asked. When she shook her head, he smiled and leaned forward. 'No, you wouldn't — but you should. You know her. You probably know her better than any of us. And even you don't know the value of that instrument.'

Confused, Erin could merely stare at him.

'Hwenfayre,' he mused. 'She could have saved us all, you know.'

'Saved us?'

Declan grinned wryly as he nodded. 'But she didn't and now she will probably destroy us all.' As he spoke, he rocked back and raised a bottle to his lips. 'I'm a little drunk,' he said. 'But you could work that out for yourself, couldn't you?' He leered at her, a look that made Erin take a hurried step backwards. 'You are a delicate little thing, aren't you? But don't worry, my life is pledged to that evil bitch we both call High Priestess. Oh, I see that surprises you. And

I would think less of you if it didn't. Not that I ever actually think of you, but well, there it is.' He took another drink, some of the liquid trickling down his chin. 'She tried to kill her. You didn't know that, did you? Our beloved Morag had the innocent Hwenfayre thrown overboard. She didn't slip or get washed away, she was thrown.' He wiped his chin with the back of his hand. As he stared at the liquor on his hand, his eyes suddenly filled with tears. 'I've killed us all,' he said. 'The gentle Hwenfayre won't be so gentle with us. Not now that we tried to kill her.'

Erin was frowning as she tried to understand what Declan meant. '*Tried* to kill her?' she asked.

'Oh, yes,' said Declan, brightening slightly. 'You can't kill the Mistress of the Waters by throwing her into the water, can you? Oh no, the Sea gave her back. But we've had our chance. She gave Hwenfayre to the Southern Raiders. And now we're all dead.' Tears started to fall down his unshaven cheeks. He raised his bottle in mocking salute to Erin. 'And so I drink to life.'

'But you . . .' Erin started.

'But I am her lover?' Declan completed for her. 'Is that what you mean, gentle Erin?'

The young Novice nodded.

'I am, to my shame, yes. But I have recently realised something about our beloved High Priestess that everyone else on the water has known for seasons.' He raised the bottle to his lips again and took a long drink. When he was finished, he threw the empty bottle against the wall of the cabin, where it shattered. 'I thought she loved me, you know,' he said. 'I always thought that beyond all the lies, the duplicity, she truly loved me. But you know what I just found out?' Declan tried to lever himself up from the chair, but failed. He slumped back down, defeated by gravity, the drink and his own weakness. 'She never loved me, not from the very start. I was always just a part of her mother's plan.' He dropped his head into his hands, so that when he spoke his voice was muffled. Erin had to strain to hear. 'All the lies,' he muttered. 'All the deaths, everything I have ever done for her, all for her, all for a lie.'

39

They hunt us.
They are too many.
We must flee!
There, go there! They do not hunt us there!
Tell the nestlings, we go there!
Run!

Shanek signalled to Raol. 'They're breaking up. Take the bolas teams and block their escape. Over there.'

Raol saw the signals and signalled his understanding. Silently he gestured to the bolas teams and they moved quietly through the long grass to where the remaining Skrin Tia'k would soon be fleeing.

One of the early things Shanek had learned about the ancient enemy was that they had poor eyesight but very good hearing. They relied upon hearing the humans' shouted commands in a battle. By using the old battle signalling, Shanek effectively neutralised one of the most powerful advantages the Skrinnies had in a fight. They could understand speech, but humans could not understand their clicking. The

Skrin Tia'k also relied upon hearing the hooves of horses, long before they saw them. By reverting to infantry, Shanek removed that advantage. Even a large command like his could hide in the long grasses of the Great Fastness and lie in wait for a knot. The only problem was knowing where the Skrin Tia'k would be. Shanek had removed that difficulty too.

Maru's company contained several skilled bolas-men. Shanek employed them to teach others in the proficient use of the ancient weapon to set up the specialist teams that now went to block the Skrinnie retreat. Whilst swords, spears and battleaxes were efficient enough, when it came to bringing down a running Skrin Tia'k nothing could touch the bolas. When thrown at the running limbs, either just the rear two or both sets, including the attack limbs, the bolas could entangle and break them. The ululating squeal of a broken Skrinnie could slow or stop others, even in the midst of a full retreat. Three well-thrown bolases could rout a whole knot.

They wait!
They know!
It is the Maimer. It hunts us!
Save yourselves, nestlings!

The Skrinnies had learned of Shanek's methods. They had learned to fear the one they called the Maimer. Shanek felt their fear and revelled in it. The whistle of several bolases, followed by the squeals of at least three Skrinnies, signalled the effective end of another battle.

A few crunching sounds, some more squealing, and the last Skrin Tia'k crackled dead to the ground, its greenish ichor seeping into the ground to join that of so many of its fellows. This vast open area had seen more than its fair share of vicious battles over the centuries.

Tonight?

Yes, tonight. Spread the word. Tonight we move.

Shanek frowned as the random thoughts drifted through his mind. He was expecting it.

Shanek's Seekers, as they now called themselves, stood and cheered. Another easy win. Another big haul of wealth. Despite their greatly increased numbers, they were all now very wealthy bandits. And it was time to celebrate, Shanek realised. Some of them had been out here in the Fastness for over a year. He had been here nearly a year himself, and he felt the need for some comfort and some luxury. He looked at Maru. The wiry Tribesman grinned back at him.

Shanek made a decision. 'Back to Mischa's Outpost!' he called. 'Tonight we feast!'

The Seekers roared in appreciation. As they turned for the ruin that they called home, Shanek pulled Ejaj aside. 'Keep a careful eye on Maru and his Tribesmen. They are treacherous,' he said.

Ejaj had long since given up questioning what Shanek told him. He'd known him to be right too often. He nodded and turned to leave. Shanek grabbed his arm.

'Stay sober and keep all of ours sober. Treachery

is close,' he hissed. 'Trust me on this. Maru is dangerous.'

They ran for the rest of the day and made Mischa's Outpost by nightfall. A campfire was already lit, prepared by the cooks. One advantage that Maru's troop brought with them was the presence of cooks, hunters and the other specialists that a band of twelve could not have. Mischa's Outpost had been rapidly transformed into a home, rather than a makeshift campsite.

A meal fit for a celebration was underway, with three large stags roasting on spits and a massive pot of bubbling vegetable stew. The exhausted but happy Seekers jogged into their new home, burdened with treasure, full of grand plans.

Skrin Tia'k had a particularly fiery liquor they called Uryt'as and the Seekers had developed a taste for it. Most knots carried at least one or two casks. Shanek normally insisted on a strict rationing of the supplies, but tonight was special.

'Break open the casks,' he said to Bartin. Maru's second-in-command had proved himself a capable leader, and Shanek sensed no guile in him. Bartin nodded.

'Good idea, Shanek,' he said.

Are you trying to make this easy for us, you
  fool?
Is he that subtle?
No, but he may be that overconfident.
How could he know? Should we wait?
He can't. No one has broken faith. Nothing has
  changed. Tonight we strike.

The night was clear, the air was sharp with the smells of ash and ice, and the wind was swirling as if unsure. Shanek's Seekers were happy. Their bellies were full of good food, their minds were full of wealth and their heads were full of Uryt'as. Laughter and song rang out across the Great Fastness as it had not done for hundreds of years. Almost, almost, Shanek could forget why he was here.

Tirace, a woman from Maru's command, sidled up to him. 'Shanek,' she slurred. 'Come dance with me.' Her brown hair was cut short and she smelt of Uryt'as, but she was willing and full-bodied. He shook his head.

'Not tonight,' he said.

She pouted. 'Why not? What is wrong with me?'

'Nothing, Tirace.'

'Then come dance, Shanek.'

'I said no.'

'You don't like me, is that it?'

'No.' He had already looked away from her, he was watching Ejaj as he moved through the happy throng, talking to the original members of his troop, making sure they stayed sober.

Tirace walked away, sullen and upset at Shanek's rejection. He barely noticed her leave, so intent was he on the party before him. Watching it with both his eyes and his mind gave him an oddly out-of-focus view. It was like two images overlaid, one showing the normal boisterous singing and laughing of a drunk and happy group of people, the other showing the slow separation of friend and foe.

There were not many foe, only sixteen, all Tribesmen. As the night progressed and the Uryt'as flowed, they gradually spread themselves out into a pattern that Shanek felt he recognised. As it became more obvious, his suspicions became knowledge. At the moment he knew what was happening, a flicker of fear was born in his breast. This was no ordinary treachery — they had structured their attack like a Skrin Tia'k knot.

Ananda was close to him, as she had been all night. He had been amused to sense a pang of jealousy, followed by an equally strong moment of pleasure when he spoke with and then rejected Tirace.

'Ananda,' he hissed. 'Come here.'

'Shanek?' she replied.

As she moved in closer, he took her in his arms and held her tight, his mouth close to her ear.

'Listen closely and don't interrupt.' For the next few minutes he spoke quickly, outlining his plan and giving orders whilst pretending to caress and fondle her. When he was finished, he said, 'Now slap me and stalk away. Go to Ejaj and alert the others.'

The slap Ananda gave him was convincing. His cheek stung and reddened. As she spun on her heel, she gave him a wink and a smile. Ananda walked away a happy woman.

Shanek touched his cheek. *I know exactly how she's feeling, and I still don't understand her,* he thought. Out loud, he said, 'Women!'

'We're not all like her,' said Tirace.

Shanek knew she had come back but acted surprised. 'I've heard that before,' he said ruefully.

'Come,' said Tirace, holding out her hand to him. 'Let me show you how different I can be.'

Shanek rubbed at his cheek and looked towards where Ananda was now snuggling up to Ejaj. He nodded. 'Why not?' he said. The small, lithe woman led Shanek away to a darkened spot, away from the firelight, where she pulled him down onto the soft, cool earth.

As the revellers slipped into blissful unconsciousness, others, all with bone-white hair and tattooed bodies, arose from feigned sleep and crept among the unaware. Swords drawn, they were looking for a specific man who was watching them from the darkness beyond the flickering light of the dying fire. Beside him, Ejaj stood silently.

'Now,' whispered Shanek.

At his word, Ejaj gave the call and ten archers stood up from behind the ruined wall that bounded the outpost's northern edge. As one, they released their arrows and ten Tribesmen died. There was a second flight of arrows in the air before the sound of the bodies hitting the ground reached their ears. Four more died where they stood, leaving Maru standing alone. His disbelief at the sudden destruction of his plan was exceeded only by his fear at the sound of Shanek's bolas. The barbed cord wrapped around his legs, the heavy balls smashing into his knees, driving him to the ground with a scream of agony. He fell heavily on a sleeping man who was so drunk he didn't even wake up.

Ejaj dashed through the snoring bodies to the screaming Maru. With a carefully weighted blow to the base of his skull, he stopped the noise. He heaved the unconscious man onto his shoulders and carried him back to where Shanek waited.

'Put him there,' instructed Shanek, indicating towards the bound, gagged but fully conscious Tirace. 'Let him seek Rest beside his slut.' Tirace stared. 'What, you think I didn't know? You poor idiot. I've had better than you try to seduce me before. You're not even very good at it.'

Shanek grabbed a waterskin and emptied it on Maru. The wiry Tribesman coughed and spluttered as he regained consciousness. He struggled against his bonds but stopped when Shanek knelt on his chest.

'See this?' asked Shanek. In his hand he held a long, needle-sharp poignard. It glowed in the starlight. 'It's called the Thane's Needle. It is given to a soldier in the Army of the World on promotion to the rank of Coerl. I took it off the body of a soldier I killed.'

Maru's eyes widened in alarm as Shanek rested the sliver of metal, point down, over his heart.

'I think your treachery is something more than simple greed. If greed was all I was concerned about, I'd just cut a few pieces off you and be done with it, but you are not a simple thief, are you, Maru?'

Despite the fear of what Shanek had threatened, Maru shook his head and tried to speak.

'Perhaps I should take that gag off to let you speak in your own defence?'

Maru nodded.

Shanek slashed upwards with the Needle. Maru shrieked with pain as the knife opened his cheek to the bone as Shanek cut the gag.

'Stop squealing or I'll hurt you,' snapped Shanek. Maru choked back his cries. 'Better,' said Shanek, resting the Needle back over Maru's heart. 'Now tell me, what is your relationship with the Skrin Tia'k?'

Maru gaped in shock. 'Nothing,' he rasped.

'No one alive knows Skrin Tia'k battle strategies better than me and your men are trained to fight like a warrior knot. I've been watching. And tonight they mounted a Skrinnie ambush. You are working with them somehow. I want to know how and why.'

'You're mad,' gasped Maru. 'The Skrinnies never work with —' He died with a surprised gasp as the Thane's Needle slid easily into his heart.

'Why did you kill him?' cried Ejaj. 'If he's working with the Skrinnies we need to know more!'

Shanek pulled the Needle out and wiped it on Maru's cloak. He stood. 'Kill her,' he said, indicating Tirace.

Ananda cut her throat with a single stroke and followed Shanek back to the campfire. Standing over the two dead bodies, Ejaj watched them go in disbelief.

Walking away, Shanek felt Ananda's thoughts. He had not paid her much heed, but tonight when he had taken her into his confidence, and then told her to kill Tirace, he sensed her infatuation with him shift into something else. She changed her relationship with him on a profound level. She no longer wanted him in the way some women want the strongest male, she shifted to being loyal. True, she still wanted him, but as she walked beside him, she unconsciously changed. With a shock, he realised she would follow him out of some totally different motivation. He tried to decide what it was but as soon as the change in her mind had happened, his awareness of her trickled away, like water flowing out of a basin. He grasped at the change but it slipped through his mental awareness to vanish forever. Within heartbeats, she had faded from his senses. He stopped to look at her. She returned his look.

'What is it, Shanek?' she asked.

'Oddly, it's nothing,' he answered. 'Truly nothing, and that's the most peculiar thing about it.'

By dawn, all traces of Maru's abortive attempt were gone. Several comrades of the missing fighters were puzzled but accepted the story that they had decided to try their luck further north. The ease with which they accepted the rather flimsy tale confirmed Shanek's suspicion; the Tribesmen were a group within a group.

The headaches and various bruises were mostly forgotten by the time the sun was halfway to its height. Shanek's announcement that they were heading to Herald's View raised spirits even more.

Herald's View was a frontier town half a day's ride south of Mischa's Outpost. It boasted a marketplace, three taverns, four brothels and a garrison of the Army of the World. If they left now they'd be there before dusk. With their accumulated wealth, the night promised much.

'Ejaj,' said Shanek. 'A word.'

'Shanek,' said Ejaj.

'I want you to take them into town. They need to let off steam. Make sure they spend as much of their money as they can. I want that Skrinnie treasure in circulation. Tell anyone anything you want them to know, except where you are based.'

Ejaj picked up the pronoun immediately. 'Don't you mean where *we* are based?'

Shanek shook his head. 'No. I have to leave you now. There's something I have to do.'

40

'Sail!'

'Whereabouts?' called the Commander.

'North and west. Coming up fast astern.'

He turned his telescope to find the sail. It was not one of theirs, and it was fast. Faster than anything he'd ever seen. 'Come about!' he called. 'Ready mangonels!'

The crew scurried to prepare themselves for the coming battle.

'What is it?' asked Hwenfayre. She had spent most of the past few days never far from the Commander. In part, it was his wish. He seemed to derive some comfort from her company and they talked often. She also took comfort from him. He was much like Wyn in so many ways: his strength, his passion for the Sea and his surprising gentleness. She knew that none of his crew would accept that last of him. On a number of occasions she had seen his hardness when dealing with some disciplinary matter, but when they were together he was different.

They learned much about each other in those days.

His wife's name was Mei Mei and they had a son and a daughter. The daughter was about Hwenfayre's age, the son younger. His wife was an islander who had had the misfortune to be on a ship he captured early in his raiding days. He saved her from mistreatment at the hands of one of his crew by throwing the man overboard.

They were married a year later and had been happy every day since. Her name meant 'beautiful flower' and she felt the lack of flowers keenly. Hwenfayre suspected the Commander's love for his wife was a part of his drive for the Raiders to find land to live on. It was clear from his descriptions that nothing grew where they lived and Mei Mei would never see another flower until he found her a new island.

For her part, Hwenfayre found herself telling him more of her childhood growing up with her mother in a walled town on a cliff. She told him of her music and her artwork. With a bittersweet smile she spoke of Niall. She told him about the fear and suspicions she had grown up with, and she told him about the wall.

But mostly she talked about Wyn.

She told the Commander about his smile, his dark eyes, his hands and his voice. She spoke about the time they spent in the small boat as they fled her home.

'You fled?' the Commander interrupted. 'Why?'

Hwenfayre did not answer, afraid of telling too much, afraid that she had already told him too much. Instead, she stared out at the Sea once more, lost in her memories. The Commander let the moment pass, allowing her the freedom of her mind. It never came up again, but his curiosity burned.

He did not say much about Wyn.

But now, as he prepared his crew for the coming battle with a fast ship of the Children of the Raft, he paused and turned to her.

'You may never see this Wyn again. Not after what is coming. I hope you told him you loved him.' Leaving her to her confusion, he went about the business of readying his vessel for battle.

The *Misty Seal* was a well-armed warship that had seen many battles and she was in a state of semi-preparedness at all times. She came about to face the oncoming Children's ship as if hungry for the simplicity of battle. The weeks of uncertain hunting and nervous waiting sloughed off her like a caruda shedding its scales. Almost like a predator herself, she sprang forward to unleash her fury at the enemy.

As they closed, the Commander squinted at the flag she flew. 'Watch!' he called to the crewman perched atop the mainmast. 'What flag does she fly?'

'Ours!' he replied.

'Do you know her?' the Commander called back.

'No.'

'Does she ready weapons?'

'No, Commander. And she is lightly manned.'

The Commander weighed up his options quickly and came to a decision. 'Hold all fire!' he called. 'Half-speed!' he ordered the crew on the sails. With the efficiency borne of much drill, the sails were hauled in and the *Misty Seal* slowed in the water. The other vessel continued to scythe through the water towards them. When it came to within hailing distance, it slowed and came about.

'Ho, the *Misty Seal*!' a voice drifted across the water. 'I bring a message for the Commander.'

'What about?' replied the Commander.

'I am Nolin, Navigator of the First Rank. A Child of Danan. I bring important news of Morag and the Danan!'

'Prepare to be boarded,' the Commander roared back.

The Commander, Officer Manno and three heavily armed crewmen boarded the *Merial* where they were met by Nolin and Sacchin. Wyn stood aside, watching, listening.

Since Wyn's heritage had been revealed, Sacchin regarded him suspiciously, but not with hostility. His time with Nolin had made him see the Children in a different light. The idea that they must always be the enemy had faded, leaving him confused and troubled. For all his life the Children, be they of the Raft or of Danan, had been people of mysticism and fear. They swept across the Sea unchallenged, ruling over her and enjoying her bounty. No one could share her or command her.

But when he was captured by the Raiders and became one with them, he learned of a new vision, one where the Children were not to be merely feared and held in awe, but to be challenged, even threatened. He shared the Commander's vision, although he never spoke of it.

Nolin had shown him the people behind the legend. He spoke often about life on the Sea, the wild and sometimes fierce joys of living without land. He told Sacchin about his early training, the teachers he had, the friends he made and the exhilaration of not only knowing the Sea with such intimacy but of seeing her commanded. For the first time in his life, the islander-turned-Raider started to see the Priestesses not as merely terrifying icons of mystical power but as the guardians of a people who used their powers to feed and to guard.

Of all the tales he heard, it was the stories of Danan that captured Sacchin's attention. When Nolin spoke to the Commander of the Danan's return to the world he felt a fire stir within him. No matter what was about to happen, he would meet this mysterious woman.

A half-heard phrase caught his attention.

'You are telling me,' the Commander was saying, 'that the Priestesses can communicate over vast distances almost instantaneously by means of their harps?'

'Yes, they can. It is a magical thing that they have kept secret for centuries. There are many, even among their own people, who don't know about it.' He shot a suspicious look at Wyn. 'But some do,' he added.

'And using this they can coordinate their attacks?' the Commander went on. Nolin nodded. 'So they are heading to the Wrested Archipelago to wait in ambush?'

'That's the plan.'

Officer Manno lit his pipe. As he did so, he frowned. 'Is there any way of avoiding the ambush? And perhaps turning the decks on them?'

'Not without being able to communicate with your own fleet and having them meet somewhere else, no.'

'Then we will face the whole fleet, which will be armed with the wild magic of this mystical Danan?'

Nolin nodded. 'Looks that way,' he said.

The Commander looked across at Officer Manno and raised his eyebrows in silent query. Manno shook his head. The Commander sighed, his eyes closing in something akin to despair.

'I can help,' Nolin suggested.

'How?' asked Manno.

'I know these waters better than any man alive,' he said. 'I can help outrun and avoid their attack boats.' He held the Commander's eye steadily, 'But I will not betray my own people to their deaths. I will not fight for you.'

'Haven't you already betrayed your own people?' asked Wyn.

Nolin turned slowly to face Wyn. 'You. I don't understand you at all,' he said. 'You left your people years ago. And yet you find the Danan and bring her home. Then you hand her over to Morag and join your sworn enemies to find her again. And you can quietly stand there and accuse me of betraying my own people. You're not consistent.'

'Only if you don't know the whole story.'

'And that is what I have been trying to find out but you have told me nothing.'

The Commander watched this exchange with interest. 'You know this Danan?' he asked. Wyn nodded. 'You may hold the key to this whole thing. If you can identify her, I can capture or maybe kill her.'

Wyn shot the Commander a hard look. 'I may have joined your people for a while,' he said. 'But I

490

am not one of you. I sailed with you for one reason and one reason only: to find Hwenfayre. When I find her, I am going to leave you and go wherever she does, and I will kill anyone who gets in my way.'

The look on the Commander's face was not what Wyn usually saw from a man he had just threatened with death. Instead of anger suffused with a tinge of fear, he saw stunned incredulity. 'What did you say her name was?'

'Hwenfayre.'

'And what does she look like?'

Wyn told him.

'I think you had better come with me.' He gestured for Wyn and Nolin to follow him. 'Officer Manno, you remain here as Sacchin's First Officer. Coordinate with him. I will send over some more men to crew and arm this vessel.'

41

As he had known so many other things he had no right to know, Aldere knew his relatives and lifelong friends would feel awkward around him after his defence of the village. He saw their faces as the strange fiery creature advanced. They were going to die and they knew it.

He had seen their faces after he had killed the creature with the river's water. They were more terrified of him than they were of their own deaths. In the few moments when the beast stood, they had faced, accepted and consented to their deaths. Aldere knew that what he had done violated everything they knew as right about the world, and rather than thank him for saving their lives, they would blame him for ruining their world view.

Of course no one came out and said this, most of them would die never knowing or understanding it, but nonetheless he knew they would eventually reject him for daring to save them. He bore them no rancour nor did he blame them. It was his fault.

On the day when he finally stopped trying to explain, only one person said goodbye.

'So you are leaving,' Michaela said.

'Yes,' said Aldere. 'It's time I stopped bothering everyone.' She stood uncertainly for a moment. Aldere smiled at her. 'You can come with me if you like,' he said, 'But I won't think ill of you if you don't.'

Her eyes brightened. 'Really?' she asked. 'I can come?'

'Of course you can come. I have no idea where I am going but I would welcome the company.'

'When do we leave?' she asked.

'Right now,' Aldere said.

'I'll just go and pack some things,' she said.

'Don't,' said Aldere.

'Why not?'

'Because if you go and do that your father will talk you out of going.'

'Oh, don't be silly,' Michaela chided.

'It's true,' he said. 'If you want to come with me, come now or stay here forever.'

Michaela frowned. 'You have always been the strange one, haven't you?' she said.

Aldere nodded, for once not sure what was going to happen.

'For years I have watched you,' Michaela went on, 'and you have never been wrong. Did you know that? Never once have you been wrong about anything. Not the weather, not relationships, not even about cooking.'

Aldere had wondered if anyone had noticed.

'So if you say that I won't come with you if I don't come now,' she went on, 'I'd better come with you now, hadn't I?'

He nodded.

They headed south, away from the Great Fastness and the increasingly angry mountains. Aldere had packed very few things: some clothes, a pot, some cooking implements and a blanket. Michaela had nothing but the clothes she wore. They were not in love, they were barely friends in the true sense of the word, but they had grown up together in a small village that had little contact with the outside world. Theirs was a relationship that went beyond words. They knew each other better than many married couples ever do.

During that first day they walked contentedly, rarely needing to speak, simply enjoying each other's company, the sun in the sky above them and the earth beneath their feet, not once looking back. As darkness fell, Aldere found them a sheltered place within a thicket. There was a small stream running by and it was easy to find some berries and roots for their meal.

They shared the blanket like children, lying close for warmth, chatting and laughing about their shared worlds with the uninhibited freedom that only darkness can bring. Dawn brought a clear and sunny day full of anticipation and adventure. They breakfasted on more berries, drank deeply from the stream and continued south.

It did not take them long to lose track of time as they journeyed. All those they met were friendly and welcoming, and they rarely lacked for anything. Aldere found that for once his uncanny gift for knowing the rightness of things was valued, not treated with suspicion. Each person, each farm, each merchant had something that they needed, and Aldere was able to help them all. He dispensed advice with quiet dignity whenever asked. Michaela watched and listened.

'Aldere,' she asked him one day, 'why is it that you are always right?'

'I don't know,' he replied. 'I have always known things that I should not know. Ever since I was a child, I knew what people felt and how to solve their problems. Even when my father was killed, I knew I had to run away and let him die. I knew I would not survive if I tried to fight the Skrin Tia'k and so I ran.'

'I heard a lot of stories about that day,' said Michaela. 'But that's the first time I've ever heard you mention it. What happened?'

Aldere shook his head. 'I don't want to talk about it.'

'Why not?'

'There are some things, Michaela, that you should not hear.'

Michaela nodded. She looked off into the distance, shading her eyes from the sun's glare. 'Where are we going?' she asked suddenly.

'South.'

'Why?'

Aldere followed her gaze. 'That's why,' he said, pointing.

In the distance smoke was rising. Michaela squinted. 'What is that?'

'Wrong,' said Aldere. Without looking back he started running.

He ran, and as he ran an anger he had known before built within him. It rose like a tide, filling his mind, driving out all thoughts of home, of peaceful times shared with Michaela. He was coldly furious. This was wrong. It must not happen!

With the anger came power. As he ran, he ran faster and faster until he was flying. His feet left the ground and he shot through the air like an arrow. He approached the fire, feeling the wrongness increase with every heartbeat until the pain of it tore a cry of anguish from his throat.

His cry rang across the plain, shocking the Skrin Tia'k into stillness. They paused from their attack on the farm and looked up to where a screaming projectile was hurtling towards them. They turned as one, clicking in a new rhythm, a harsh, jarring call to their Azar'Methyst to cease its devouring and face a new threat. The fire pulled back from its meal and rose above the smoking wreckage. It roared in anger and surged towards Aldere, sparking new fires wherever it moved. The Skrin Tia'k also stood to meet the threat, bursting into their full battle form, their wings and strike limbs ready.

Aldere slowed and dropped to his feet. His eyes shone with anger, his whole body twitched with the barely contained power within.

As one, the whole battle knot of Skrin Tia'k sprang into the air, screeching in rage, sending a shattering wave of sound across the plain. Even so far away, Michaela threw herself down to the ground in pain, clutching at her ears. Aldere stood, icy-cold calm ruling his anger, watching their display.

They swirled in the air above him, rising ever higher until they abruptly ceased their screeching and dived. Aldere called out in a language he did not know and punched a fist towards them. With a mighty crack that rang out for miles around, a huge bolt of lightning shattered the clear sky and smashed into them, sending them fluttering to the ground in pieces.

The Azar'Methyst paid no attention to the lightning. Being a creature of flame, it had no fear of superheated gas. It advanced upon the puny man-creature, seeing only food. Aldere cried out again, raising his other hand, open to the heavens, calling down the only thing a creature like this would fear — rain.

Clouds formed out of nothing, swirling into vast heaped masses that towered above the smoking, ruined farm. With another cry, Aldere summoned the waters.

They poured down, sending the Azar'Methyst into a frenzy of writhing agony. It smoked and steamed, screaming as its life was extinguished.

Aldere watched dispassionately, keeping the waters on it until its final flickering flame vanished. Only then did he stop the rain and send the clouds on their way, and only then did Aldere look at the destruction the knot had wrought.

By the time Michaela had staggered to where the farm had once stood, Aldere was on his knees, weeping. He held a dead child in his arms, and around him lay the rest of the family, all burned, all dead. Michaela watched him, wondering how he could weep so and not make a sound. She reached up to rub her ears, and pulled her hands away. They were soaked in blood.

Aldere wept to the unheeding skies.

42

Hwenfayre watched the boat as it made its way back from the *Merial*. She could see immediately that there were different people on it, but she was beyond caring. The Commander's words still troubled her.

Love? Wyn? She had tried to kill him. *What sort of love was that?* How could she love a man she had tried to kill? But he had left her.

Or had he really? She only had Morag's word and the High Priestess herself had tried to kill her.

With a cry of exasperation she spun away from the railing. These thoughts had been plaguing her ever since the High Priestess had so casually dismissed Wyn as both not who he claimed to be and dead by her hand. Despite the High Priestess's betrayal and lies, she simply could not rid herself of the fear that some of what she had said was true.

And if none of it was true, she had herself tried to kill him.

Do I really love him?

Rather than face the news that the ship had brought, Hwenfayre went below to the small room that had become her cabin, sat on the low pallet bed and stared at the bulkhead.

She was still there, wrestling with the confusion and frustration that tormented her mind when a firm knock at the door interrupted her thoughts.

'Hwenfayre?' It was a crewman's voice. 'Hwenfayre, the Commander wants to see you in his cabin immediately.'

She paused at the Commander's closed door as the crewman knocked to announce her arrival. From inside she could hear muffled conversation, but she was still so distracted that she did not pay it any heed. She was totally unprepared when Wyn opened the door.

'Hwenfayre!' he exclaimed.

She froze in the doorway, unable even to complete the step she had started to take into the room. Motionless, she could only stare at him.

Staring at Wyn, this man who had dominated her thoughts and heart for so long, she felt her world crash in about her.

Every emotion she knew rose like a wave within her, each clamouring for attention, threatening to overwhelm her. She stood, unable to speak or move. Each breath was a struggle, each heartbeat an effort. It seemed to her that time stood still as she looked at him.

She saw afresh his fighter's stance, remembering how he had killed the Raider as they talked. She saw his coarse, unrefined features, comparing them with the more cultured, educated features of the long-gone Coerl. His hands twitched as she continued to stare, reminding her of the time he had so gently undressed her and eased her pain. She could feel again the hardness of his calluses against her soft skin. He breathed and she took in the massiveness of his chest, recalling his strength and how he had carried her, cradling her against that powerful chest, protecting her with those arms. Her heart started to beat faster as the images of the times they had spent together flitted through her head. How she had missed him, his quiet strength, his confidence, his eyes. She looked up into those dark eyes. Once again she saw the hardness that allowed him to kill, the distance that had allowed him to leave her in the hands of Morag.

Hwenfayre felt herself beginning to move towards him, intending to throw herself into his arms and plead for his forgiveness and promise again never to let him down, when another thought intruded. It was as if the thought had come from somewhere outside herself, yet it was so powerful that it drowned out every other idea in her mind. *He left me to Morag!*

He had left her! The pain of that betrayal, the danger he had left her in, jolted through her. She blinked and stepped back, a fire growing in her eyes as she felt again the dagger cut of anguish. Her heart slowed and went cold. All her life she had been treated as an outcast. In her home town, among the Children, even here and now. In a flash of insight, she realised it was not because of the way she looked, or her heritage: it was because of how she had acted. With the coldness heavy in her heart, she knew she was about to do it again and there was nothing she could do about it. No matter what might happen, she could not give in to the emotions that urged her to go to him. There was nothing he could say that could deflect her from whatever was about to happen. She looked away from him to regard the Commander and the other men in the room.

'You wanted to see me?' she said, proud of how even and cool her voice sounded. Out of the corner of her eye, she saw Wyn's face fall as he stepped aside to allow her to pass. She ignored the pain she caused him.

The Commander regarded her thoughtfully. He was a man who commanded men, and he recognised that something significant had just happened. His curiosity was piqued, but he could wait.

'Yes, Hwenfayre,' he said. 'I think there are some things about yourself you have neglected to tell me.'

'Really?'

'Yes. Your name, your real name for one thing, and what exactly is your relationship with the Children of the Raft.'

She shook her head slowly. 'I don't know the answer to the second one.'

One of the other men, the one with the intelligent eyes and sun-bleached hair, stood up abruptly. 'How can you not know? You have been with Morag! Surely she told you who you are.'

She looked at him. There was something about him that made her suddenly nervous. Behind her she heard Wyn move, his sword rattling slightly as if he had grasped its hilt.

Swallowing hard she forced herself to be calm. 'I have spent time with Morag and she assured me I am nothing but an ordinary, perhaps even less than ordinary Novice. I am nothing to her. She tried to kill me when I offended her.'

Nolin nodded sadly and slowly sank back into his chair. 'As I feared,' he muttered.

'What?' asked the Commander.

'Morag and her mother have been trying to deceive our people for years and now she is attempting to keep the truth from even the Danan herself.'

'The Danan?' asked Hwenfayre.

Nolin nodded. 'Yes, you are the Danan. Any of our people should have known it the moment they laid eyes on you. If you have spent time with the High Priestess and no one recognised you, then her victory is all but complete. We are lost.' He leaned forward, resting his head in his hands.

'You may be,' growled the Commander. 'But we are not.' He shot Hwenfayre a hard look, a look that would brook no refusal. 'You are presently without people,' he said. 'I offer sanctuary.'

Hwenfayre hesitated. Something was happening that she did not understand. She looked about the room: all eyes were on her and none were friendly. Not even Wyn's. He refused to hold her gaze, looking away, his face set hard.

Once again she felt alone among people.

'Sanctuary from what?' she asked finally.

'Do you mean to tell me you don't know?' asked the Commander.

Several glib retorts from her past rose to her mind but she paused before speaking. This was no silly bully-boy with childish taunts come to torment her, this was a formidable man who commanded respect. Instead of attempting to fob him off with an inane comment, she merely shook her head.

He frowned, regarding her with a wary eye. Another man, an officer whose name escaped her, made as if to speak, but the Commander waved him to silence. After a few moments, he nodded.

'I am inclined to believe you,' he said slowly. 'Which leaves me with yet another dilemma. What to do with you.'

'Don't do anything with me. You have offered me sanctuary, let me live in peace.'

The Commander shook his head slowly. 'Peace is something I cannot offer you now. Not if this Navigator is to be trusted.' Nolin stirred as if affronted by the words, but he was silenced by a hard glare from the Commander. 'Do not forget, Navigator,' he said, 'despite your story, you remain one with my enemies until you prove yourself.'

Nolin subsided, insult written clearly across his face.

Hwenfayre looked at him closely. Beneath the bleach of the sun, his hair would have been dark. His eyes looked out of a face that had seen many sunsets on the open Sea. Those eyes turned on her as if feeling her gaze. They were not friendly but neither were they unkind. Rather he regarded her with speculation. She returned his gaze with all the courage she could muster and was surprised to see him lower his eyes and look away.

A sudden thrill ran through her as she realised that she was not powerless here. All the fear and uncertainty of the past parted briefly to give her a glimpse of something more, a chance that she might be what she had barely allowed herself to think she was. A reckless courage flickered across her mind as she permitted herself a tiny smile. She turned slowly back to face the Commander. 'If I accept your offer of sanctuary, what will you expect of me?'

'The same as any of the Southern Raiders,' he said. 'Loyalty and obedience.'

'To whom?'

'Me. Or whoever holds the rank of Commander.'

'Not good enough,' she said. 'I have listened to you for some time. You do not "offer sanctuary" to the sailors you defeat on the seas. You take them. No,' she said, lowering her voice, 'you are not telling me close to the whole story.'

The Commander's face was mottled with anger as she spoke. With barely contained fury he surged to his feet, his eyes flashing dangerously. 'How dare you!' he roared. 'I will not tolerate insolence!'

Even as she watched him in his anger and outrage, she recognised something else, something she had started to see on the *Kelpie* — fear. With a strange sense of detachment she looked away from the Commander and observed the others. All those years spent watching the people around her, learning to know without words what they were thinking, clicked together in a single moment of clarity. *Everyone in this room was terrified of her!*

Everyone except Wyn. He was feeling something else entirely. She paused as she looked at his plain warrior's face. She knew she should recognise this feeling, she had seen others show it, but not to her. What was it?

She became aware that everyone was watching her, waiting for some form of response, but nothing seemed right. As she waited, the Commander's anger seeped from him and he sat back in his chair. Words that she might have said flowed away from her like a receding tide. She stood, silent, still, powerful. Her silence eased away from her, filling the room, until the only sounds were those from outside, the random noises of a ship waiting. Muffled voices of sailors calling out, seabirds crying, the Sea lapping at the hull, sails flapping while ropes, taut and stressed, creaked. Hwenfayre became aware of her own heartbeat, her breathing, the blood surging through her veins. Each breath brought with it new knowledge, new tastes, new scents. She felt time slow as she stood encased in her silence.

How long she would have stood like that, holding herself and those around her in silence, she never knew, for a sudden shout shattered the moment.

'Sails!'

The cry cut through them, galvanising them all into action. As one, the Commander and the other officer leaped to their feet and they were gone, leaving Hwenfayre with Wyn and Nolin.

The three Children of Danan regarded each other warily, none of them speaking. Above them, the sounds of running feet and shouted commands increased as the *Misty Seal* made ready for battle. They felt her begin to shudder and move as the sails were unfurled and the wind started to fill them. Nolin looked up, feeling the ship through his feet. He frowned.

'That's odd,' he observed.

'What?' asked Wyn.

'We are either running from Morag's fleet or something very strange has happened to the weather.'

Hwenfayre stared at Nolin in shock. 'Morag's fleet?' she gasped. 'What fleet?'

'Morag has called her entire fleet of attack ships here to wipe out the Southern Raiders,' said Wyn quietly.

Hwenfayre spun around to face him. 'Why?'

Wyn shrugged. 'Power,' he said. 'If she thinks you are dead, there is nothing left to stand in her way.'

Nolin shook his head. 'She would know if the Danan were alive, I think,' he suggested.

'How?' asked Hwenfayre.

'Was there a sailor named Declan with her?'

Hwenfayre nodded. 'He is the one who threw me overboard.'

'Declan?' asked Wyn. 'Tall, fair-haired, slim build?'

Hwenfayre nodded. 'I trusted him too,' she added, staring at Wyn.

'I knew someone called Declan once,' said Wyn, either ignoring or not understanding her look. 'What does he have to do with all this?'

Before Nolin could answer, the *Misty Seal* heeled over alarmingly as the wind shifted again. He looked up with concern. 'Not good,' he muttered. 'Morag has some Priestesses with some power with her, I think. The wind doesn't do that sort of thing, not even this far south.' He regarded Hwenfayre speculatively. 'I think, Your Highness, that the time has come for you to decide whose side you are on.'

'"Your Highness"?' asked Hwenfayre.

'No matter what anyone says, you are the Princess and High Priestess of my people,' replied the Navigator. 'I will serve you whatever you decide.'

'Why?' asked Wyn.

'Morag has betrayed us by her actions and if, as you say, Your Highness, she attempted to have you killed, then she stands condemned and unfit to be High Priestess.' He gave Hwenfayre a short bow. 'What are you going to do, Your Highness?'

On deck, the crew of the *Misty Seal* hurried about their tasks with the skill borne of years of living at sea. Preparing for battle, even against a fleet that spanned the horizon, was as natural as breathing for the Southern Raiders.

They were about a day's sail away from the Wrested Archipelago, but the Commander was confident that they had enough distance between them for him to be able to keep ahead until the rest of his fleet could join the attack. He sent a message to the *Merial* instructing them to make all speed to the Archipelago and bring the Raiders' fleet to meet them. He toyed briefly with the idea of sending Nolin with Sacchin, but he did not fully trust the Navigator. It would be best to keep Nolin here, under his watch.

And you never know, the Commander thought, *he may even be useful in time*. He muttered a curse as the wind, already a little fluky, swung around again.

'If the wind keeps doing this we'll be fighting the whole fleet alone,' he grunted at the helmsman, who grinned wryly. The Commander was about to join the helmsman in a laugh when the truth of his own words struck him. Morag had power over the weather! He turned to a nearby sailor and roared, 'Get that Navigator up here on the double!'

The sailor went to obey but Nolin had already made his way up on deck.

'There's no need to shout,' he said to the Commander. 'I felt the wind change from down in your cabin.' He looked up at the fleet visible on the horizon. 'Morag has brought someone of talent with her.'

'So she is playing with the wind then?' the Commander growled. 'I thought as much. Is there anything you can do?'

'Me?' said Nolin with surprise. 'I am a Navigator of the First Rank, it is true, but there is nothing I can do about the wind.' He looked back towards the fleet. 'They seem to have a different wind to us,' he observed calmly.

The Commander glared at him with murder in his eyes. 'I noticed,' he growled.

Nolin half-smiled. 'Would you like me to be of assistance?' he asked.

'I thought you said there was nothing you could do.'

'About the wind, no. But I can help your crew deal with these unnatural changes.'

The Commander frowned, then nodded. He turned to the helmsman. 'He has the bridge,' he snapped. The helmsman gave a small salute.

Nolin took command of the *Misty Seal*. For a moment he stood still, watching the water and the clouds and smelling the air. He smiled gently, then called for a realignment of the sails into a configuration the Commander had never seen. The Navigator ordered a new course, the helmsman spun the wheel and the *Misty Seal* eased to a dead stop. The sails hung limply in the still air, the ship rocking gently as the low swell marched past her.

Behind him Nolin could hear the Commander take a deep breath, a precursor to some sort of roaring complaint, he supposed. To forestall the imminent eruption he held up his finger and pointed at the sails.

'Wait,' he said without turning. His finger seemed to be tapping a beat, counting the seconds. 'Now,' he whispered. As if at his command, the sails flapped, billowed and filled as the wind shifted. Like a caruda at bait, the *Misty Seal* sprang forward, white water suddenly appearing at her bow as she took the wind eagerly.

'How did you. . . ?' the Commander started to ask but Nolin laughed before he could finish his question.

'Morag may have someone of talent with her,' he explained, 'but whoever she is, she has no imagination. That is one of the first tactics they teach Novices.' He turned away from his scrutiny of the water to regard the Commander. 'Didn't I tell you I was a Navigator of the First Rank?' He laughed, a rich, deep laugh, full of the fierce joy of the Sea. 'Let's sail!' he roared in jubilation.

The *Misty Seal* might have been the finest vessel the Commander had ever sailed but he had never imagined she was capable of the speed or manoeuvrability he witnessed during that mad dash. They sailed before the wind, whatever wind Morag threw at them, like a greyfin scything through the waters. The Children's fleet followed, never losing touch, but never closing.

Ahead of them the Wrested Archipelago waited. Like a sleeping whale, it crouched in the black waters of the untamed South Ocean Reaches.

43

'Your knowledge of history is very limited,' Mayenne said. The table was set with simple fare. Mayenne sat opposite Leone with a book opened in front of her.

Leone hid her distaste of the woman behind her normal mask. Ever since she had, as Zatopek believed, sold herself to this rebellion, Mayenne had taken on the role of her teacher. Mayenne's view of history was skewed, to say the least. Instead of a unifying influence that brought the centuries-long internecine feuding to an end, she saw the Empire as a brutal invading force that destroyed all in its path.

Mayenne tapped her finger on the table. 'Leone, focus!' she snapped. 'You have many years of false teaching to unlearn and it will take a lot of concentration.'

Leone nodded, allowing a small smile to cross her face. She had learned that Mayenne had an excellent mind for facts and details but not the slightest understanding of people. Little signs of interest were all she required to maintain her faith in Leone's complete belief in the new cause.

'Yesterday,' she continued, 'we started to consider

the Triumvirate, the three mystics that use their power to dominate and cause so much evil within our world ...' Mayenne raised her eyebrows, expecting Leone to supply the rest.

'The Guardian, the Weapon and the Danan,' said Leone.

'Very good,' said Mayenne.

'What is the Weapon?'

Mayenne took a deep breath. Leone had seen her take that breath many times so far; it always happened just before Mayenne was about to tell her something that would precipitate argument. Leone smiled, knowing it drove Mayenne to distraction.

'The Weapon was killed by a Skrin Tia'k years ago.'

'The whole line?'

'No, the Weapon is different from the rest. Its powers lie dormant until needed. There is no place in a peaceful world for power like that.'

Leone pondered for a moment. 'One thing troubles me, though,' she said.

'What is that?'

'If these three people are so dangerous to us, why don't we just extinguish their lines?'

'The Danan is the ancient guardian of the Sea. She comes unpredictably every few generations to the Children of the Raft. When she comes, she brings enormous power over the waters. It makes the Children invincible. She has not come for more generations than normal and there are those of us who believe her line has already been extinguished.'

'But I heard Cherise call a woman Danan when we stopped in Ys' home on our way to Ajyne,' Leone protested.

'Cherise is one of our most useful recruits but his understanding of the legends is tainted by his lifelong adherence to the Way of Purity. He has, like so many, assumed that the Danan's colouring is due to a Tribal heritage. A lot of the tribes up there revere any woman born with lavender eyes, expecting her to be the Danan, but of course no one ever is. She must be on or near the oceans for her power to awaken.'

'How will you counter her if she does come?'

'We won't need to,' said Mayenne with a smug expression. 'The Children of the Raft are slowly weaning themselves off the ancient mysticism, like your people, and when, or if, she comes again, they won't accept her.'

'How can you be sure?'

'As sure as we are that the Guardian's powers lie forever dormant now.'

'And who is the Guardian?'

Mayenne burst into laughter. 'How the mighty are fallen!' she chortled. 'You have spent years defending it in the army, and you didn't even know.'

'What?'

'The First Counsellor is the Guardian, and his son after him will carry that burden with him.'

'What?'

'The First Counsellor has a mystical link with the ground. It speaks to him, telling him what his enemies are doing.'

'How can the ground do that?'

'No one knows, but it happens. How else do you think the First Counsellors make such brilliant generals?'

'Training, intelligence, skill,' said Leone.

'They do things that can't be explained away by such qualities.'

Leone nodded, remembering the day in the Training Arena, the aroxii, Tapash's arrow. 'But why don't they know about this? How is it that you know all this and the finest minds in the best Loci across the Empire don't?'

'They all have the same books I do, they just don't believe.'

'It's just that? A matter of faith?'

'That and centuries of decadence and depravity. Think, Leone,' Mayenne said. 'This is a society that has elevated human suffering to an art form. They condemn an entire species, not just a race, to perpetual slavery.

'Mix that with an army so vast it can overwhelm every opponent on the continent by simple numbers and you have the perfect recipe for forgetting the truth of the past.' She stared at Leone with hard eyes. 'Why do you think the Thane never touches the ground with his bare feet?'

Leone shook her head.

'It's because the ground is sacred. Only the First Counsellor should enjoy its caress. What was once a sign of respect has become a meaningless tradition. Did you ever notice how many ancient traditions are to do with the ground and how to make contact with it?'

Leone nodded, whole sections of Asan tradition suddenly making sense in a way they never had.

'But who carries this power now?' Leone asked.

'The First Counsellor, but he hasn't touched bare soil for decades,' said Mayenne. 'Only Shanek could

513

possibly have reawakened the power, and now that he is dead, it is gone forever.'

'Forever?'

'Yes, it is carried through the family. Have you ever noticed that every First Counsellor has only ever had the one son? Lots of daughters, only one son. And that son has always followed in his father's path as a brilliant general. So unless Shanek has a son, the power is gone.' Mayenne's face showed such a glowing contentment that Leone had to physically grip the table to prevent herself from striking her. Despite the outlandish nature of her story, too much made sense for Leone to dismiss it outright. Abruptly she stood.

'I need some air,' she said.

Without waiting for Mayenne's response, Leone strode from the room and out into the street where the air was cleaner and life seemed simpler. She stood in the road outside Zatopek's home and breathed deeply. The smells and sounds of the Widows' Quarter enveloped her, reminding her that while she had been cloistered within the house learning a new vision, the rest of the world had continued, unheeded. She was shocked to discover that she did not even know what time it was. With a glance up to the sun she realised that the morning had passed and the afternoon was well advanced. Her stomach suggested that a meal was overdue.

Leone was filled with a need to remind herself of that world, to remind herself that the normal still existed, untouched by mystical powers and battles behind battles. She turned and strode away from Zatopek's elegant house.

The market was bustling and noisy with the afternoon crowd. Vendors called the virtues of their wares, women talked and laughed, men bargained, children ran and played. Even here, Leone realised, amid poverty and hardship, life went on. She looked around, aware that her own disfigurement, whilst bad, was not the worst here. There were veterans bearing horrific injuries, those born with defects, the blind, the sick and those whose minds were damaged. Leone was suddenly struck by the pointlessness of what she was doing. Why learn an arcane history of the world when there was so much suffering around her?

She reached into her purse, filled with coins that Zatopek gave her from time to time. With a feeling of mounting anger she pulled out a handful and started handing the coins to beggars.

Within moments she was surrounded by a crowd of reaching hands, of crying voices, of desperate faces. She felt herself being grabbed, handled and pulled at by the dozens of hungry beggars that surrounded her. Their cries clamoured against her, pounding at her mind and setting her ears ringing. The sheer volume of their noise, the insistence of their need threatened to overwhelm her. She threw the purse in the air. The last few coins fell into the crowd, but none of them hit the ground.

Still there were beggars swarming around her, clamouring for her attention and her money. She felt her emotions rise, anger and frustration battling for control. Instinctively, she reached for the knife that hung at her side. As soon as her hand made contact with the hilt, those closest to her fell silent and stepped back. Leone heard the whispered word 'knife' rustle through the rapidly quietening crowd. Within a matter of a few heartbeats, the whole mass of people was quietly muttering and starting to fall back. Leone stood, watching them back off, the hope in desperation she had seen in their eyes replaced by the return of fear.

She stood, alone in the market, watching the beggars and the hungry slowly vanish back into the niches and dark corners where they spent their lives, the day's excitement over.

'I'm sorry,' she whispered, 'I'm sorry, I didn't mean to frighten you.' No one heard, no one seemed to care any more. Leone stared around her, anger and frustration fading to be replaced by hollow sadness. 'How can you live like this?' she said softly. 'Who did this to you?'

Even as she asked the question she knew the answer. In part, she had done this. She had spent her life defending the structures that made this place and kept it the way it was. Her training, designed to be used to defend the Empire from threats without, had been spent mostly to protect it from threats within. If the Empire was the benign force she had been told about, why did so many people want to rebel against it? A sudden chill ran through her. Had she been wrong all her life?

All the violence, the ritual torture, the oppression, the heavy-handed treatment she had dealt out to civilians, it all crashed in upon her. The weight of it all drove her to her knees. She slumped forward, visions of her life as a soldier flashing across her numbed mind. Unnoticed, her blade slipped from her grasp as tears trickled down her cheeks. Leone knelt on the dirt, unaware of the market resuming its normal bustle around her. Where a woman with a knife was noticeable, a woman crying alone was not.

Slowly the tears dried up. The chill faded and reality once more intruded. Leone stood and looked at a world that seemed darker somehow. *Now what?* she wondered. She needed to talk to someone, but who? Could there be anyone in this world that even knew all of this, let alone someone who knew it and held an open mind on it? She needed someone who could tell her who was right.

Something nagged at her, a name. Something Shanek had told her. What was it? The thought of Shanek, hacked to pieces by a wild Skrinnie and left to the elements somewhere by a river, left her hollow and aching. Despite Mayenne's insistence Leone could not shake the feeling that, had he lived, Shanek might have been able to ...

To what, exactly? Change the Empire? Alter the direction of hundreds of years of decay and decadence? Refocus the mindset of thousands of wealthy nobles? Leone shook her head. Perhaps it's just as well that he was dead. Maybe Mayenne was right, that this Empire might have served its purpose. What if it is time for a new force to rise?

Bedi!

The name came to her. The old man who had spent so much time with Shanek. That was who she could talk to, presuming he was still alive, of course. *But where to find him?*

Now that she was remembering Shanek's time here in the Widows' Quarter, it all came back.

Hashan, the merchant and criminal. Bedi was near his stall in the Lesser Market. And that was ... Leone turned around, looking for the landmarks that would lead her there. Her eyes narrowed. A smile slowly formed when she recognised an alley. *Down there*, she thought.

The route to the Lesser Market was tortuous, but once she started she remembered it all. She had walked this way many times, following Shanek as he wended his way 'home' after a busy day harassing merchants and extorting protection money for Hashan. After the first few days he had either decided to ignore them or forgotten their presence. Leone knew Shanek's skills well enough to realise that no matter how good she and her men were, he was better, and they could never hide from him. Now, believing what she did of Shanek's abilities, she found herself wondering how much of that was his skill and how much was mystical gift.

The Lesser Market gained its name from location rather than size. In truth it was larger, busier and louder than the main market but was further from the edge of the Widows' Quarter. Being deeper in the poor region, it attracted none of the wealthier clients who would frequent the main market. Not many dared venture into the Widows' Quarter, even in search of bargains or other services that were on offer, but the few who did never went beyond the main market.

Leone had also never given much thought to those who frequented the market or their motives. She did not want to now either, as she approached the Lesser Market.

It was as she remembered it: loud, stinking and threatening. Everywhere she looked there were people yelling, either selling or buying or simply trying to talk over the clamour.

Hashan, seated behind the counter of his stall, was fatter than she remembered, but just as smug, just as slimy. She looked to where Bedi used to sit. A smile slowly formed as she saw the old man sitting cross-legged on his mat. A young man was seated opposite him with his back to her. Her heart lurched briefly when she saw him. *Shanek?* she wondered. But no, he was dead and this youth was a boy, not the powerfully built man left dead by a river.

Leone made her way through the crowd towards Bedi. Before she arrived, the boy stood, bowed and walked away. When her shadow crossed over the old man's rug, he looked up. He frowned.

'I know you,' he said. His voice was rasping and old. He squinted up into the setting sun. 'You followed Shanek around. How is the boy?'

Leone shook her head. 'Dead,' she said.

Bedi's frown deepened. 'And his son?'

'What son?'

'He has a son.'

'No he doesn't,' said Leone. 'He has no children.'

'Then he is not dead,' said Bedi. 'The world would not allow it.'

'What are you talking about?' asked Leone.

'All this time with the First Son and you know nothing?' the old man said with a scowl. 'Sit, sit.' He gestured to his rug. Leone hesitated, and then sat cross-legged opposite Bedi.

'Why do you think he has a son?' asked Leone.

'The line must be maintained,' said Bedi. 'It extends back to times before the Empire and it will outlast the Empire.'

'How can you say that?'

'The line you people call the First Counsellors is a power that transcends the simple temporal power of any Empire. It dates from the oldest antiquity and it has a purpose that extends beyond the trivial military one.'

'So you believe all that?' Leone asked.

Bedi laughed, a harsh cackling sound. 'Believe it? Do you believe the sun is in the sky?'

Leone scowled. 'There's no need to believe what is in front of your eyes.'

'Indeed, Caldorman Leone, indeed.'

'Caldorman?' she asked. 'How do you know about that?'

'The same way I know the arox beast that took your arm was not a wild beast, but a trained one.'

'What are you talking about, old man? No one can train the aroxii. They're too savage.'

'The Tribesmen of the north hide many secrets. That's just one of them.'

Leone was confused. This was not what she wanted to hear. She just wanted the old man to tell her if anything Mayenne had told her was true, not more riddles.

'Old man,' she snapped. 'I've heard tales about the Guardian, the Weapon and the Danan. I need you to tell me if they're true.'

'What have you heard, Caldorman?'

'Stop calling me that,' she said. 'I have been dismissed in disgrace. I hold no rank.' Even after all this time it still cut to acknowledge it. To say it out loud was almost as much as she could bear. With pride she held her head up as she said it.

'And yet you still carry the Needle,' said Bedi mildly.

Her hand went instinctively to the scabbard. It was empty. The sadness bit again. Her last link was gone; she was truly cut off.

'No, old man,' she said. 'I don't carry the Needle. I lost it.'

Bedi reached under his scruffy robe and pulled out a dagger. He handed it to Leone, hilt first. 'Is this it?' he asked quietly.

Leone stared at it, recognising her own Needle. 'How did you ... ?' she started to say as she grasped the hilt.

Bedi shook his head. 'It means so much to you?' he asked.

Leone nodded. 'It does.'

'Even after the Thane dismissed you and cut you so badly?'

Leone was unsure whether Bedi meant the scars on her face or the emotional cut that still pained her. Either way he was right. She nodded.

'You must believe in the Empire,' he observed.

'Yes, I do.'

'Despite what it has done to you?'

'Done to me? What it has done to me? The Empire trained me, gave me skills, gave me a position, a role, a meaning. It fed me, clothed me and taught me the Way of Purity,' she said.

'So why do you come to me to question it?'

'If the First Counsellors have all this power, why is the Empire the way it is? Why does all this,' she

521

waved her arm to encompass the poverty that surrounded them, 'exist? Can a society that does this, that elevates torture to an art form, be anything but evil?'

'An evil act does not make something evil.'

'The power that the First Counsellors have, is that evil?'

Bedi shook his head. 'It is the choices that the wielders of the power make that determine their evil, not the power that enables them to make the choices.'

'So the Empire is not evil?'

Bedi shrugged. 'It is, or it isn't, but it is not the power of the Guardian that makes it so.'

'Why does the power exist?'

'At last you ask a good question, Caldorman.'

'You're a very irritating old man, Bedi,' she said. 'Just answer the question.'

'I don't know the answer, Leone. I wish I did.'

Leone rose to her feet. 'You're not irritating, you're a disappointment.' She turned to leave.

'Before you go, Leone, I'll ask you a question. How did I know your name?'

Without turning Leone said, 'Shanek told you.'

'Yes, he did. But ask yourself this. Why did he tell me?'

Leone stopped and turned back. 'What do you mean?'

'Is it the Empire you believe in?'

She stared down at him.

'I'll tell you one thing about the Weapon, the Guardian and the Danan. They are never alone. They always have a companion. Think about why it is that the First Counsellors have not married for generations. Not one First Counsellor since Gyran has been married. All First Sons have been born to concubines.'

'What's your point, old man?'

'Leone, you are at an important moment in history. The Weapon is active, the Danan is back and the Guardian is missing. But more importantly for you, you need to decide what side you will be on. If Shanek is dead, as you suggest, you must find his son. If he is not dead, you must find him and ask him the questions you didn't ask me.'

44

Officer Manno shaded his eyes against the rising sun. Behind him, Sacchin breathed a curse.

'Will you look at that?' he gasped.

'Big, isn't it?' replied Manno.

'I had no idea,' said Sacchin, still unable to take his eyes off the sight.

'No one did. It's one of our best-kept secrets.'

'How did you manage to hide it?'

'Why do you think we always have such a fast turnaround of ships when they come into harbour? This is the first time that the whole fleet has ever been gathered.'

'But surely ...' his voice trailed off in disbelief.

Manno chuckled. 'The size of our fleet will hopefully be as big a surprise to Morag as it was to you.'

Sacchin shook his head slowly. 'How many?'

Manno shrugged. 'Don't rightly know,' he said. 'I've never counted but there are a lot of them, aren't there?' He looked at the Raiders' fleet. 'And if you allow for our superior weapons, the fight may not be as one-sided as the Children hope.'

'Will it really come down to a fight?' asked Sacchin.

Officer Manno nodded. 'Yes, I think so. It's been going this way for years now and something has to give eventually. We've been dancing around each other for too long.'

'What about the Priestesses? And this Hwenfayre?'

'The Priestesses are overrated,' Manno assured him. 'We've been collecting information about their abilities for a long time and most of their so-called powers are myth and threat. In truth there's not much they can do.'

'And Hwenfayre?'

'A wild card to be sure,' Officer Manno conceded. 'But she's only a girl, and I doubt there's much more to her power than legend.' He lit his pipe, puffing heartily. Blue smoke wreathed his head. 'But I'm not sure,' he muttered. 'I've seen some strange things in my years at sea, but nothing like her.'

Sacchin looked at Manno with surprise. 'What is so strange about her?'

'Not her so much as the way she came aboard.'

Sacchin raised his eyebrows quizzically. Manno did not turn to face the big islander, continuing to stare out at the huge fleet. After a few moments he started to tell the story of Hwenfayre's unorthodox arrival on the *Misty Seal*. By the time he had finished, Sacchin was wide-eyed.

'So is she more than just a girl?' asked Sacchin.

'Perhaps.'

'And if she is?'

'If she is half what the legends say she will kill us all.'

'But don't the legends say that she protects the Children?' protested Sacchin.

'Not all of them, Sacchin,' Manno said softly. 'Not all of them.'

The *Misty Seal* rode the swell easily, spray pluming and sails taut. The rigging hummed as the wind bore them with ever-increasing speed towards the Wrested Archipelago. Hwenfayre stood alone in the prow, the white spray enveloping her in its icy embrace. Her eyes stared unseeingly at the rocks that surged starkly up from the black depths. Spread out around the brutal archipelago was the Southern Raiders' fleet.

She had not said a word to anyone since they'd begun their mad flight from the Children's fleet. After Nolin took control of the *Misty Seal*, she and Wyn emerged from the Commander's cabin. They had not spoken to each other since, nor had they mentioned to anyone what they spoke of while together in the cabin. Their faces, hard yet broken, told their own tales of what had passed between them. Wyn took up duties as befitted a seaman and Hwenfayre took up station in the prow. No one came close enough to hear her song.

Even if they had, none of that vessel would have recognised the words or understood their meaning. Hwenfayre sang from her confusion, her sense of loss and betrayal. She gently called to the Sea to hear her pain.

As she sang, the Sea heard her and felt her pain.

Far to the south, untamed winds, vast currents and awesome surging masses of icy dark water started to merge, building the watery avatar of Hwenfayre's aching emptiness.

No one heard, but Wyn watched in pain. He silently ached for the anguish of regret, the words spoken in haste, the voice raised in misunderstanding, the slowness of mind that would not allow him to consider before speaking. Hwenfayre's words of accusation had cut deeply, leaving him reeling in disbelief.

Left her? How could she have thought that? What lies had Morag told her?

He stood up from his task to stare once more at her rigid back. She stood motionless, staring at the Wrested Archipelago as they raced towards the barren rocks. Already he could see signs of habitation clinging tenaciously in the face of the Sea's onslaughts. The sheer size of the Raiders' fleet, the chilling harshness of the Archipelago, the power that he had already seen Hwenfayre wield, the malice of Morag, the duplicity of Declan, all whirled in his struggling mind. He could not see any way out that would not involve death, and once a battle on the seas was joined, there was always death and no way of ever being sure of keeping out of its wake.

With a pain so sharp, so clear he gasped with its clarity, he had a sudden vision of a pale face surrounded by limp, white-blonde hair with lifeless lavender eyes staring up at him out of freezing water. A dagger-thrust of agony was as sudden as it was unexpected and he cried out at its harsh touch. Icy tendrils of terror clasped his heart, leaving him gasping for air. His whole body shook, his eyes blurring as the image of Hwenfayre's inert body sinking beyond his grasp into the Sea filled his mind.

527

As if feeling his pain Hwenfayre suddenly turned from her distant regard of the waters to look at him. Wyn was so overwhelmed with the image of her dead body that he was unable even to return her gaze. Instead he went back to his task, all the while cursing his weakness in the eyes of the only woman he had ever loved.

Hwenfayre continued to watch him, her eyes a mystery. By the time she looked away, Morag's fleet had come into view behind them.

Declan was the first to see the *Misty Seal*. He was having a spell as watchman on the high watch at the top of the mainmast. For the past few days he had found more and more reasons to be away from Morag's side. She was becoming increasingly distasteful to him. It seemed that everything she did or said jarred with him in some way. Where before he had seen leadership, he now saw manipulation, where he had seen intellect, he now saw deceit and where he had once seen the woman he loved, he now saw betrayal.

There was no mystery in his sudden awakening to new vision; he knew to the moment when his eyes were opened. She had never loved him, never sought him out on the *Two Family Raft* because she saw his potential. No, she had cynically manipulated him, played with his simple emotions, torn him away from one who was as a brother, poisoned his mind against his own people, all with this moment in mind. Today he knew Morag's triumph would be complete. She had the whole Southern Raiders' fleet before her and her own fleet would fall upon them like ravening caruda, tearing them apart, scattering the only opposition to her total command of the seas. His heart sank as he contemplated his lot under her. She would rule with a whimsically iron fist. Everyone on the water would be subject to her every careless fancy. Without the Southern Raiders and their increasingly sophisticated battle strategies to keep her and her loyal warboats in check, no one would be safe. Once again he marvelled at how easily she had achieved total loyalty from the attack fleet's captains.

His morbid reflections were interrupted by a flicker of something he half-saw. He stared at the horizon beyond the *Misty Seal*.

There it was again. A sail. No, he thought, *not a sail. A number of sails*. With mounting concern, he looked wider, then wider still. *What the . . . ?*

'Sails!' he bellowed. 'Sails!'

'Whereabouts?'

'Everywhere! They are everywhere!'

Below decks, Morag smiled grimly. She ran her fingers lightly across the strings of her harp. It murmured gently in response. 'So it has finally come,' she whispered.

Summoning her concentration she started to relay her instructions to the Priestesses scattered among her fleet. They in turn passed on her instructions by more prosaic methods to the ships around them. Like a school of fish, the whole fleet turned as one in preparation for the battle.

Between the two fleets, the *Misty Seal* with Nolin at the helm strove to join the Raiders before Morag caught her. But the High Priestess had something special planned for her that she had been saving until the rest of the Raiders could see it.

From the first rank of her attack boats, three unfurled new sails. They billowed out, catching the wind, and the three vessels surged forward. With breathtaking speed they easily outpaced the *Misty Seal*, drawing level with her in what seemed like seconds. Behind them Morag grinned at the irony. The additional sail plan had been first designed by Nolin and his own idea would be his undoing.

She watched with building excitement as the three attack boats opened fire with their heavy crossbows and short-range cannon. The bark of the cannon carried clearly across the water as they shot their canisters of hundreds of small pellets. They were designed to cut through rigging, tear sails and pulverise living flesh.

Their canisters ripped through the *Misty Seal*'s rigging and sails leaving tatters in their wake. Across the water Morag heard the cries of injured men. Her breathing quickened as she saw, in her mind's eye, the wounds inflicted by the jagged, high-speed projectiles. She always enjoyed the opening volley of a battle. With a gentle caress she invoked the soothing melody of her harp. The strings responded to her almost sensuous pleasure with their own song, a song of eagerness that she interpreted as reflecting her own desire for destruction.

It was a song she did not recognise, and for a moment she allowed herself to enjoy its rich, full melody, its subtle counterpoints and its surging energy before reality struck her. With shock she stopped playing and rested her hand on the strings to still their unfettered song. They acquiesced, reluctantly it seemed, and murmured into silence.

Morag, High Priestess of the Children of the Raft, stared in growing wonder at her harp. For years she had been studying the legends of the Danan and her harp, dismissing most of it as superstitious nonsense, but now, *What if a harp carved from bleached driftwood and strung with fibres spun from the gills of the caruda indeed had the powers spoken of? What if she now commanded them?*

New vistas of power opened before her. If the powers were not legendary ... She stared without seeing the horizon, dotted with more sails than any had expected, contemplating what could now be.

Her expansive contemplations were interrupted by a rude shove. In surprise she spun around to regard the one who dared to touch her.

It was Declan.

'Call them back!' he bellowed at her, waving at the battle. 'Can't you see what is happening?'

Too confused to be angry, Morag followed the direction of his gesture. To her shock she saw what was left of her three special attack boats. One was already sinking, another was aflame and the third was listing heavily. Even as she watched, the *Misty Seal* fired again, unleashing a brutal storm of hot metal and flaming bolts from her catapults and mangonels.

The sheer destructive capability of just this one ship shocked her. If all the Raiders' ships were armed like this one, the battle she had spent so long manoeuvring for would be much too close. Even with her Priestesses, the outcome could yet be in doubt.

She was just about to give the order when the two remaining boats slipped beneath the waves.

Something like a sigh eased its way across the whole fleet as the Children contemplated the loss of their fastest vessels.

'Summon the Navigators and Priestesses at once!' she snapped. 'And have the fleet drop back, we need time to plan.'

'Can't you ...' Declan started, but his voice died as Morag shot him a glare of pure venom. He nodded and dashed to do her bidding.

Far to the south, the Sea felt pain. The waters heaved and piled up in wild disarray, whitecaps dancing, tendrils of spume trailing in the building winds. Anguish shared is not always halved, sometimes it is doubled. Sadness will sometimes feed upon itself. Fear can rapidly turn to anger.

'But you saw it!' said Navigator Lamar, plaintively. 'If they are all armed like that they will cut us to pieces!'

'You are supposed to be the greatest seamen who ever sailed. Deal with it!' screamed Morag.

'How?' asked Lind, another Navigator.

'Perhaps we should focus on our strengths rather than theirs,' observed Sirran. He leaned forward, resting his elbows on the table. 'As the only remaining Navigator of the First Rank, I would like to remind everyone here that we have the fastest, most manoeuvrable fleet the Sea has ever borne. We also have a level of command over the winds and the waves. I suggest that these two things, together with the skills of the Children of Dana — sorry,' he caught himself before finishing the word and nodded in deference to Morag, 'Children of the Raft,' he continued, 'we should have more than enough advantages to put paid to these pirates.'

Sirran was an old man with hair so bleached by the sun it was white, a face made leathery by the winds and eyes perpetually watery from staring at too many sunrises. He was held in a regard bordering on awe by all Navigators by virtue of his decades of flawless sailing. Despite his age and increasing infirmity, he was still the finest Navigator and the only person who dared question the High Priestess. Even Morag would not challenge him in council for he only ever spoke of the things he knew best, the Sea and navigation. When he gave his direction on any issue to do with the Children's travel, all listened. As they did now.

'This is how we can use our advantages,' he continued. At his gesture a chart was unrolled across the table. It showed the Wrested Archipelago and the surrounding waters in exquisite detail. He rose slowly to his feet and started to give orders. As he spoke, Morag felt her anger subside, to be replaced by relief.

The old fool has his uses after all, she thought. *Declan was right to stop me from killing him.* At the thought of his name she looked around for Declan. He had been increasingly distant of late and it bothered her. He knew far too many of her secrets to be allowed too long a line. It was time to reel him in a bit.

With a gesture she summoned Erin. 'Go and find Declan,' she said. 'And bring him here.'

Erin scurried away in search of the Sailer. As she went, she remembered the drunken conversation she had had with him. Ever since then he had been polite, almost deferential to her, as if he feared he had said too much and she would betray him. Erin, however, was thinking something else entirely. Her anger that had started with Morag's uncaring behaviour grew with the knowledge of her duplicity. Declan had unwittingly provided Erin with the last piece of the puzzle. She had already begun to believe in Hwenfayre and when Declan called her the Mistress of the Waters her last doubts vanished. Hwenfayre was the Danan and Morag had tried to kill her when she could not control her.

She went looking for Declan, knowing what she must do.

By noon the two fleets had readied themselves. During the hours of morning they manoeuvred, circling warily, seeking the best positions, testing the water. Some shots had been fired, falling harmlessly into the cold, black Sea. None but the three attack boats had been lost. Aboard the *Misty Seal*, the damage was repaired and the weapons reloaded. Nolin watched the winds with intense concentration while Wyn relayed to him the movements of the Children's fleet. Just before noon, the Navigator smiled broadly.

'We have them now,' he said. 'Old Sirran has taken command. He taught me everything he knew.' He turned to Wyn. 'He is a brilliant tactician. If this fleet was not the size it is there would be no hope. But as it is, who knows?'

'And the Priestesses?' asked Wyn.

'If Sirran has set up the attack plan I think he has, they will all be coordinated. So there won't be anything unexpected. We can allow for them.' He called to the Commander and the Raider fleet closed for battle.

The ships of the Raiders were larger and more heavily armed, but the attack boats, although smaller, were faster and more manoeuvrable. The light winds the Priestesses summoned were perfect for the smaller vessels and they were able to make lightning passes through and past the Raiders. They were hard to hit, but when the Raiders' weapons landed the damage was terrible. In a short time the air filled with smoke, the Sea was littered with burning wreckage and the cries of the wounded were carried on the light winds.

But Hwenfayre was oblivious to the carnage all around her. She stood in the prow of the *Misty Seal*, lost in the cries of the Sea. Despite the furious sounds of battle raging about her, she heard only the turmoil of the waters. It was unlike anything she had ever experienced.

When she had called down the storm on the Raiders as they attacked the wall, she had felt a great anguish. The violence of wind and water mirrored her own pain, and as she sang the torment within her found expression, took form and achieved release. As the storm died down, so did her pain.

When she summoned the storm to hunt down Wyn and kill him, she did so out of her anger and sense of betrayal. The storm that sought him was the simple expression of her soul. On any occasion that she had sung to the Sea, she felt at peace. Even when the Sea responded to her in violence, she had felt nothing like what she was feeling now.

This was pain, a crying out in anguish that made her troubles over Wyn seem trivial, childish in comparison. Her soul ached as the waves of torment washed over her. Her head spun with a tumult of conflict. Never before had the voice of the Sea come to her; always she had called out to the Sea. And when she did, the Sea affirmed, enhanced and strengthened her own emotions.

But now Hwenfayre reeled under a relentless flood of emotion that threatened to overwhelm her mind. This emotion surged in on her, over her and through her. She felt herself begin to drown in the alien flow, gasping at the energy and intensity of feelings so basic, so raw. They tore at her mind and heart, threatening to unravel her completely, leaving her with nothing.

She stood, swaying unsteadily as the world turned into smoke and fire around her. Without consciousness she sang, her hands caressing the strings of an unseen harp. Her song was of pain, of loneliness, of desperate longing for peace. She sang without realising what she sang.

Slowly, the tide of the battle turned. Despite its larger vessels and superior firepower, the Raider fleet was being undone by the speed of the attack boats and the fluky winds. They simply could not manoeuvre fast enough in the conditions to be able to bring their weapons to bear on the Children's boats. They were being progressively annihilated. Onboard the *Kelpie*, Morag saw it and rejoiced.

She turned with her eyes shining to Declan, who stood silently beside her. 'You see, my love,' she said, 'it is all going beautifully.'

He nodded, not trusting himself to say anything because he saw things differently. Where she saw victory, he was seeing his friends being killed. Despite the fact that they were clearly winning this battle, victory would come at a vast cost. Already a third of their fleet was destroyed, vanished below the icy waters, with a third of what remained heavily damaged. Inwardly he burned with the fleet, yet his heart was strangely cold as he reminded himself of what was to come.

He reminded himself about how she had used him, had taken him away from the only family he had ever known and now how she was leading his people into destruction in her vainglorious quest for power. Mostly he simply despised her for pretending to love him.

'Yes, my love,' he muttered. 'It will all go well.' Quietly, and without Morag noticing, he slipped away.

As she watched the battle the High Priestess saw what she knew would happen. It was what Sirran had promised her. The Raiders' fleet broke and turned. Like a school of fish herded by caruda, they sought the protection of closeness, safety in numbers. Knowing they were beaten, they hastened towards the Wrested Archipelago, no doubt seeking to lose their attackers in the maze of islands. But even though they owned the archipelago, they still could not know it like a Navigator of the First Rank. Their ploy would be their undoing.

Sirran, expecting this, sent word for the Children's fleet to follow.

And this was what Declan and Erin had also been waiting for. As the orders were shouted and the *Kelpie* swung around, Erin moved up behind Morag.

'High Priestess,' she said.

'What is it?' asked Morag without turning.

'High Priestess, Declan would like to speak with you.'

'He knows where I am,' she said, her eyes still focused on the Raiders' retreating fleet.

'He said,' Erin hesitated, 'he said he would like to speak with you in your cabin. Below.'

Morag turned, noticing his absence for the first time. 'Would he now?' She smiled, imagining the passionate embrace that awaited her. Declan was a superb lover, and now that she had rid the seas of the Southern Raiders forever, she would finally take him as husband so that they could rule together. *Yes, I will tell him now*, she thought. *I'll make it my gift to him*. Without a glance at Erin, she swept past her and hurried down to her cabin to tell him. Erin followed her at a distance.

'High Priestess! The Raiders!'

Morag turned, on her heel, almost colliding with Erin. 'Out of my way, girl,' she snapped. The Novice, following close, stepped hurriedly aside, bowing her head deferentially. The High Priestess paused briefly, fixing her with a steely gaze. 'Now what, I wonder, are you doing?' she asked. The seaman who had called did so again, distracting Morag. 'I think you and I will need to have a conversation about your role,' she said as she walked away.

'What is it?' Morag asked the seaman.

'The Raiders, High Priestess. They are fleeing!'

'I knew that! It was Sirran's plan to drive them into the Archipelago where we could cut them to pieces.'

'No, High Priestess, they are fleeing, not heading into the Archipelago. They are scattering and heading north!'

'What?' She dashed to the prow, where she stood, watching as the still-large Raider fleet scattered. They had turned away from their strongholds on the Archipelago and were fleeing north under full sail. In the stronger winds, the Raiders were pulling away from the pursuing attack boats, slowly moving out of range of even their own weapons. She watched her quarry escape her, puzzled by their sudden change of heart.

Why would they flee when they had the superior weaponry, as well as the possession of the Wrested Archipelago? She knew from bitter experience that the settlers on the rocks would have been well prepared to sink any attack boat foolish enough to stray too close. Even with a Navigator of the skills of Sirran, a battle through the Archipelago would have been dangerous.

'Damn you!' she screamed at the retreating fleet. 'Cowards!'

'Do we continue to chase, High Priestess?' asked the sailor who had called her.

She did not turn around, preferring to watch as the Raider fleet escaped her, feeling the cold wind on her back that whipped her cloak around, carrying with it the sharp tang of the frozen waters far to the south. It had increased enough in strength to give the Raider fleet the speed they needed to get away.

'No,' she said. 'Let them go. We can't catch them now, not with this wind —' She stopped suddenly, realising what she was saying. *We control the wind!* she thought. Something colder than a southern wind chilled her suddenly. Slowly she turned away from her contemplation of the fleeing fleet.

On the southern horizon she could just make out a build-up of cloud. 'Lookout!' she called. 'To the south, what do you see?'

'Storm.'

'What quarter?'

'Both of them.'

Morag was about to reply when Sirran grabbed her by the arm and wrenched her around. 'Don't you smell it?' he asked.

'Smell?'

'The ice. You know where that wind is coming from.' He roughly shoved her towards the railing. 'Look. Do you see what is coming?'

She stared at the vast purple-black thunderhead that rose over the horizon, her mind unable to comprehend what the old Navigator was saying.

'Do you know what you have done to us?' he screamed. 'You have unleashed the Danan upon us!'

Even in the few moments she looked at it, the storm seemed to come closer. 'How fast is that thing moving?' she whispered.

Sirran shook his head. 'We are lost. Even this fleet cannot outrun it.'

'But the Raiders? They are lost too, aren't they?'

Sirran stared over the High Priestess's head at the onrushing storm. 'No,' he said. 'They saw it before we did and they fled. Someone knew what it was and they will probably survive.'

'But who?' asked Morag. Her eyes were blank, uncomprehending, as if unable to recognise what was happening.

'It doesn't matter who, you fool!' Sirran said. 'All that matters is that we get away, now!'

Morag nodded dumbly. Sirran shook his head and then turned to give the orders.

The fleet followed the Raiders north. As they scudded past the Wrested Archipelago, they ignored the frantic calls and signals from those onshore. The Raiders on the naked rocks had also seen the storm, and they could not escape its fury, but the Children of the Raft had neither time nor inclination to rescue their enemies, so they left them to their fate. Morag wondered why they wasted time going around the Archipelago rather than cutting through, but Sirran ignored her question.

'We would stand no chance if we were caught in among the islands,' Erin told her. 'We may be able to survive in open water.'

But the time they lost was more than they had. Barely had they cleared the last of the islands when the storm hit them like a hammer.

Within seconds they were plunged into a world of screaming winds and driving rain. Mountainous seas, steep and black, soared around them, tossing the small attack boats like so much flotsam. They smashed over the islands of the Archipelago, sending white spray high into the winds. The terrified screams of the dying were lost in the deafening anger of the storm.

Lightning shattered the inky blackness, illuminating the nightmarish scene. More than one sailor was hurled into the ravening sea as they released their grip to cover their ears as the thunder, so close as to be a single eruption, cracked across the wind.

With every lightning strike a new scene of terror flickered into view. They were coming so frequently that it was like a blink; each time another face starkly imprinted its mindless horror on Morag's broken mind.

She clung for her life to the mast as the *Kelpie* alternately climbed up a wave face then plunged down. Her mind was beyond numb; it had simply ceased to function. No new information registered as her eyes jerked through stark scenes, each one a deeper trip into madness. She saw sailors, Novices, Priestesses hurled into the water or broken like dolls by the force of the winds. A fragment of her mind reminded her of Sirran. Of how he had been picked up bodily by a wave and carried away, cursing her as he died. At least she thought he had been cursing her; his words were lost, whipped from his lips before they found form.

Her arms, locked around the stub of the broken mast, burned with the pain of holding on. But what was left of her sanity would not allow them to move. She knew she was screaming but her voice was lost, shredded into the storm. Somewhere within her broken mind, she registered that her clothes had been torn from her and she lay naked before the Sea. Another part of her mind told her that this should mean something, but it was beyond her to know what it was. So she hung there, naked, frozen, battered by the wind and the waves, waiting to die.

Somehow, a thought intruded. *I lost*, she thought. *I tried, I tried so hard — but I lost.*

But that was just one thought. It rose then subsided to be replaced by another. A face. A young girl with lavender eyes and wild, white-blonde hair stared at the High Priestess with pity in her eyes and a smile on her lips. The girl said something but the storm she had raised took the words away. Morag was left screaming, not knowing what the Danan would say to her.

Still screaming, she looked up at a wall of water that reared above her, poised to bear her down into the black depths. There, within the pitiless water, she saw a blaewhal.

It was swimming with the wave, surging through the waters of its home, revelling in the ferocity, finding basic joy in the wonder of unleashed power. The blaewhal, she knew, was a true creature of the waters. Not for it the cringing fear of waves, the running from the storm. The blaewhal knew and understood what she did not. It knew that *this*, *this* was life.

But the *Kelpie* did not die, not then. Rather it rose with the wave, riding over the wall to dive back down again, past the blaewhal, back down into the trough. And Morag kept screaming.

Declan. The name, the face, suddenly blazed, beacon-like, across her mind, illuminating the darkness that had overwhelmed her. In this glimpse she saw his dark eyes, his sun-bleached hair, his callused hands that had so lovingly caressed her, his lopsided grin. His unquestioning love and support were all that had really sustained her. And she loved him. Needed him. *Where are you, my love?*

But sanity was fleeting. Madness is forever. The terror of the storm struck back into her mind; another lightning flash ripped the darkness open, revealing a different scene. Amid the destruction, the shattered planks, the sundered ropes, the bodies, she saw a cleat, torn from the deck with ropes still wrapped around it, swinging towards her.

The brilliant light of lightning vanished, only to be replaced by the white-hot glare of agony as the cleat smashed into her side. She felt flesh tear and bones splinter. In the shocking pain she lost her grip on the mast.

Once more, the *Kelpie* surged up, driven over another icy wall. Morag, High Priestess of the Children of the Raft, slid screaming down the deck. She slid over broken planks, past splintered stays down towards the hungry storm. Her legs dropped over the side, her feet touched the water.

She stopped.

And looked up.

Declan had hold of her. He held her by the arm, keeping her out of the water, saving her life. Despite the violent heaving of the *Kelpie*, the battering of the wind and the blasts of thunder that still assaulted her senses, she could see only him. He spoke, and she could see his lips move, but could not hear him. Yet knowing that he spoke to her was enough.

She felt strangely safe, despite hanging over the edge of a battered ship in the midst of a storm, as Declan held her hand in his. With his other hand, he reached out to her, offering her the bleached white harp. He saw her grateful smile as her hand grasped it.

Morag gripped the harp, feeling its power stir as her hand closed on it. Even above the clamour of wind and wave she heard its song. Her heart was filled with love for Declan who understood, even now, her need for this. She tore her gaze from the harp to look into his eyes, to find bitter anger there. Disbelieving, she saw him mouth the words 'Take it!' as he released his hold on her.

To the north, the remnants of the Raiders' fleet flew before the winds. They had seen the storm before the Children's fleet and put on all sail in an attempt to escape. The *Merial*, the *Misty Seal* and the rest scythed through the water with the terror behind them.

Hwenfayre remained in the prow of the *Misty Seal*, never looking back, hardly aware of looking forward. She was lost, deep in the anguish of the Sea. A song was torn from her lips, a song she barely understood — but she was becoming conscious of its intent.

As had happened on the wall, she was losing herself in the power of the Sea, the mystical energy of which she was the avatar, the conduit. As she sang, the torment, the pained confusion she had felt as Morag and her Priestesses had driven the Sea to act as a weapon for their selfish bidding was slowly abating. In its place a vast anger was growing that threatened to overwhelm her. She knew she needed to break free and take herself back but she did not know how. Instead she sank deeper and deeper into her own power, a dark well of raw emotion that knew no diversion. It would take her completely, emptying her of Hwenfayre, replacing her with only the Danan. Distantly, in a world beyond her, she heard the cries of seamen as they strove to put on yet more sail in an attempt to outrun the storm she was bringing upon them. She knew it was pointless. This storm would destroy them all. She knew because the storm was hers.

'Hwenfayre!' The voice cut across her thoughts as the hand grabbed her arm. Roughly she was wrenched around. 'Hwenfayre!' the man repeated. 'What are you doing?'

'Doing?' she asked. 'Nothing.'

'I know that storm,' the big man yelled. He shoved her harshly, making her look at the purple-black cloud. 'That is not natural!'

She shrugged, hoping this interruption would go away so that she could return. But he would not, he kept talking at her, at times shaking her, insisting that she look at the storm. Why look at it? She knew it was there, she had called it.

And still she sang, without even being aware.

'Hwenfayre,' the rude man said again. 'Look at me!'

She took her eyes off her storm and looked at him. He was a big man, heavy, with coarse, almost brutish features. His long black hair was whipped back by the harsh cold wind as it blew in from the sea. And he was afraid. But not of her, he was afraid of the storm. 'Why are you afraid?' she asked, her song stilling.

'Hwenfayre, I have seen a storm like this, once before. We cannot survive.'

'I will,' she said. 'I cannot die in the Sea.'

'But you can die on it!' another voice said.

She looked at the newcomer. He was also a big man, but dark-skinned and without any hair. She was confused. 'What do you mean?' she asked.

The second man did not answer, he drew a sword and raised it to Hwenfayre's throat.

'No!' cried the first man, drawing his own sword. He swung his weapon, forcing the other sword away from her. With deliberation, he put his own bulk between them. 'You will have to kill me first!'

'I don't have a problem with that, Wyn,' the dark man said.

Wyn? I know that name, Hwenfayre thought. *Why do I know that name?*

'Don't make me hurt you, Sacchin,' Wyn said. 'But you touch her and I will kill you.'

'She is killing us all anyway,' Sacchin said. As he spoke, he lunged at Wyn.

Wyn was a fighting man and saw the trick, parrying the blow. Sacchin swung again. The two of them fought as the storm grew closer.

'Why are you fighting?' Hwenfayre asked. She knew there was something she should know, but her mind was still in thrall to the power of the Sea. Neither Wyn nor Sacchin answered. They continued to fight.

Others saw. Some drew their swords and advanced, some looked away, continuing to work to escape. Within moments, Wyn and Hwenfayre were surrounded by muttering, angry men. Sacchin lowered his sword and backed away, joining the others.

'Let us have her, Wyn,' Sacchin said. 'We don't want to kill you. But we will if we have to.'

'Then kill me.'

Something inside Hwenfayre was screaming. Dimly she almost remembered, but the memory retreated as she grasped at it. 'Why are you doing this?' she asked.

'Because you are my Princess,' replied Wyn without turning around.

'No,' she said. 'That's not right.'

'You are my Princess,' he repeated.

Hwenfayre nodded. 'Yes, I think I am. But that is not why you are doing this.'

'I love you, my Princess,' he said.

A wall crashed down at his words. Her mind returned. 'You love me?' she asked.

He still did not turn.

Her song had already ended, but as she saw him nod his head the pain and anger flooded out from her. In its place a new feeling grew. With it came understanding. She was not merely the Danan. She was Hwenfayre as well. And Hwenfayre knew what the Danan could not.

Hwenfayre knew love.

But as she looked at the horizon to the south she remembered that she also knew hate. And she had killed in hate, killed in revenge, killed in uncaring power.

The sudden knowledge was almost too much for her. With a cry of grief she crumpled to the deck, tears welling in her eyes.

'No!' she cried out. 'This must stop!' She did not hear Wyn drop his sword, neither did she hear the cry from the lookout, but she did feel Wyn's arms as he gathered her to himself and lifted her up.

* * *

The storm blew itself out within hours, leaving the Raider fleet essentially untouched. They had lost three ships to the savagery of Hwenfayre's vengeance, but it was a small cost compared to what had happened to the Children's fleet.

There had been no question that they would turn south to seek to help any who might have survived. No matter that they had been enemies; there were people lost on the waters. The Southern Raiders went in search of the Children of Danan once more.

They came upon a scene of despair. Maybe a tenth of the mighty fleet of attack boats was afloat, and every one that still sailed was heavily damaged. Hundreds had drowned in the deep waters. Bodies floated, some still grasping the shattered remnants of their vessels. The Raider fleet rescued any they could, taking aboard shivering, terrified sailors and Priestesses. Most were too far lost in shock to tell their stories, but no one really wanted to know. None who sailed wanted this fate for a fellow seaman.

The Wrested Archipelago was scoured clean. Not a remnant of the Raiders' settlement remained, but as the *Misty Seal* sailed close people started to appear from cracks and caves in the rock. They had not survived so far south without knowing how to escape wild seas, but even from the deck the Commander could see their faces. Despondency was etched into every brow. They would have to start again.

Hwenfayre stood motionless on deck. Every broken spar, every broken plank, every body tore a new wound into her soul. She had done this. It was all her fault, and nothing could ever make it right. All around her she felt the stares of the Raiders, the silent watching. And every shaking Child of Danan they pulled from the water filled her with such guilt. So much guilt that she feared she would die of it.

No one spoke to her. Their eyes were filled with loathing, horror and fear in equal amounts. When they pulled aboard the plank bearing the name *Kelpie,* the tears finally came. She collapsed in sobs of anguish.

Or she would have collapsed had Wyn not held her close. His arms encircled her as she wept into his chest. There was nothing he could say, so he just held her.

Later, when they finally stopped looking for survivors, they turned north again. The few remaining attack boats limped along with them, sheltered by the Raider fleet.

The Commander spent hours on the journey talking with the only surviving Priestess. They were hesitantly exploring the possibility of peace. It was clear that the Children would not be a force on the sea again for a generation. And with a Princess returning to them, they had much to rebuild.

Hwenfayre heard them talking about her.

'Wyn,' she whispered. 'I cannot go back with them.'

'They are your people,' he said. 'They need you.'

'No. They don't. You saw what I did. You know what I can do. Power like mine is too dangerous.'

'She's right, Wyn,' agreed Nolin. The Navigator had quietly joined them. He looked at Hwenfayre with compassion in his eyes. 'Power like yours is not needed now. Morag was wrong in what she did but right in what she tried to do. It is time for us to sort ourselves out without the ancient power.'

'But what can we do?' asked Wyn.

'I know,' said Hwenfayre. 'We should run away. Far from here. Far from anyone that I can hurt.'

'Do you think that is the best way?' Wyn asked. 'Can't you just not use the power?'

Hwenfayre shook her head. 'No. It is a part of me. And it always will be. Who knows when I might get angry again? I cannot do all that again. I just cannot.'

'But to just run away . . . '

'It's the only way. All we need is somewhere that the world can be safe from me.'

'I know a place,' Nolin said. 'I can take you.'

45

Shanek stared at the mountains ahead of him. They stood at the edge of his world. Beyond them stretched the Blight, a wind-blasted, icy wasteland where, legend told it, the Skrin Tia'k lived before the great wars. Now, it was believed that they had left their ancestral homeland deserted, but Shanek had detected too many knots heading north to accept this any more.

He had heard so many things over the past months that he dared not share with anyone. The Skrin Tia'k were a far more subtle species than he had ever suspected, and, he knew from his years of studying them, more subtle than anyone else suspected either. They lived in a complex society with an alien social structure that he had not even started to unravel, but one thing was clear: the enslaved Skrinnies were at the lowest end of their society. Beyond the Arc Mountains lived Skrin Tia'k who had never been slaves, and had never been seen by any Asan still alive.

Shanek knelt on the cold ground and rested his hands on the soil. So much pain had been felt here over the centuries. It was here that the great battles of the Skrin Tia'k wars had been fought, it was here that so many bloody skirmishes had been fought and so many Skrinnies had been killed or taken. So much suffering. The Asan Empire believed it was still in control over this continent, but Shanek now wondered whether the Skrin Tia'k held the same view.

'Tired already?'

Shanek leaped to his feet and spun around at the interruption. Ananda stood about ten paces away, regarding him quizzically.

'What are you doing here?' Shanek snapped.

'Following you, what did you think?'

'Why?'

Ananda shrugged. 'Nothing else to do,' she said.

'Find something,' Shanek said.

'Don't want to.'

Shanek was in turmoil. He knew how she regarded him, he didn't need mystical powers for that, and he knew that she was an excellent tracker, but she would almost certainly die if she came with him. Even though he did not return her feelings, he did not want to be responsible for her death. Ever since she had faded from his awareness he had tried to keep away from her. He was in touch with the ground, and he had had no warning of her approach, and he had come to depend on his extra awareness. The last thing he wanted was someone close whom he could not sense.

'I don't want you, I don't need you and I refuse to be responsible for you,' he said harshly.

Ananda snorted. 'Responsible for me? No one has ever been responsible for me.'

'If you come with me, you will die, Ananda,' Shanek said. 'And if you die it will be your choice.'

Ananda nodded. 'I know, Shanek. But I've watched you over the months and you know things. I don't think I will die, not with you.'

'You know where I'm going?' Shanek turned and pointed at the Arc Mountains. 'Beyond that lies the Blight, the ancestral homeland of the Skrin Tia'k. I am going to seek them out and destroy them.'

Ananda nodded again. 'That's fine with me. If I want to go and die in the Skrinnie homeland, it's my choice.' Her eyes went hard and the half-smile that characteristically played about her lips vanished. 'But it *is* my choice, not yours.'

'Fine,' said Shanek. 'Follow if you want.' He started jogging away but a sudden shock of pain shot through his body.

Wrong! So wrong!

Shanek cried out in pain and fell to the ground. Beneath him the ground heaved in anguish. Like a knife, its suffering cut into Shanek and he lost consciousness.

It was nearly dawn when he stirred. Ananda sat cross-legged nearby, watching him. When she saw him open his eyes, she frowned.

'What was that about?' she asked.

Shanek shook his head and struggled to sit up. 'Pain,' he muttered. 'So much pain.'

'Are you injured?' she asked.

'Not me,' Shanek said. 'But something is in pain. Something over there.' He gestured beyond the Arc Mountains. He lowered his eyes and regarded Ananda. She returned his gaze with guileless love. 'If you still want to make your own choice,' Shanek said, 'I am leaving.'

Ananda smiled and stood up. She held out her hand and offered it to Shanek. He took it and stood beside her.

'Let's hunt.'

Without a backwards look they started to run.

46

The *Merial* sailed south and east to an island that existed on no maps or charts. Nolin navigated alone, allowing only Sacchin to share the tiller. Aboard they carried the small boat that Dinah had given Wyn, together with supplies to build a small shelter and other essentials to live.

During the day, Hwenfayre and Wyn sat close together in the prow of the ship, watching the waters flow by. They were often accompanied by blaewhals who slid alongside the ship, their dark shapes appearing as shadows in the immeasurable deep. Sometimes they would ease their way alongside the *Merial* and keep her company for hours before silently vanishing into the inky blackness of the deep ocean. Other times they would suddenly appear, leaping high out of the water before crashing down with a thunderous detonation of spray. At such times, Hwenfayre would squeal with delight, clapping her hands like a child as the icy waters soaked her. But as the water dried, her smile faded and she went back to silently watching the dark sea.

She spent most of the day sitting, leaning against

Wyn, staring. He sat with her, content to know she was alive. His arm wrapped around her shoulder gave her the strength to go on living from one day to the next. She did not say much; there seemed neither need nor much to say. Instead she sat with Wyn, watching the deep water slide past, lost in her thoughts.

Wyn was content to enjoy her silence. They sat together, scarcely speaking, rarely looking at each other, but in complete communion. Sometimes she would stir briefly and look up at Wyn to make sure he was still there, and smile. He would smile back, their eyes meeting briefly.

Nolin sailed them far into the deep waters to the east. After a few days, Wyn stopped trying to measure how far they had gone or even what direction they were taking. He was with Hwenfayre and she loved him as he loved her. They could be sailing forever and he would be happy.

One cold morning when the sky was grey with cloud, an island came into view. It was little more than a low mound in the ocean, covered with trees, with a small sandy beach in a sheltered bay. Nolin steered them unerringly towards the beach until they were within the shelter of the bay.

They dropped anchor and loaded the small boat. There was little to be said, so Wyn and Hwenfayre climbed down the rope ladder into the boat and rowed ashore.

Watching them go, Sacchin shook his head. 'I can't help but feel this is a waste,' he said.

'A waste?' asked Nolin.

'There is so much to do and those two could make such a difference.'

Nolin watched them as they pulled the boat up on the shore. 'I know where this island is,' he said. 'And so do you, friend Sacchin. When we need them, we know where to find them.'

'Will it come to that?'

Nolin stared as Wyn and Hwenfayre, hand in hand, walked across the white sand and disappeared into the darkness beneath the trees. 'It will come, friend Sacchin. One day it will come to that.'

Character List

Adam — a journeyman harper
Akash — a member of Shanek's Fyrd
Akem — Master Torturer to two Thanes and three
     First Counsellors
Aldere — a peasant
Alyce — Priestess of the Children of Danan
Ananda — a member of Ejaj's troop
Andrine — a northern tribeswoman
Anwyn — a former High Priestess of the Children
     of Danan, mother of Morag
Arden — a thug in the Widows' Quarter
Arragone — an islander girl
Aristide — Master Carver of the Children of Danan
Ashfaq — a member of Shanek's Fyrd
Audra — Priestess of the Children of Danan
Badghe — a member of Shanek's Fyrd
Bakht — a member of Shanek's Fyrd
Bartin — a member of Maru's troop
Bedi — a beggar in the Widows' Quarter.
Brin — a member of Shanek's Fyrd
Burgen — a barbarian Chieftain
Cadock — Commander of the Army of the World

Cherise — Diplomat in the Thane's service

Danan — the mystical leader and founder of the Children of Danan

Declan — Sailer of the Children of Danan

Dinah — Guide unto Death, an islander

Domovoi — The Appointed One

Dushyan — a member of Shanek's Fyrd

Egon — a member of Shanek's Fyrd

Ejaj — Leader of bandit group in the Great Fastness

Ekaterina — a member of Shanek's Fyrd

Erin — Novice Priestess

Eustaquio — a Caldorman in the Army of the World

Feargus — Harper of the Children of Danan, father of Hwenfayre

Garel, The Commander — Leader of the Southern Raiders

Garth — a Southern Raider who sailed aboard the *Gretchen*

Garpatrao — a member of Shanek's Fyrd

Gayathri — a member of Shanek's Fyrd

Gerhay — a member of Shanek's Fyrd

Gyran — a former First Counsellor

Hadrill — a shepherd at Aldere's village

Hagan — Novice Priestess

Harald — a villager

Harin — a member of Shanek's Fyrd

Hashan — Trader and racketeer in Widows' Quarter

Hasibu — father of Tapash

Hemant — a member of Shanek's Fyrd

Hofie — a member of Shanek's Fyrd

Hwenfayre — Lander child of Feargus

Hylin — The old Teacher of Novices

Jaya — a woman from Aldere's village

Kasimar IV — Thane of the Empire of the World

Katya — Aldere's mother

Kelsy — a Southern Raider who sailed aboard the
    Misty Seal

Lamar — Navigator of the Second Rank

Lane — a Southern Raider who sailed aboard the
    Misty Seal

Leone — Coerl of the First Son's Fyrd

Lind — Navigator of the Second Rank

Lyaksandra — a member of Shanek's Fyrd

Maeve — Novice Priestess

Maire — Novice Priestess

Malik — a member of Shanek's Fyrd

Manno — Officer of the Southern Raiders

Marcene — Noble daughter in the court of the
    Thane

Marek — Captain of the *Gretchen*, a Southern
    Raider

Marran — an islander girl

Maru — Tribesman leader of bandit troop

Mayenne — a servant of Zatopek

Merryk — husband of Silvia, blacksmith from
    Aldere's village

Michaela — a friend of Aldere

Morag — High Priestess of the Children of Danan

Morgan — the hero of a legend

Muttiah — Caldorman in the Army of the World

Myandra — soldier in Muttiah's Fyrd

Niall — Captain of the Guard

Nicole — Novice Priestess

Nolin — Navigator of the First Rank of the
    Children of Danan
Petran — mother of Leone
Raol — a member of Ejaj's troop
Roshan — a member of Shanek's Fyrd
Sacchin — a Southern Raider
Salen — Noble in the Thane's court
Samba — Coerl of legend
Sandor — First Counsellor to the Thane of the
    Empire of the World
Sara — Novice Priestess
Shanek — First Son of the Empire Son of Sandor
    First Counsellor
Shar — Southern Raider woman, partner of
    Sacchin
Silvia — wife of Merryk, from Aldere's village
Sirran — Navigator of the First Rank of the
    Children of Danan
Tanit — a soldier in Muttiah's Fyrd
Tapash — a northern Tribesman
Tillekeratne — father of Virender
Tirace — a member of Maru's troop
Urtane — a Tribesman guard
Virender — a merchant
Wellfyn — an islander girl
Wyn — a fighting man, a Child of Danan
Yesmah — woman from Aldere's village
Yngwie — a travelling minstrel
Ys — a northern Tribesman
Zatopek — a trader in the Widows' Quarter
Zahir — a noble in the Thane's court

Ships

Gretchen — Southern Raider vessel, commanded by
    Marek

Kelpie — personal transport of Morag, High
    Priestess of the Children of the Raft

Learning Raft — vessel of the Children of the Raft,
    on which Navigators are trained

Merial — vessel of the Children of the Raft, taken
    by the Southern Raiders

Misty Seal — the flagship of the Southern Raiders,
    commander by the Commander of the Raiders

Southern Scend Raft — second largest vessel of the
    Children of the Raft

Two Family Raft — large vessel of the Children of
    the Raft

Voyager
online

for travellers of the imagination

Booklovers of science fiction and fantasy have a new destination! Voyager Online has the latest science fiction and fantasy releases, previews of upcoming titles, book extracts, author information and weekly competitions. It also features exclusive contributions from some of the world's top sci-fi and fantasy authors.

There's a message board where you can discuss books, authors and anything about sci-fi and fantasy with other fans, a place for you to read and submit book reviews, and there are special offers and competitions for members.

So why not visit Voyager Online today at:

www.voyageronline.com.au